❧ More Praise for The Lone Snake ❧

"In The Lone Snake, Lisa Vihos celebrates the inspiring power of Renaissance painter Sofonisba Anguissola, a woman determined to follow her dream. Sofonisba transforms old stories into new realities for herself and for others. Full of 'joyful surprises,' The Lone Snake transforms our understanding of the past and bolsters our hope for the future."

Margaret Rozga, author of *Holding My Selves Together: New & Selected Poems* and poet laureate of Wisconsin, 2019-2020

"Meticulously researched and beautifully written, this novel in the form of a memoir reads as if experienced firsthand by the author herself. We walk right alongside the painter Sofonisba Anguissola as she makes her way in the male-dominated art world of Renaissance Italy and Spain."

Chris Keledjian, editor and playwright

"The work of the sixteenth-century painter Sofonisba Anguissola whose career was resurrected during the feminist revolution of several decades ago, has since been admired primarily for her intimate and inventive self-portraits. Building on that phenomenon, Lisa Vihos's vibrant, empathetic novel offers a beautiful and reflective account of the artist's life and career. The Lone Snake is a brilliant self-portrait in words of the woman and the artist."

Joel Isaacson, painter and professor emeritus of art history, University of Michigan

D1599832

Books of poetry by LISA VIHOS

Fan Mail from Some Flounder
This Particular Heaven
The Accidental Present
A Brief History of Mail

THE LONE SNAKE

The Story of Sofonisba Anguissola

LISA VIHOS

Nov. 22, 2022

WATER'S EDGE PRESS
SHEBOYGAN, WI

Printed in the United States of America

ISBN: 978-1-952526-10-7
Library of Congress Control Number: 2022930949

Water's Edge Press LLC
Sheboygan, WI

watersedgepress.com

Credits:
Author Photo by Michael Hoover
Cover Design by Water's Edge Press

Cover Image licensed through the Museum of Fine Arts, Boston

Sofonisba Anguissola, Italian (Cremonese), about 1532–1625
Self-Portrait (DETAIL USED)
about 1556
Varnished watercolor on parchment
8.3 x 6.4 cm (3 1/4 x 2 1/2 in.)
Museum of Fine Arts, Boston
Emma F. Munroe Fund
60.155

To all the artists in my family

FOREWORD

by Michael Rothenberg

From the moment of first breath, a craving for immortality seizes the heart and soul of the artist. This is a story of that. The artist seeking truth and insight in every strike of brush to the canvas, the unveiling of the adorned, reflecting the secret magic behind the world of nature and static privilege, from a stick in the sand to the Spanish court.

With an acute awareness of the fragility of life, wonder and passion drives the artist to be eternally manifest. And the impulse of this artistic passion winds together in one serpent coil, the theme that resonates throughout the many stories of Lisa Vihos's caring work, *The Lone Snake: The Story of Sofonisba Anguissola.*

Yes, this is a book of many stories as much as it is one story. It is a fictive memoir. The story of humanity, the individual, the child, the daughter, the woman, the wife, the lover, the poet, and the biographer, waking from slumber and isolation to engage and display the prophetic that lingers within the constraints of a society, much like our own, which is rarely prepared for a free spirit like Sofonisba Anguissola to rise.

The Lone Snake is a story of innocence and wisdom, hope and embrace. An exquisite portrait of an inspired and innovative portrait artist, in which the author introduces the reader to a lineage of dream weavers who adorn the world, and history, with a threaded light that makes the imagination tangible, possible, memorable.

MICHAEL ROTHENBERG is the Florida State University Libraries Poet-in-Residence Emeritus and the author of numerous books of poetry, most recently, *Drawing the Shade* from Dos Madres Press.

Anguis sola fecit victoriam.
The lone snake achieved victory.

—Anguissola family motto

PART ONE

Sofonisba

Until today, I have never been asked to prove my existence. A messenger arrived this morning bearing a letter from King Philip III of Spain. Long ago, I served at his father's court in Madrid as a painter of portraits. Now that I have reached the advanced age of seventy-two, there is some question as to whether or not I am still breathing. In order to continue receiving my pension from the Spanish court, I must sign a paper to verify that I am not dead.

For the last quarter century, I have lived on a narrow street in the heart of Genoa. My painting studio—a spacious room with good light—is on the top floor of my house, and a steady stream of portrait commissions keeps me busy. My husband, Orazio Lomellino, is a ship's captain. Just now he is out at sea. My dear husband—who is twenty years younger than me—lives by the rhythm of the waves, the fire of the sun, and the force of the wind. He finds his way home to me by his guideposts, the stars.

If my husband were here, I know he would laugh at the notion that I am no longer alive. He would contact his notary friend and ask him to draw up the necessary paperwork, a *fides vitae*, it is called. Orazio once told me that the longer I live—if I hoped to continue to receive my pension—there might come a day when I would be asked to sign such a paper. Well, he was right. I must send a messenger to this notary today. As quickly as we can sign, I will exist once again.

Meanwhile, my work continues. My current portrait subject is an acquaintance of Orazio's, the shipbuilder Matteo Bruzzone. Signor Bruzzone came to me several weeks ago to discuss how he wished to be painted. He had some specific ideas for what he hoped to see in his

1

portrait. He wanted a workbench with the tools of his trade nearby—wood, hammer, nails, a plan drawing—and a view of the Ligurian Sea in the background. I was pleased to oblige. His first three sittings did not go well, however, as he was quite impatient and always arrived late.

Patience is not a virtue I possess. While I waited for him to arrive today, I tried to distract myself from my rising frustration by sketching the lemon tree in our courtyard. Finally, my dear housemaid Giulia called out. "Signora! Your guest is here!"

"Take him up to the studio, Giulia. I will be right there."

I took a moment to calm myself and prepare to meet my sitter. I felt the stiffness in my knees as I climbed the stairs to my studio. When I got to the top, Signor Bruzzone was already there, pacing back and forth.

"I am in a hurry, Signora."

"Greetings, Signor Bruzzone," I said, holding back my annoyance. "As you are in a hurry, let's waste no time. Please stand still in your spot near the window, would you? We've nearly lost the afternoon sun."

My subject wiped the sweat from his brow. "It is much too hot up here," he said.

I ignored his complaint and picked up my palette, dotted with colors I had laid out before his arrival—burnt umber, red from cochineal, white lead, and a bit of verdigris for the shadows.

"When will my portrait be done, Signora?"

I was tempted to reply "not soon enough." If he was not always late, we would be much further along by now.

"Soon," I promised. "Please hold still."

"I am holding still," he said, turning his head from the window, wiping his brow again.

It has always been my method to have my subjects sit for me only when I am working on their faces. All the details of clothing and setting can be done without the sitter present. At that moment, I was grateful for my working practice and looked forward to Signor Bruzzone's departure.

"Might you give me a bit more smile, Signor?"

"Smile? What is there to smile about? I am behind on several projects, yet here I am having my portrait painted."

I did not want to argue with him, so I just continued to work quickly, laying down the colors that captured the tones of his face.

"I have much to do, Signora, and my customers hound me daily to finish their projects. Unlike you, I am a busy man."

With that remark, I had the urge to throw my palette at him. "I understand," I said as I worked on his forehead and cheeks. Unpleasant as he was, Signor Bruzzone was quite handsome when he was not scowling. When he commissioned my services for half of what it would cost to secure a male painter, I suppose he did not realize that sitting for a portrait—no matter who paints it—would take a bit of patience on his part.

At our first meeting, I saw in Signor Bruzzone's eyes something that I thought could be anger, but I think now it is the urge to create. Whether one paints, builds ships, or bakes bread, such desire can be found in the eyes. With all my sitters, I look for that passion and do what I can to make it shine.

"The sun has shifted, Signor, so unfortunately, we must stop for today." I set down my brush and palette. "When can you return?"

"Return?" he wiped his brow yet again. "I cannot return until next week, perhaps Thursday."

"Thursday is fine," I said. "Please come earlier, though, so we can make use of the light."

"If you insist," he said. With one last look of irritation, Signor Bruzzone was on his way.

Apparently, many people are thinking of me of late because this morning I received another letter, this one from my brother Asdrubale.

Dearest Sofi,

I hope this letter finds my only remaining sister significantly better than it finds me. Since Mama's death, the last many years have been a time of gloom for me in Cremona. Nothing feels right anymore— not even my Latin translation work—and with each passing day, I wonder why I am still alive. I think fifty-four years is long enough among the living. You must understand what I am saying. With finances dwindling, I cannot continue to pay the maid or the boy who works in the stable. It pains me to rob them of their livelihoods, but what else can I do? I will just have to make my own soup and feed my own horse.

Please write to me and tell me what is new in Genoa. Do you have any new commissions? How are your eyes? I should tell you that Lodovico da Viadana is the new choirmaster at San Luca. Perhaps you would like to come home and meet him, perhaps even paint his portrait. I know how much you enjoy his choral compositions.

Your loving brother,

Asdrubale
21 June, 1605

Though we are separated by eighteen years—and for most of our lives, great distances—Asdrubale has always been close to my heart. Perhaps we share a special bond being the oldest and youngest of seven siblings in our family. As soon as I receive verification that the authorities know I am still alive and my pension is secure, I will write King Philip and ask him to transfer my monthly payment directly to my brother.

I will not miss the pension much. I am comfortable here in this house and have no need for extra money. I have plenty of time to paint the portrait commissions that come to me, and even some religious images of my own choosing. I am content and would not think of living anywhere else. But my brother's letter has stirred memories of my family home in Cremona. Reading his letter, I could almost smell the fragrance of my mother's garden filled with roses, lavender, and basil.

Mama was a humble soul, born Bianca Ponzone. She cared for her children and her garden, stitched banners for San Sigismondo church, and could often be heard singing in her sweet soprano voice. My mother was always giving, and through her example, I learned to be kind to other people, no matter what their station in life.

As for my father, Amilcare Anguissola, I picture him seated at his desk leaning intently over his account ledgers. He collected and sold Latin manuscripts and also helped other men start businesses. He wanted everyone, including his daughters, to succeed. He had been born illegitimate and had to earn his name from his father. I think that effort made him value determination, something he most certainly passed along to me.

Our house on the edge of the city was only a short walk into the heart of Cremona. When I was twelve, I often went with our housemaid, Antonella, to the market in the central square. The square was flanked by the cathedral, the Baptistery, and the Torrazzo, an imposing clock tower built in the fourteenth century, and according to Papa, the tallest tower ever built.

I was proud that our city had such a grand and noble structure watching over us. While Antonella haggled with the vendors, I would slip away and climb the five hundred steps to the top. From such a height, I could survey the land around Cremona and the River Po snaking its way through green fields. I felt like a bird, or an angel, looking down upon all creation. I remember the distinct feeling of wanting to bring something of value to the world. And now, the older I get, the more I wonder, beyond my paintings, what am I leaving behind?

Asdrubale's letter and my memories of home are inspiring me to write about my life. I know I have a story to tell. I will gather paper and find the leather portfolio that once belonged to Papa to store the pages as I fill them. My story will be a long one. I want to go back to the very beginning and document how my journey as an artist began.

PAPER AND CHALK

If someone were to ask me how I became an artist, I would answer that I began on the ground, in the sunshine. Out there in the grass for hours with my sister Elena—sometimes sitting, sometimes lying on our backs and looking up at the clouds. We would put our ears to the ground and listen for messages coming up out of the earth itself.

I was born in Cremona in 1532 and Elena came two years after me. As we grew, I felt it was my duty to watch over her. When she was eight and I was ten, I taught her all manner of things. How to make clover crowns, how to make mud cakes, and how to follow ants on their journeys across forests of grass. Inspired by the reflections in rain puddles, Elena and I made up a world of brave princesses who rode wild horses and did important things.

It was not easy to sit on the ground in our corsets and the wooden frames that shaped our skirts. So, I showed Elena how to undo our garments, which upset Antonella. She would act the good housemaid and always scold us at first, but then she'd laugh and let it go, and we were free to play and dream, unbound.

From an early age, I was fascinated by the look of things: flowers, rocks, birds, butterflies, the glimmer of light on a drop of dew.

Everything I saw around me had a shape to it. One day, I picked up a stick and started to scratch some lines into the hard-packed earth near where the cypress trees stood tall to mark the edge of our family's property. Elena picked up a stick too. We drew circles, squares, and triangles, then flowers, trees, our house, and the sun.

"Draw me!" Elena said, giggling. "Try to draw my face, Sofi. Make it look like me!"

I looked carefully at my sister, the oval shape of her head, the way her light brown hair swept back in a gentle curve to the ribbon loosely tied at the nape of her neck. Her eyes were shaped like little fish darting toward each other. Her nose was both round and pointy, like a button, or a mushroom. Her mouth turned up in a smile, the shape of the small boat that our father docked on the Po. I did my best to inscribe all this into the earth with my stick.

Elena looked down at the ground where we were kneeling. "Is that me?"

"That is you," I said.

Elena ran toward the house. "Papa," she called. "Come quick and see what Sofi has done!"

I could picture Papa at his desk in his office, looking up from his ledger and sighing. I wished that Elena had not bothered him at his work. He was a kind and loving man, our Papa, but he did not like to be disturbed while he was tracking his numbers, amounts in, amounts out. He was always looking for a profit so he could feed the growing number of daughters in our family—five of us at that time—and save enough to someday provide dowries for all of us: myself, Elena, Lucia, Minerva, and Europa. It was a daunting future and Anna Maria, daughter number six, had not yet been born. And then there would be Asdrubale, the first and only boy.

"What have we here, my ladies?" he asked.

"Sofi drew a picture of me in the dirt with a stick! Look at what she did, Papa! It's me!"

Papa rested his knees on the ground and tipped his head to one side, surveying my work.

"My, my," he said. "That is lovely, Sofi. How did you know how to do that?"

I didn't understand his question. How did I know? I had just looked at Elena and followed her lines and shapes with my stick in

6

the dirt.

"I don't know, Papa," I said, looking down, ashamed that I could not answer his question.

Papa put his finger lightly under my chin and lifted my face so that he could look into my eyes. "Dearest Sofi, what you have done is most lovely." He was smiling at me, so I smiled back.

"You are an artist, my child. Did you know that?" I shook my head.

Elena jumped up and down. "My sister is an artist! I want to be an artist, too! Can I Papa?"

Papa stood up and dusted the dirt from his knees. "It is entirely possible, yes, that you will be an artist, too. My daughters. Artists."

As he said this, his mind seemed to be somewhere far away. I was too young to understand that he was seeing into the future. At age ten, I did not have a sense of the future much past the evening meal. But I could see Papa was thinking.

"I will get some paper and chalk. Young ladies need the proper tools to be artists."

Elena continued to jump up and down. "Paper and chalk, paper and chalk!"

As for me, all my jumping took place on the inside. I had captured the essence of my sister's face with just a few lines in the brown earth. I was proud to realize that I was, myself, a creator. Of course, had I known then about all the challenges being an artist would entail—a woman artist, especially—I might not have been so elated. But my papa was going to give me paper and chalk so I could draw. What more could a girl who was an artist ask for?

As I begin writing down my memories, much is stirring inside me. Unfortunately, the task of writing is causing some strain on my eyes, more stress than painting alone provokes. For years, I've suffered from an ailment that causes my eyes to swell and ache from time to time. The feeling is of something pushing on my eyes from inside my head. I blame this mysterious condition for also causing my eyelashes to fall out, which was quite distressing when it first began to happen just before my eighteenth birthday. I looked in the mirror one morning and thought, "Oh, dear God, what is happening to me?" I thought perhaps this loss meant I would

7

die. While several doctors assured me that lost eyelashes were not a sign of imminent death, none of them ever had a remedy.

Eventually, I accepted the fact that I could not replace my eyelashes. However, alleviating the swelling has been something I have dealt with continuously throughout my life. Antonella taught me to place a cool compress soaked in lavender water on my eyes. This has always brought relief, but lately, I notice that I have a sharp new pain that I've not had before. I must be careful. I have too much to do yet in this life to lose the ability to see.

This morning, the notary came and we both signed the *fides vitae*. He will send the document to the authorities. After he left, I finished my letter to King Philip III, the son of my former patron, to ask that he transfer my pension to my brother. I have called for a courier and hopefully this whole process won't take too long. Asdrubale is in need of my help, and I wonder if perhaps I should go to Cremona myself and deliver some money. As he suggested, I could also meet the composer, Lodovico da Viadana, while I'm there. That sly Asdrubale. He knows how to catch my attention.

While I was thinking about making a trip home, I heard Giulia addressing someone at the front door. "I am looking for Signora Anguissola," a man's voice said.

"Do you have a letter of introduction, Signor?" she asked.

"I do not, but I have read about the Maestra in *The Lives of the Artists* by Giorgio Vasari. He describes her as one who has created figures in her paintings that seem truly alive, lacking only in speech. I would like to meet her."

The word "Maestra" and the mention of Vasari stirred my curiosity. I ventured into the front hall to get a look at my visitor and found a young man standing in the doorway, covered in dust from the road. He held a large leather bag in one hand, and there was a satchel over his shoulder. Tall and slender, he had a gentleness in his demeanor that drew me to him.

"It's all right, Giulia. You can let him in."

"Allow me to introduce myself," he said, setting down his bag to offer me his hand. "I am Francesco Rossi of Florence."

The smile on his handsome, young face touched my heart.

"It is a pleasure to meet you, Signor Rossi. What brings you to Genoa?"

"You do, Signora," he said. "If I may be so bold, I am in search of a teacher."

In recent years, many novice artists passing through Genoa have stopped at my doorstep to meet the "lady artist," but none have ever asked for training.

"Let's sit and talk about your search. I will ask Giulia to bring some wine. Come, tell me your story."

Once we were seated in the courtyard, he said, "Thank you for inviting me in, Signora. My story is that I have worked in my father's vineyard since I was nine, but I have always had this inclination to draw."

He pulled a sheath of papers from his satchel and placed them on the table between us. He showed me drawings of houses, trees, flowers, and faces. I could see that he had potential.

"I want to learn how to draw better, and ultimately, to paint."

"You know, being a woman, I am not allowed membership in any guild, and so I cannot offer true apprenticeship."

"I am not the typical student," he said. "Don't most boys begin training at age nine or ten?"

"That is true. And I am not the typical teacher, even though I have taught many. How does your father feel about you seeking this new path in life?"

"My father was hesitant at first, but he gave me permission to leave the vineyard if I could find a teacher. When I read about you, I hoped you might take on a student like me."

"I have heard versions of Vasari's words often repeated, but I've never seen the book."

"He gives you high praise, Signora. Did you ever meet Vasari?" Francesco asked.

"I did not. He visited my father's house in 1566 when I was already long gone to Spain. My father showed him my work, and it seems that he liked it."

"Indeed, he did, Signora. What do you think? Will you take on a student?"

The look on the face of my visitor was one of hope, and I must admit feeling rather hopeful myself. It will be good for me to pass along some of my knowledge to a willing student. His presence and the desire to learn from me are proof, no doubt, that I am still alive.

"Yes, I will do it. I will teach you."

"Oh, thank you, Maestra! That is all I ask."

Francesco

Each morning, I wake up and pinch myself to make sure I am really in Genoa. I am renting a room above a taverna on the wharf, and through the open window, I can smell salt air and freshly caught fish. I hear seagulls calling and the voices of the fishermen as they unload the morning catch. I am grateful that my father released me from my work at our family's vineyard to pursue my artist's dream.

My room is a short walk to the palazzo where my teacher lives. I am two weeks into my studies with her. Every few days, she gives me a new assignment. Today, when I brought her some sketches of my hands, I found her enjoying the morning sun in the courtyard.

"These are wonderful," she said as I showed her the drawings. "It is clear you look at the world with a sharp eye."

I was so pleased by her approval of my efforts. "What do you think I need to do next?"

"Good that you should ask," she said. "I think we need a sketching trip in the hills."

"That sounds wonderful, Maestra. I look forward to it. When should we go?"

"Well," she said as she pulled a basket out from behind her chair, "I've already asked Giulia to pack us a lunch. Can you go today?"

I peeked into the basket to find a loaf of bread, cheese, smoked sardines, and two pears.

"I certainly can. Thank you for this invitation, Maestra. And for providing this fine feast!"

She set the basket at my feet. "There is something else." She paused and studied her hands, which were clasped in front of her. In the short time that I have known her, I have not seen her look nervous about anything. Signora Anguissola is an extremely well-possessed woman. She continued looking down and said, "I have started writing the story of my life."

"Oh, Maestra, I'm sure your story will be something quite wonderful. Something that everyone will want to read."

She looked up, eyes wide, "You think so?"

"Indeed, I am sure of it."

She took a deep breath. "I have a favor to ask."

"I am here to help in any way I can, Maestra. What can I do for you?"

"I've been plagued most of my life with a recurring pain in my eyes, and lately it is becoming more acute. When I write, the pain is worse. I need the help of a scribe. Would you be willing to write down my stories?"

"Whatever troubles your eyes, Maestra, it seems it has never diminished your ability to paint beautiful portraits. But yes, I would be honored to help you."

She smiled and there was a new lightness about her, as though a weight had been lifted off her shoulders. The carriage pulled up out front and I picked up our food basket. She held a second basket containing her portfolio, a quill, ink, paper, and chalk.

As we settled into the carriage, she said, "While we are out on this sketching trip, perhaps I will tell you a story. You could try writing it down."

"I am ready to give it a try."

"I want to take you a little way up into the hills. From there, we'll have a wide view of the sea. There are olive trees up there that make good subjects for sketching. If they could talk, I think those trees would have their own stories to tell."

The carriage went back and forth up the side of the hill, and we gradually made our way to higher ground. We stopped at a place near a grove of squat, sturdy olive trees. The carriage driver hopped out and placed a small stool in the shade for the Maestra. For me, he spread out a blanket, and I leaned my back against one of the trees.

"Did you know," she said, "that the best way to understand a thing is to draw it? Sketching teaches us the essence of things."

I looked around at the grove of trees, and the first thing I noticed was that their gnarled trunks made them appear to be in some form of agony, twisted as they were. I settled on one especially anguished tree and put my chalk on the paper. I wanted to show how the tree was rooted to the land, how its trunk met the ground. The trunk came straight up out of the dry earth, with no indication of any roots below. As I focused on the tree trunk, I saw hollowed eyes, bulbous noses, and sagging mouths that seemed to be crying out. The trunk was a collection of these tortured faces, all braided together and twisting their way up the branches that clawed their way to the sky. I saw the lance-shaped leaves that were dark green on one side, silvery on the other, and how they were organized in patterns on the branches with every leaf met by a partner on the opposite side of its twig. Buried among the leaves were the olives, mostly green, some pale purple, all dangling from their drooping spindles amid the forest of leaves.

It was not easy to draw these things, but I persevered. I noticed that if I stopped my mind from thinking too hard and allowed my hand to take over, the vision of the tree in front of me began to emerge on the paper. The Maestra was right. By looking carefully enough with the intent to translate the tree into chalk on paper, I could see many things about the tree that I might have otherwise taken for granted or missed entirely. The Maestra looked over at what I was doing.

"I see that you are seeing," she said.

My heart swelled with pride. "Thank you for showing me how simple it can be."

After we sketched for a while, we opened the lunch basket and ate. It was a good meal, and we didn't say much, just enjoyed the view and the food together. When we finished, she pulled a portfolio from the other basket.

"Would you mind reading out loud what I have written?" she asked. "I'd like to hear it."

I was happy to oblige. As I read to her, she closed her eyes and smiled. It was especially interesting for me to learn that she made her first drawing in the dirt since I myself have spent so much time digging in the dirt in my father's vineyard.

"Do you want to tell me more?" I asked.

"I do!"

I rested my back against the tree and put the portfolio on my lap. I would have preferred a desk to write on, but I did my best to write quickly and legibly, eager to hear everything that Signora Anguissola had to say.

After Papa gave me paper and chalk, I woke up early each morning, gathered my supplies, and slipped out to the garden. I drew roses, jasmine, bluebells, and the leaves on our lemon trees. I drew the lemons. I drew insects. I would pull off my shoes and draw my bare feet. Again, and again, I drew my own left hand. I discovered I could draw equally well with both hands, so then I drew my right hand too. I drew the patterns of tree bark and clouds in the sky. I tried to draw the water pouring from the fountain at the far corner of the terrace. Water is difficult to draw. I did my best. Papa kept replenishing my supply of paper, so I kept drawing.

Most days, Elena would join me before lunch. She did not have as much patience for the work as I did. I tried my best to share my self-taught skills with my sister. Sometimes she would listen to me, but most times, she did not.

At lunchtime, Antonella would call us in. Elena always ran ahead. I went reluctantly, wanting to put one last line down on my page before I took a break.

"Sofi! Come! Your soup is getting cold."

"I'm coming."

"Now, young lady!" Antonella commanded.

And so I would put down my chalk and go. If I had completed a drawing, I would take it in to show Papa and Mama. They always responded with smiles and praise. I felt important.

When I think back on that time of my life, it appears in my mind's eye like one long, sunny afternoon in the garden. So often I was at the edge of the terrace drawing while my father and his companions sat around the table, drinking wine and talking. There was one man, Signor Barosi, to whom my father had loaned money for the purpose of starting a cheese shop. There were also two brothers—I forget their names, but I remember that Papa helped them start a grain and produce business. All these men were good men, I'm sure. But they were all completely certain that women could never amount to anything.

I can still hear Signor Barosi's deep voice booming across the table, "So, Amilcare. What makes you think you should educate your daughters?"

"All daughters should be educated, my friend. Yours too."

"I would say you are asking for trouble by educating daughters. No amount of education will allow women to function as men do. They don't have the capacity."

"Ah, good sir, I disagree," Papa said.

"Well, then, it will be a very long time, well past our lifetimes, before women can even come close to being the equals of men."

"Perhaps you are right, my friend. But that doesn't mean we don't start."

My father was very proud of our family coat of arms and the Latin phrase that graced it, *anguis sola fecit victoriam,* the lone snake achieved victory. The design showed a snake rising up in the center of the image toward a golden sun, and above that, a crown. Everything about the coat of arms was a source of pride for Papa, especially because it was something he had earned.

He was born outside of marriage, and only after much hard work did his father make him a legitimate heir to the name Anguissola. Thus, he became a member of the minor nobility of Cremona. He then used his privilege to repay his father's grace by helping others. This is why, I am certain, he was so dedicated to the notion of educating all his daughters. He was not afraid to see our value, and to make sure that each of us saw it too.

Papa was a student of Roman history and he liked to tell us stories of ancient times. One figure he talked about at great length was the Bona Dea, the Good Goddess, the protector of women. Papa said that snakes were her special symbol, representing her roles in both healing and birthing. He told us how a snake sheds its skin, and that this was seen by the Romans as a symbol of fertility. He said that consecrated snakes were kept at the temples of the Bona Dea, sanctuaries that were for women only. This intrigued me because I had never heard of anything that men were not allowed to do.

All the while Father was providing us with an education, Mother kept to a wife's duty, overseeing the household, bearing the children. She was skilled at embroidery and had a singing voice straight from Heaven. She was a kind and humble person, my mother. I wish I had thought to paint her portrait more than once.

Signora Anguissola stopped speaking and looked at me, tears in her eyes.

"What is it?" I asked.

"I have never said that out loud about my mother, that I wish I had painted her more."

She wiped her eyes with the back of her hand.

"I can see that speaking my stories like this will bring up many regrets. But perhaps that is a good thing, a necessary thing. What about you? Are you close to your mother?"

Her question caught me off guard, bringing up painful memories for me as well. "My mother died when I was just a lad of nine."

"I am sorry to hear that."

"She was giving birth to her fourth child, our family's first girl. Sadly, the child died too."

"I can imagine the pain that someone as young as nine must have felt, losing a mother."

"It was painful at the time, that is true, and sometimes I still feel the loss. You know, I cannot clearly picture her face anymore, but I do remember her as a force of great love. My father did his best to make up for the loss then, and even now. I think that is why he has allowed me to journey to Genoa—to you—to pursue my dream."

"He sounds like a kind and loving man, your father."

"That he is. I hope you will meet him one day."

"I would like that, my dear."

In that moment, when Maestra called me *dear*, I felt a pain in my heart, the sting of losing my mother. Emotion welled in my throat. To avoid any embarrassing display, I busied myself with packing the baskets.

The Maestra woke the sleeping carriage driver, and soon we were on our way down the hill. It had been an enlightening day, and I could see that helping Signora Anguissola write her stories was going to be a moving endeavor that would teach me many things. It was interesting to hear her speak about what the men at her father's table had said regarding the education of daughters. I looked forward to hearing more about her father, and also her journey to becoming an artist.

The room I rent is above a taverna called the Barbarossa, a popular drinking establishment with wide front windows that open to the sea. My room is small but clean, and the proprietor, Giuseppe, is a kind and cheerful fellow, bald with a round face and bushy black mustache. His thick arms are perpetually raised in the task of drying mugs, and the corners of his mouth are turned up in a bright, welcoming smile.

The Barbarossa has a mix of clientele from fishermen and laborers to merchants and minor nobles. In my short time in Genoa, I have found respite there and have enjoyed wine and a bit of food on several occasions. This evening, after my day in the olive grove, I was not surprised to step into the taverna to find a group of men my age who visit every night.

They are a rowdy bunch of fellows, with one among them who is clearly the leader. He stands out from the rest because his face is in a perpetual snarl, as though he is chewing hard on something he wants to spit out. His name is Dario Bacigalupo, and his family name reflects him perfectly: "The one who annoys others." His nose is crooked, and I imagine it must have been broken in a fight. Or several fights. Dario's main purpose in life seems to be insulting others, instigating quarrels, and then winning them at all cost.

"Artist!" he called above the din of the gathered crowd when he caught my eye. "Come join us! Remind us again what you are doing here in Genoa."

I placed some coins on the bar and retrieved a mug of wine from Giuseppe. Why can't Dario remember what I've already told him at least twice? I thanked Giuseppe and took a sip of wine to fortify myself before making my way to Dario's table.

"Good evening, gentlemen," I said, more to Dario's companions than to him.

"You didn't answer me," he said, almost daring me to respond.

"As I've mentioned before, I'm here from Florence." I took another sip of wine. "I've come to study with Signora Anguissola."

Dario pushed himself up out of his chair and headed to the counter. "Anguissola?" he said over his shoulder, laying down his mug for a refill. "The wife of the sea captain? What could that woman—what could any woman—possibly teach a man?" As he returned to his chair, he came very close to my face, narrowed his eyes, and leaned in. "You are a man, aren't you?"

His friends chuckled into their mugs.

I hate his contempt, and also his ignorance. Everyone I have met in Genoa knows exactly who Signora Anguissola is and admires her artistic talent.

16

"Sofonisba Anguissola is a painter of great renown who served at the Spanish court. She creates beautiful portraits that breathe with life."

"He even talks like a woman, doesn't he?" Dario looked at his friends for some sign of agreement.

"You should have more respect," I said, setting down my mug.

"Respect? For a woman? You Florentines are so weak and stupid, so full of art. Women have nothing to teach us. All they are good for is between their legs!" Dario's friends roared with laughter.

"Hey, Bacigalupo," said Giuseppe from behind the counter. "Calm yourself."

Dario drained his mug and wiped his mouth with his sleeve. Then his face brightened. "Oh, you sly dog. Maybe that is what you are doing?" With a wink, he said, "She is a little old for you, don't you think?"

Dario burst into laughter, and all his friends raised their drinks and laughed too.

"You fool," I muttered under my breath. I set my unfinished wine on the counter, nodded to Giuseppe, and made my way to the door.

"Forget about art," Dario called after me. "It will get you nowhere!"

I went up the outside staircase to my room, stretched out on my bed, and thought about how rude some men can be. Not all men—not Giuseppe, nor my father. But I have read Castiglione's *The Book of the Courtier* and I don't see most of the men I have met in my twenty years displaying any of the qualities that are espoused therein.

Castiglione puts forth that courtly men should exhibit a calm mind and a voice that speaks "elegant and brave words." Most men I know— my father a prime exception—rarely exhibit a calm mind. Rather than speaking words that are elegant, men like Dario speak words that are rough and intended to offend. Rather than being truly brave, a man like Dario puts on the illusion of bravery, when in fact, he is fearful of life.

I have concluded that this fear is something that passes from one generation to the next. My father had a different way. His example of how to treat others—men and women alike—came from his experience in the vineyard, where rain and sun cannot be controlled. He taught me and my brothers that there is more to life than being in command of all things at all times.

Dario's behavior is laughable, but I have found that laughing in the face of fearful men does no good. It only riles them more. And I have not come to Genoa to change men like Dario. I only want to learn to draw and paint.

Sofonisba

LESSONS

My father was unique among men. He believed that young women should be educated, so he hired a succession of tutors to school his daughters. All men, of course. Some did not stay long because Papa sent them on their way as soon as they acted contemptuously toward us. The nicest and most respectful tutor we had was Signor Alessandro Cavallaro. He taught us for two years before he was called to return to his home in Sicily. I learned so much from him. He encouraged curiosity and creativity. He appreciated my questions, and I can remember him saying often, "Let us find the answer together."

I am guessing now that Signor Cavallaro was only about twenty years old when he came to teach us, but to a young girl like myself, he seemed quite old and wise. He was from Palermo and brought with him the mystery of a faraway place. He kept his curly black hair cut short to crown the top of his head, and he had a pointy little beard that I wanted to pull on—which, of course, I did not do. Signor Cavallaro had deep, dark eyes full of secrets and knowledge—all the collected knowledge of the world, I imagined.

He was with us at a time when only Lucia, Elena, and I were old enough to participate in the lessons. The three of us would wait for him each morning at the large wooden table in father's sitting room with our slate boards and chalk ready. We knew when our teacher was coming because we could hear him singing as he came up the garden path. He had a clear tenor voice and the songs he sang expressed a kind of joy—but also a melancholy—that I did not fully understand but felt in my heart.

What impressed me about Signor Cavallaro from the first day he came to teach us—aside from his beautiful singing—was that he did not stand over us at the head of the table as other tutors had done. He sat at the table with us and made every lesson a game. We had four hours of study each day and we would jump between Latin, history, poetry, and even some theology.

We also learned mathematics, which was most unusual. Girls were not considered intelligent enough to learn how to manage numbers, but Papa wanted to prove that theory wrong. Signor Cavallaro was an excellent teacher, and we went from simple mathematics, like counting hazelnuts laid out on the table, to learning the abstractions of geometry. We learned French and Spanish, too, which later became quite valuable to me. I would never have been able to survive my years at the Spanish court or become a confidante to the queen had I not been fluent in these languages.

But as I consider all the things he taught me, I think I am most grateful to Signor Cavallaro for introducing me at an early age to Dante's *Divine Comedy*. Together, with our teacher as our guide, we followed Dante through the realms, the *Inferno*, *Purgatory*, and *Paradise*. Most of the things we read were not easy for me to grasp, but there are certain passages that hover in my memory and that I carry with me to this day. In the *Inferno*, Dante's guide tells him that if we do not act to awaken who we are, any trace of ourselves will vanish in time the same way that smoke dissipates in air or foam dissolves on a wave.

This thought haunts me now as I dwell on how much I want my name and art to be remembered. Perhaps I am being presumptuous, but I have always felt I have something to give to the world. The older I get, the more urgency there is for me to secure my legacy. Whether a blessing or a curse, I think Signor Cavallaro was instrumental in placing this desire in me. He used to say, "Never forget that your life is important, Sofonisba."

I realize now how contrary his view was to the prevailing thought of the day. When I was young, women had no power whatsoever, which was a shift—Signor Cavallaro taught us—from the Middle

Ages, when women could own property and make decisions. With the rebirth of antiquity in the 1400s came a new imagining of the human being in nature. Male and female alike were depicted more realistically in art than they had ever been before, but women's roles in the affairs of the world suffered, and women were not free to make decisions or pursue their talents. Things have gotten a bit better, as there are now women being recognized for painting: myself, Lavinia Fontana, Barbara Longhi, and a few others. In music, women composers are being published and their compositions performed: Paola Massarenghi, Vittoria Aleotti, and my favorite, Maddalena Casulana. It is a new century, and I do have hope.

But it is not just my artistic legacy that weighs on me. As I think back on Dante's journey in pursuit of higher realms with his beloved Beatrice, I worry the sins I have committed in this life could land me—if not in eternal hell—in purgatory for a very long time. Through it all, I have aimed to stay close to God in my heart. One reason I want to write down the story of my life—aside from being remembered—is that in doing so, I can repent my youthful transgressions. I hope I will be forgiven by confessing my sins. I pray that my place in paradise will not be denied.

It was a sad day for all of us when Signor Cavallaro was called home to Sicily. He gave us his copy of the *Divine Comedy* with an inscription: *To the daughters Anguissola, may each one prosper in her own way.*

I have kept the book all these years, and whenever I read his kind words, I am filled with emotion. I wonder what became of my dear Signor Cavallaro. After he left us, we did not hear from him again. I imagine by now he is dead. I trust he found his Beatrice and made his own way to Paradise.

Orazio is home! I am so happy to see him. My husband makes eight to ten sea voyages each year. Sometimes he is gone for just a week or two, sometimes for more than a month. When he is away, I devote myself to my commissions. When he returns, my heart lifts at the sight of him. Orazio is a man who is rich in spirit. I believe he is closer to God than the rest of us. I think this comes from spending so much time on the open sea, where there is nothing between him and God but the stars.

Orazio's eyes are as blue as the sky, and his face is framed by brown curls streaked with a few strands of gray that have recently begun increasing in number. He is a man of compact build, not much taller than me. His arms can lift great weight and his hands are calloused from long years of handling the rigging of his ship, the *Sant'Agata*. His ship is his child, and the sea his other wife. I don't mind. Orazio's heart is big. There is room in there for both me and the sea.

Being married to this man who is two decades my junior makes me feel much younger than my seventy-two years. He is generous and thoughtful, always bringing me a gift from wherever his ship has taken him. Sometimes he brings fabric, sometimes a ceramic piece, sometimes sweets. Today's gift was a stack of sheet music.

"I know how much you like to have new music for the clavichord," he said. "I purchased these sheets in a music shop at the port of Livorno."

I sifted through the pages to see compositions by all my favorite composers: di Lasso, Palestrina, Casulana. I chuckled when I saw the name Lodovico da Viadana.

"What makes you laugh, my love?" he asked.

"I received a letter from Asdrubale the other day telling me that da Viadana is the new choirmaster at San Luca. I think my brother wants to lure me home to bring him some money. It seems he is nearly destitute."

"Maybe you ought to go see him."

"I've been thinking that will be best. But first, I must finish the portrait of Signor Bruzzone, and there is one more reason to delay. I have a student."

"A student? This is news."

We sat down to eat the meal that Giulia had set out for us.

Orazio bit into a fig. "Tell me about this student."

"His name is Francesco Rossi. He left his father's vineyard in Tuscany, just outside Florence, in search of me and arrived at our doorstep two weeks ago."

"Surely he desires to learn from the very best."

My husband's flattery hit his mark, causing a blush to rise in my cheeks. "He has a good eye, and he is making progress. I enjoy having a student."

"I am glad to hear it. I look forward to meeting him soon. And what about Signor Bruzzone? How is his portrait coming?"

"That man is tiresome! He is always late, and I can't seem to get his face right."

"Maybe that's because he never smiles," Orazio said. "Whenever I see him at the dock, he looks so grim. You should paint a smile on his face and be done with it."

We laughed. "I think you might be right, dear Orazio."

My husband poured me another glass of wine. After taking a sip, I said, "There is one more bit of news to share."

"And what would that be, my love?"

"I have begun to write down the story of my life to document how I became an artist."

Orazio set down his fork, taking hold of my hand. "Sofi, you have been busy! I am delighted to hear this news, but does writing trouble your eyes?"

I was not surprised that he would ask me this. He knows how easily my eyes tire.

"It does cause some strain, but I am being careful."

Always wanting to find a way to help me, he said, "Maybe we should look for a scribe to write down your words for you."

"I had the same idea. In fact, and I've asked Francesco for his help."

"That is good. I am even more eager to meet him, and I look forward to reading your story."

"Oh, I forgot to mention—at long last, I received the *fides vitae*!"

"You did?" As I suspected might happen, this made Orazio laugh. "If only they would come visit, they would see how truly alive you are!"

"I contacted your notary friend and it is all taken care of. I have sent it off and have also sent a letter to King Philip asking that my pension be assigned to my brother. But, it could be several months before the funds arrive in Cremona."

"Well then, my love, you must go see your brother and rescue him from becoming a pauper! But, let's wait until after we celebrate your birthday. We need to pick a date."

I have no birth certificate and don't know my exact date of birth. My father always told me I was born in 1532, sometime in autumn. Each year, Orazio and I celebrate whenever it is convenient to do so, and often, the celebration extends over a period of weeks.

"I think we should do something elaborate for your seventy-third birthday, don't you?"

"You mean, in case I don't make it to seventy-four?"

"That wasn't my intention, but now that you mention it, I'm so glad that you have signed the *fides vitae*!" At that, we both laughed again.

Orazio always brightens any situation. No doubt, his ability to make me laugh helps keep me among the living.

Giulia cleared away our plates and brought some sweets.

"Let's read the manuscript," he said. I handed him the pages, and while I savored a piece of honey cake, my husband read my own story out loud to me. When finished, he reached out and embraced me.

"You have a great story to tell, my love. I look forward to seeing what comes next."

APPRENTICED

One day toward the end of my thirteenth year, Papa came into the garden with a chair and sat down to watch me and Elena draw. Mother stood behind him with her hand on his shoulder and her gaze turned down. She looked tired and her face was lined with worry.

After a few minutes, Papa cleared his throat.

"Girls," he said. "Can you please stand for just a moment?"

We obediently stood, and he looked at us with so much love. "Your mother and I have discussed this, and we feel it is time for you to have more formal instruction in the art of drawing and painting."

Elena and I turned to look at each other, her eyes questioning mine. *What does this mean?*

"What shall we do, Papa?" I asked.

"I have a colleague who is known to me because of my service to the Church of San Sigismondo. His name is Bernardino Campi and he is an artist. In fact, he just recently completed a project to decorate the interior of the church with the most beautiful frescoes."

Papa looked at Mama, who gave a slight nod.

"Mama has finally agreed with me and so I have arranged for the two of you to live with Signor Campi and his wife, to be apprenticed to him in his studio. There you will learn the art of drawing and painting."

Elena grabbed my hand. "You mean we are leaving home?"

Mama put her hands to her cheeks as if to press back her tears.

"We will be happy to go, Father," I said, squeezing Elena's hand hard. *Don't ruin this, sister*, I thought. I also tried not to look at my mother because I did not want to see her crying.

"You will still be in Cremona, so you will not be far away," Papa said. "But yes, you will go to live with Signor and Signora Campi. You will come home for a few days at the end of each month. If all goes well and you make progress, we will think about what should come next."

"This is a great opportunity," Mama said with tears in her eyes. "I will miss you both, but I know that your father is thinking of what is best for you. I give you my blessing to go."

"Oh, Mama, Papa. This is a true gift. Thank you!" I said.

"We look forward to great things from both of you," he said.

Elena squeezed my hand harder, and Mama embraced us each in turn.

One week later, we left home and found ourselves in the home of Bernardino and Anna Campi. The boy apprentices—seven of them—slept in a common room attached to the studio, but Elena and I were treated more like house guests. Tucked under the roof, the small room we shared in the Campi's home had slanted walls on two sides. Elena made me laugh when she said, "We are sleeping in a triangle!"

I loved our little triangle room. There was a window on each side of the triangle, right over the bed we shared. Our first night there, we lay together with our arms around each other and looked up at the stars.

"Why do you think Papa sent me here too?" Elena said. "I cannot become an artist." We had known for many years that as the second daughter, Elena was destined for the convent.

"But you might still be able to paint inside the convent," I told her.

"That is not my destiny. If anyone will be an artist, it will be you, Sofi," she said, turning her back to me.

I knew her frustration was real, and I felt guilty knowing I would be free while my sweet sister would not be. But she was trying to take her fate in stride, while I was trying to fight fate on her behalf. My sister did not like to fight. She was willing to accept things, whereas I was always looking to change them.

Every morning, I awoke before the sun. I loved the sound of songbirds beginning their choirs just as the sky let darkness slip. I awoke to their trills and peeps, and I moved around in the nascent light to pull on my clothes and rouse Elena. It was always a struggle.

"Get up, sister! The day is here."

"No, Sofi. Let me sleep," she would say.

My sister had never liked waking up early. This was not something new that came with living with the Campis. Ever since I could remember, I had risen before dawn while Elena had wanted to sleep until well after the sun was high in the sky.

"Let's go," I'd say, pulling on the bedclothes to unwind Elena from her dreams.

"No. You go without me."

"Elena, you can't not go. Get up!" My sister could be obstinate, and I sometimes felt more like her mother than her sister.

I was excited to wake up every day, get dressed, and sit at the table where we had our morning meal. Even though Signora Campi had a housemaid, she prepared and served our bread, cheese, fruit, and warm milk herself. She was always a source of morning cheer. She made me feel at home, and because she and Signor Campi had no children of their own, it seemed to me that she thought of all the apprentices as her children. I think she was especially glad when Elena and I came. We were her first and only daughters.

In addition to our daily drawing assignments, all of us swept the floors, cleaned the workbenches, and washed the brushes. We organized tools and put things away in their proper places. We learned to stretch and prime canvas, grind pigments, and use oil to turn the colored powders into paint.

The boys were not terribly friendly, at least not at first. They kept to themselves and mostly ignored us. They put on airs of being superior artists to us when, in fact, they were just as much novices as we were.

From the oldest to the youngest there was Nico, Angelo, Pietro, Jacopo, Giuseppe, Massimo, and Bepe. I was younger than Nico and older than Angelo. I decided that if the boys were going to ignore me, I would ignore them in turn. So, I did not trouble myself with them too much. Over time, they let down their guard a little and seemed to acknowledge both me and Elena as fellow students. I so much wanted them to like me. Mostly, it seemed they did not, but there was one exception.

Nico's feelings for me did not start out as love, nor mine for him. In fact, at first he was jealous of me because I was more skilled at drawing than he was. I tried not to outshine him, but there was nothing I could do. I could not hide my ability to draw any more than I could willfully stop myself from breathing. My drawing just was.

One day, we were outside doing studies of flowers. Like my mother, Signora Campi kept a beautiful flower garden, and there was much to see and draw there—violets, lilies, roses, cyclamen, bougainvillea, and more. Signor Campi assigned us to select two different flowers that were not growing near each other, asking us to put them together in a composition so they appeared to belong together. It was not a particularly difficult assignment, but it did have its challenges related to scale and perspective. The task was to bring two disparate things together so they appeared to be related to one another, and to make the composition look realistic as well as interesting and pleasing. I got straight to work.

Signor Campi expected us to be quiet as we worked, but on this particular day, Nico would not stop troubling me with questions.

"What are you doing?" he asked.

"What do you mean?" I said.

"I mean, what flowers are you putting together?"

"Why do you care?"

"I just want to know what you are choosing, Sofi."

We weren't supposed to be talking. We were supposed to be drawing, and if he needed help choosing a flower, how could I possibly do that for him?

"I am drawing that rose, there," I said, pointing to a large bloom in the middle of the garden.

"Why that one?"

"Why not that one?"

He frowned at me and dropped his eyes back to his paper. I saw it was blank, and then I felt sorry for him. How can one aim to be an artist if one doesn't know how to make choices as far as what to draw? My heart softened. "Do you see one that you like?"

He looked up at me again. "Not really, no."

There was a fearful look in his eyes. I wondered if poor Nico worried that his inability to find something in the garden to draw meant his future as an artist was grim. Like all of us, he had been sent by his father to learn the craft of painting, but he seemed to have no real skill for the job, and it was quite possible that he might never amount to anything at all.

"Try, Nico. There must be something here you see that is beautiful."

"Maybe," he said, dropping his eyes.

I went back to my two flowers and tried not to pay him any mind. And yet, I felt sympathetic to his plight. It was possible that, like Elena, he was not destined to be an artist.

Soon after this conversation among the roses, Nico and I began our secret meetings. Somehow, we would suddenly find ourselves near the wood bin, or the scrap pile, or the well. We might be sitting together one day at the pigment table or putting tools away at the tool shed. Whenever we found ourselves in proximity, I could feel our hearts beating in unison. Soon, when we met, we found a way to touch, to have some piece of our clothing brush the clothing of the other person, so softly it barely made a sound, but I could feel it like a spark of fire flying up through my body. The look in Nico's eyes told me he felt it too.

Soon, we made it a point to find each other somewhere, anywhere, and for just a few seconds, to hold hands. The first few times we did this, nothing else passed between us, just holding. Then one day, this holding of hands shifted. We were near the woodpile. It was high sun and very warm. There was the slightest breeze and the smell of roses. We clasped hands and for the first time, we raised our faces and our eyes met. I felt myself being pulled down into the deep well of his eyes. I thought I might faint. We heard the voices of the other boys coming and let go of our hands. We said nothing to each other, just smiled.

The very next day at our morning meal, Nico was not there.

"Where is Nico?" Bepe asked. Bepe, in particular, looked up to Nico like an older brother.

Signor Campi told us that very late the previous night, Nico's father had taken him away. "Nico has gone to Milan to the cloth guild. He was not progressing here. His father did not want to invest any more money training his son in the wrong profession."

Bepe's face fell in disappointment, and no one at the table—not even Elena—knew how deeply I also felt this loss. Thinking of this moment now, sixty years after it happened, the pain is still sharp in my heart. Someone I cared about had been taken away without warning. We did not get to say goodbye. We never kissed. We just held hands and looked into each other's eyes.

I often wondered if Nico felt the same pain I did. I wish I could have given him a drawing, a poem, anything to remember me by. Nico's departure put the first crack in my heart. Still today, my eyes get moist at the smell of roses.

Francesco

When I arrived at the studio today, Signora Anguissola was sitting in her chair with her head tilted back on a cushion and a cloth lying over her eyes. Upon hearing my footsteps, she pulled the cloth away.

"Ah, Francesco. I'm glad you are here."

"I hope I'm not too late. How are you?"

"You are not late, but I am upset with myself. I think I have been doing too much writing and stirring too many memories." She dipped her cloth in water, wrung it out, and repositioned it on her eyes.

"Do you want me to help with writing today?"

"I do," she said. "Today is a good day for you to be my scribe because I will share information you need to know if you are going to be a painter."

I went to her desk to retrieve the portfolio, the inkwell, and a quill.

"Please look under the desk," she said. "Do you see a plank of wood?"

I picked up the lap-sized piece of varnished oak and tested its weight in my hands.

"Orazio made that for us, thinking you could use it as a portable writing surface."

"What a thoughtful gesture," I said, then settled myself into a chair next to my teacher. "I'm ready now, Maestra. Please, begin."

LAPIS LAZULI

One of the most important things I learned from Signor Campi was how to grind pigments and make paint. He used so many interesting materials. Some were quite common, like bone black, sienna, and umber. There were other pigments much more precious—like carmine from the New World, which is made from the dried, crushed bodies of cochineal insects and results in a bright red pigment that is perfect for rendering the robes of clergy.

And then there was the most expensive of all, lapis lazuli—a hard stone that takes a lot of time and energy to grind. It is a rock that comes from the Far East and makes a deep, rich, mystical blue called ultramarine, so called because it literally comes from beyond the sea. This very special hue was reserved for the sky and for the robe of the Virgin Mary. It cost Signor Campi dearly, and he taught us to be careful in preparing it.

The first time I sat down to grind lapis lazuli, I could not do it. I tried again and again, but the stone would not break.

"Slow down, Sofonisba," Signor Campi said. "Push very hard."

I tried to follow his instructions, but it still did not work, and frustration welled up inside me. My teacher just smiled.

"I know how you feel, Sofi," he said. "I had this same problem when I first tried to grind lapis. Just keep trying. Take a deep breath and press down hard."

I closed my eyes and inhaled. I opened my eyes and looked into the bronze mortar. The blue pebble looked so firm and defiant. I put the pestle against it, and as I exhaled, I pressed hard. The stone broke.

"You see?" he said. "Breathe and press on. Never give up when you want something."

Once the stones had been ground into powder, there was still much to do to make ultramarine. We used as our guidebook Cennino Cennini's manual for artists, *The Craftsman's Handbook*. This text became like a Bible for us, detailing all the technical processes artists needed to know. Once we had a good quantity of blue powder ready, we blended beeswax, pine rosin, and gum mastic over a small, contained flame. Once these ingredients were combined, we put the sticky mixture into a white linen cloth and strained it over a washbasin. Into the mixture would go the blue powder and, with much stirring, we'd make a thick, doughy substance. This blue dough had to sit in the washbasin to harden.

It took three days for the mixture to reach the proper consistency.

Then, over the hard dough, we poured warm lye. We took turns using two paddles to knead the mixture, just like bread dough. Eventually, the lye became bright, bright blue and we collected that into a bowl and covered it. It thrilled me every time I saw the first yield of ultramarine from the lapis lazuli I had ground. We poured more lye and continued to knead the blue dough, and each time, we pressed out another yield of blue liquid. The dough was like a sticky sponge that retained all the impurities of the original pulverized rocks. The startling blue liquid was released through the process of cooking, hardening, soaking, and kneading. It was magic.

To this day, my teacher's words still echo in my ear: "Breathe and press on. Never give up when you want something." Although I was young, I knew Signor Campi was not talking only about grinding lapis lazuli. He was talking about life. But at that time, I did not know what I wanted. He must have sensed my uncertainty because he also said, "Remember, Sofonisba, the meaning of your family name."

I was fourteen. What did I want? I certainly had no desire to be a lone snake. It was not so much the word "snake" that troubled me. It was "lone." Even though I could see that I was on a singular journey in life, I did not want to be alone. The one thing I wanted was to become a skillful painter. I listened to my teacher and pressed on. My path would not be not easy, and while my father opened many doors for me, there was still much that stood in my way. There was always something I was pressing against. And now, I am pressing against time itself.

"What do you think?" the Maestra asked.

"I think making ultramarine sounds like magic. Thank you for explaining the process to me."

"You are welcome. Thank you, Francesco, for writing for me today. I hope you and I can make ultramarine together soon," she said. Then she studied her hands in that same anxious way she had done when she first asked me to be her scribe.

"What is wrong, Maestra? Are your eyes hurting?"

"Actually, my eyes feel better. I think perhaps it is healing to me to share my memories with you, my eager and thoughtful student."

"I'm so glad, Maestra. You must always let me know how I can help you."

"I do have another small favor to ask of you," she said, twisting the cloth in her hands.

I set the writing board down on the floor at our feet. "Anything you need, I can help."

"I'd like it if you could call me Sofi. I know it is unusual to be so informal, and I do appreciate 'Maestra.' But, if you are agreeable, Francesco, I would like to be Sofi to you. Your presence is such a gift to me."

"And yours to me—Sofi."

I walked home through the market, feeling lucky to be learning things from a teacher as kind and knowledgeable as Signora Anguissola—Sofi. I will have to get accustomed to calling her that. And despite Dario's ignorant disdain, it feels good to have a feminine force guiding me. Look at Dante and Beatrice. Look at all the artists who have put their trust in the Muses—women, every last one of them. I wish I could make Dario understand, but I don't think it's possible. He is who he is, and I cannot change him.

As I passed the front windows of the Barbarossa to head up to my room, Giuseppe saw me and beckoned me into the taverna.

"I have something for you," he said, setting down the mug he was drying and handing me an envelope with a red wax seal stamped *DB*. I turned the envelope over a few times, aware it could only be from Dario. I couldn't imagine what he would have to say to me in a letter.

"Aren't you going to open it?"

"I suppose so," I said, then broke the seal. In angular, scratchy script was an invitation.

"Dario is inviting me to compete in a foot race, to be held tomorrow on the path along the sea at the city's southern edge."

"Interesting." Giuseppe picked up another mug to dry.

"He says it will be good entertainment and he hopes I will show myself. He writes, 'You should forget about art and old crones who think they have something to teach you. Join our crew. We know how to have a good time.'"

"Will you go?"

"I'm not sure. Do you think he hopes to humiliate me in public?"

"I wouldn't put it past him. Be careful, my friend."

"Thank you, Giuseppe. I will think about it."

"Thinking requires some sustenance. Here, take this." Giuseppe handed me a hunk of bread, a plate of sardines, and a mug of wine.

It was not even close to sunset yet. I sat down at a table looking out toward the sea. As I ate, I pondered Dario's request. It seemed highly unlikely that he truly wanted to befriend me, and more likely that he planned to do me some harm. I reminded myself I am a good runner. After my mother died, I ran up and down the rows of my father's vineyard trying to make myself whole again. At nine years old, it was the only way to allay my grief. I think I did not even know what grief was back then. I just knew that I needed to move my body as fast as I could to make the pain of losing her go away.

Last night, I lay awake thinking about my mother, Dario's invitation, and my desire to paint. I eventually drifted off to sleep and dreamed that I was on a ship at sea in the middle of a dreadful storm. The sky was pitch black and lit by bolt after bolt of lightning that spread across the night sky like white fingers. Thunder boomed and waves rolled over the deck of my ship, drenching me at every turn. It occurred to me that I might very well be washed over the railing to be devoured by the waves.

Then, the oddest thing happened. I saw in front of my face a little sparkle of light, almost like a candle flame. It hovered in front of my eyes and seemed to beckon me. I heard in my heart the words of God from the Book of Isaiah in the Old Testament: *Fear thou not, for I am with thee.* With those words, everything shifted and the storm vanished. The flicker of light expanded before my eyes until it became the entire sunlit sky that cast a field of shimmering diamonds across the breadth of the newly calmed sea.

Standing before me was an angel whose radiant face was framed by golden-brown curls. I opened my mouth to speak, but the angel put its finger to my lips to silence me. It took hold of my hands and lifted me off the deck of the ship, and we rose high into the pink morning sky. The higher we went, the less and less I could sense my body, and I seemed to become only my thoughts, looming in the vast sky. The last thing I remember from the dream was a thought: *This is all that matters.*

Whether it was the angel and its divine light or Sofi's faith in me, I woke up this morning realizing that I must meet Dario and his friends to show them exactly how fast a man who is learning to be an artist can run.

I arrived at the meeting place a little before the sun was at its height, just as Dario's invitation instructed. He was already there with a number of other runners.

"Artist! Greetings!" Dario called, as though we were the oldest and dearest of friends. "Come and get ready for the first race. We need to do some weeding of this crew."

Twenty young fellows were scattered about, bending and stretching, preparing to run.

"There will be three races," Dario announced. "The first will narrow the field to the top ten runners. The second race to five. And the final race will name the winner."

He paused and rubbed his hands together, a sly grin on his face. "And the four losers will do the winner's bidding for an entire week!"

All the fellows laughed heartily, as though this kind of declaration came often from Dario, a man accustomed to being the victor in all things.

A boy of about twelve sat on the sidelines with a barrel of fresh water. Dario ruffled the boy's hair and said, "You all know my brother, Agnolo. Listen for his whistle to begin the race."

We lined up, took our marks, and waited. At the shrill sound of Agnolo's whistle, I leapt. Like a herd of wild horses, we were off. I found my pace quickly and put myself at the front of the pack. Dario, smaller than me and with shorter legs, was nonetheless a strong runner, and I could see him at my side. When the first race ended, about a hundred meters from where we began, we were both in the group of ten that finished first.

"You have done some running in your day, artist," Dario said, panting to catch his breath.

I did not give him the satisfaction of my story. "Only the usual child's play," I said as we made our way back to the starting line with all the other fellows.

"Drink up everyone," Dario said. "The second race begins soon." Then, we lined up and Agnolo whistled once again. The men on the sidelines shouted to spur us on. My heart pounded like a beating drum and I had no doubt that I would finish ahead of most of the other runners. The second race ended with both Dario and me in the final five.

We were all breathing heavily as we walked back along the seashore to begin again. "Let us rest for just a few minutes," he said, cupping his hands in the water barrel. "Don't you think you ought to have some water, artist? Or are you too good for that?"

I shrugged my shoulders and took a little water in one palm.

"You are fast," he said, "but this time, I will get you."

When Agnolo whistled a third time, I used every bit of power left in me to take the lead from the beginning and hold onto it. I felt confident in my ability even though I was aware of Dario on my heels. I kept in mind the image from the dream, that moment when I flew up into the sky with the angel. I knew I would win if I just held that vision of flight.

I crossed the finish line first. Dario was right behind me.

Breathing hard, and quite red in the face, Dario said, "You are fast, artist."

He sounded surprised.

"You should forget about art, you know—become one of us."

I was drenched in sweat and breathing heavily myself. "Thank you, but I am happy as I am," I said, and with that, I dipped my hand into the water barrel one last time. Agnolo looked up at me with the slightest smile on his face and winked. I winked back. Then I took my leave of Dario and his friends.

Sofonisba

I have finished Signor Bruzzone's portrait, despite the fact that he did not return for a final sitting as we had discussed. Nevertheless, I decided to move forward and work from memory. While I did not take Orazio's advice and give the shipbuilder a full smile, I did put some warmth in his cheeks and made his eyes sparkle. I am pleased with the result, particularly the view of the sea through an open window behind him. I sent a messenger yesterday to invite him to view the painting today.

I continue to wonder why Signor Bruzzone was so disagreeable during his sittings. My thought is that perhaps, like other people I have known, he has experienced too much hardship in his life. He has become bitter and hardened on the outside, while inside he is just another lost soul looking for human kindness.

"Signora," Giulia called. "Your guest is here!"

"Please send him up," I said from the doorway of my studio, where I waited for him.

Signor Bruzzone arrived at the top of the stairs, wiping his brow.

"Forgive me, Signora, for missing the last sitting. How did you finish without me?"

"Your face is not one to forget," I said. "I hope it will please you, Signor." I pulled the drape off the painting.

He looked at it for a long moment. Then he put his hands upon his chest and said, "Oh Signora, it is stunning!"

"I am so glad to hear you say that, Signor."

"I was worried that I was not a very engaging subject for you, Signora."

I could not quite believe what I was hearing.

"I will hang this in the entry hall of our new palazzo on the Via Garibaldi so everyone will see it when they enter my home." He paused to wipe his brow. "Signora, would you have time to paint a portrait of my wife—and perhaps my children, too?"

How is it that someone who was so unpleasant the whole time I was working on his portrait is suddenly my most faithful customer? Is it possible my patience won him over? Since I can't ask, I suppose I will never know for sure. Perhaps my painting shows him a side of himself he did not realize was there.

"I will be going to Cremona soon, but—"

"But of course, when you return? Then will you honor me? For now, let me revel in this grand image you have created of me."

We stood together quietly for a while, taking in the painting. I had to admit, I did well.

He fished around in the pocket of his coat and pulled out a cloth bag. "And now, your recompense, Signora, for this great work you have done."

As he handed me the money, Matteo Bruzzone actually smiled.

FIRST LIE

One day, Signor Campi arranged for all the apprentices to visit the morgue and witness a dissection. Because I knew that girls were not allowed there, I asked Angelo if I could borrow a pair of trousers and a cap in order to disguise myself. He provided what I requested and seemed excited to be my accomplice. "I hope this works," he said.

Everyone gathered to get in the horse cart. I had hidden my hair under the cap, certain I must look like a boy. As I approached the cart, Signor Campi put his hand on my shoulder.

"Sofonisba," he said. "I know you want to go, but I cannot take you to the morgue. I will get in trouble with the authorities if I bring a girl to witness the dissection of a cadaver."

"But Signor Campi. I must go. I must learn. No one will recognize me."

"I'm sorry, Sofonisba. You must stay here with Elena and Signora Campi. Make some sketches of your hands for me. Cadavers are something you are not permitted to know."

Signora Campi was standing at the door, watching this unfold.

"Come, Sofonisba," she said. "I will take you and Elena out for an adventure. We'll take paper and chalk and make some sketches from the figures in San Sigismondo." She smiled and held out her hand to me. "Come, my dear. We'll have our own good day."

And so we did. Signora Campi packed a lunch basket and we set out in the carriage for San Sigismondo, well past the edge of the city. It was a hot, still June afternoon. As we entered the church, I felt as though the world outside had come to a halt. It was so much cooler inside, and the air smelled of frankincense. The frescoes on the nave's walls and ceiling inspired a feeling of soaring toward Heaven.

"The frescoes are so beautiful," I said, awestruck. "Did Signor Campi do all this?"

"My husband comes from a whole family of painters. Some of these were done by his brothers. But, he did quite a few. Here is one of my favorites," she said, pointing to an image of Saint Philip and Saint James talking together under a fruit tree. I was intrigued by the colors and the gently swaying forms and so I settled myself to make a drawing of the two figures.

After some time, Elena looked over my shoulder. "What are you doing?"

"What do you mean, what am I doing?"

"Sofi, you are not drawing what you see, you are drawing what you want to see."

I tilted my head side to side to see if by changing my viewing angle, I would understand what my sister was talking about. Her criticism made no sense to me.

"I am drawing what I see," I said softly, "and how it makes me feel." We were the only three people in the church, but still, I felt we should keep our voices down. Having an argument in God's house would be ill-mannered.

Elena shook her head but did not lower her voice. "You are not supposed to do that," she said. "You are supposed to copy *exactly* what you see."

Her idea to copy exactly what is seen was not the lesson I had learned from the teachings of Signor Campi. Elena's interpretation confused me. For me, an artist was to observe, feel, and then create something new.

"And who said that?" I asked.

"Our teacher! We are supposed to imitate nature, not make it do our own bidding."

"Well, this is not even nature, here. This is art. We are looking at Signor Campi's interpretation of two apostles. They might not even be real."

Elena's face turned bright red and her voice got even louder. "How can you say that? Of course they are real!" I had never seen my sister so angry. Signora Campi looked up from her prayer book.

"It upsets me that you take these liberties," Elena continued. "You do whatever you wish. Today, you dressed up like a boy hoping to get to the morgue. That is not the way God wants us to be. God wants us to follow the example of good people, and to do as we are told by our teachers."

"So, this is about the morgue, is it?"

"No!" Elena turned away from me. "It is about you, my sister, being a liar."

I felt her words like a blow to my stomach. And, the reason it hurt so much is that what she said was not completely untrue.

At this point, Signora Campi set down her prayer book and came over to us. "Girls," she said. "No more fighting. Let's pack our things. It is time to go home."

On the carriage ride home and for the rest of the evening, Elena did not look at me or speak.

After that episode with Elena, I began to think a lot about what God was asking of me. I feared that things were only going to get worse the older I got. I began to think that perhaps my life was a test. I knew I would burn in Hell for the thought, but I wondered if God might possibly be female. Perhaps God was She, and She was testing to see if a woman could do something that had been only in the purview of men. I wanted so much to prove Her right.

I'm not sure how it is happening, but despite all this writing, my eyes are bearing up well. Orazio says he thinks it must be because I am writing with my heart, not my eyes. I think I understand what he means. Writing about my life brings me joy—mostly joy, but sometimes sorrow. Who I once was and who I am now are connected. I would like to understand better how I got to where I am, and what it has meant to be the lone snake.

The last week of each month, Papa came to Signor Campi's house with the horse cart to collect Elena and me to take us home. The first time he came, I was happy to go. I missed my mother and father. I missed my sisters and Antonella. At first going home for a few days was a welcome respite, familiar and comforting. But, as time passed, the daily routine at the studio became my life, and going home was a disruption. More and more, I did not want to leave my lessons or the chores. None of the boys went home. They continued working and practicing and learning. I did not want to fall behind.

It was not the same for Elena. She could not wait to go home. Every day, she questioned why Papa had sent her to study with Signor Campi, and every day, I tried to convince her that being trained as a painter might serve her well, even behind the convent walls. I didn't have any solid proof of this, so one day after Signor Campi excused us all from the studio for the day, I told Elena to go on without me and I fetched the broom to do some sweeping.

My sister sighed and said, "You do too much, sister, but carry on. I will gladly go."

She left and I began to sweep. When Signor Campi realized I was still in the studio working, he said, "Thank you, dear Sofi, but you don't need to do that. Things are tidy enough here. Go outside and enjoy the afternoon sun with your sister."

"Signor, it is Elena I want to ask you about. She feels she does not belong here."

"Is that so?"

"She questions why our father sent her to you when she is destined for the convent."

"Ah, I see," he said, pausing to think for a moment. "You must tell Elena about Antonia Uccello, the daughter of the painter Paolo Uccello. She was a Carmelite nun who painted in the convent. There is also Caterina de' Vigri, a nun who was both a painter and a writer. Being behind the walls of the convent does not necessarily mean your sister will not have the opportunity to create things."

"Thank you, Signor Campi. I will tell her."

He held out his hand and I gave him the broom. "You are a good sister," he said.

That night, when Elena and I lay in our bed in the triangle room, I shared with her what I had learned from Signor Campi.

"I don't know," she said. "I still don't believe I am destined to be a painter. Your drawings are so much better than mine, and in fact, better than what any of the boys can do. You are going to be an artist, dear sister. I am not."

She looked up at the night sky. "I am afraid, Sofi," she said, breaking down in tears. "I just want to take my vows and be done. This waiting for the inevitable is so difficult for me. What will I do when I do not have you to hold me any longer?"

I put my arms around my sister, and together we cried. I knew that a great deal of my strength came from her presence. As much as Elena feared leaving me, I feared letting her go.

Francesco

I hope my prowess on the running field has finally ended Dario's low opinion of me. Today I came to the church of San Siro, which is not too far from Sofi's home. I wanted to clear my mind of all the contempt that Dario has for me. Being in a church always reminds me of the peace of the vineyard. It brings me comfort to sit with God.

When Mass ended, I followed the crowd heading to the door. Just before passing the threshold into the sunlight, I passed the priest. He held out his hands to stop me.

"Greetings, my friend. You are new here," he said. "May I ask your name?"

"Greetings, Father. I am Francesco Rossi. From Florence."

"How nice to meet you! I am Father Valeriano. What brings you to Genoa?"

"I have come to learn drawing and painting from Signora Sofonisba Anguissola."

"Signora Anguissola! What a gift she is to us. And what a noble pursuit for you."

I was about to thank him for his kind words but found myself rendered momentarily speechless by a most arresting sight. A young woman with dark eyes and raven hair approached the door near where we were standing. As she and her chaperone passed, the priest touched her arm to stop her. "Paola Vespucci, how are you today?"

"I'm very well, Father. Thank you. And yourself?"

"I am well. May I introduce you to someone new to Genoa? This is Francesco Rossi. He has come to us from Florence to study art."

The young lady paused and looked straight into my eyes. I was awed by her face—high cheekbones, slender nose, and a wide, inviting smile. Her hair was pulled back tightly in a bun, making her face all the more splendid. It was a face that ought to be immortalized in a work of art. The impertinence of my thoughts brought me back to earth.

She held out her hand. "I am pleased to meet you, Signor Rossi."

I took her hand, which was soft as velvet. Dumbfounded by her beauty, I nevertheless managed to speak. "Signorina, the pleasure is mine."

"Paola is the daughter of one of Genoa's finest cloth merchants," Father Valeriano said. "She does a great service for the Church by helping me transcribe my letters, and she has exquisite handwriting. An art in itself."

Paola blushed. "Father, please. It is my honor to help you."

Something or someone caught the priest's eye and he said, "Excuse me, I must go. I hope we will see you again at Mass, Francesco. Welcome to Genoa!" With that, he was gone.

And yet, I was not ready for Paola to vanish as suddenly. With boldness in my heart, I asked, "Would you ladies have time to walk with me?"

Paola looked at her chaperone, who nodded. Together, we walked out of the church and headed into the street, following the crowd toward the market and the sea.

I wasn't sure what to say and was relieved when Paola began. "So, you are studying art?"

"Yes, with Signora Sofonisba Anguissola."

"I have heard this name," she said, "but we have not yet had reason to meet one another."

"She is a remarkable woman."

We made our way through the market, past the stalls of fresh herbs and vegetables, loaves of bread, iron shoes for horses, ceramic pots. Paola stopped at a fruit seller's stand.

"Are you the same Francesco Rossi who won a foot race the other day?" she said, handing the vendor some coins for two ripe pears.

"Indeed, I am. How did you hear of it?"

Paola tipped her head toward her chaperone and smiled. "It was Fabia who told me."

"Yes," said Fabia. "The defeat of Dario Bacigalupo is already legendary. You are a famous man, Signor Rossi."

I laughed, perhaps a bit nervously. While I wanted to know more, I decided it was better to change the subject.

"What about you, Signorina?" I said. "Please tell me about yourself."

"Well..." she hesitated. "I am eighteen years old and have lived in Genoa my whole life."

"And your father is a cloth merchant?"

"That he is. My mother died four years ago, and Father is preparing me to take over the family business one day."

I had not expected to hear so many personal things so quickly. "My sympathy to you on the loss of your mother, Signorina. I lost my mother, too, many years ago. And what a responsibility it must be to take on your father's business."

"True. I miss my mother terribly, as I'm sure you understand. My sympathy to you as well." She paused. "And honestly, I have no desire to take on the family business."

"Forgive me if I am prying, Signorina, but what would you hope to do instead?"

"I am a poet. At least I aspire to be one. What's more, I dream of one day having my own printing press. I want to bring words into the world."

Paola laughed and drew her hand over her mouth. "I have told you all my dreams, Signor, and all I know of you is that you study art and are fast on your feet."

"You have an impressive dream," I said.

"I have never told anyone my idea about the press other than my father—who is very much against it—and so your words are encouraging, kind sir."

I was becoming more admiring of Paola Vespucci with every passing moment.

"Have you ever heard of Vittoria Colonna, the poet from Pescara?" I asked her.

"I have not," she said.

"Colonna was born to a noble family and experienced many losses in her life. She journeyed to Rome and became famous for her poetry and her friendship with Michelangelo."

"Have her poems been published?" the Signorina asked. "I would like to read them."

"Yes! I have brought a book of Colonna's sonnets with me from home. I would be happy to bring it to Mass next week and lend it to you. I think you will find her work most inspiring."

"That would be wonderful," she said.

The light in her eyes lit a flame in my heart. Just then, the church bell began to toll the noon hour.

"I must say goodbye for now, ladies. I am almost late for an appointment with Signora Anguissola. But I will see you again next Sunday."

"Yes, you will!" Signorina Vespucci said. "Please remember to bring the book of poetry!"

"I will remember."

⁂

Today, Sofi's eyes are once again troublesome. She blamed her condition on too much writing on her own during the week. Of course, it is not my place to stop her from taking on so much without me. But I do worry about her. She is old in years, and I don't want her to strain her eyes so badly that she can no longer paint. But, I must trust her to be the judge of her own abilities. When she asks for my help, I will always be ready to oblige. Today, I will write down her words as best I can. But the whole time I write, I am sure I will be thinking of the beautiful, aspiring poet who wants to read my book of poems by Colonna.

THE PRINCE

In the spring of 1548, we learned that our city, Cremona, would be a stopping place for Prince Philip, heir to the Spanish throne, as he made his way from Madrid to Brussels to visit his aging father, Charles V. It was said that the king suffered terribly from gout and other ailments and, anticipating his own demise, he wanted to prepare his son's reign. The domain of Charles V included Spain, Austria, Germany, the Netherlands, large swaths of Italy, and all the lands recently conquered in the New World. A descendant of the Habsburg dynasty, Charles had always ruled his vast empire from the court in Brussels. The purpose of the trip, as I understood from the talk I overheard between my father and his friends, was for Philip to make himself known to the people of his future realm.

At that time, Cremona was an outlying place, not a major city center. We could, however, lay claim to the fact that Andrea Amati, the great innovator of the violin, was born and worked in our city. He had come on occasion to my father's terrace for discussions with the other men, and I knew him to be a kind and gentle soul.

45

His brilliance in relation to geometry and sound is what led him to transform the violin from a three-stringed farmer's diversion to a refined instrument that could vibrate with a range of emotions from joy to sorrow and back again. I have often wondered if it was Amati's violins that put Cremona on the map of the world, making it a place that a king-to-be would wish to visit. What else would bring Prince Philip to Cremona?

At the time, I was sixteen and still a student of Signor Campi's. I learned about the prince's pending arrival when I was at home visiting my family. I overheard my father talking to his friends one afternoon out on the terrace.

"It is a long journey, made even longer because he is stopping in so many places," Signor Barosi, the cheesemaker, said. "Prince Philip is scheduled to arrive in Cremona early next year."

"Yes, and you know, Jacopo," my father replied, "the noble families of Cremona must receive the prince in high style."

"Absolutely, Amilcare, my friend. Philip may be young now, but one day he will be a great king. He is an ardent protector of the Catholic faith. I am confident he will go to any lengths to expand upon his father's work of making sure Protestants and other heretics are destroyed. Already there are Muslims in the south of Spain who Charles has forced to convert to Christianity. Did you know that?"

"Yes," my father said. "I do know, and I find it appalling. I would hope that acceptance, not judgement, would be the mark of our next ruler."

Papa's statement ignited a barrage of words between him and his friends about the attributes of a good ruler. Wine was poured and they battled over the topic for the rest of the afternoon. I tried to stop listening and focus my attention on sketching their faces, but I knew I agreed with my father.

I was dismayed to hear—if Signor Barosi was to be believed—that Prince Philip intended to rid the world of anyone who spoke of reforms to the Catholic Church, such as those put forth by Martin Luther. In my heart, I was fully with Luther's ideas, although I would never say so out loud. What did I, a mere girl, know about such things?

Upon returning to Signor Campi's, I learned that preparations to welcome Prince Philip at various celebrations had already begun in other quarters, and my teacher was just getting his workshop involved. He made an announcement to all of us that he was looking for willing helpers. I stood right away and looked around for who else would join me. No one else stood, not even Elena. I was alone.

"Come now, fellows," our teacher said. "Where is your civic spirit? Is Sofonisba the only one I have taught to be ready when new work presents itself?"

One of the boys said that painting canopies was "girls' work."

"Nonsense," Signor Campi replied. "All work is honorable when it comes to welcoming the prince. Since no one but Sofonisba has volunteered, I will make it mandatory for you all to contribute to this effort."

And so, side by side with the boys, Elena and I painted flowers, leaves, and scrollwork along the sides and borders of the canvas canopies. I was proud to help prepare for Prince Philip's visit, even if—in my opinion—he had some questionable ideas about the future of the Church. It was exciting to be involved and hard to believe that someone as illustrious as the prince would find his way to Cremona.

Months later, I stood in a long line of people with my father at my side—under a canopy that my sister and I had helped decorate—to meet Prince Philip. As each person approached the throne, an aide asked for names to announce the guests.

"Amilcare Anguissola and his daughter, Sofonisba Anguissola," the aide said.

My father put me in front of him and gently pushed me ahead toward the prince.

As Prince Philip offered his hand to me, he said, "Sofonisba Anguissola. I have heard this name. This is the maiden painter who is raising up Cremona with her fine work."

I was stunned to know that he recognized my name, and I could not speak. My father was standing at my side, and he spoke for me. "We thank you, most honorable and gracious sovereign, for your kind words. My daughter and I are humbled by your lordship's praise."

Papa pressed on my shoulder and I smiled and curtsied, holding out my hand, afraid at first to raise my eyes. But, raise them I did. The prince, only a few years older than me, looked at me with a heartening smile. It was hard to believe he could hate anyone.

"Signorina Anguissola," he said, "I have heard so much praise about your work and I was eager to come to Cremona, hoping to meet you for myself."

My legs almost gave way underneath me. The prince came to Cremona hoping to meet me? The defender of the Catholic faith had heard praise about my work? How and from whom? I wondered if word had gotten out about me through the men who know my father, men like Signor Barosi and all the others.

"The pleasure is all mine, Your Majesty," I said and wondered if I truly meant that, knowing that he had views about the role of the Church that were different from mine.

That was how I first met the future King of Spain, the man who would expand the brutality of the Spanish Inquisition and burn countless poor souls—alleged heretics—in the name of the Catholic Church. The same man who would one day employ me long into my old age.

When Sofi stopped speaking, I looked up from the page. "You have done so much, Maestra. To have a prince know your name—I am inspired by your story."

"It always gives me great joy to know that I have inspired someone," she said.

"I have an idea," I said, putting down the board and standing to stretch my legs. "Just this morning, I met a young lady, the daughter of the cloth merchant Lorenzo Vespucci."

"I know that man. I have bought many bolts of cloth and much lace from him over the years. I did not know he had a daughter."

"He does. And I met this young lady this morning after Mass. Her name is Paola. Father Valeriano said that she writes down his correspondence for him."

"So she has experience transcribing. That's very interesting," Sofi said.

"We took a stroll through the market—" The look on Sofi's face displayed some surprise. "With her chaperone, of course."

"Of course!" she said, nodding, and with a slight smile on her face. "Please continue."

"And what do you make of this?" I said. "Paola told me that her greatest passion is to write poetry. She said her father has educated her because he expects her to take over the family cloth business."

"That is wonderful, to educate a daughter."

"Yes, except that Paola does not want to take over the cloth business. She wants to start a printing press. She wants to publish books.

"And you say she is a skilled scribe?"

"Indeed. That recommendation comes from Father Valeriano himself. I think you two should meet each other."

Sofonisba

Francesco's suggestion that I meet Signorina Vespucci is intriguing. Perhaps I could engage her to help me with my story. It would be lovely to speak about my life to a young woman, in particular one who has some dreams of her own. Francesco has offered to serve as my emissary to present Signorina Vespucci's father with the idea that I am in need of a scribe and ask if he would allow his daughter to serve me in this manner. I hope he will say yes. I am very curious to meet this young lady. Meanwhile, Orazio has gone back to sea unexpectedly. He left early this morning for Barcelona with a load of cargo and a few passengers. When he gets back, sometime in October, we will celebrate my birthday.

I did receive a letter from a secretary of King Philip, and my request to transfer my pension to my brother has been granted. It will take several months to arrange for the first installment of money, but it will happen. I don't understand the reason for the wait, but I am grateful. I will write to Asdrubale this morning to tell him the good news. After my birthday celebration, I will pay him a visit, just to keep him solvent until the pension transfer is complete. But for now, I will return to my story.

DEPARTURE

The prince's visit in 1549 also marked the year that my teacher, Bernadino Campi, was called to Milan to paint a portrait of a noble lady. Signor Campi seemed to be riding a golden chariot. One day soon after he returned to Cremona, he gathered us all together and announced that he would be moving his studio to Milan.

My heart broke to know that he would leave. Signor Campi had taught me so much, not only about line, composition, contrast, and the recipes for painting, but more importantly, how to trust my artist's eye—to believe I even had an eye, my own vision. He taught me to stand up for myself. Without him bringing me to my life as an artist, I would not be the person I am today.

During the years when I was under his tutelage, I developed a habit of slipping into the studio in the late afternoon while Elena was reading her Bible and the rest of the apprentices went off to swim in the River Po or toss a ball in the street. The studio had large windows facing west, and I liked to go there to sit and watch the sunlight move across the work tables. Sometimes I would sketch or straighten up a bit.

One afternoon, close to Signor Campi's departure, I was in the studio dusting the pigment jars and organizing them on the shelf in chromatic order. I started with yellow ochre, then lined up all the umbers and siennas, moving onto carmine, verdigris, lapis lazuli, and ending my rainbow of colors with black gall. I was deep in thought, imagining what life would be like without Signor Campi, trying to picture what would come next. Papa had already arranged a new teacher for me, another prominent Cremonese artist named Bernardino Gatti. I was anxious about building a relationship with a new teacher, for I felt that no one could possibly replace the patience and wisdom of Signor Campi.

"Aha!" Signor Campi said, catching me in the act of dusting the pigment jars. "I always knew you were the sprite who has been keeping things neat and tidy around here."

"Maestro! You startled me."

"Forgive me," he said, smiling. He reached under his desk, bringing up a narrow wooden box.

"For you," he said, pushing the box toward me. "A parting gift to my best student."

I lifted the lid and found a set of pigment jars.

He had included not one but two jars of ground lapis lazuli. Looking at the rainbow of colors and knowing that soon he would leave me, I burst into tears. Signor Campi wrapped his arms around me.

"Shhh, shhh," he said. "Of all my students, you are the one that has the stamina, the intelligence, and the talent to go far. I know there will be walls you will have to knock down, but I am sure you have it in you to do that." Then he handed me a kerchief to dry my eyes.

"Thank you, Maestro," I said. "I will never forget you and all that you have taught me."

"And I shall not forget you, dear Sofonisba. One day, your art will be well known."

Coming unmoored from my teacher's safe harbor was difficult. But it was equally hard to leave the care of Signora Campi. She had become like a second mother to me. On the day we said goodbye, we sat in her garden under the lemon tree.

"You know, I have no daughters of my own," she said, her voice cracking as she handed me a small box. Inside the box was a heart-shaped gold locket on a chain. "This is something my mother gave me when I married Bernardino," she said.

"Signora, it is beautiful. Are you sure you want me to have this?"

"I do. This heart must go to someone special."

With tears in her eyes, she put the necklace around my neck and closed the clasp.

"Make your teacher proud, Sofi," she said. "I know you will."

Francesco

Today, after Mass, I watched for Paola and her chaperone as they left the church, and I pushed through the crowd to catch up with them. When I presented the book of Colonna poems to Signorina Vespucci, she smiled and turned the book over several times in her hands.

"I can't wait to read this!" she said. "Thank you so much for loaning it to me."

With Fabia a few paces behind us, Paola and I began to make our way through the market.

"I remember Father Valeriano saying that you transcribe his letters for him."

"Yes, I do," she said.

"You know, Signora Anguissola is writing the story of her life, and because of an eye ailment that she suffers, she needs the aid of a scribe. I have been serving in this role, but I believe she would find great value in telling the story to a young woman. Like you. Would you be interested in helping her?"

"I don't know," she said. "I mean, I would love to meet her, and I would be honored to help. But I don't know if my father would allow it. He already has trouble with me using a small portion of my time to help Father Valeriano, and he is the priest. I'm not sure he would give me more time away from our business."

"Do you think it would help if I were to make the inquiry to your father on behalf of Signora Anguissola?" I asked.

"That is an interesting proposition," she said. "An inquiry from a gentleman representing the artist might give the request some merit. If you are willing, let's try it!"

I held out my hand to her and she took it without hesitation. Briefly, our eyes met and I felt as though I were floating on a cloud.

"Can I buy you something?" I asked. "Maybe a bag of pistachios? Some pears?"

"A gift is not necessary. I am happy just to walk with you." Her words made my heart pound in my chest as though I had just run around the entire city.

My moment of bliss ended when we came around the corner near the wharf and encountered my nemesis Dario and his friends. They stood right in our path in front of the Barbarossa, already quite far into their cups, it seemed.

"Artist!" one of them called. "Done any more running lately?"

I put my arm around Paola to hurry us along, and Fabia came up quickly from behind.

I did not wish to engage these men, not knowing how far they might go to embarrass us all, so with Fabia now at our side, the three of us kept walking.

"Is that your teacher?" another asked. "She's a beauty! And much younger than you described her."

Dario called out, "Artist, have you dipped your brush in her paint yet?"

Fabia turned, shooting back, "Shut your foul mouth, Dario Bacigalupo, you stupid ass!" As we continued quickly on our way, he responded with the braying sound of a donkey.

"Run away, little rabbits," he called after us, amidst more laughter from his friends.

Once we turned the corner, we stopped. "I am sorry, ladies, for so many rude remarks."

"So that is Dario," Paola said. "The one you defeated in the foot race."

"He is big trouble, that one," said Fabia, who seemed to be speaking from experience.

"He has been taunting me ever since we first met because I came to Genoa to learn to paint. He thinks I'm a fool to believe that a woman has anything of value to teach me."

Paola wrinkled her forehead in great concern. "Should I tell my father about him?"

"Oh no, please don't do that. I'm sure he is harmless."

Fabia shook her head. "Just be careful, young friend. Bacigalupo is

notorious for starting fights, which always finish badly for his opponents."
She then turned to Paola. "It is time for us to go."

"Goodbye, Francesco. Please be careful. Don't forget the plan to approach my father."

"I will not forget."

Paola

I am happy Francesco thinks I would be a good scribe for the aging
artist. I must admit, I hope he finds me pleasing in other ways as well.
I would like Father to meet him. All of my friends have been sent off with
their dowries to enter into marriages that are not about love or choice, but
instead are "good for business."

My father is not so eager to marry me off. Perhaps it is because I am his
only child. He is proud of his clients and wants to keep this enterprise in
our family. It is not my desire, though, to be Genoa's first female cloth and
lace merchant. I have long dreamed of making books. Writing them, and
also printing them. To me, a book is a living, breathing thing. If you hold
it gently in your hands and give it your undivided attention, it will speak
to you.

When I was a little girl, my mother would sit me on her lap and read
books of poetry to me—excerpts from Dante, Petrarch, and Boccaccio. I
did not often understand the words, but I absorbed rhythm and rhyme,
and I wondered if someday I might be able to write my own poems. I did
not know then that most women in this world do not even know how
to read. My mother was rare in this regard, and she formed me to be a
person equally rare. Father not only allowed but supported my education.
I suppose he saw the value in having a child—even a girl—who could
inherit the family business. I think both my parents put all their hopes in
me because I was their only offspring to survive.

My mother became pregnant on several occasions after I was born, but
each time, the pregnancy ended badly. Once, when I was six, I witnessed
my poor mother's agony and I secretly agonized with her. I was frightened

by all the blood on the floor and my mother bent over crying in pain. I thought it was my mother herself who was dying.

Then, when I was seven, a boy was born. My parents named him Tomasino, and I loved him from the moment I saw him. Everything about my little brother was sweet and in need of protection. I couldn't wait for him to grow up so we could run and play.

In the winter before Tomasino turned two, he became quite ill. For two weeks, he could not keep down our mother's milk, and with each passing day, he became weaker. It was a dark and terrible day for all of us when my brother died. I saw my mother and father sitting at our kitchen table, holding each other, crying bitterly. I hid behind the door and heard my mother vow that she did not wish to be pregnant ever again. "Paola is enough," I heard her say. Those words have hung on my heart ever since.

When I was fourteen, Mother caught a fever and took to her bed because she was having trouble breathing. The doctor came but could offer little to improve her situation. He told us to stay near her and do our best to make her comfortable. For days, Father and I took turns sitting by her side, keeping a cool lavender-soaked cloth on her forehead. Each day, I read poetry to her.

On the evening before my mother died, she gathered enough strength to pull me close to her. "Paola," she said, "The world needs poets. Women poets." Then she smiled at me and brought my hand to her lips. "I love you, dear daughter." She closed her eyes and Father and I sat with her into the early morning hours. We prayed for her soul as we let her go.

As I grieved her death, my mother's words led me to begin writing my first verses. I found solace in the act of putting words down on paper to keep her memory alive. I wanted to pay homage to her, using words built upon the poetry she had read to me when I was small.

Now, I am finding new inspiration in the book that Francesco loaned me, the poems of Vittoria Colonna. Her poetry has been like a bolt of lightning to my heart. Unlike Petrarch, who spoke grandiose sentiments to the wide world, Colonna speaks only of herself, her own turmoil, her own grief. Colonna has given me courage to write as though I am speaking to a friend and to speak of things that are personal to me.

When Death Came

When was the day I looked upon you last?
What world was split, never to be the same?
My joy cut short when merciless death came
on a day like no other, now long past.
Once darkness fell, on wings my sadness cast
like a melody with sorrow's refrain
or a chariot I could not detain
that carried my loss, running swift and fast.
Now that you are gone, nothing can soothe me
and nothing lends a hand of kind relief
like your motherly touch that softly drew
our hearts close together with poetry.
And so, I hold this thread of lasting grief,
bringing measure to the memory of you.

Today, according to our agreement, Francesco came to see my father, ostensibly to purchase some lace. I watched in secret from the adjacent room as Fabia let him into the house, and I marveled—as I do each time I see him—at his exquisite good looks. He is tall with a mane of chestnut brown curls, an angular jawline, deep brown eyes, and a bright, alluring smile. I remained hidden so I could listen to his conversation with my father. After exchanging pleasantries and information about lace options, I heard Francesco say that the artist Sofonisba Anguissola was looking for a scribe.

"Ah, yes. Signora Anguissola," my father said. "She has been a customer of mine for years. I'm afraid I know of no scribes. For what purpose does she need one?"

"As you may know, she paints beautiful, lively portraits. She is currently writing the story of her life and how she became an artist. It is taxing on her eyes to do this work on her own.

"I have seen her portraits. They are indeed life-like. But why are you telling me?"

"Well, I have heard it said that your daughter is an aspiring poet. I thought, perhaps, that having the opportunity to serve as a scribe to a woman artist would be good for your daughter."

"Good for my daughter? What knowledge do you have of my

daughter?"

It pained me to hear him respond so harshly to my handsome friend, who was speaking kindly on my behalf. I wanted to run into the room and beg my father to let me help, but I restrained myself.

"Forgive me, Signor. I do not mean to alarm you. I have met your daughter at San Siro, where I have been going to Mass since I came to Genoa. Father Valeriano introduced us and told me that your daughter is well-known for her beautiful script and her ability to transcribe for him when he needs help with his correspondence."

"That is true, yes. But the work she does for Father Valeriano already takes her away from the account books and the work I need her to do here."

I wanted to burst into the room and tell my father that I was not born to be an accountant. But I held myself back.

"I understand, but perhaps there is a way to seize this opportunity," Francesco said. "I respect Signora Anguissola a great deal, and I see that she needs help. Bringing together your daughter with the artist seems to me to be a fruitful partnership for all parties concerned."

"Fruitful partnership? All parties concerned? Think again, young man, because I will have none of it. My daughter is not for lease to an artist to do work she should do for herself."

"Sir, I'm afraid you misunderstand me. This is not anything your daughter would be paid to do. This is a service she would do for Genoa, recording the life of a major artist living here. Your daughter would be highly esteemed and gain valuable skills and knowledge."

Although I could not see him, I imagined my father's face turning bright red at this suggestion. His voice exploded, "Get out! I don't know who you are or why you have come here. Your suggestion is preposterous. My daughter will take over the family business. She cannot serve as a scribe to everyone who needs assistance. Now, good day, sir."

"Signor Vespucci, please—"

"Good day, sir."

I heard the front door open, then slam.

The more I think about how rudely my father treated Francesco, the angrier I become. I am living between two worlds and I don't know how to step in or out of either one. Francesco supports my dreams. Mother would like him for that. But unyielding as ever, Father refuses to consider what I want. He sees only one place for me in this world, and that is tied to his account books. I must make him see that I envision another place.

Today at our morning meal, I set down my fork and gathered my strength to speak.

"Father, please, can we talk about the printing press?" The look on his face was stone cold, as though had not heard me. But I pressed him. "Why are you so opposed to this?"

"A printing press is too expensive." This is something he has said to me many times. "There is too much equipment needed and too many laborers to make it all function."

As he put more butter on his bread, he added new reasoning to his argument. "Furthermore, it is too revolutionary. Printing makes room for ideas, and ideas bring change," he said. "Tradition must always come first."

"But I am not interested in fabric, Father. You know I love books. You educated me!"

"Your mother and I educated you, that is true. I love you and I want to see you successfully carry on this family business."

"You mention mother. What do you think she would say?"

My question clearly flustered him because his knife fell from his hand and clattered on his plate. "I don't know what she would say. But, I know that if you were a boy, I would apprentice you to the cloth merchants' guild and then you would learn what is important."

If I were a boy? My father had never said anything like that to me before. His words fell on my heart like boulders, more painful than if he had hit me on the face with his hand.

"Father! I have heard you say that your business is struggling. Instead of letting this situation drag us down, perhaps it is time to make a change."

"You have a duty to this family, Paola. I gave you an education so you could carry on my work. A printing press is out of the question. You must stop thinking that because I have educated you, you are free to do whatever you wish. You are not free."

A fire flared inside me from the pit of my stomach to the top of my head. I wanted to scream at him. Instead, I pushed back my chair and calmly left the table. I went to my room, sat down on my bed, and cried.

Today, I met Francesco in front of San Siro. Fabia was with me, but she gave her permission for me to walk with him on my own while she kept pace a short distance behind. My new friend was taking me to meet Signora Anguissola. I had not told Father about this meeting, as helping her is yet one more thing I desire to do that my father opposes.

"Something is making you sad today," Francesco said. "What is it?"

I could not repeat out loud what my father had said to me. *If you were a boy* and *you are not free.* The cut of those words remained like a knife in my heart.

"My father continues to oppose my printing press dream. I feel hopeless."

"I'm sorry to hear that, Paola. Perhaps the Maestra will have some ideas on how to convince a father to change his mind."

"That would be a miracle."

We arrived at our destination on the Carubeo Auri Genue, a narrow street that comes off the main thoroughfare, not too far from the Via Garibaldi where all the most illustrious palazzos are being built. A maid let us in at the gate and we entered a peaceful courtyard with ivy-covered walls. Under a potted lemon tree, an elderly woman sat on a wooden chair that had a tall back and was couched with large, embroidered cushions— almost like a throne.

She stood and held out her hands to welcome us. "Francesco, greetings! How are you today?"

"I am well," he said. "Allow me to introduce—"

But before he could finish, Sigorna Anguissola said, "And you must be Paola Vespucci. What a pleasure it is to meet you! Come, come sit down. We must talk!"

There was a vibrant warmth in her presence giving me the feeling that not only did I know this woman, but that she knew me.

Francesco pulled two chairs out from the table and offered one to me.

"First of all, let me say what a pleasure it is to meet you, Signora Anguissola."

The artist smiled. "Ah, the pleasure is all mine. But please, tell me about yourself."

"Well, I am eighteen, and I am trying to find my way in the world. I write poetry."

"Poetry! I love poetry. I hope you will share some of your poems with me."

"I would be happy to." I looked at Francesco again. He looked at me

61

with a smile on his face, so I continued. "Francesco tells me you are writing down the story of your life."

"Yes, that is true. Francesco has been helping me on occasion by transcribing my words. I understand that you are a gifted scribe yourself."

"He is too kind, but yes, I do help Father Valeriano with his letters. If I can do so, it would be my honor to help you write your story."

"As I understand from Francesco, your father has not approved this endeavor."

"That is true, Signora. He has not given me his permission to help you."

"Since I know your father, perhaps it would help if I were to ask him myself. Would that be agreeable to you?

"Certainly, Signora. Thank you."

"And, I have one more favor to ask."

"Anything Signora."

"I feel like we are going to be great friends, and I like my friends to call me Sofi. Can you do that?" She held out her hand to me.

I clasp her outstretched hand in both of mine, "Sofi."

PART TWO

Sofonisba

I sent a letter yesterday to Signor Vespucci seeking his daughter's help. For many years, I have been one of his loyal customers. Surely, he will see that my intentions are good and that his daughter would be of great help to me. And now I find I am truly in need of her services, when before I simply wanted to work with an eager young woman. This morning, Francesco came to tell me he must return home to Tuscany for a few weeks to help his father with the grape harvest.

"I'm sorry, Sofi, because I knew all along that I would have to go," he said. "I should have told you sooner. This is all the more reason I was determined to find you a new scribe."

I assured him I understood. I hope Paola's father will give his blessing to my request. While Francesco is away, and without access yet to Paola, I will just have to take good care of my eyes so that I can slowly and carefully continue writing my story myself.

I have been thinking about choices of late and how women do not have the freedom to make choices for themselves. Looking back, I wonder if I would have chosen to be an artist without my father's encouragement. I like to think this path was my choice, but without him clearing the way at every turn, I might not have gone this way. And I think of Elena, destined from birth for the convent. Would she have chosen that of her own accord?

THE CONVENT

The day that Elena left us in 1551 was a hot, humid summer day much like today. Every flower in my mother's garden was bursting

65

with color, and the aroma of roses was strong. Our entire family stood in the garden waiting for the carriage that would come to fetch Elena and take her away from us.

Asdrubale was only a little over a year old, still a baby in Mama's arms. All five sisters stood around Elena and tried not to cry. Papa and Mama stood off just a bit to keep out of the sun. The carriage was late and we were all hot and tired from waiting. At one point, my mother set my brother down on the grass to rest her arms. Asdrubale crawled over to the flower beds. He pulled up a handful of violets and crawled right to where Elena stood. When he tugged on her skirt to lift himself onto his feet, the movement made Elena gasp and we all turned to see my brother raising his hand to offer his sister a bouquet.

Any fortitude each of us had exhibited up to that point, including Papa, completely collapsed. Every last one of us, except Asdrubale, burst into tears. He looked around with an expression of surprise on his face. Of course, that was the very moment the carriage arrived. We loaded Papa, Elena, and her trunk onto the open carriage. We all stepped back and saw that she was safely ensconced with Papa at her side. The driver snapped the reins and the carriage slowly pulled away from us. Elena raised her arms over her head in a gesture of victory, smiling through her tears. With one hand, she held onto Papa, whose raised arm shared in her triumph. In her other hand, which she placed near her heart, she held Asdrubale's bouquet of violets.

In the days and weeks after my sister left us, I missed her terribly. Three months into this enduring sadness, I asked Papa if I could go to Mantua and visit her. As I was going on nineteen, he gave me his permission to journey to the convent with a chaperone so I could paint her portrait.

The Convent of the Holy Virgin at San Vincenzo was cloistered, meaning no one was allowed inside the walls for any length of time, but because I was going there to paint her, Papa gained permission from the Mother Superior. I was allowed to stay with my chaperone at a nearby pensione and visit every day for two weeks. My job was to capture her likeness in paint.

When I arrived at the convent, it looked inviting enough— certainly it was no prison. The ivy-covered edifice was surrounded by towering oak trees, and lilies of the valley lined the path to the entrance. The Mother Superior herself met me at the door, greeted me warmly, and led me to a sitting room where Elena was waiting for me. I almost did not recognize my sister dressed in her white habit. But when she jumped up and embraced me, I knew she was still my Elena.

I followed her through hallways of cold stone that were devoid of any touches that might add warmth or comfort. Elena's room was quite sparse, with just a bed, a washbasin, and two hooks for her habit and undergarments. We went together to the noon meal, a simple repast of broth with root vegetables and a bit of bread. I was fascinated by all the nuns, young and old, eating together but not conversing and certainly not laughing. It seemed to me to be an isolated and lonely existence. We went back to my sister's room to begin the portrait.

All I could think about was that I wanted to take her home with me. I confessed my desire to her and she sighed.

"Sofi, I am all right. Please don't worry about me."

As I progressed with the portrait, the image that emerged captured her peace. I showed her thumbing through the pages of a Bible, trusting this detail would point to her devotion to God. I hoped this devotion would carry her through the years of quiet isolation and keep her heart rich. Maybe I painted what I wanted to see, her acceptance of her new life. If I had been in her place, I don't think I would have found contentment.

I was able to finish the painting during my short visit with her, and Papa and Mama were glad to have the portrait when I brought it home. Saying goodbye to Elena at the convent was every bit as hard as it had been when she departed from Cremona. We promised we would write. I have saved all her letters, and I read them from time to time. The one letter I cherish the most always reminds me that we each have a unique path in life. Although Elena has been dead twenty years now, her sweet, kind nature is always with me.

My dearest sister,

Greetings to you from Mantua. Thank you for visiting me when I first arrived at the convent to paint my portrait. I am happy to tell you that I am doing well. The sisters are so kind and I am adjusting to this new life of prayer, study, and work. We wake before dawn for Lauds, the first prayer of the day. I know you would be surprised that I am not having trouble with this. At least not too much trouble.

We end the day with Compline, before we go to sleep. In between, we have prayers every few hours, Prime, Terce, Sext, Nones, and Vespers. That one is my favorite, as it is in the evening, just as the sun is setting. It makes me think of you and the many times we watched the colors change on the River Po at sunset. Did you know that the Po comes all the way here to Mantua where it is met by the Mincio? It makes me feel like home is not so far away. My least favorite prayer is Matins, because we have to wake up in the middle of the night. But I am learning.

I think about you every day and wish the very best for you. I know you are going to be recognized as a great artist one day. We are fortunate to have a father who was determined to educate us. As Signor Cavallaro once wrote to the daughters Anguissola, "May each one prosper in her own way." I am sure we will. I am sending you all my love.

Yours forever,

Elena
18 May, 1552

Elena and I were born just two years apart and we came from the womb of the same mother. We learned to draw together in the sunshine, each of us blessed by a father who was devoted to us. But, we were different. And so, while my sister prospered in her soul through prayer and service behind the cool walls of the convent, I kept moving forward into the heat of the world.

THE STUDIO

When I met my new teacher, Signor Gatti, I was nineteen. He was thirty-seven years older than me but full of energy. He was a different kind of teacher than Signor Campi had been, but maybe that is because I was a different kind of student than I had been six years earlier. I did not live in Signor Gatti's home. I stayed with my family and visited my new teacher each day.

When I began my studies with him, Signor Gatti was starting a large fresco for the refectory wall at San Pietro. I would go there and watch him paint in wet plaster directly on the wall. While his apprentices assisted him, I would work on sketching or painting assignments he had given me. I did not let it bother me that being female, I was not allowed to paint in fresco. It is strenuous work, and I was happy instead to perfect my skills with oil on canvas.

One morning when I was about a month into my studies with my new teacher, Papa and I were sitting at home together on the terrace, admiring Mama's garden.

"Sofonisba," he said. "What do you think about having your own studio here?"

I told him this was a wonderful idea, but where? Our house had no rooms to spare.

"I'm thinking of turning the sitting room into a place where you could paint."

"But that room is yours, Papa!"

It was the same room in which Signor Cavallaro had conducted our morning lessons long ago. It was also the room in which Papa entertained his friends on afternoons when it was too wet or windy to be on the terrace. And yet it was perfect for a studio, jutting out on the south side of our house with windows on three sides so all day long it received good light. The windows on the east faced the garden, and my mind filled with thoughts of how pleasant it would be to call this room my own.

"I can make do elsewhere, Sofonisba. If it is raining and I must meet with someone—or ten someones—we will find someplace else to sit. We can sit in the main room, or even in the kitchen. I am not worried about that at all. It is more important that you have a place to paint."

"Oh, Papa, thank you! I will use the table to grind pigments and I'll set my easel near the window where the light is best."

"This will still leave you plenty of room to stretch and prime canvas," he said.

At the mention of priming canvas, I wrinkled my brow.

"What is it?" Papa asked.

"Will Mama let me cook rabbit skin glue for priming canvas in her kitchen?"

"I have already asked her," he said.

"And?"

"And, she has given her blessing."

"Antonella too?" I asked, for I knew who reigned over that domain.

"Antonella, too."

That very morning, we set up my studio. We moved the long, central table against the wall. I set up my easel, and he brought me a mirror and set it on a stand, adjusting it to the height where I could get a good look at myself while painting my own face.

I went to my room and pulled out from under my bed the box containing the jars of ground pigments that Signor Campi had given me. As I was arranging them in chromatic order on a shelf built into the wall above my new work table, Mama came in to examine our progress.

"I have an idea," she said. "What do you think about having Papa bring the clavichord into your studio?"

"Oh, yes!" I said. I was so pleased that she thought of this because it meant that she might join me in the studio at times to sing. "May we do that, Papa?"

"Of course!" he said "I will get some help later and we will move the clavichord."

I laid my brushes, palette knife, and clean palettes on the table. When I had all my tools and materials organized, I stood back to view my new studio. The room glowed with morning light. I took a deep breath. This would be the place where I would become a painter. That day, when I left to join Signor Gatti at San Pietro, I carried with me a new feeling of purpose.

I woke early and worked in my studio every morning before I went to meet my teacher. Some mornings, I would devote myself

70

to sketching. Other mornings were filled by stretching canvases and preparing them to receive paint. There were mornings I would grind pigments and others when I worked on a self-portrait or had one of my family members sit for me.

And some mornings, I would do nothing other than sit in my chair and look at myself in the mirror. I saw a girl in plain, dark clothing who kept her light brown hair parted in the middle and pulled back. I looked into my hazel eyes—my eyes with no lashes. They would change color at times, appearing sometimes more green, sometimes more brown, depending on the time of day and the angle of the light. Looking into my eyes every morning, I became familiar with the spark of creativity, of life, that was in me. That spark has stayed with me, and it is the thing I aim to capture in the eyes of my sitters when I paint their portraits.

On many occasions, I depicted myself sitting at the clavichord. I liked showing the world that I was passionate about music as well as painting. I hoped that my self-portraits at the clavichord might inspire fathers to ensure their daughters received musical training. It is my firm belief that everyone should be musically trained. Music is a gift to the soul.

During my three years with Signor Gatti, I painted many self-portraits. With each new depiction of my own face, I learned more about who I was. I wanted to show the world that I was Sofonisba Anguissola, the lone snake, a woman who truly believed in herself.

Paola

Today, I went with Fabia to meet Francesco at the church to say goodbye before he goes home to his family's vineyard. He and I have not known each other long, but he has won my heart. First of all, he is quite handsome. No one could deny that. But, more than the way he looks, I value the way he understands me. I never imagined I would meet a man who believes my dreams are worthy. I will miss Francesco when he goes.

As we came around the corner onto the Via Garibaldi, I saw him sitting on a bench at the edge of the piazza. He was bent over his sketchbook, engrossed in his work. He was so absorbed he did not realize, at first, that we were standing right in front of him.

"What are you drawing, sir?" I asked, pretending we were strangers.

He looked up, perplexed at first. Upon seeing who was interrupting him, he immediately put down his sketchbook and stood to greet us.

"Paola, Fabia! Good day to you both. I was sketching the pigeons."

"May I see?"

He handed his sketchbook to me, and I was delighted by his renderings of the birds. Together on one page, he had drawn some pecking the ground, some looking up at the sky, and some dipping their beaks in a puddle of water.

"This is so lovely," I said.

"Would you like to keep it?"

When I nodded with enthusiasm, he removed the drawing from the sketchbook, rolled it up, and presented it to me as though it was a royal scepter.

"For you, my lady," he said. "I'm glad you like my birds."

"I do! I like them very much."

"You know, I believe that birds are spirits of the air watching out for us."

"What a lovely thought," I said. "That should be in a poem, you know."

"Maybe you will write such a poem for me one day," he said and offered me his hand. I gave him mine, and he bowed down and touched it lightly with his lips.

"And while I am gone," he said, "look for feathers. If you see a feather on the ground, you will know I am thinking of you."

I reluctantly let go of his hand. I looked at Fabia, who smiled and said, "We will keep watch for feathers, no doubt. You have a good trip, Francesco."

"I will. I will be thinking of you often, Paola, so you should find quite a few."

We said farewell and went our separate ways. The whole way home, I had my eyes on the ground, looking for feathers.

"He hasn't even left Genoa yet!" Fabia teased.

"I know, but I am searching, nonetheless."

It has been three days since Francesco left, and this afternoon, I told my father that I was going to the market with Fabia to buy peaches. He loves peaches and we did go to the market, but the errand was only a pretense for the real reason for our excursion. It was the artist I wanted to visit. When we arrived at Sofonisba's house, Giulia welcomed us in.

We found the Maestra in the courtyard, having a glass of wine in the afternoon shade.

In a burst of courage, I said, "I would like to help you."

"Has your father received my letter?"

"He has. I saw it on his desk. But he has not said a word about it to me yet and I wonder if he ever will. I am a grown woman now. I feel I must make my own decisions."

"Oh, my dear," she said. "I value your desire to help me. But the last thing I would ever want to do is come between Lorenzo Vespucci and his daughter. Talk to him. Let's not begin this effort until you have his blessing. Otherwise, there will always be a dark cloud over us."

I had to admit, she was right.

"I have had my share of dark clouds in this life," she said. "They are not easy to live under."

Her statement intrigued me, but it did not seem my place to ask her for more details. I left Signora Anguissola knowing I must gain my father's permission.

"I agree with the artist," Fabia said. "Talking to your father will be the best thing."

"I know that Father has other plans for me, but why does helping the artist negate these other plans? Why can't I do both? How can I make him understand that this is something I really want to do, something that feels important to me?"

"Just tell him," she said.

I must work up my courage to tell him that I can do both tasks. I can balance the books for him and I can transcribe for Signora Anguissola. Together with the peaches, I hope he will accept my offer.

Lorenzo

I find comfort at the sight of this familiar view from my desk, a view that spans the rooftops of Genoa. I think of Rossella, my dear wife, who was also my business partner. While I was out and about attracting new clients to buy fabrics and lace, she was here at this desk, surveying this view, keeping track of orders, income, and expenses. Fellow merchants in the guild were incredulous that I had my wife assist me in this way. They would ask, "How can you do that, Lorenzo?" But my Rossella had been born to a father from a branch of the illustrious Spinola family in which learning was highly valued. She was his only child and he put all his stock in her, nurturing her intelligence by granting her an education.

Rossella's mother died in childbirth when Rossella was seven, and the baby died too. It was a death that came after losing several other pregnancies. I have often wondered what was passed from mother to daughter because Rossella struggled in the exact same way. After Paola was born, my wife had three pregnancies that did not hold.

And then Tomasino came. What a blessing he was, a piece of my heart forged in the fire of my body and delivered into the world. And when God took Tomasino away, my heart broke into a million shards. Perhaps in my grief, I have put too much pressure on my one remaining child. I haven't made plans for her to marry because I have selfishly wanted to keep her here, working with me.

Yesterday I was at the guild house, where word is out that the cloth market is failing. One would think that as Genoa prospers, the result would be more prosperity for all. Instead, the glut of new sellers means the producers cannot keep up the needed quantity of product. As my inventory of brocade, velvet, and lace suffers, my income follows the downward flow. This business was given to me by my father, who received it from his father, who received it from his. I am the steward of a family dynasty, and I cannot let it collapse.

There is a rumor among the members of the guild that the new path to stability in the cloth market is "Every man for himself." As my fellow merchant and longtime friend Federico Barbieri said, "What should we do, kill each other to decrease the competition?"

I have a letter on my desk from the illustrious and much-admired painter of portraits, Signora Sofonisba Anguissola. She has been a customer of mine for many years, and I have always valued her integrity. She has never quarreled over price with me and has always paid on time. In her letter, she is asking me to allow Paola to serve as a scribe for a story she wants to tell. I know Paola wishes to do this for her.

Should I let my daughter take on this task? I am not happy to be standing in the way of my daughter's dreams, but what am I to do? To become the artist's scribe might improve her stature in Genoa. Might this arrangement also improve mine?

For so long, Paola has talked about her dream of owning a printing press, and I have dismissed it as folly. I confess I have failed to hear the words from my daughter's heart. What is God asking of me? Perhaps I cannot look to God for the answer. God has not treated me very well all these years, taking away my only son and then my dear wife. It looks like God is about to take away my family business and my daughter as well. I don't have a lot of faith in God. But I have faith in Paola, and I know, too, that if I sit here quietly looking out over Genoa, Rossella's calm, steady mind will come to me. If I listen, Rossella will tell me what to do.

Sofonisba

While I wait for Signor Vespucci's answer to my query, I will continue writing on my own. This past week, my eyes have not been giving me too much trouble. And today, I have a story that would be hard for me to say out loud, for I must admit to a great indiscretion as well as a long-maintained and ignoble lie.

RINALDO

My new teacher, Signor Gatti, had many students under his wing, all young men. Just like the boys apprenticed to Signor Campi, they viewed me as inconsequential and ignored me, except for one. His name was Rinaldo, and he was full of life and exuberance. Every day when I arrived at San Pietro to observe my teacher's progress on the fresco, Rinaldo spoke to me, always wanting to know how I was doing, what I was doing. He praised my work and asked me questions about materials and technique that no fellow student had ever asked me.

On many afternoons when the painting day was over, he walked toward home with me and Antonella, and he would always stop in the market to buy me flowers or some fruit before he excused himself and went on his way. I had just turned twenty and was not used to flattery and attention from men, and it did not take long for me to fall in love with Rinaldo. The way I felt in his presence reminded me of how I had felt with Nico when I was just a girl, except that I was a grown woman by the time I met Rinaldo—although thinking back on it now, I was no doubt as inexperienced as ever.

Eventually, Rinaldo and I began spending afternoons alone together at his place, and we were not painting. I think Antonella was aware of more than she let on. "Be careful, Sofi" was all she ever said. I considered myself grown, wise, and certainly not foolish. But I should have done a better job of heeding Antonella's warning.

I have never told anyone this story, not even in the confessional, because if it had ever become known that I was not a maiden, my reputation as the "virgin painter" would have been destroyed. But there is no longer a need for concealment. I am old now, and perhaps soon I will be gone. I think it is best to confess my sin at last.

In the autumn of 1553, Rinaldo was called home by his parents in Naples to fulfill an arranged marriage. He had kept this information from me, hoping he might be able to convince his parents to undo the contract. At least this is what he told me. He swore he loved me and told me he was sorry to break my heart. I wanted to believe him, but his deceit made me question everything he had ever said or done. I let him go with no further argument because I had no recourse. I was devastated, but what else could I do?

Soon after he left, I missed my monthly flow. Sick with worry, I had no one I could turn to. Elena was in the convent, and besides, she would have disowned me to know that I had been so careless. I could not tell my parents, who had done everything to give me the gift of an education and the opportunity to become an artist. I should have known better. And I did not want to tell Antonella because she stood to lose her job for her negligence, and I could not have that. Shame enveloped me in a dark cloud and I considered that I might have to end my life. What else could I do?

Then, one morning about a fortnight later, God intervened. Antonella came to my room at first light with a pitcher of water and found me sound asleep in sheets covered in blood.

"Sofonisba, wake up!" she hissed in my ear, shaking me awake.

I looked at the pool of blood around me and burst into tears.

"Is this what I think it might be?" she asked.

"I have sinned," I said through my tears.

"I should have taken better care of you," she said, holding me in her arms while I cried tears of shame, and also relief. Then, she gathered the sheets and took them away. She never asked me any more questions, and I never told anyone what had happened.

Part of me wanted to erase the entire episode, but I also wanted to remember my transgression so that I would never allow such a thing to happen again. I developed an idea for a miniature self-portrait on parchment. I wanted to create something that I could carry with me always, to remind myself what can happen when one falls prey to one's desires. In this small image of myself, I hold a medallion that displays an emblem of interlocking letters that spell my father's name to remind me of him, my protector, someone I must never disappoint. I gave special emphasis to the *R*, to remind me of Rinaldo. As for the *I*, I looped it around the crossbar of the *A* as a kind of diversion, and to create an unexpected visual effect.

Around the rim of the medallion, I invoked the spirit of my old teacher, Signor Cavallaro, and included a title in Latin that reads SOPHONISBA ANGVSSOLA VIR[GO] IPSIVS MANV EX [S]PECVLO DEPICTAM CREMONAE, which means "The Maiden Sophonisba Anguissola painted this by her own hand from a mirror, Cremona." I wrote in Latin because it seemed more authoritative than to write in the Italian vernacular. And, I very purposely positioned my thumb to obscure the last two letters of the word *Virgo*, because as I have explained, I was not that.

Thinking back on all of this now, I am reminded of a passage from Dante's *Purgatory* in which Beatrice leads him on toward Paradise, admonishing him to let go of his shame. Although I long ago released the shame I carried because of what I did, I have never completely forgiven myself for my sin. Now that I have written my confession, I think I can wake up and pardon myself, and finally make peace with that young and errant woman who once was me.

Paola

Father called out to me from his study. It occurred to me that this could be the moment when I would confront him with my offer. I have been avoiding the conversation, so afraid he will reject the idea of letting me help both him and Signora Anguissola at the same time. I brought the bag of peaches with me, hoping that my gift might sway his response. I found him pacing, his hand pressed against his brow.

"What is it, Father? Are you feeling ill?"

"No, no, not ill. Perhaps anxious, but not ill."

"I have some peaches for you. Fabia and I got them at the market yesterday."

"Thank you, my dear. How kind of you."

He put the bag of peaches down on his desk and took both my hands in his. "My daughter, have I been a good father to you?"

His question surprised me. For a moment, I thought of bringing up his dismissal of my printing press dream but decided against it.

"Of course you have. You have been a very good father. What is wrong?"

"I want you to know that...I mean...I will let you go. To work with Signora Anguissola. You have my permission to go."

"Oh, Papa!" Tears came as I threw my arms around him. "Thank you so much!"

He held me close and stroked my hair, just as he had done when I was small. I could have stayed there for hours, but he backed away a bit so he could look into my eyes.

"I know your mother would want you to have this opportunity to assist the artist and to learn from her. I do not want to stand in your way. But..."

He cast his eyes downward as though ashamed to admit what he said next. "I still need your help, if you will give it."

"Father, of course I will! That is exactly what I came to tell you—that you should let me try doing both tasks. If things start to fall behind here, you will let me know and we will make an adjustment. I do not want the business to suffer because of me."

He smiled. "How did God give me such a daughter?"

"You made me. You and Mama. I stand here, the person I am, because of you."

I embraced him again. "I promise, I will not fail you," I said.

"I love you," he said, placing his hand on top of my head as if to bless me.

"I love you, too."

He reached into the bag, pulled out a peach, and bit into it. "Delicious," he said. "Thank you."

A Father's Love

When small, I sat upon my father's knee
and no day journeyed into night without
his kind words bringing a smile from my pout
and all the charms with which he conjured me.
He saw my soul, a spirit bright and free
and I raised up my voice to meet his shout.
Under fatherly gaze, from seed to sprout
to maid, my branches blossomed as a tree.
A father's love is delicate as lace
for daughters dear, we treasured ones who know.
We hold this filigree of truth and grace
and rue those bards who say it isn't so.
No man will ever take a father's place,
despite the fact that we are bound to go.

As if one miracle was not enough for this week, something lovely happened when Fabia and I were standing at the doorstep to Signora Anguissola's palazzo today. I knocked on the door and looked down to see a white feather on the ground, right at the toe of my shoe. How I had not seen it moments before, I cannot say. The feather appeared seemingly out of nowhere.

"Look!" I said as I bent to retrieve the feather and tuck it into my bag. "At last, a message from the birds. Francesco is thinking of me."

"He loves you, that one," Fabia said. "Mark my words, one day, you will marry him."

Before I could address her comment, the door opened and I was surprised to be greeted not by Giulia but by the artist herself. "I had a feeling it was going to be you," she said. "Please, come in!"

"I have good news, Signora Anguissola," I said. The artist looked at me with mock dismay. "I mean, Sofi," I smiled, remembering that she had asked me to call her by this name.

She nodded at my correction. "You are here, so I can guess the news. But, please tell me anyway!"

"Your letter to my father got through to his heart. I have his permission to help you!"

"This is wonderful news," she said. "Come in, come in, dear girl. Come, Fabia. Let's sit in the courtyard together and make a plan for when we will begin."

"You know," I said, "I would be happy to start today, if you like."

She thought for a moment. "I can do that, yes! Let's start! You couldn't have come at a better time because I am eager to tell the story of my time with Michelangelo. It is a long story and it may actually take us several days."

"I'm ready to begin."

We followed the artist into the courtyard as she called out, "Giulia, can you please bring us some wine? We are going to need refreshment."

TO ROME

On so many afternoons when I was growing up, I listened to the conversations of the men who met on Papa's terrace. They gathered with their glasses of wine and chunks of cheese to talk of Neoplatonism, Leonardo, and the new age of genius. Under dappled light and shadow cast by our lone olive tree, they spoke of Martin Luther, Copernicus, and Michelangelo, the man who could make men (and women, I hoped) emerge from blocks of stone. As I continued my studies with Signor Gatti, I felt I was ready for new challenges, but I did not know where or how to find them. Luckily for me, Papa never slowed his plans to continue my education.

Unknown to me until much later, Father had engaged the help of Annibale Caro, the esteemed poet, writer, and translator of Virgil, to facilitate an introduction of my work to Michelangelo Buonarroti. *The* Michelangelo. To explore what might be possible, Caro sent the artist one of my drawings along with a drawing by Signor Campi. The result—so I eventually learned—was that Michelangelo sent word back saying he was impressed by my skills as an artist and was willing to meet me, if ever I should come to Rome.

In 1554, with my father's blessing and a small traveling party that included two porters, my sister Lucia, and my chaperone—an old family friend named Manuela Cavalieri—I headed south to Rome. I was a girl from Cremona, not yet twenty-two, and I was on my way to meet one of the century's greatest minds. I felt nervous and excited all at the same time.

As our carriage journeyed to Rome, I recounted to my sister and my chaperone what I had heard the men around my father's table say about Michelangelo. *Il Divino*, they called him. I reviewed for my traveling companions what I knew of Michelangelo, how he had begun his studies at age thirteen in the workshop of Ghirlandaio, the great Florentine master, and how he had learned to grind and prepare pigments, just like I had.

"He sounds quite human," Lucia said.

Her comment surprised me, but I suppose it does no good to hold someone up so high that we forget their humanity.

"We all begin as babies," Manuela said.

"True enough," I said. "And as we grow, we learn the nature of our vocations. Michelangelo learned the techniques of painting, but his passion was for carving marble, which, at that time, was considered menial labor."

"Ah, yes," Manuela said. "All that pounding and chipping and fighting the marble with one's hands. That was not viewed as noble work, was it?"

"No, it was not. Carving sculpture was seen as the work of the laborer, like the stonemason or foundryman. But Michelangelo changed all that and brought carving stone to the level of poetry. His talent for carving was well known, and while he was still quite young, he was summoned to the court of the Florentine statesman and art patron Lorenzo de' Medici. Then, in his twenties, Michelangelo took on the challenge of working with a large, unyielding block of Carrara marble that was thought by those who had quarried it to be completely unusable."

"I've heard about that," said Manuela. "Is that the stone that became Michelangelo's David?"

"Yes. From that flawed block he released his David, a monumental statue that stands now in front of the Palazzo Vecchio in Florence."

I'd seen sketches of the sculpture when my father and his friends passed them around the table, and I'd heard their musings about the raw strength inherent in this depiction of David, the young hero who stood up to Goliath. This story of triumph over power resonated deeply in my heart. I hoped the artist who had created this David would pass some of that triumph on to me.

Michelangelo followed in Leonardo da Vinci's footsteps by employing the dissection of cadavers to understand the structure of the human body. I told my traveling companions about my youthful attempt to visit the morgue to view a dissection.

"Why did you have to disguise yourself?" Manuela asked.

"Being a girl, I was not permitted to go."

"Did your ploy work? You've always liked to have things your way," my sister said.

"It did not. Instead, I learned to make do with the outer trappings, focusing on the details of elegant clothing and facial expression, the things that can be seen. Not what is under the skin."

Lucia was right. I was determined—not necessarily to have things my way, but certainly to acquire knowledge. I was on my way to meet the greatest artist alive, and it was my goal to impress upon him my readiness to learn.

The artist stopped her story and took a sip of wine.

"Have I worn you out?" she asked.

"Not at all. I captured every word. Are you getting tired?"

"Maybe just a little. Can you come back tomorrow?"

"Indeed, I can. I look forward to seeing you again tomorrow, Sofi."

Sofonisba

The Damned

We arrived in Rome at dusk on a cold evening on the first night of February, 1554. We settled into a pensione, a cozy little place with a common eating room. There was a fire roaring in the hearth, and we took our evening meal there, resting after so many long days of travel. The proprietor was kind and attentive. After dinner, he brought us sweet custard drizzled with honey and pine nuts. It was delicious.

"So, my dear, how do you feel being in Rome?" Manuela said.

I thought for a moment. "Maybe a little uncertain."

"In what way?" Manuela asked.

"Well, what will I do here? What will I learn? Will I really meet Michelangelo?"

Manuela smiled with compassion in her eyes. "Sofi, you will do much here. You will see much here. And yes, I am certain, you will meet Michelangelo."

"I think you can believe Manuela," my sister offered. "Papa would not send us all this distance without paving your way. *Il Divino* knows you have come here to see him. It may take some days or even weeks, but you will have an audience with him."

"In the meantime," Manuela said, "we are going to see Rome together!"

Her enthusiasm was contagious, so I let my worries dissolve. "Yes!" I pushed my dessert plate away, taking my chaperone's hands in mine. "We will see Rome together! Thank you for being here with me, both of you."

The next morning, we summoned our coach and made our way through the streets of Rome. The city surprised me. It was more rustic than I expected it to be. There were cows and goats everywhere, eating grass that sprouted between the paving stones of the streets. Everywhere, there were crumbling walls, stone reminders of Rome's previous glory.

We entered the Sistine Chapel as the morning sun was pouring in through the upper windows. Straight in front of me was Michelangelo's *Last Judgement*. The fresco spanned the entire wall above the altar, and the sheer enormity of the image, which was filled by a multitude of writhing figures, took my breath away. High up and in the center of the composition, a muscular Christ reigned over the scene on a swirl of clouds while his mother, Mary, sat demurely at his side. His raised right arm invited the blessed to rise up to Heaven. His left hand turned downward, casting the hoard of sinners on the other side down into the fires of Hell.

Standing so small in front of this overwhelming image, I could not help but think of my own sins. There were the minor things— like taking something from my mother's sewing basket without telling her—to the major transgressions, like my sin of the flesh with Rinaldo and the ensuing lie surrounding my status in the world. And even those things seemed potentially small when I considered my whole existence, in which I dreamed of a life of creative endeavor, a life inappropriate for a woman.

The vision of the damned with their twisted bodies underscored my fears regarding where I might end up someday. It brought to mind the eternities of grotesque suffering that Dante had chronicled in the *Inferno*. As I looked at Michelangelo's vision of the damned, my heart raced. I did not want to think about the tortures that might await me.

I turned my eyes away from all that and set my attention on the ceiling, to *The Creation of Adam*. Michelangelo had bravely moved all the figures to the edges of the composition and left the center nearly empty, except for the almost-touching fingers of Adam and God. I was fascinated by Michelangelo's placement of Eve under God's cloak, as though she was already in existence before Adam came to be. Perhaps Michelangelo was suggesting that woman was not a mere graft of man. But then I noticed that the artist showed the creation of Eve in the next section of the ceiling, and she did indeed seem to come from Adam's sleeping body. So, I wasn't sure what to think or what the artist meant to imply.

One more section over, I found Michelangelo's fascinating depiction of the snake, its sinuous body wrapped around the tree of knowledge of good and evil. The snake's figure ended in the breast and head of a woman. I had never thought of the snake as female before. Most interesting, Eve was not offering Adam the apple. Instead, he was reaching for the forbidden fruit himself. It seemed to me that in his images on the Sistine Chapel ceiling, Michelangelo was suggesting some different versions of both Genesis and the Fall. If anyone could have rewritten Scripture, it would have been *Il Divino*.

WAITING

About two weeks into our stay, I was getting tired of all the sightseeing, and I began to miss my studio. I tried to spend some time each day drawing, but even that was tedious because I wasn't sure where all the looking and drawing was headed without someone to critique my work.

One morning, Manuela, Lucia, and I were in the pensione having breakfast, preparing for a visit to the Pantheon. A boy came running into the dining room from the courtyard. "A message for Signorina Anguissola!" he said, catching his breath and holding out a scroll.

The scroll was held shut by a wax seal with the intertwined letters *MB*. My hands were shaking as I picked at the wax to unroll the paper. As the page unfurled, I saw that Michelangelo had sent me a drawing. Out of the scroll fell a letter written by *Il Divino* himself.

Dear Signorina Anguissola,

I welcome you to our fair city of Rome, where antiquity and the new age meet. My friend, the translator of Virgil, Annibale Caro, forwarded to me a letter from your father. This communication included a pair of drawings, one by you and one by your teacher, B. Campi. I can see that your work shows promise and I understand that you have come to Rome seeking knowledge. Although I don't keep a typical workshop of apprentices with all the responsibility that entails, I am always happy to make the acquaintance of a young artist.

My preoccupation with the building of St. Peter's Basilica does not allow for an in-person meeting at this time. Let us begin by exchanging drawings. I enclose a sketch of mine for you to copy. I ask that you send me back two things, a copy of what I have provided as well as one drawing from your own mind. It will help me to see where you are in your development, and I promise to respond with my thoughts to help you grow in your work. If you can be patient with me, I promise we will meet soon.

Yours sincerely,

M. Buonarroti
18 February, 1554

I could hardly believe my eyes. Michelangelo had said that my work had promise. I wanted to run into the street and yell at the top of my lungs. I wanted to dance, sing, and immediately communicate with Papa this miracle and thank him for all the work he had done to get me this far. But first, I needed to reply.

Lucia had already gone in search of quill and paper. "I knew you would want to reply right away," she said, "and send your response back with this fine boy." The boy blushed and bowed his head.

I remember writing something along the lines of the following:

Dear Signor Buonarroti,

I have received your letter and your sketch. I send many thanks to you, kind sir, for taking time from your work to write. I look forward to providing what you have requested of me. I am eager to learn.

I signed the letter "Sofonisba Anguissola, the daughter of

Amilcare." Once the scroll was sealed, I handed it to Manuela, who passed it back to the boy.

"Please take this scroll to Maestro Buonarroti," she said. "Here is another coin for your effort. Godspeed!"

"Of course, Signora. I will run."

As I watched him go, I whispered a prayer that my few words would impress upon *Il Divino* my gratitude and desire to study with him. Then I turned my attention to the sketch he had sent me.

It was a chalk drawing of a woman's stern and foreboding face. The drawing was labeled *Cleopatra*. I stared at the drawing, thinking about what the artist had asked me to do.

Lucia broke my trance. "You should finish eating, sister. We have a day of sightseeing ahead of us. Our carriage will be here soon."

"Perhaps I should stay here and begin my assignment..."

Lucia looked at Manuela, who chuckled as though she could have predicted this is what I would say.

"I think you should continue with your plans as they were laid out for you today," Manuela said. "We will visit the Pantheon and see one of the ancient wonders of Rome. I think the experience will teach you something and help you with your drawing. You will see."

I knew Manuela was right. I put the drawing away for later and prepared myself for the day as planned.

A temple for "all the gods," the Pantheon was a massive structure. The front portico was a deep, shaded space, its roof supported by sixteen tall, thin columns. As I approached the entrance, I felt as if I were wandering in a dark forest. It was a great surprise to pass through this shadowy arcade and enter the building itself, which was filled with light topped by a breathtaking, coffered dome. At the top of the dome, a large opening, an oculus, revealed the sky. I stared at that circle of blue.

Manuela asked, "What do you see there, my dear?"

"I see a doorway," I said, "showing me that the things we need to learn will find us if we remain open to powers higher than ourselves."

"I told you the Pantheon would have something to teach you," Manuela said.

On the way home, our carriage driver took us along the Tiber River and we viewed the seven hills of Rome. As we slowly wound our way along the Aventine Hill, we passed a crumbling marble temple quite near the road. I noticed a niche next to the temple's ruined entryway, and in this niche was a statue of a female figure holding in one hand a cornucopia filled with fruit and grain.

"Stop!" I commanded our driver.

"What is it?" Manuela said as I jumped out of the carriage, sketchbook in hand.

Lucia recognized the figure too. I heard her telling Manuela the story of the Bona Dea. I was thrilled to find the goddess without even looking for her. Close up, I could see the sinuous snake curled around her arm, whispering in her ear. The goddess's demeanor told me there was nothing to fear. I saw that being a "lone snake" was perhaps not the worst thing in the world.

Later that day, when we returned to the pensione, I admired my sketch of the Bona Dea and felt joyful that I would bring it home to Papa. I set that drawing aside and turned my attention to Michelangelo's *Cleopatra*. The intensity in her eyes made me feel as though I could see right into her mind, and her mind was on fire. I looked at myself in the mirror. I felt that same fire, but I also felt the potential of so much else that pushed against me. Would I ever be taken seriously as an artist? If I thought of the encouragement of Papa and my teachers, the answer was yes. But if I thought of the men sitting around my father's table, arguing that women had no intellectual capacity, no inherent worth beyond bearing children, I felt less confident. I knew they were wrong, but I also knew they were in charge.

The only thing I knew for certain was that I needed to respond to Michelangelo's drawing, and so I set to work. I made several practice versions of Cleopatra until I got one that pleased me. I set down my chalk. I needed to think before I began the next task. "To make something *from your own mind*," he had said.

I decided to do a self-portrait. Thanks to the example of the German artist Albrecht Dürer, self-portraits had gained momentum in the previous fifty years or so. Prior to Dürer, no artist had made a formal painting of his own face. Sending Michelangelo a self-portrait would show that I knew about art, and it would also proclaim, "Here I am, Michelangelo. See me."

The next morning, I sent off the drawings. And then, I waited.

Paola

I have placed the white feather I found at Sofi's front door the other day on the little table next to my bed, where I can look at it each morning when I wake and each night before I go to sleep. I think about Francesco and wonder how he is faring. I have only found this one feather, so I must wonder, *Is he thinking of me, too?*

Today, after we left Sofi, Fabia and I made our way through the market and turned to walk along the wharf.

"How is your hand?" Fabia asked. "Is it hard to write for so long?"

I held out my arm and opened and closed my fingers. "My hand does get a little cramped, but I think it's fine. I enjoy hearing her story."

"As do I," she said. "It will be interesting to learn how her meeting with Michelangelo unfolds."

Our route led us past the Barbarossa, and as we passed, I thought of Francesco. We were perhaps twenty paces past the taverna when a whistle made us both turn.

That awful fellow who has been troubling Francesco was standing in front of the taverna, leaning back on his heels, looking at us with his arms across his chest. His eyebrows were raised and his toothy smile gleamed with bad intent. Seeing that he had our attention, he thrust his hips forward and held his hands out, as if holding onto something, or someone. The rudeness of his gesture made me turn away, and I grabbed Fabia's elbow as though I was now the chaperone.

But Fabia loosened herself from my grip, turned toward Dario, and made her own gesture, smacking her fist into her bent elbow. She yelled, "Take it elsewhere, idiot!"

91

We picked up our pace and re-entered the market, safely mingling with the crowd.

"That Dario Bacigalupo," Fabia said, her eyes burning with anger and disgust. "He is a devil, that one."

"What can we do about him?" I asked.

"Nothing, except stay out of his way."

"I'm sure you are right," I said. It would be easy enough to avoid the taverna, I thought, for Francesco was not there. "Mention nothing of this to my father, Fabia," I said. "He would only want to protect me, and if that meant keeping me home, keeping me from my service to Sofi, I—"

"Do not worry," Fabia said. "I will not let Dario Bacigalupo ruin things for you."

Sofonisba

The Invitation

It took nearly three agonizing weeks of waiting after I sent Michelangelo my first drawing assignment, but at last, his second letter arrived.

Dear Signorina Anguissola,

I am in receipt of your recent drawings. Thank you for doing exactly as I requested in order to allow me to critique your work. Your rendition of Cleopatra is to be applauded. You have done a wonderful job capturing the intensity of her gaze, which seems of the utmost importance to me when I think of her story.

You clearly demonstrate that you understand line, and I invite you to continue to explore its many nuances, especially the different qualities that can be depicted by thin lines or thick lines. If I could give you any advice on how to make the drawing even better, I would say pay close attention to how you choose the width of the line, especially around your subject's eyes. As for your self-portrait, what a gift! I was hoping you would draw a picture of yourself so I could begin to know you.

I continue to labor on the basilica, and so I enclose a new image for you to copy, a Madonna and Child. I also ask for another original image from your own mind. Until we meet, I am sending heartfelt encouragement.

M.B.
7 March, 1554

I could hardly believe it, but there it was, in writing. Michelangelo was impressed by my work. He was pleased that I'd sent a self-portrait. I was so proud of myself for thinking of it that I wanted to get on top of the roof and sing. *What a gift*, he'd written.

During the next month, we exchanged drawings two more times, but still there was no invitation to meet with him and I began to worry that might never happen. I'd allowed myself to feel excited when I first received his letters, but the delay of our meeting began to plant doubt in me. Manuela and Lucia encouraged me to keep my spirits up, but I could see by the looks in their eyes that they were beginning to have their doubts as well.

Then one excellent morning, a messenger came to the pensione. He carried with him an invitation from Michelangelo announcing a meeting. A carriage would be sent in two days. I was going to meet *Il Divino*. I could hardly believe it was true.

On the evening before the big day, Manuela, Lucia, and I ate our dinner as usual. Well, they ate. I was nervous and could barely touch my food. Finally, Manuela broached the topic that was hanging between us, "So, do you feel ready for your meeting tomorrow?"

"I think so," I said. "No, not really."

"But Sofi," my sister said. "He wrote and told you that he has been impressed with your work. Why do you doubt yourself?"

"He was probably just being kind," I fretted. "And what does one say to a genius?"

Manuela smiled. "What would you like to say?"

I had so many questions. "I would like to ask him where his ideas come from. I would like to know what he thinks about when he is walking in the countryside."

"Those are good questions, Sofi," my sister said. "You should ask him."

"I would like to know how he maintained calm when he was pulled away from his work on the Tomb of Pope Julius by none other than the Pope himself. What was it like to turn his attention to designing the frescoes for the Sistine Chapel? How did he know how to properly proportion figures that would be seen on a ceiling?"

"More good questions, my dear," Manuela said with a firm nod.

"I would like to know what he dreams about, what he eats for breakfast! I would like to know everything inside his head!" By now, the three of us were laughing.

"Anything else?"

"I want to ask if he thinks a woman can be an artist."

Manuela looked into my eyes. "I can answer that, Sofi." She reached out for my hands. I gave them to her as though I was holding onto a rope that was saving me from a fast-rising river.

"No matter what the genius Michelangelo may tell you, the answer to that question is *yes*. Never forget that, dear girl."

I wanted so much to believe her. "I will not forget."

The next morning, we arose before the sun to get ready. I had brought my most beautiful brocade dress for this occasion, and there was a fair amount of binding and tying that had to be accomplished to get the dress looking just right. I always hated the restrictive corsets we wore, our skirts held out by wooden frames. It made dressing such a chore. I would have been equally happy in nothing but a cotton smock. Of course, this is not how decent ladies dressed for the world, and so I put up with the preparation.

Before I left the pensione, Lucia embraced me. "You look beautiful, Sofonisba."

"But do I look like an artist?" I asked.

"Indeed you do," said Manuela. She placed her hand on the top of my head, on the place where my braid made a crown, as if to bless me. Her blessing sealed the fact that I was indeed an artist. I would not let the genius of any man, not even *Il Divino*, take that away from me.

CHERUBS

You might think that visiting someone as famous as Michelangelo would involve complicated arrangements. However, while there are certain rules to follow with kings and queens, meeting an artist—even one as famous as Michelangelo—posed no particular difficulties. One just walked in, and on that day in April of 1554, that is exactly what Manuela and I did.

Manuela's knock on the heavy wooden door at Michelangelo's house summoned a slight young man in a cotton work smock.

"Good morning," Manuela said. "I bring you Signorina Anguissola, who has an audience with Signor Buonarroti."

"Si, Signora. Please follow me."

We followed the young man down a hallway until we found ourselves in the central courtyard of Michelangelo's home. In its center, there was a fountain ringed by roses. Facing the courtyard, across from where we entered, wide doors opened onto a room. In that room—very close to the edge of the courtyard—there was a large desk cluttered with books, piles of paper, plaster sculptures, and various hammers and chisels. Behind the clutter sat a wiry old man with a mass of white hair. Manuela and I stood nearby in the courtyard, but he did not look up until the young man coughed and said, "Maestro, guests."

At that, Michelangelo stopped what he was doing and looked up. He squinted at us, and within an instant, he sprang to his feet—which was very surprising, given that he was in his eighties. Then he was in front of his desk, standing with us in the courtyard. The young man slipped away without even announcing us by name, and I was surprised when I heard the Maestro say, "Signorina Anguissola, welcome!"

He held out his hands to me as though I was his oldest and dearest friend. I wasn't quite sure what was appropriate, but Manuela nudged my back, so I went forward and took his hands, bowing my head and curtseying deeply.

"Maestro, it is an honor."

"The honor is mine, Sofonisba!" He leapt back into his study and pulled forward two wooden chairs, one for me and one for Manuela. "My dear ladies, sit. Please!"

We sat as Michelangelo pulled up his own chair, and there we were, sitting in the artist's study. All I could hear was the sound of the fountain trickling lazily behind us.

"And so, tell me Sofonisba, how are you?"

"I'm fine, thank you. I'm very much enjoying our travels."

"What do you think of this place?" he asked.

"I think it is quite old." Immediately, I felt that was the silliest thing I could have said.

He laughed. "Ah, yes. Everything is old here, myself included. Where have you been?"

"To the Colosseum, the Baths of Trajan, the Pantheon, Aventine Hill. And of course, to the Sistine Chapel. Your frescoes there are beautiful."

"Thank you, Sofonisba. I'm glad you like them."

There was silence then, but not really an awkward silence. It was more of a quietness, broken only by the chirping of birds and the sound of the fountain.

"You know," he said. "You are a very good artist."

I felt my cheeks turn red. "You are too kind, Maestro."

"Sofonisba, please. Call me Michelangelo. I may be old enough to be your grandfather, but as artists, we are ageless. And you, my young friend, are an artist."

"Thank you, Maest... Michelangelo," was all I could think to say. I wondered if he was only being kind or if he really saw something of value in my work.

"I have been happy with the drawings you have returned to me, and with each one, I see that you accept my comments and work to improve your hand. This is not always easy to do, to learn from criticism. But you have shown yourself more than capable in this regard."

Now his words were starting to make some sense. I found myself trusting him, and I became aware that he would not have met with me at all if he did not see some promise in me.

"You know, when I was your age, no one wanted me to be an artist. My own father thought such work was beneath me. He yelled, he cajoled, he actually hit me once or twice, trying to beat my creativity out of me. He would have preferred me to be a grammarian, a banker, or a government administrator like him. Anything but a carver of stone."

I was uncertain what to say, and so Michelangelo continued.

"You are lucky, on one hand, because you have a father who believes in you completely. He has provided you with many opportunities that most aspiring artists don't get."

I remained silent, waiting for him to say next how unlikely it was

97

for a woman to ever be a great artist. It is a man's world.

Instead, he said, "Even though our world is slowly changing and we have come to recognize the beauty of forms as described by Plato, we have not yet advanced to our highest capacities, have we? A world in which men and women are equals."

"That would be a very different world, wouldn't it?" I said.

"It would," he said, and then fell silent himself. As he sat thinking, a smile gradually grew on his face, as though his mind had settled on a most pleasant thought from some faraway place in his memory.

"You know, I had a wonderful friend, a poet named Vittoria Colonna. She died seven years ago now. She was from a noble family in Pescara—a woman who was brilliant, strong, and fearless in all things. From her, I learned a great deal about poetry and also about how men are only half of the story."

Michelangelo came out of his reverie and looked straight at me. He said, "You know you have a place in the story, don't you?"

Something about the way he looked at me in that moment encouraged me to be totally honest. I took a deep breath. "Since you ask, I do not know my place in the story. I am not at all certain what my purpose is."

He smiled. "That is a good answer," he said. "Humility is the beginning of all greatness."

I looked at him, astonished by the turn of this conversation.

"Tell me about something that you do know to be true," he said.

"Well, I..." Panic rose up my back and made the top of my head tingle. I looked at Manuela, totally unsure what to say. "Well, I think..."

I wanted to speak well, so as I searched for the right words, I looked up. And there, on the ceiling of Michelangelo's study, there were cherubs. Chubby flying angels formed from luscious pink- and peach-colored strokes of paint. These little figures were tumbling over each other through the clouds and I burst out laughing.

"You like my cherubs?"

"I do, Maestro, very much. They make me smile."

"Why is that?" he asked.

"They surprised me. They remind me that there are many unseen things all around us. I think that when I am drawing or painting, I am looking for these things that are hidden from sight, and I try to bring them into view, to unlock the mystery of what I see."

"My dear Sofonisba," he said. "You will go far."

"Please. Tell me what I must do to improve. I know there is much to learn."

"Exactly, yes, and this attitude is why I know you are going to succeed as an artist."

I lowered my gaze. I felt naive and exposed. I had no idea that talking to Michelangelo was going to be like talking to a friend. I had not been prepared for this.

"I am not saying it will be easy." He paused. "Why do you want to do this thing, Sofonisba? Why do you want to make art?"

I was flooded by another wave of doubt, so afraid to answer his question. But I knew what I must say. "To be truthful, it is not something I ever chose. I believe it chose me. Whenever I pick up a piece of chalk and start to draw, I feel like someone is standing over my shoulder, helping me to get the lines just right."

Michelangelo nodded and gestured for me to continue.

"You asked me before to tell you something I know to be true. What I know is that the world is full of light and shadow."

"Ah, yes, light and shadow. Tell me more."

"You could be looking at a woman's face. She may be smiling, but if you look carefully, you can see that there is hurt behind her eyes."

"That is true, Sofonisba. I have seen that look often enough on a woman's face."

"Or," I continued, suddenly feeling as though I had something worth saying, "you may see a man's face and think he looks bored and aloof, but his mind is full of righteous and uplifting thoughts. He could be thinking of inventing something never seen before."

"Yes!" the Maestro said. He stood up from his chair and began to pace back and forth. "He could. He could indeed. Or he could be preparing for battle and he could be thinking about his mother and how much he loves her, thinking he may never see her again."

Michelangelo stopped moving then and looked at me. "Sofonisba," he said. "No matter how hard this road gets for you, being an artist who happens to be a woman in a man's world, you must never stop. Never surrender to those who will attack you, block your way, or criticize your work. Promise me that you will always speak through the language of pigment on canvas that which is in your heart."

"I promise."

At that moment, the young man who had first brought us into Michelangelo's house arrived with a tray of honey cakes and a carafe of wine.

"Ah, Giancarlo, thank you!" the Maestro said. "Some refreshment is exactly what we need right now, and some wine to toast this promise."

The boy set down the tray and began passing out plates of cake and pouring wine. When each of us had been served, Michelangelo raised his glass.

"To the promise," he said.

"To the promise," Manuela and I responded.

Michelangelo bit into his cake and said, "I'm going to tell you a story in the hope that it will inspire you always to take credit for what you do. After I had carved the *Pietà* and it was placed on display, I was admiring my work one day and I overheard a group of visitors from Lombardy talking about the sculpture. Have you ever seen my *Pietà*?"

"I have just seen it here in Rome. It is beautiful."

"Thank you!" he said, taking another bite of cake. "But let me tell you what happened. In the presence of my own creation, I overheard two men commenting on my *Pietà*. They were extremely complimentary, but they attributed my sculpture, *my* carving, to the work of other hands, a second-rate carver from Milan whose name escapes me now. I was aghast. I almost spoke up, but instead, I devised a plan. Late that night, I slipped into the place where the sculpture was kept, bringing my hammer and chisels. By candlelight, I carved my name on the sash across Mary's gown. The *Pietà* is the only work I ever signed, but I would not have anyone mistake my work for someone else's ever again. Always stand up and be proud of your work."

"Yes, Maestro, I will," I said and nodded at him. He winked at me and put the last bite of cake into his mouth.

The sun had shifted in the sky and rays of golden light were coming into the studio from the courtyard. The birds continued their chirping. The fountain continued to trickle. Above us, the cherubs were tumbling and laughing.

"It is a beautiful world, is it not?"

"Indeed, it is, Sofonisba. Indeed."

Before we left, Michelangelo rummaged through a stack of drawings on his desk and pulled one out. It was one of my original subject matter drawings, and I was startled to see it mixed in with his own work. The drawing depicted my little brother, Asdrubale, getting his finger pinched by a crab.

This was one of the assignments that I had created from "my own mind." *Il Divino* had asked for something showing an unexpected emotional response. I remembered once seeing Asdrubale reach his hand into a basket of crabs and then get pinched. He had cried inconsolably. When I first thought to make this drawing, I wasn't sure if I could replicate my brother's expression of pain because Asdrubale was not sitting in front of me. I was drawing from memory.

But I must have captured the emotion reasonably well, because as the Maestro handed my drawing back to me, he said, "I liked your depiction of the boy expressing a moment of pain so much..." He pulled a second drawing out of the pile and said, "I was compelled to make my own copy of your work. What do you think?"

"I think it is the most wonderful thing I have ever seen!" The most renowned artist of our time had admired something I had invented enough to make a copy of it with his own hand. That was a compliment like no other, and I have kept his admiration in my heart to this day.

We had many other visits, Michelangelo and I. And contrary to what some lecherous minds were heard to whisper after I returned to Cremona, there was never anything inappropriate between us. Michelangelo was always looking beyond the physical and directly into the soul. Besides, as you may have heard, it was said that the Maestro was one who loved men. This I only learned later, but truly, I'm not convinced that he was unwavering in this preference. I think Michelangelo could have loved deeply both men and women alike.

Paola

Yesterday was another long day of storytelling. When Sofi finished speaking, I was exhausted but full of admiration. How wonderful that she developed—during that year and a half she lived in Rome—a friendship with an artist as monumental as Michelangelo. How many people in this world can say such a thing? What a surprise to learn that Vittoria Colonna—the poet Francesco has introduced me to—had been an influence in Michelangelo's life. All this information gave me much to ponder.

I told Father when we sat down to dinner last night that I am learning a great deal about Signora Anguissola's life, and he told me he is glad I am helping her. His comment felt like a small triumph after he was, at first, so opposed to the idea. Maybe someday he will soften on other matters as well.

When Fabia and I arrived at Sofi's palazzo today, Giulia led us straight up the stairs to the studio. The artist was seated near an easel on which sat a most interesting painting. It depicted three girls seated at a table playing a game of chess. An older woman watched over them. In the far distance, there was a mountainous landscape shrouded in blue mist.

"What a beautiful painting," I said. "The girls look as though they are about to speak."

"Thank you, Paola. It is one of my most prized creations. I call it *The Chess Game*."

"What inspired you to paint it?"

"Get your quill and ink ready," Sofi said. "I will tell you."

102

VICTORIES

I returned home to Cremona in 1555 full of pride about my studies with *Il Divino*. I was happy to be in my studio again and to have my family members serve as the models for my paintings. In addition, my sisters Lucia and Minerva wanted to learn to paint, and they were eager to have me pass to them anything I had learned in Rome. And so, I became their teacher.

Soon I came to realize that people in Cremona viewed me as an oddity. They knew that Amilcare Anguissola had a daughter who had studied with Michelangelo. However, not even that fact opened the door for me to obtain church commissions, which is something I desired to have. That kind of work was the purview of men only. Papa presented the idea to the church fathers that I might create a series of easel paintings for the side chapels at different churches throughout the city, but they would have none of it.

So instead, Papa set about making a name for me as a portrait painter. In this realm, the notion that I was somehow of "lesser value" than my male counterparts actually worked in my favor. My commission fee was significantly lower than what male artists asked for their work. It became known that my portraits were life-like depictions and that I took my work seriously. Soon people sought me out to have their portraits painted because they knew they would get something good for half the normal price.

Throughout the autumn of 1555, I was quite busy. Along with commissioned work, I began experimenting with something that was very interesting to me—that is, portraits of people in groups. As you might imagine, it is much more complex to paint a group of people engaged in an activity than to paint just one person. Not only does the artist need to ensure that the figures inhabit a logical shared space, but each individual must also display their own inner light. Each one must appear unique from the others.

My sisters Lucia and Minerva were captivated by the game of chess, having learned to play from our father. I did not have patience for the game myself and preferred instead to sketch them playing. When I was ready to paint my sisters at the chess board, the idea came to me that the scene would be more interesting if I added two observers. The first observer was our next youngest sister, Europa, who was always laughing and smiling. That is how I showed her in the painting. And the other was our maid, Antonella, who I portrayed with her usual motherly concern. I am fairly certain no one had ever painted such an image of a group involved in a common activity before.

So you see, it was my lack of access to grand commissions for churches that forced me to look at the world immediately around me for inspiration. Had I been given commissions to decorate church altars and ceilings like Campi, Gatti, and Michelangelo, I would have been required to stick to the prescribed subject matter dictated by the Church. Even the great male artists were subject to a higher authority. I think being female worked in my favor in this regard.

"Did you ever feel like you would just give up?" I asked.

"Never. I think the isolation that I had to endure being a woman is what provided me a doorway to explore new kinds of imagery, like this painting of my sisters playing chess."

We sat quietly then and I studied the painting for a while. I admired the different expressions on each sister's face. Little Europa was joyful in the presence of her two older sisters. Minerva raised her hand to admit defeat. Lucia looked out at the viewer, her steadfast gaze saying, *I won*.

"I had to be resourceful," Sofi said. "I had to be the lone snake, traveling my own course. I learned that I must never avoid the things that seemed to be my stumbling blocks. In fact, I always did my best to turn those obstacles into my victories."

I will take Sofi's words to heart. The fact that Father will not even consider my idea of starting a printing press is my obstacle. But I will not give up. I know it will take a long time for my dream to come to pass, and I don't know yet how it will happen. But someday, like the lone snake, I will be victorious.

Francesco

My time in the vineyard harvesting grapes these last weeks has replenished my soul, something I had not realized I needed. I am beginning to think that as much as I have enjoyed my studies with Sofi, it is possible that being an artist is not my destiny after all. The vineyard is where I grew into manhood, in fields lined by trellises bearing the weight of fruitful vines.

That weight was a comfort to me after my mother died, when my father began teaching me to tend the vines and placed the mantle of the family business on my shoulders. What I learned by going away for a while and then returning to the vineyard is that this load does not weigh me down. Instead, it has the effect of making me feel light. I don't understand this other than to say that home, the vineyard, the place I come from, is the place I feel most myself.

On my last afternoon in Tuscany, and after a long day of harvesting, Father and I brought chairs to the edge of the vineyard. We sat together under the waning sun, sampling a bottle of last year's yield. The clouds above us turned fiery yellow and orange as the sun slowly dropped toward the edge of the sky.

"Tell me what it is like in Genoa," my father said. "Tell me about your teacher."

"Genoa is a beautiful city by the sea, and my teacher has been so generous with her time."

"I'm glad to hear that. What have you learned from her?"

"Her drawing lessons have allowed me to see the world in a fresh way. I now see everything—from trees and stones to buildings and

105

fishmongers—as connected parts of a whole."

"I'm not sure I understand what you mean," my father said.

"When you truly look at something in order to recreate it on the page, you become one with it. You see it as part of yourself."

"That is the way I look at grapevines. If I look at the vines carefully, they tell me what they need. I may not be recreating them on paper as you are, but I do want to see them thrive."

I touched my glass to my father's. "Here's to thriving."

"To thriving!"

I was eager to tell him about Paola even though I knew he would have many questions. I, myself, was still not sure what our friendship meant, or if her feelings for me were as deep as mine were for her. "I have met a young lady."

"A young lady?" Father took a sip of his wine. "Tell me about her."

"She is kind, intelligent, and beautiful. She is also a poet and dreams that one day she will have her own printing press."

"An ambitious young lady, it seems."

"She is. And would it shock you to hear that I have fallen in love with her? She has shown me that whether painter or poet, an artist brings added meaning to all things."

"I had no idea you would go to Genoa, fall in love, and come home a philosopher," my father said.

We sat in silence for a while, listening to doves call. The air grew cooler and the colors in the sky began to dim.

"You know," he said. "It was your mother who first had the idea that you should be given artistic training. She used to watch you draw, and she told me she thought it was your calling. If I had listened to her, I would have apprenticed you to an artist when you were much younger."

"Really? I had no idea."

"I know," he continued. "I suppose I felt lost when she died. I did not like the idea of sending you away to live with someone else to be trained in something of which I knew so little. I selfishly needed to keep you nearby. You, the first born, reminded me so much of her."

"You did what you had to do, and that is all we can do in this life."

He clinked my glass again. "Well said. Someone very wise must have raised you!"

"Indeed!" I wanted to tell my father about Dario. I didn't want Angelo Rossi to think his oldest son was weak, but I knew he would have good advice for me.

"There is one other thing. There is a fellow, Dario Bacigalupo is his name. He finds me laughable because I am studying art with a woman."

"Bacigalupo? He sounds like trouble. What is his story?"

"Every time I see him, he taunts me and insults both me and my teacher. I did, however, beat him in a foot race once. That was quite enjoyable."

"Well done!" Father was quiet for a moment. "Has he ever threatened you in any way?"

"No, but I worry that he will say something I can't accept, inciting me to attack him. I think that is what he wants, because he knows I could not possibly win. He is a fighter. You did not train me to be a fighter."

"That is true," Father said. "Ignore him, as I'm sure you do. But, if it should come to fists, you may surprise yourself."

Sofonisba

When Orazio returned home a few days ago, the house erupted in a flurry of activity as preparations for my birthday celebration began. I have not had a single moment of quiet in which to paint or write. Of course, I'm not complaining. Wherever Orazio is, joy always follows.

He and Giulia have been working together to make a gathering fit for a queen. Giulia asked her sisters to come from Mantua to help with the cleaning and baking, while Orazio has dashed all over Genoa inviting our many friends and buying food and fresh-cut flowers. He said he would like to create something theatrical for our guests, so he has opened the doors between the great room and the courtyard and has draped silk banners from ceiling to floor. Everything smells wonderful—a mixture of honey cake and jasmine.

"Why so much commotion for my seventy-third birthday?" I asked Orazio as he stepped down from a ladder, having just hung the last banner.

"Because you are a wonderful person, my dear. The people of this city love you. I love you." Orazio kissed my cheek and went off to get the wine.

By mid-afternoon, he returned with three barrels, which he placed in the courtyard. He brought a chair for me to position myself in the entrance hall so I could greet each guest. I spent the rest of the day welcoming my wonderful friends, each person bringing something they had made or had a hand in making. I received drawings, bolts of fabric, ceramics, jewelry, carvings, poems, and musical scores. Their generosity was overwhelming, and I felt blessed.

I was pleased and a bit surprised to see Signor Bruzzone, the dour and always-late shipbuilder. He brought his wife, daughter, and two young sons. One of the boys approached me. He held a carved sailing vessel.

"Happy birthday, Signora," he said, handing me the ship. "Papa made this for you."

"How lovely it is! I did not know you carved wood, Signor."

"I used to. I mean, I have taken it up again. You know, your portrait of me reminded me of my youth and the person I used to be. I cannot thank you enough, Signora, for seeing the person I forgot I was. And, I still want portraits of everyone in my family."

"I am ready any time," I said. "Just name the day!"

"I will, I will," he said. "Actually, allow me to introduce you to my wife, Roberta." He gestured to the woman standing at his side. "It is she who keeps track of what we do and when we do it." And with that, he dashed off toward the wine barrels in the courtyard.

"What a pleasure it is to meet you, Signora Anguissola. Ever since Matteo brought home the portrait you painted of him, he has been a different, much happier person. I don't know what you did, but I must thank you!"

"You are most welcome, Signora Bruzzone. I am glad the painting makes him happy. Let me know when you want to set up your first sitting."

"I will do that soon," she said, then curtseyed. "Happy birthday to you, Signora." With that, she turned and led her children out to the courtyard.

Right behind her was my dear Francesco, returned from Tuscany. He looked as handsome as ever with Paola on his arm, and to my great surprise, her father on his other side. I was so happy to see the three of them together.

"Welcome home!" I said as Francesco approached.

"It is good to be back," he said, handing me a bottle of wine. "From our vineyard."

Signor Vespucci took my hand. "Now that my daughter is helping you, Signora Anguissola, I think I should keep a closer eye on you." He winked and presented me with a small package wrapped in paper. I opened it to find a gorgeous piece of silk bobbin lace.

"This is absolutely beautiful. Thank you, Signor Vespucci."

"Happy birthday!" he said. "I hope we'll see more of each other in the time to come."

"I hope the same, kind sir."

And then it was Paola's turn. She glowed with happiness, and I was certain it had everything to do with Francesco's return. She handed me a small scroll.

"Open this later," she said. "It is a poem I wrote for you. I made you two copies so you can always keep one in a safe place. I hope you like it."

"I'm sure I will. Thank you, my dear." I squeezed her hand, and then the three of them moved toward the food and wine and I lost sight of them in the crowd.

Once all the guests had arrived, Orazio moved my chair to the courtyard so I could join them. The rest of the afternoon was a delightful mixture of blue sky, smiling faces, wine, cake, and conversation with many dear companions. As dusk approached, a violinist began to play. I was delighted to see many couples begin to dance, Paola and Francesco among them.

As the piece of music came to its climax, a calamity of shouting came from the front of the house. A man's voice said, "I want to meet the artist who drew the boy bitten by the crab!"

Orazio jumped from his chair when he heard the sound of furniture scraping the floor and something ceramic shattering. He did not get far before a disheveled, wild-eyed man burst into the courtyard. Giulia and our stable boy, Luca, were holding the tail of the man's coat, trying to restrain him, but their effort was as futile as attempting to hold back a tempest.

"I need to meet the woman who drew the boy bitten by the crab!"

"Sir, calm yourself. If you wish to meet me, I am that woman," I said.

The man dropped to his knees and crawled toward me. It was comical to see, but the look on his face was serious and I did not dare laugh at his show of humility.

"Signora! Maestra!" He bowed his head at my feet. "It is I, Michelangelo Merisi da Caravaggio. I have come to meet you."

"Caravaggio the painter?" I said. "Welcome."

He clasped his hands to his heart and pulled on the front of his shirt as though to tear it off his chest. "Oh, dear lady! You honor me. I have admired your work for so long. You have no idea how much you have inspired me."

Caravaggio's wild entrance and effusive praise had drawn the attention of all the party guests. Everyone was listening.

"Your drawing, the one you gave to *Il Divino* in Rome. The one of the boy crying after being bitten by a crab. Do you remember that drawing?"

"I do." That was the drawing that *Il Divino* himself had copied, which made me so proud.

"I saw a copy of Michelangelo's copy of your work. I could not have made my painting *Boy Bitten by a Lizard* without the inspiration of your drawing, Signora."

Like a magician, Caravaggio pulled a rolled-up paper from inside his cloak. "You see? Here is a drawing I made of my painting. I left Rome ten days ago, being in some trouble with the law. I wanted to get as far away as I could. I decided to come to Genoa to find you, to show you this drawing, to let you know how much you mean to me."

"Well, my young friend, I am amazed and honored. You could not have come to find me on a better day, because today we are celebrating my birthday. You must join us!"

"Happy birthday, Maestra! I am here to celebrate with all my heart."

Orazio, always astute, escorted Caravaggio to the wine and food, allowing me the chance to settle myself a bit. My surprise was certainly still on my face when Paola's father approached me and asked, "Who is this fellow, Signora? Is he trouble? Shall I call the authorities?"

"No, Lorenzo. Thank you. I think he is fine. Caravaggio is the fiery young artist from Rome who, at the beginning of this new century, has begun to revolutionize painting."

"Caravaggio. Is he the one who has used a prostitute as a model for the Virgin Mary?"

"He is the one. He even painted the bottoms of peasants' dirty feet as they knelt to honor Mary and the child in her arms."

"There is something else about him," Lorenzo said, pausing for a moment, looking for the right word. "Chiaroscuro?"

"Yes, exactly. Not only are his depictions of traditional subjects new and shocking, but he has taken the use of chiaroscuro—the treatment of light and shadow—to new heights, thus greatly enhancing the dramatic impact of his work."

"I will keep my eye on him for you."

"Thank you, Lorenzo. I'm sure he means no harm."

Along with the violinist, Orazio had hired a group of women singers to regale us with madrigals. The singing carried on far into the night. We all drank more wine and everyone danced. Even I joined in. But mostly, I sat in my chair and watched Paola and Francesco dance. They made a beautiful pair. I hope only the best for them.

I also watched Caravaggio as he moved in and out of light and shadow.

I hoped this volatile and innovative young artist would find a good resolution with the law in Rome. When people are too far outside their time—the way Caravaggio is—things do not always go so well for them. As I watched him among the partygoers, I hoped he would have many years ahead of him to create more remarkable works of art. His presence on my birthday was a most unexpected gift, reminding me that I have certainly been an oddity in my own way, and yet I have survived.

Paola

At breakfast Father said, "That was quite a celebration last night."

"Yes, it was. I'm glad you joined us."

"I am, too," he said. "I think that Signora Anguissola is adding something new and wonderful to our lives. I hope you agree."

I wasn't sure why my father would say this. "Of course. Yes! Is anything wrong, Father?"

"Wrong? No, no. Everything is good. I am pleased with your work, Paola. I am just wondering how you are feeling."

"I'm feeling very well. I am happy." I still felt there was something he wanted to tell me that he was not saying.

"And Francesco? How are you feeling about Francesco?"

"I'm feeling good about him, too. Why do you ask?"

"He is a fine young man." Father took a bite of bread and then continued. "Last night, Francesco told me his father would like him to go to Sicily to care for a new vineyard. He wanted to know if I thought this move would distress you. Has he told you about this?"

"No, he has not." I felt heat rising in me. "I wonder why he told you first and not me."

"I think he just wanted some reassurance that you would listen and accept his plan."

"Accept his plan? What plan? We are going to walk in the market this afternoon. I will have to talk with him about this."

My father reached out to cover my hand with his. "I think that would be a good idea," he said. The look in his eyes expressed the unmistakable desire to protect me.

113

When Francesco came to fetch me for our walk, he was as cheerful as ever. Fabia was with us, of course, and I was glad to have her nearby. I planned to ask him why he was keeping secrets from me, and it was possible that things might become difficult.

As we walked through the market toward the sea, Francesco said, "I meant to ask you, how many feathers did you find while I was gone?"

"Feathers? One."

"Only one? I thought of you so many more times than that. You must not have been looking hard enough." Perhaps he thought that was humorous, but his comment made my ire rise.

"I looked every day. I only found one. I imagined you were too busy harvesting grapes to think of me."

"Paola, no! I thought of you every day, many times. It seems that my messages were not getting through to the birds."

"Apparently not."

"What is wrong today, Paola? You seem displeased with me."

"Displeased? Yes, I am displeased. When are you going to tell me about Sicily?"

His face fell at my words. "You heard about Sicily. I asked your father not to tell you."

"Why did you tell him first and not me?"

Francesco didn't speak right away. He seemed to be looking for the right words. "I wanted to know if he thought you would accept my departure. And he said he thought you would understand. I was going to tell you about all this on our walk today."

"So, tell me."

Francesco sighed. "My father has a new venture that needs my help. Through a cousin of his, my father is in the process of obtaining a vineyard on the island of Sicily, in a place called Alcamo. He would like me to go there to oversee the work."

"So you would be leaving Genoa."

"Yes, and it would likely be for quite a while. I'm sorry you did not hear this from me first."

"And this is definitely going to happen?" I asked, turning my shoulder away from him. How could he leave me again? All that business about feathers! Such nonsense to fool me into thinking he cares.

"Yes. But, Paola—" He took my hand and drew it to him. "There is something else. Once I get settled, I would like you to join me there. Would you?"

"Would I join you? Are you asking me to marry you? That is a question you would need to put to my father. And I know what his answer would be."

Francesco's face fell into a look of despair. "Paola, please listen. I know your father needs you here. That is why I want to go to Sicily and establish myself. Then, I will be in a better position to ask him for your hand in marriage. You do understand, don't you?"

I had to admit that his reasoning made some sense, as far as Father was concerned. But still, I could not fathom why he had discussed his intentions with my father at all before having first spoken to me. His actions seemed like a betrayal. It made me wonder what else he might be keeping from me. Men do these things. Pretend devotion when they do not plan to follow through on their promises.

"I am not sure," I said. "I will have to think about all this."

Francesco stopped walking, took both my hands in his, and looked straight into my eyes.

"I love you," he said. "I hope that one day, you will join me."

I sensed he spoke the truth, but suddenly, the truth was not so simple.

"I think," I said, "that right now, I need to go home."

"I understand," he said. At the door to my father's house, Francesco pulled a feather from his pocket and pressed it into my hand.

"Remember," he said, "I am always thinking about you."

Sofonisba

As planned, once my birthday had been celebrated, I packed my bags to head for Cremona. The trip from Genoa only takes a few days. I was excited to see my brother and had a sack of money to deliver. I also brought painting supplies, just in case I should happen to meet the composer da Viadana and have the opportunity to paint his portrait.

As I watched the countryside stream by, I pulled out the poem Paola had given me at the party. I saved reading it for the journey to Cremona. I carefully untied the red silk cord around the scroll, unrolled it, and read.

What Life is This?

What life is this in which our stories blend?
You the painter and I the humble scribe.
I gather up the colors of your life
and stand aside, this gentle arc to bend.
For life's deep hues will shadow and portend
to readers reading at some future time
while I can only see you in the prime
of this radiant tale we weave and mend.
The words you speak become the tale we spin
and every month we know the waning moon
will wax anew to share this life in verse.
With threads rejoined, we aim to live again,
ensuring that you do not fade too soon,
for your life lost to us would make ours worse.

How beautiful it was to read these words of my young friend. I will read this poem each morning upon waking and again each night before I go to sleep. I am grateful to know she is invested in helping me keep my story alive. How lucky I am to have Paola and Francesco in my life.

I laid my head back on the coach seat and gazed at the passing world marked by crumbling stone walls and recently harvested fields. What unexpectedly came to mind was Canto V of Dante's *Inferno* and the characters Paolo and Francesca, the lovers whose union sprang from a lie. Francesca was tricked into marriage by an evil man who put forward his handsome younger brother, Paolo, as the groom. One day, while reading out loud together the legend of Lancelot, Paolo and Francesca fell unexpectedly into the throes of passion. The two slipped deeper and deeper into a long love affair. When Francesca's husband discovered his wife's infidelity, he was enraged and killed both his wife and his brother. Of course, he had brought it all on himself, and Hell had a place for him, as well as for the two lovers. Paolo and Francesca remained caught in the second ring of Hell, swept about by a rushing wind that kept them within sight of each other but unable to be united for the rest of eternity. What a terrible fate that was.

I have seen the signs that my two friends are in love, and I am pleased. I see nothing indicating that anything awaiting Paola and Francesco will include eternal suffering. In fact, I see them creating a life that is the exact opposite of Dante's ill-fated lovers—a life that will be full of great joy. As someone for whom marriage came late in life, I hope that soon enough everything will work out well for my two young friends.

As my carriage approached my family home, I could see that my brother was bent over in Mother's garden, pulling up weeds. He wore a wide-brimmed straw hat to protect himself from the sun and, at the sound of the horses' hooves, he looked up. *How much he looks like Papa*, I thought. How did my Asdrubale get so old?

"Sofonisba!" he called as the carriage pulled up to the side of the house. "I was not sure you would arrive today. I wanted to tidy up a bit and have the place looking good for you!"

"Oh, dear brother, it looks beautiful just the way it is."

And yet I could see that the garden had grown ragged and unkempt over time, and those years had not spared my brother either. His thick mop of hair was completely white and he had quite a few wrinkles, especially around his eyes, especially when he smiled.

As I stepped from the carriage, he grabbed me in his arms, lifted me, spun me around, and set me on the grass at the edge of the garden. Apparently, although he looked older, his physical strength had not waned one bit.

"You are here, dearest sister! Welcome home!"

"Oh, dear brother, in troubled times, you have been my rock. Now it is my turn to do something good for you."

"Let's get your things off the carriage and then have something to eat. Are you hungry?"

"I am starving!"

Asdrubale lifted my bags off the carriage and I paid the driver. Then I followed my brother into the house. We went straight to the kitchen and sat down. He placed before me on the table a loaf of bread, a fresh ball of mozzarella, and a large bowl of beans marinated in olive oil, lemon, and dill.

"So, how are you?" he asked.

"I'm very well. The more important question is, how are you?"

He finished chewing his bread and took a sip of wine.

"I'm well, especially now that you are here!"

I took his hand. "I love you, you know."

"And I love you," he said. "It's ironic because just two days ago, a man came to the house on horseback and delivered the first disbursement of the Spanish pension."

"So, you are saying I did not need to come with the satchel of money?"

"No! I'm saying now I am a rich man." He raised his glass high. "More wine!"

I raised my glass to meet his and we burst into laughter.

Asdrubale

The first time Sofi left me was to go to Rome. I was not quite four, and I don't have a clear picture of her departure—only an aching memory of loss. As far as I knew, she was gone for good. Her return from Rome a year and a half later, however, is clear in my mind. It was a sunny day at the end of summer when she stepped down from the carriage. I was standing on the terrace watching, so amazed to see her before me that I couldn't move. I'm sure Mama and Papa must have been there too, but all I remember is Sofi picking me up, lifting me high into the air, and carrying me off into the garden, dancing and singing.

After my sister returned from Rome, I became her shadow, following her everywhere. I sat next to her when she worked and felt proud when she made sketches of me. I loved to sit in her studio, watching as she put paint on canvas and made images appear like magic.

There were five other sisters between us and I loved them all, but Sofi held the prime place in my heart. I wanted to please her. She did not ask much of me, but I would have done anything for her. I still would.

Not only was my sister an artist, but she was also an excellent storyteller. Many an afternoon, Sofi and I sat together under the lemon tree while she invented stories in which I was the hero. She made me the brave knight on horseback, saying it was I who slayed the dragon, saved the village, and married the beautiful princess.

"You, Asdrubale," she would say, "are named after a real warrior whose name was Hasdrubal who lived a long time ago in a place called Carthage. He had an older brother named Hannibal, and together they would go on military campaigns with their father, whose name was Hamilcar, just like our father, Amilcare. They were fighters, those brothers, and they were on a mission to overthrow the unjust power of the Roman army."

"How did they fight?" I would ask.

"With swords and lances, riding on horses or even on elephants. They led huge armies of soldiers through Spain, along the Mediterranean coast, and all the way here, to Cremona. And even though Hasdrubal and his brother did not defeat the Romans, they were both very brave and good warriors. You should be proud to have this name."

And so I was.

Years later, after Sofi had gone to the Spanish court, I learned more about Carthaginian history from my father. For one thing, our family had a deep-seated connection to Hasdrubal and Hannibal and their efforts to defeat Rome in the Punic Wars. It wasn't a blood relationship but more of a moral connection, a connection in spirit. In ancient days, there was a Roman garrison in Cremona and our city became the stage for much fighting. The local people resented this violation of their city, first by the Romans, and then by the Carthaginians. Yet, they did admire the bravery of men like Hannibal and Hasdrubal, who desired to see Rome crushed.

There was another important character in the story that Sofi never talked about, although I'm quite sure she knew of her. Hannibal had a niece by marriage named Sophonisba. She was extremely beautiful and highly educated in music and literature. She was known to be clever and personally captivating. As happens sometimes to beautiful women of noble birth, she became a pawn between two kings. She was in love with the Carthaginian leader, but the Roman king was also smitten with her and wanted her for himself. When the Roman authorities tried to take her away from her true love—in order to solidify their own power—Sophonisba chose instead to drink poison. That is how brave she was, willing to end her life rather than allow the Roman leader a foothold into Carthage by marrying her.

But Sofi never told me that part of the story. I must ask her why.

Sofonisba

I have been going slowly through each room of the house letting memories of home flood over me. Asdrubale has taken over the room that was once my studio and has made it his study, a place where he can work on his Latin translation projects and practice music on the clavichord. This light-filled room has always been a place of intellectual pursuit.

As I sit in my old studio, the scent of roses wafting from the garden reminds me of Mother. Bird songs remind me of my sisters. Visual details bring Papa back to life as though he might appear at any moment. I am touched to see that the little altar he enlisted me to decorate in the front entryway is still there. Asdrubale found me gazing at it.

"I pay my respects here every day," he said with a wink. "Remember the story Papa told?"

THE LARES

Papa told many stories from antiquity that I did not completely understand. One such story was that of Mercury and Lara. It seems Jupiter became angry when the nymph Lara—who could not keep secrets—spread the news of his philandering. Jupiter ordered Lara's tongue cut out and sent Mercury to escort her to the Underworld. Mercury and Lara fell in love as they journeyed, and when love happens, children are often the result.

The children of Mercury and Lara became associated with the

Lares, household gods that were said to protect hearth and home. Roman houses often had a place near the entrance called a *lararium*, a place to honor these deities.

Despite being forward-thinking when it came to educating his daughters, my father appreciated the rituals of history. So, he built a niche in the wall near our front door and had me decorate it with snakes, flowers, and vines. I felt important the whole time I was painting the decoration, and I hoped that someday I would have the opportunity to paint sacred subjects for the walls of a church. The paint around the niche has faded, but I can still see traces of color here and there. I am proud of the work I did when I was still quite young.

The altar was a special place, and I often said a prayer when I passed the niche. More than once, I left a spray of violets as an offering in the hope that the Lares would bring good fortune and abundance to our home. I have often wondered if I owe some portion of my success in life to the Lares. God knows I left many offerings for them all the years that I was growing up in my father's house.

Today I went to San Luca to hear a performance of choral music composed by Lodovico da Viadana. Many of the pieces were familiar to me, having been moved to joyful tears by them on more than one occasion at San Siro. Afterward, I sought out the new choirmaster—who is also a Franciscan monk—and introduced myself.

"Sofonisba Anguissola!" he said. "You are the painter who studied with Michelangelo and went to the Spanish court. What a pleasure to meet you!"

"It is my pleasure to meet the composer of 'Exsultate Justi in Domino.' Bravo to you for your music and all the new things you are doing with basso continuo."

Brother Lodovico smiled. "You know," he said, "it seems that we have a lot to talk about. Is it possible that while you are in Cremona, you might have time to paint my portrait?"

"I'm pleased you should ask because I was planning to ask you to sit for me."

"Well, I guess we are even in our thinking, then. Do we have a deal?" he reached out his hand to me.

"We have a deal," I said. "Would you be free tomorrow? I will only be in Cremona a short time before I must return to Genoa. But if I can begin right away, I should be able to make you this gift."

"Signora, I would be honored. Let us begin tomorrow."

When I returned home after the concert, I went into my old studio to find the materials I would need to paint Brother Lodovico's portrait and looked through old canvases in search of something I could use. To paint over an old painting would have taken time, so I was delighted to find a blank stretched canvas already primed with rabbit skin glue. It only needed a bit of cleaning. I also found several additional prepared canvases tucked away, and I wanted to take them all home to Genoa with me. I could use them if Matteo Bruzzone followed through on his desire to commission portraits of his family.

Among the old canvases, I found a large group portrait I started in 1557 depicting my father, Asdrubale, and Minerva. I created it not long after I returned home from Rome, and I was pleased to be reminded that I had incorporated some Roman ruins into the background. It has been almost fifty years since I've laid eyes on this painting. Looking at it again, the first thing I noticed was how successful I had been in showing Asdrubale's love for Papa. I also saw quite a few elements lacking the proper finish—for example, Asdrubale's feet and hands, my father's feet, and the bottom of Minerva's gown. While I'm here, perhaps I can spend some time filling in what is missing. Of course, my priority is to complete the portrait of Brother Lodovico.

This morning, Asdrubale loaded up the carriage with all my materials and took me to the Church of San Luca. Upon arriving, we found Brother Lodovico waiting under the stone archway that shades the front entrance.

"Greetings, Signora," he called out, raising his arms to receive me.

A short, stocky gentleman with a square face, strong nose, and full lips, brother Lodovico does not have a shaved tonsure the way some monks do. Instead, a thatch of dark curls crowns the top of his head. We exchanged pleasantries and I introduced him to Asdrubale, who quickly unloaded my supplies.

"Good to meet you, Brother," Asdrubale said. "May your sitting be fruitful. I will return before sunset."

Brother Lodovico and I stood on the cobblestone terrace in front of the church.

"What do you think of this ancient edifice?" he asked. "It was built in the twelfth century, so it's just a bit older than I am."

"It is decidedly medieval," I said.

"Do you know what prompted the unusual addition?" he asked, referring to the six-sided temple dome that juts out from the facade of the old church. "It is so elegant and lovely, clearly built much later, but I haven't found anyone to tell me about it."

"Indeed, I do," I said. "My father told me that the temple was added by the city fathers in the early 1500s to give thanks for the fact that Cremona had escaped the plague."

"What a wonderful story," he said.

"I have always loved this church, and now that you are here—no doubt to make beautiful music—I will love it even more."

"I certainly hope I will not disappoint you, Signora."

"And I feel the same regarding your portrait. So, once again, we are of like mind!"

"So we are!"

With that, he picked up the box full of supplies, I picked up the blank canvas, and we entered the church to start his portrait.

When Asdrubale and I sat down to a late dinner, I was almost too tired to eat.

"How did it go today?" he asked as he passed me a plate of marinated artichoke hearts.

"I made fast progress on Brother Lodovico's portrait. I was able to lay down the basic composition and started to work on the undertones of his face. He asked me to show him sitting at his desk, working on a musical score, and I'm pleased with what I have accomplished so far."

I noticed that Asdrubale was not eating much and was instead moving his food around with his fork.

"Dear brother, did you spend too much time in the sun today, weeding the garden?"

"No, no. I'm fine, but I do have a rather odd question for you." He continued to push his food back and forth.

"What is it?"

"Remember how you used to tell me about Hasdrubal and Hannibal?"

"I do."

"Why did you never tell me that you were named for a Carthaginian as well? The Sophonisba who ended her life rather than be given over in humiliation to Rome."

It was a good question and deserved an honest answer. "You were a child, and I didn't want to put the idea into your head that people could choose to end their own lives."

"Ah," he said, chewing on a piece of roast chicken. "Perhaps that was wise of you."

"Frankly, that part of the story has always disturbed me. I didn't exactly understand why our parents chose this name for me. Her story was not joyful. It was tragic."

"Did you ever ask Papa about it?"

"I did get up the courage to ask him why he gave me this name, right at the time I was getting ready to start my studies with Signor Campi. I was thirteen going on fourteen."

"And what did Father say?"

"At first he pressed his lips together as though he was pained by my question. I had never seen Papa be slow to speak. He suggested I focus on her strengths, not her demise. He said, 'The history books tell us what happened to her, but perhaps you, Sofonisba, can someday tell us how she felt.'"

Asdrubale took a swallow of wine. "What kind of answer was that? How did that help?"

"At the time, it did not help much. But over the years, I have thought of Sophonisba often."

"In what way?" Asdrubale asked. "I mean, besides sharing her name?"

I took a sip of wine and decided that the moment of confession had arrived. "When I was in my early twenties and a student of Signor Gatti's, I became pregnant by one of the other students, a man I loved and who I thought loved me. But, he left me. I was so afraid to confess my sin to our parents that I contemplated ending my life."

"Is that where all the blood came from?" Asdrubale asked.

"What?" I said, stunned by the question. "What do you mean?"

"My bedroom was across the hall from where you slept. It was early morning and I heard sounds. I went to my bedroom door and cracked it open. I saw Antonella leaving your room with sheets that were covered in

125

blood. I had no idea what that meant. I pushed myself through the crack in the door and opened my mouth to speak. Antonella put her fingers to her lips and kept moving."

"The blood was due to the loss of the child, not to any action to end my life."

Asdrubale nodded. "And you kept this secret all this time?"

"I did," I said. "And you never told Father or Mother what you saw?"

"I never did," he said.

I put my head in my hands. "I can't believe you remember that. You were only three. You must have been so frightened."

"Confused, maybe. But not frightened."

"How did you know to keep quiet about what you saw? I would have been ruined if anyone had learned about what had happened."

"Being so young, I could not understand what I was seeing, but I could tell that whatever it was, Antonella had it in her control. Her silent admonition to stay quiet was all I needed."

"Oh, Asdrubale, thank you. Thank you for keeping my secret."

"Ah, Sofi." He brought my head to rest on his shoulder. "That is what brothers are for."

Asdrubale

My sister's visit will come to an end in one more short week, and I am not looking forward to her leaving me. Today I convinced her to take a break from painting and walk with me around the city a bit. We sat in the Piazza del Comune in front of the Cathedral, flanked by the Baptistery on one side and the town hall on the other. The Torrazzo loomed over us.

"Sitting with you beneath the Torrazzo makes me think of climbing to the top when I was a girl," she said.

"Did you do that alone?"

"Sometimes, yes, just me. I would go to the top while Antonella was down in the market. Sometimes Elena and Lucia came with me and we would sit up there at the top of the world and tell each other stories of knights and princesses."

"That's nice. I wish we could have made that climb together."

"You and I never got to do that, did we?"

"No, we did not. And now we are far too old to ascend all those steps."

"That is true," she said. "It saddens me that there are many things I never got to do with you, Minerva, Europa, and Anna Maria. You were all so much younger than me, and eventually, I left to go to Spain."

"I know. You and I missed sharing many things, except that now that you have lived so far into your old age, I feel as though I have caught up with you!"

"Indeed! We are both old people now, aren't we?"

This made us both laugh, and when we looked into each other's eyes, we both teared up. The sun was slipping down the sky and the flower

127

vendors in front of the cathedral began to pack their wares. People were out strolling and a cool breeze came across the piazza.

"You know, brother, I would love to see the sun reflecting off the River Po this evening. Elena and I used to ride the horses to the river late in the day. Do you think if we were to jump in the carriage right now, your horse could get us to the river before sunset?"

"Most certainly."

"Let's go!"

We made it to the river while it was still light and we settled ourselves on a fallen log near the water. The riverbank was quiet and peaceful, except for a soft breeze that made the surface of the water ripple and catch the light, a blaze of golden orange. From not far away, an owl called.

"He is out early," said my sister.

"He knows you are here, and he doesn't want you to leave." I took her hand in mine. "I don't want you to leave, either."

"I know. I will come back."

The owl called again.

"You see?" I said. "The owl heard you. He will be waiting for you." Now it was my turn to put my head on my sister's shoulder.

"This is what sisters are for," she said.

Sofonisba

Today was my last day in Cremona, so I spent the early morning with Brother Lodovico in his office in San Luca. He sat by the window and I put the final tones on his cheeks and chin, adding just that bit of warmth that his smile so readily exudes. In our short time together, he has become a true friend. I will miss seeing him. With a few final strokes of the brush, I was done.

"Are you ready to see yourself?" I turned the easel toward him so he could see the result of our many sittings.

"Signora, it is wonderful!"

"You like it? You feel it captures who you are?"

"Oh my, yes. Yes! Thank you. I will treasure this always. I will get some help tomorrow from the church caretaker to frame this and hang it."

It pleases me to know that he is happy with the portrait and that something I painted—even though it is not a traditional religious image—will hang in a little church that I have always admired.

"I have something for you too," he said. He went to this office and returned with a folio. Inside was the sheet music for "Exsultate Justi in Domino," inscribed by him on the title page: *For Sofonisba, to keep us even. Blessings, Brother Lodovico*

"We are most definitely even, my friend! Thank you so much! It has been a pleasure to get to know you."

"Yes, it has," he said.

I heard the carriage pulling up. Asdrubale had arrived to collect me.

"Goodbye Brother Lodovico," I said and held out my hand to him.

He took it in his and then wrapped me in a brotherly embrace.

"Goodbye, Sofonisba. Godspeed to you on your journey home to Genoa!"

Back at the house, I found that Asdrubale had packed up those old—but quite usable—canvases that I'd found wasting away in the studio. I will put them to good use. I was sad that I had not made time to finish the group portrait of him, Papa, and Minerva.

"I'm happy to keep it safe. And besides," Asdrubale said with a grin, "it is good that I keep something in Cremona that will lure you back here sooner rather than later."

"You know, brother, you don't have to wait for me to come to Cremona. You are welcome in Genoa anytime."

"I will remember that, dear Sofi."

Soon, the coach will come and take me back to Genoa. For now, I will spend this last bit of time in Cremona in my mother's garden with my dear brother. He is the one whom I regaled with Carthaginian tales when he was but a boy. He, the one who cried when bitten by a crab, a memory I drew from that impressed not only Michelangelo but Caravaggio, too. He is the one who saw bloodied sheets and kept my secret.

Paola

Every day for the past three weeks, Francesco has done something nice for me. He is trying hard to make things right again, back to the way they were before the misunderstanding that followed Sofi's party. I know he wants me to trust that his love for me is real.

This morning, he came to fetch me for a walk to San Siro. He brought a leather-bound journal as a gift—"to fill with poetry," he said. "We can sit together on one of the benches on the piazza outside the church. You can write while I sketch."

Fabia accompanied us to San Siro but then went on to the market alone. I honestly think she's in love with the idea that I am in love, so she finds ways to give me time to be alone with Francesco. He and I sat on the same bench where once I found him sketching the pigeons. I opened my new journal and stared at the blank page. I was not able to write a word.

I looked over at Francesco and saw that he was looking at me and also at the paper in front of him. He appeared to be in a kind of reverie.

"What are you sketching?" I asked.

"You," he said. "I want to take your face with me to Sicily."

I felt the color rise in my cheeks. "Really?"

"Yes, really. The first time we met, do you remember that day?"

"I remember it well."

"I knew when I looked at you that you should be depicted in a work of art."

"Is that so?"

"Yes, and I'm trying to show the contours of your face not with lines, but rather with shading, with the play of light and shadow on the forms of

131

your face. This is something Sofi has been trying to teach me."

Having Francesco look at me, his eyes filled with so much attention and tenderness, kindled a desire impossible to ignore. I am ready to start believing in him again.

⁂

Sofi is home from Cremona. When Fabia and I arrived today, she answered the door herself and we embraced. She looked weary from her travels, but her smile was as welcoming as ever.

"Come in, come in," she said, "Tell me what you have been doing while I was away."

"I devoted a lot of time to working on the accounts for Father's business. I think it made him feel secure to have my undivided attention on the ledgers for a while."

"That's good, to build some trust. And how about Francesco? How is he?"

"You have not heard?"

"Heard what?"

"Francesco is leaving Genoa."

"Oh dear," she said. "What has happened? Where is he going?"

"To Alcamo, on the island of Sicily. To oversee a new vineyard there for his father." I could not hold back my tears.

Sofi wrapped me in her arms and stroked my hair. "This is a big change. Do you want to just sit and talk today? We can put transcribing aside."

"No, let's work. Doing something productive with you will distract me from my woes."

THE CALL

After my time in Rome, I settled back into a quiet life in Cremona. For the next three years, I put my full attention on painting portraits of either myself or my family. In addition, I continued to teach my sisters Lucia and Minerva how to paint. But this quiet, tranquil life would change in 1558 when Signor Campi called me to Milan. He needed help fulfilling portrait commissions. I was deeply honored that my former teacher would ask for my assistance.

I had cousins in Milan I could stay with, and so, with the spirit of adventure fully alive inside me, I went. Although the churches in

132

Cremona had turned me down, I thought perhaps the churches in a bigger city like Milan might appreciate my ability.

After nine years apart, it was a great joy to see both Signor and Signora Campi. My former teacher seemed slightly awed by me. I was surprised at first, but I also knew how much I had grown as an artist. I knew full well what I was doing. Signor Campi turned over several of his portrait commissions to me and I took care of them with ease.

In Milan, I followed through on my plan to visit churches in search of work. Unfortunately, just like in Cremona, I was told by all the church officials I approached that a woman could not possibly produce the level of quality required. They would not even look at my work samples or letters of recommendation from my teachers. In contrast to the polite denials I had received in Cremona, the Milanese church elders acted almost as if I were not there. They all sent me away. Their attitude toward me was wretched, but I should not have been surprised.

I had to accept that I was an anomaly. A woman like me had no precedent in the world. I would have to make whatever art I could, as best I could. It was some consolation that my cousins in Milan were impressed by my talent and my courage. They could not believe the little girl they had once seen running about with a clover crown in her hair had grown into such a self-assured and determined painter.

Their awe was even greater when the first portrait commission that came directly to me—and not through Signor Campi—was a request in a letter from Fernando Alvarez de Toledo, the third Duke of Alba. Even I was stunned, but only for the briefest while. After all, hadn't I conversed at length over many months with Michelangelo, and hadn't he copied one of my drawings himself? Why shouldn't a duke seek my painting skills?

I'd first met the Duke of Alba when Prince Philip had come to Cremona many years before. Since that time, the prince had become King Philip II of Spain. What I remembered of the Duke of Alba was that he was an extremely energetic person. He had been the man in charge of making sure that all activities for the prince's visit to Cremona were properly planned and carried out. He was the one making sure the Cremonese nobility did their best to honor their future king. The Duke of Alba had been to my father's house many times, and I was quite honored that he remembered me as someone who could paint a good portrait.

My Milanese cousins had given over a room in their home for my studio, and it was here that the Duke of Alba came for his first portrait sitting. The last time he'd seen me, I'd been a girl of seventeen. When we met in Milan, I was a grown woman of twenty-seven with much more experience and knowledge of art and life.

The first thing he said when he walked into the studio was "My, how you've grown!" Since I was not any taller than I'd been ten years earlier, I assumed he meant that I had aged.

"So have you," I replied, which made him chuckle and I think introduced him to my sense of humor, putting him immediately at ease.

"I hear you spent some time in Rome with Michelangelo," he said. "What was he like?"

"He was a kind and encouraging teacher. He helped me see my value as an artist."

"And Rome, what did you think of it?"

"It was very old," I said, and that made him laugh again.

I invited the duke to sit near the window so I could make some preliminary sketches of him, and while I drew, we chatted. I told him about Michelangelo, and he regaled me with his efforts to bring unity to the large and sprawling domain of King Philip.

"Sometimes," he said, "there is no good choice other than military force."

Being the daughter of Amilcare Anguissola—who believed there is always a better way than exerting might—I wanted to argue, but I said nothing. What interested me more was his ability to speak and write three languages: Italian, French, and Latin. I'd not practiced my Latin since the days of our tutor Signor Cavallaro, so I tried a phrase or two.

"*Bene conatus,*" he said—a good attempt.

"Perhaps it is fortunate that I am a painter, not an orator," I said, making him laugh again.

The Duke of Alba was a willing and companionable sitter, and after that first time, we spent many pleasant afternoons together talking about art and poetry. He did not dwell too much on life at court, although the final time we were together, he did mention that Philip's second wife, Mary Tudor, had recently died and that the king was about to marry a third wife, a young French girl named Elisabeth de Valois. And this girl had let it be known to her future husband that she would like to learn how to draw and paint.

"Have you ever taught anyone how to draw and paint?" the duke asked.

"I have. When I returned from Rome, I spent three years in Cremona and taught two of my sisters as much as I could from all that I had learned."

"And is that something you found enjoyable?"

"I did, very much. Teaching has helped me better understand and perfect my own craft. It is also a gift to see another person learn to trust their eyes."

"That is a gift, indeed. Thank you for teaching *me* something today, Sofonisba," he said.

Francesco

I went down to the Barbarossa a little early this evening, hoping to get something to eat before Dario's arrival. It was a quiet moment when I entered the taverna, with the final golden rays of the late afternoon sun streaming in. Giuseppe was there by himself, smiling behind the counter, drying mugs.

"Ah, my young friend, what can I get for you?"

"A plate of cheese and olives with some bread, if you please."

As I was the only customer, he came out from behind the bar with the food, sat down with me, and poured us some wine. He lifted his mug and touched it to mine. "Salute," I said.

"Tell me about your trip to Tuscany," he said. "Tell me about the vineyard."

"The vineyard was bursting with grapes. My father was glad to have my help."

I picked up the loaf of bread, broke off a chunk, and offered it to him.

"You know," I said, "I brought with me some bottles of wine from last year's harvest. Would you like one?"

"That would be wonderful!" he said.

Just then, our peaceful repast was broken by the creak of the door, a clattering of footsteps, and a riot of voices. I had my back to the entrance and turned to see Dario saunter in as if he owned the place, filling the small taverna with his customary scowl and his band of rogues.

"Giuseppe!" he called. "Drinks for my boys, and be quick about it. We are thirsty!"

My friend went behind the bar. I continued chewing my bread, bracing myself for what might come next.

"Ah, the artist who runs so fast is back. I haven't seen you in a some time, my friend." He took an olive from my plate, popped it into his mouth, and spit the pit onto the floor.

"How is your lady teacher?"

I locked eyes with Giuseppe but continued chewing my bread and cheese.

"So, are you making any progress? Have you finally managed to grind her colors?"

"That's enough from you, Dario," Giuseppe said.

I seethed inside, restraining myself from responding and wondering when he would ever tire of making his lewd insults.

"Is she any good? Should I try her?"

I could restrain no more. I leapt from my chair and lunged at Dario, swinging my clenched fist at him. He ducked his head and I missed. His friends broke into laughter and cheers, calling for a fight. Dario rolled up his sleeves and said, "Would you like to try that again, little rabbit?"

Instead of swinging, I threw the contents of my mug at his face. He howled at the sting of wine in his eyes, rubbing them with his sleeve.

"Bastard!" he yelled and dove toward me, but I did not want to fight. I flew through the door and up to my room on the second floor, taking the stairs two at a time.

Thankfully, Dario did not attempt to follow, and I could hear him laughing through the floor of my room for quite a while. I'm guessing he had plenty to say about me being a coward. I wondered what Giuseppe was thinking. I understand there is not much he can do. Dario and his friends are longtime customers. And I will soon be gone to Sicily.

I swear, it was a good thing I didn't have a knife. If I'd had one, I might have pulled it out. I must not cause any trouble, not now. Someday soon, I hope to ask Signor Vespucci for his daughter's hand in marriage. I need him to see that I am a good and honest man, not some hot-headed knave who fights in public. I may not have turned myself into an artist in Genoa, but I did accomplish a few things. First, I found Signora Anguissola a skillful and dedicated scribe to help her write her story. Second, I fell in love. Third, I threw a mug of wine on that idiot, Dario.

Paola

It is the last day of January, 1606, and perhaps I should be cheerful, but how can I be happy knowing that Francesco will leave tomorrow? All through Christmas and Epiphany, we spent a great deal of time together, sketching, writing, walking, and strengthening our bond. I know he is doing what he needs to do to help his father with the new vineyard, and I suppose I understand. It occurs to me that I ought to apply Sofi's philosophy of turning stumbling blocks into victories. Maybe things will turn out much better for us than I can possibly imagine.

My love and I took our final walk through the market today. Fabia has given up trying to watch over us. She lets me go alone with him now. At the edge of the market where all the stalls of fish, fruits, and vegetables come to an end, in sight of the sea, Francesco held me in his arms.

"Tomorrow is the day when Orazio will take me on the *Sant'Agata* to Sicily," he said.

"I know."

"It is agony for me to think of leaving you," he said. "You know that, don't you?"

"I do."

"We both know that your father wants you here, so it will take some persuasion for him to allow us to marry. We will have a much better chance, though," he said, "if I can assure him that I will be able to provide for you. For us."

He looked into my eyes as he said this, and I wanted to believe him. His logic made sense, but who knows what will happen when he goes away? What beautiful Sicilian woman might he meet? How might he change?

He could see that I was worried. "Please believe me, Paola."

"I do," I said, but I knew my words were not completely true.

Then he reached into his coat pocket and pulled out a white feather.

"Another reminder of me. Keep it close." Then he walked with me to Sofi's door and kissed me goodbye. "Will I find you here tomorrow morning? Will you come with Sofi to the dock to say goodbye?"

"Of course I will." We kissed once more and then we parted.

Sofi opened the door herself after Francesco left and pulled me to her. She knew too well the pain in my heart.

"Giulia has made lemon tarts," she said. "I hope that along with my story today, they might be just the balm you need."

DESTINY

One day, a courier dressed in fine livery displaying the seal of the King of Spain arrived on a white horse at my cousins' house in Milan and delivered a letter to me. I, Sofonisba Anguissola, had received an invitation written in the hand of Philip II. The king began by reminding me of our meeting in Cremona many years prior. He went on to say that the Duke of Alba had spoken highly of my skills as a painter. He then asked me to come to the Spanish court and serve as a lady-in-waiting to his soon-to-be wife, Elisabeth de Valois.

From what I had heard about her, Elisabeth was a girl of fourteen, the daughter of Catherine de' Medici and Henry II. Her union with Philip was a condition of a peace treaty between France and Spain. She was half my age, and I imagined she had a lot more riding on her shoulders than I did, becoming a queen so young.

I was honored to be asked, but I knew if I went to Spain to serve the court for some undetermined amount of time, I might never see my family again. It was no small decision. I sent a letter to Father and Mother, to request their thoughts on this matter. I also talked to Signor Campi. Of course, they all felt it was not only the right thing for my career as an artist, but it was also my duty. I knew I had to go.

The most compelling thing pulling me toward the Spanish court was the fact that a girl, like me, was being called to leave her home. I felt that she was going to need a friend, and because she wanted to learn to paint, I realized I was that friend. It seemed that some force beyond me—dare I name it God?—was calling me to go. More than anything, it was my concern for this girl that pulled on my heart and sealed my fate. I accepted the call to go to Spain, moving forward to meet my destiny.

Before I left Milan, my father wanted to commemorate my call to serve at the Spanish court, so he commissioned a portrait medal in my honor. It was designed and cast in bronze by none other than the great maker of medals, Leone Leoni. It shows me in profile, and around the edge is a Latin inscription stating: *Sofonisba Anguissola, Daughter of Amilcare.*

This medal was my father's way of telling me how much he loved me. I know people had often speculated that the only reason my father educated me and my sisters was so that he would not have to pay all our dowries. By educating us, they gossiped, he ensured that we would not be desirable marriage partners. No man would want an educated wife. I know my father was a good businessman, but I do not think he did all he did for me just to save money later.

As Sofi was talking, Giulia brought us the lemon tarts and left them on the table. Once Sofi finished speaking, I wiped the ink from my fingers and helped myself to a tart. It was delicious. Sofi went to a drawer in her desk and pulled out a small wooden box. She opened it and held it before me. Inside was the medal her father had commissioned in her honor. She was depicted in profile, as illustrious people so often are. She wore a jacket laced up the front with puckered sleeves that puffed at the shoulder, and she had an elaborate braid wound around her head. She looked serious. And timeless.

"How does one meet their destiny?" I asked.

"That is a good question. There are many false paths and sometimes roadblocks."

"Tomorrow," I said, wiping lemon curd off my fingers, "Francesco will leave."

"Yes, and it is hard, isn't it?"

Sofi pulled me to her and I cried in her arms.

This morning, Fabia was with me at Sofi's doorway when Francesco came, as promised, to pick us up in the carriage. Orazio had already gone to the dock to ready the ship. We settled into the carriage for the short trip to the wharf. As we neared the Barbarossa, we saw Giuseppe out front, sweeping.

Francesco asked the driver to stop, then jumped from the carriage and into the arms of the taverna owner.

"A hug for you, my young friend. Best of luck down south."

"You've been a kind host, Giuseppe, and I will miss our talks."

"Again, I'm sorry my clientele did not treat you well. I told Dario many times he needed to leave you alone, but he simply would not listen."

"Some people are just like that, Giuseppe. I always knew you were on my side."

"I hope you will come back and see me sometime. Bring more wine!"

"Thank you, Giuseppe. I will."

We arrived at the wharf and stepped from the carriage. The driver unloaded Francesco's *cassone* and a couple other bags and put them all onto a cart to load them onto the ship.

"There's Orazio," Sofi said. "It always makes me happy to see him on the *Sant'Agata*."

Orazio stood on deck amidst a flurry of deckhands. Some ran with supplies and cargo while others tied ropes and lifted sandbags.

"I'm glad that Orazio is taking my beloved to Sicily," I said. "I know Francesco will be safe."

"He will be safe on his journey," Sofi said, putting her arm around me. "And also once he arrives at the port of Palermo. From there, he will make his way to Alcamo. Try not to worry, my darling. I know Sicily well, and he will thrive there. He will fulfill his promise to you, I am sure of it."

Francesco finished settling the fee with the driver, and after making sure everything was in good order to be loaded onto the ship, he turned toward Sofi and me. Together, we walked him to the edge of the dock. Before heading up the plank onto the ship, he gave Sofi a hug.

"Goodbye, my teacher."

"Goodbye, my student," she said. "Keep sketching."

Then, he turned to me. When I looked into his eyes, I saw at first a boy who was afraid to go. We kissed, and when I looked again, I saw a man determined. I put a scroll into the pocket of his shirt. "Promise me you will read this poem every night before you go to sleep."

"I will Paola, I promise. I love you."

"And I love you."

Francesco

We are far out to sea now, with no sight of land. After giving me a tour of the ship, Orazio invited me to dine with him in his quarters. The meal was simple fare—smoked sardines, bread, and olives—but it was nice to talk with him and begin the journey with a friend. I was worried I might not be able to eat with the motion of the ship, but he assured me it's best to eat a little the first day out to keep the stomach calm. And I do feel better.

After our meal, we went up on deck to take in the night air before retiring to bed. Looking at the immense dome of the sky speckled with so many stars, I remembered the dream I'd had on the night before the foot race. That was a different sky, one filled with terror. This new sky was awe-inspiring, a gift from God, and it took my breath away. I could hardly wait for the day when I would be able to call for Paola to join me, and she would see this same sky. I was sure she would write poems about it.

I'm settled now in my cabin below deck and am calmed by the ship's gentle rocking. I know I should sleep, but I can't stop thinking about what lies ahead and how hard it was to say goodbye to Paola today. I purposely saved unrolling her scroll until now. I wanted her words to be the last thing I ponder on this momentous day.

One Day

As seasons come and go without end
and birds, the spirits of the air, fly free,
I hope one day we'll meet again.

Steadfast vines grow tall then bend
to drop their fruit and give back seed,
as seasons come and go without end.

The gardener stoops upon the earth to tend
his tender, greening sprouts along the lee.
I hope one day we'll meet again.

Tides rise and fall and rivers wend
and only we lament in misery
as seasons come and go without end.

With this ebb and flow we must contend
and aim our hearts to reunite across the sea.
I hope one day we'll meet again.

And so, my love, we can't pretend
that change will not burden you and me.
As seasons come and go without end,
I hope one day we'll meet again.

How like Paola to remember what I once said to her about birds being spirits of the air. Her words fill my heart. Reading her poem, I know I will do everything within my power not to keep her waiting too long.

PART THREE

Sofonisba

I am ready to begin the complex tale of my time at the Spanish court. When Paola came today, I warned her there is a lot to tell, and I will keep her very busy. I am finding it best not to tax my eyes too much these days and save them for painting. Matteo Bruzzone has commissioned me to paint a portrait of his wife. I'm glad I brought those prepared canvases home with me from Cremona. I had a feeling I would need them.

Paola arrived today looking sad and tired, her usual inner light not shining. I imagine that Francesco's departure is weighing heavily on her heart. I hoped that sitting with me in the courtyard with the fountain sparkling in the morning sun would lift her spirits a bit, and I trusted that she would share her sorrows with me when she was ready.

"We are embarking on a new part of the story today," I told her, hoping this might be a cheerful thought. "There is a great deal to tell!"

"I am ready, dear friend," she said, as she opened the portfolio and set her ink bottle and quill nearby. "Can you take me somewhere far away today?"

"I most certainly can."

TO SPAIN

Early in 1560, I joined the Spanish court—not at its home in Madrid, but in Guadalajara, where the wedding of King Philip and his new queen would take place. My journey to Spain began in Milan, where I was working at the time with Signor Campi. Winter

147

was coming when I left, and the king had requested that I make haste so as to avoid bad weather and arrive prior to the queen. My father met me in Milan to see me off. That is when he gave me the commemorative medal that I so treasure. We held onto each other at the dock, and he told me he was proud of me. We both shed some tears. I wish I could have detoured to Cremona to also say goodbye to my mother, sisters, and brother, but there was no time.

My first stop was Genoa, where there was much for me to see. What I noticed immediately upon arrival was how different the geography was from the mostly flat farmland around my home in Cremona. Genoa is built around the port, so there is a vast expanse of water to contemplate. Then, the hills rise up quickly. Everything seems to be piled on top of itself, with the feeling that one should be ready to leap at any moment. It is a city that inspires action.

I had to wait a few days for our ship to set sail, so I had time to visit the many lace shops. I was well aware that Genoa is known for its beautiful lace, along with banking, shipping, and Christopher Columbus. I bought quite a bit of lace, thinking I might need to refer to its patterns for cuffs and collars in the portraits I would paint at court.

As I passed through Genoa on that trip to Spain, I had the distinct feeling that I would come back someday. I had such premonitions often, glimpses of the future. At that point in my life, I had not yet realized that these persistent thoughts meant something. Little did I know then that one day I would move to Genoa permanently and live a rich, full life.

At the port of Genoa, we boarded a ship and made our way across the Ligurian Sea to Barcelona. I spent the voyage mainly below deck, where my food was brought to me, because it was not safe for a woman to wander around above deck. Besides, the motion of the ship made me feel uneasy unless I was lying down. So I stayed under my blankets. Once we reached Barcelona, we still had a long journey by coach through the mountains. After three more weeks of travel, we finally arrived at Guadalajara.

While I made this arduous journey from Genoa, the new Queen of Spain was making a similar journey from Paris. While I was traveling the vast sea, she was making her way across the snowdrifts of the Pyrenees to unite with her soon-to-be husband. While I made sketches of sea birds and deckhands, she practiced Spanish. Her mother advised her that such study would serve her well if, when she met him, she could speak to her new husband in his native tongue. Along the way, Philip sent his couriers to check on her progress, to ensure that she was being well-cared for, and to see that court protocols were being followed according to his wishes. It was on this journey that her name changed from Elisabeth to her Spanish name, Isabel. She told me all this later, once we became friends.

Luckily, I arrived at the palace at the end of January, just a few days before she did—as the king had requested. The castle was more of a fortress than a palace, a foreboding structure of brown stone with crenelated walls and towers rising up out of the landscape, echoing the distant mountains. It looked like a place made to keep people out, and I wondered how the young queen would feel when she saw it.

My entourage stopped at the entrance to the imposing structure, and the feeling of being unwelcome immediately faded when the Duke of Alba appeared. He greeted me with open arms and a wide smile.

"Sofonisba! I am so glad you are here," he said, wrapping his arms around me.

"So am I, my friend." It felt good to be held after such a long trip. I just wanted to rest in his embrace.

"You must be very tired." He gently pushed me back and looked into my eyes. "I have arranged that tonight you will be treated like the royalty you are. You will have a hearty meal and a soft bed."

"That sounds more than wonderful, Your Excellency. Thank you."

I must have appeared to him as weary as I felt, for he conveyed to me that for the first few days, I would have no duties to attend to.

"The wedding celebration has everyone preoccupied, as you can imagine," he said. "You will have some time to settle yourself."

The duke delivered me to a housemaid who in turn took me to my room. I ate, slept, and dreamed of marriages. I didn't know when or if I would ever have one of my own, but when I did, I hoped it would be with someone as strong and steadfast as the Duke of Alba. I remembered all the engaging conversations we'd had when I painted his portrait multiple times in Milan. I was embarrassed to admit it, but I realized how often I had wished we could have been more to each other than mere friends, which of course we could not be. He was such a busy man, but also, he was married. Not that marriage stopped most men from doing whatever they pleased. But the Duke of Alba was a man of virtue and he was dedicated to his wife, even when he was far from her, one more reason I was drawn to him.

The fact that I even considered him in this light was surely another blight on my soul and put me on the side of the damned in any Last Judgement. I resigned myself to my thoughts and knew they would not come to pass. Still, I held them. I awoke the next morning with sunlight pouring into my room. I had the feeling that life would be good at the Spanish court.

Paola

As I transcribe Sofi's story, I can't let go of the notion of my own destiny. For the time being, I live two lives—one helping my father balance the account books and the other helping Sofi with her story. I think Father is satisfied that I am capable of doing multiple tasks. Like a juggler who can keep more than one ball in the air through the swift and steady movement of his hands, I am proving myself to be adept at all my work.

I continue to study the sonnets of Vittoria Colonna, reading over and over the book that Francesco loaned me. Her verses bring me some amount of comfort whenever I think of him, which is always. Colonna began her poet's journey by writing love letters to her husband, Fernando Francesco d'Avalos, who was far from her when he was wounded in battle. She set out to go to him in his time of suffering but received word that he died before she got very far. She returned home and remained devastated by this loss. For the next several years, she wrote poems to alleviate her grief and even considered suicide. As she wrote her verses, she realized it was better to keep living than give in to the desire to die. She contemplated entering a convent to live out her days in seclusion. But Pope Clement VII had other plans for her.

He recognized that Colonna had important, influential familial and political ties; he needed her out in the world. He would not give her permission to cloister herself. She did find refuge in a convent for a while, but he forbade her from taking the vows that would take her from him as a useful pawn.

How frustrating that must have been for her. How is it that a man can determine what a woman will or won't do with her life? But he was the pope, so she had no choice but to obey his wishes. Eventually, she left the convent and made her way to Rome where she became a friend to Michelangelo. He wrote some of his finest sonnets in her honor and spent a good deal of time in the company of Vittoria Colonna, his Muse.

Colonna's work inspires me in my own time of sadness and uncertainty to focus on my own poetry. As she had to face the reality of her own life— her own destiny—I must also. My Francesco is not dead, only starting a new venture. He says he loves me and I must trust him. Poetry will help me in my resolve. I have a plan to write a set of poems, a heroic crown, and I have just completed the first sonnet. There will be much to do, but thanks to Sofi's example and all that she has accomplished, I know I will achieve my goal.

I

If ever from myself I wander far
I'll turn my gaze upon the waiting soil,
this ground where I began my worldly toil.
I'll search to find a flame, a buried star
and nothing I encounter there will mar
my movement toward that light. I'll spin my coil
'round blood and bone. No raging fear can spoil
the promise that God made us who we are.
This knowledge carries no small price, my friend,
for persistence pays, the reward is great.
This spark possessed will raise me from the fall
and light my sacred worth and origin.
And so, I forge myself in Heaven's shape
and reconfigure every earthly wall.

Sofonisba

My eyes are troubling me today, but I could see well enough to recognize the look of creative spark in Paola's eyes when she arrived today to transcribe for me.

"Something exciting is happening," I said. "What is it?"

Paola seemed hesitant at first to speak. "Well," she said, "I have set myself a daunting task."

"Tell me!"

"Have you ever heard of a heroic crown?"

"I have a vague understanding, but please, remind me how it works."

"A heroic crown is fourteen sonnets, linked by having the last line of each sonnet become the first line of the poem that follows. Then, in the fourteenth sonnet, the last line is the first line of the very first poem in the cycle."

"And that makes the crown!"

"Indeed. Last of all, there is one final poem, the fifteenth, made up of all the first lines of the other fourteen poems."

"Daunting, indeed," I said. "How will you be certain that the fifteenth sonnet will make sense and that the rhyme scheme will work properly?"

"Well, I'm not sure what other poets have done, but I've created a rough plan of that final sonnet first to guide me in writing the other fourteen."

"An excellent idea," I said to my ambitious friend. "It is always advisable to plan ahead!"

"I agree," she said. "But for now, let's write your story."

The marriage of Philip and Isabel was a condition of a treaty between Spain and France, and the young queen was already being heralded as "Isabel of the Peace." The House of Mendoza spared no expense for the ceremony, and in fact arranged to have a grove of flowering trees brought to the palace from a great distance and set up on the lawn in large clay pots in the dead of winter, just for her. The Duke of Alba was in attendance, of course, along with numerous other members of the Spanish court.

Isabel wore the most splendid dress I had ever seen, off-white satin encrusted with seed pearls, tiny rubies, and lace across the bodice, with a train of French lace that flowed behind her. She was petite but held herself with great confidence, impressive for one so young. Philip wore a white silk suit with gold embroidery, a change from his usual dour black. They made a shimmering spectacle.

In the midst of all that light, there was one rather dark spot, and that was the king's own son, Don Carlos, age fourteen at that time. He was born to Philip's first wife, Maria of Portugal. I was struck by what a sour-looking lad he was. His mother had died three days after his birth in 1545, and immediately Philip asked his sister, Juana, to care for the sickly child, who had been born with a curved spine. I thought it was odd that the king had abandoned his first son because Don Carlos was technically heir to the throne. I could only guess it was because Don Carlos was born deformed, and thus viewed by his father as damaged. But ignoring the child only damaged him more. Over time, I would come to know Don Carlos, and I found that beneath his dark armor, there was a spirit deeply hurting.

No one from Elisabeth's family was able to attend the wedding, and I wondered if that weighed on her heart. Her mother had ensured, however, a hint of her presence at the festivities by commissioning a special violin by Andrea Amati, the master violin maker from Cremona. There was quite a stir among the guests knowing that the instrument was among us, and I was especially proud to be connected to this feeling of awe and excitement in some small way, having been born in the same town from which it came. The violin not only looked stunning, but in the hands of the player who bowed the strings, its sound brushed all the hearts in attendance like a reed swaying gently along a riverbank.

It was surprising to me that after the ceremony, when the feasting and merriment began—and Amati's violin held center stage—no one stepped up to dance. The king himself asked for a certain dance, a galliard. The music began, but no one moved and the king looked visibly disappointed. A nobleman from Mantua approached me and asked me to be his partner. I accepted his offer and once we began to dance, other couples joined us. I saw Philip's face brighten with a smile. It made me happy to know that Cremona was making a strong showing in the eyes of the king. Not only the joyful sound of Amati's violin, but my very presence and my willingness to participate was pleasing to him. Already, I was gaining favor—so I hoped—in the eyes of the king.

BEING QUEEN

After the wedding, we—one very large retinue of nobles, ladies-in-waiting, cooks, seamstresses, stable boys, and more—made our way toward Madrid, stopping first in Toledo. Along the route, the young queen became ill and there was great concern all around for her welfare. Personally, I wondered if her illness was a sign of fear and worry more than some physical ailment.

Once we arrived in Madrid, another week went by before news spread throughout the court that Isabel's health was much improved. And so the day came that I had my first audience with the new queen. I was led to her chambers by one of the maids and found Isabel sitting on a throne. She was dressed in a blue velvet gown with pleated tucks down the arms, which added to its rich texture. She looked so small and alone. When our eyes met, I smiled. My heart melted for her. I decided at that moment to be a sister to her and do whatever I could to bring her joy.

"Greetings, my Queen," I offered in French as I curtseyed before her. I knew a little of her birth language, and I thought it might make her feel more at ease to hear her mother tongue.

She looked surprised and replied also in French. "Greetings, Mademoiselle Anguissola. It is a pleasure to meet you." She did not look very happy, though. In fact, she looked like she might cry at any moment. She pointed to a chair.

"Won't you sit down?" she said. "Should I ask for something warm for us to drink? It is so cold in this palace, don't you think?"

"Thank you." I took the chair she offered. "Whatever pleases Your Majesty. And I agree, it is very cold in the palace."

"I am surprised by the cold," she said, "I thought it would be warm in Spain."

"Yes, me too."

We sat in silence again. Then she said, "I am going to ask for some warm mead. I hope you will join me." She rang a bell and a maid came immediately.

"Your Highness," the maid said, curtseying deeply. "How can I serve you?"

The queen responded in Spanish. "Marta, please bring a jug of warm mead and two cups."

Marta nodded and departed the chamber, and as soon as she was gone, the Queen of Spain crumbled into uncontrollable sobbing.

I sprang from my chair, my first instinct being to take her in my arms and comfort her.

She cried into her hands. "May I call you Sofonisba?"

"My Queen. Call me Sofi."

"Oh please, please, don't call me that. Can you please just call me Elisabeth?"

"Of course, Elisabeth," I said, holding her as her body shook. "What troubles you so?"

She looked up at me and, through her tears, said, "I don't know how to be the Queen."

I could imagine the grief she must have felt, leaving behind all that she knew to take on this unfamiliar role in this unfamiliar place. I was in a similar position, perhaps, but I was thirteen years older and had seen a bit of the world, although clearly, I was not a queen. However, I had the ability to paint, and I felt this connected me to something much higher than myself. It gave me a kind of power, even if I could not wield it to alter the course of history. I could at least use my abilities to calm my heart and create something beautiful out of nothing.

When I saw Isabel cry, and knowing how sad and uncertain she felt, I was determined to help her realize that she, too, was a creator. I wanted her to know that as confined as she may have felt by her station in life, which was nothing less than the Queen of Spain, she, too, had something to offer. She could learn to draw and paint.

Soon after that day, our lessons began. It was too cold in February to sit in the garden, so we started indoors, sketching our hands and objects like candlesticks and vases. By mid-March, the world began to warm up just enough to venture outside. Isabel must have felt freer when we were beyond the castle walls because she began to ask me many questions. She wanted to know, for example, all about what it had been like to meet Michelangelo.

"He did not try to have his way with you?" she asked one day.

"Heavens, no," I said, a bit amused. "He was kind and well-mannered."

"I am surprised," she said.

"I do think men have that ability," I said. "Consider the Duke of Alba."

"You are right. He is kind enough," she said.

"And what about your husband, the king? He is also kind, is he not?"

"Yes, mostly kind."

I did not dare pursue this matter of kindness in men. While I knew many kind men, Rinaldo had been unkind, using deception to have me for a time. I was not a good person to advise her.

"He is not here that often," she said. "And when he is here, he is nice to me. But I have overheard the ladies-in-waiting say that he has a mistress at court. I am only here to give him an heir."

I had heard this same rumor, about the mistress, but I was too new at court myself and did not know for certain that this was true, so I said nothing to confirm her suspicion.

"I think he likes me," she continued. "I wrote to my mother and told her how lucky I am to have married such a charming man. But, we are in different worlds. I am a child to him. A wife, but a child. I know he is thinking of other things whenever he is with me. There is nothing for me to do but satisfy his needs and carry on."

She said this with such resignation that I was torn inside. I had no way to help her, other than doing what I could to strengthen her ability to draw lines on a page. That was all I could give her to help her feel she had control over some part of her life.

My situation at the Spanish court was quite unusual. No one had ever existed in my position before, and I did not fit into any of the usual categories. Sometimes, I was referred to on various lists as a lady-in-waiting to the queen. My specific role was to teach the queen to paint and also to paint portraits of court members and visiting dignitaries. However, I could not be called the "court painter." First of all, I was a woman, and a woman could not be a court painter. Second, there was already a court painter, and his name was Alonso Sánchez Coello.

From the moment I met Coello, I knew he was not interested in me or in having our efforts align in any way. Soon after my arrival, the Duke of Alba brought me to Coello's studio and introduced me to him. The fact that Coello actually had a studio said a great deal about my place at the court. I had no studio. I was expected to paint in the same chamber in which I slept.

When I met the court painter, he was occupied with grinding pigments, and he barely looked up from what he was doing. He had a girl with him who looked to be about ten years old, busy with her own mortar and pestle. I had been told by the duke that Coello's wife had died in childbirth and this child, also an Isabel, was the artist's daughter. Unlike her father, she was welcoming and cheerful.

She held out her hand to me and said, "What a pleasure to meet you, señorita!"

"The pleasure is mine, señorita!"

Isabel Coello was the exact opposite of her father in terms of manners, and she and I grew to be good friends during my years at the court.

Coello viewed me more as an oddity than a colleague. However, given the amount of work there was to do, he often required my assistance—though ever so begrudgingly. There were so many portraits of members of the court that needed to be painted, as well as portraits of frequent visitors—noblemen and ambassadors passing through—that he could not keep up with the demand by himself. But he never bothered to talk to me about these projects. Instead, he would have one of the maids bring an unfinished canvas to my chamber with an unsigned note: "Finish." He ignored my contributions, but he could not get along without me.

His daughter was another story entirely. Like many artists' daughters, she helped her father grind pigments and prepare canvases. I had no assistant and had to do all these things by myself, but sometimes, Isabel Coello was able to turn her attention from her father and offer her help to me. I, in turn, imparted to her some of what I had learned from Signor Campi, Signor Gatti, and of course, Michelangelo. Bright and inquisitive, Isabel had a good eye and I wanted to help her develop her talents. I do think I was able to impart some useful information to her. If nothing else, perhaps I was an example of how women are capable of far more than they are given credit for in this world. I was certain her father would not have thought to tell her so.

One day, Isabel asked me how I had become an artist. "Did your father also make you do all the tedious tasks?" she asked.

"Oh no," I said. "No, I am lucky to have a father who was not an artist. My father simply believed in me and wanted to see me succeed.

"How unusual!" she said. "Tell me, what must I do to become an artist?"

"Well, to be an artist, you must work every day. You must never listen to anyone who says you cannot do this work. And, you must always take the time to know your subject."

"What do you mean Sofonisba? How would I do that?"

"I have found the best way to really get to know my subject—whether that subject is a person, a dog, or a tree—is by sketching. In fact, sketching for me has always been a way of seeing better."

I told Isabel the story of the time I drew my sister's face in the earth behind our home. She liked that story and said it made her wish she had a sister. I assured her we could be honorary sisters.

"I know my father loves me," she said, "but he does not see me as an artist."

"Let's prove him wrong," I said. "We'll do it gradually. One day, you will be painting wonderful portraits of the nobles here. Mark my words!"

One day when Isabel arrived to help me prepare some pigments, her face was flushed red. I asked her if something was wrong, and she explained that she'd gotten into an argument with her father.

"We were preparing canvases when he began to say disparaging things about you. He said you were a mistake of nature."

"My goodness. But that is no surprise coming from him."

"He said you could not paint a good likeness of anyone," she said. "I told him he was just envious of your ability to breathe life into your figures. I told him you were without a doubt the better, more genuinely talented artist." Tears formed in her eyes as she spoke. "That is when he hit me."

"Dear girl, I am so sorry." I wrapped my arms around her and let her cry.

"He said that I must never utter such lies again."

"I will speak to your father. He mustn't treat you so."

"Please do not approach him. I don't want him to know I told you."

I honored her wish, but I found myself doing things to make his life a little more difficult. I would hide a tool or neglect to remind him of something that needed completion. I was usually a forgiving person, but it was hard to forgive Coello. The male artists I had known—Campi, Gatti, and Michelangelo—had all let go of the notion that only men have value. Michelangelo once pointed out to me that all the Muses are female. Apparently, no art can happen without the presence of the feminine. And while Dante looked to the reasoning skills of the poet Virgil as his guide through Hell and Purgatory, he knew he could not get to Paradise through reason alone. Dante's one aspiration was to achieve the approval of Beatrice. Only Beatrice could lead him to Paradise. Only she had the key to Divine Love. *She.*

Paola

Over the last few weeks, at Sofi's request, I reviewed some earlier passages in the manuscript—events she wrote herself—and was struck by the story of Rinaldo and his betrayal. I did not hear her speak this story, but reading the words made her hurt feelings palpable to me. I hope betrayal is not what I should expect from Francesco. Before he left, he promised he would eventually call for me, but how can I know for certain that he will keep this promise?

Now more than ever, it is necessary that Francesco keep his promise, and not only because of me. No, just like Sofi long ago, I have missed my monthly flow. I have missed it twice now. A child is coming, and I can no longer hope there is some mistake. I was caught up by Francesco's gaze upon me that day he sketched my face in the shade of San Siro, and now I am on a path from which I cannot turn back.

In her telling of the story of Mercury and Lara, Sofi observed that "when people fall in love, children are often the result." I am living proof of this. I have not told anyone yet. After I transcribe today, I will confess my sin to Sofi. There is no one else I can tell right now. I only hope she can guide me. I need to know what to do.

QUESTIONS OF POWER

My time at court was divided into three main pursuits. First and foremost, I was there for the queen, to teach her how to draw and paint. Second, I was there to produce portraits of the many nobles who came to visit the court. Finally, I had a fair amount of idle time to sit with the ladies-in-waiting and talk. On countless afternoons, we sat together in a circle in the queen's antechamber, a spacious room with walls covered in rich tapestries. We conversed about reports we'd heard of battles, alliances, or grievances—whether worldly or personal. Now and then, something occurred that caused a great deal of disruption, like the day in 1562 when a painting arrived at the Spanish court all the way from Venice.

The Rape of Europa by Titian, the Venetian master, was the final canvas in a series that the king had commissioned from the artist many years earlier. Titian had proposed to make a series of six mythological subjects, which he referred to as *poesies*—painted poems—all inspired by tales from Ovid's *Metamorphoses*.

The painting depicted the princess Europa—shown floundering with her clothing in disarray—clinging in terror to the back of a white bull as he carried her across the open sea. There were flowers wrapped around the bull's horns, a garland put there by Europa herself just moments before she was taken. As the story goes, Jupiter—king of the gods—desired the princess, so disguising himself as a gentle bull, he lured her away from her companions and then carried her off to Crete. There she had three children by him, one of them Minos, who became the King of Crete. Titian's painting showed Europa, precarious and vulnerable, holding tight to the bull's horns as her friends gestured wildly and ineffectually from the distant shore.

If I looked past the distressing immediacy of the abduction, the first thing I noticed was that the image was beautifully painted. Titian was—and still is—well known for his luscious brushwork and rich, vibrant color. These qualities are typical of Venetian art, with Titian recognized as the greatest master of all. The beauty of painterly execution made the image all the more disturbing. How could it be right, I wanted to ask, to make terror look so lovely?

The first time the ladies-in-waiting gathered after the painting had been unveiled, not a word was spoken about it. The talk was of inconsequential matters—the weather, new dresses, and who had said what to whom. But I could not let the moment pass. I raised the issue by asking my question.

"How could it be right to make terror look so lovely?"

All the women fell silent and looked at me in disbelief. Then, the king's sister spoke.

"You are brave to raise this question," Juana said. "I am not sure it can be answered in any other way than to say that this is just the way things are. Women can be taken by gods or by men and no one will make a fuss about it. There is no way around it. Titian's painting proves the point."

Her words opened a torrent of commentary as all the women at last had something to say. In the cacophony, words blended together and it was difficult to hear any one woman's voice.

"Silence!" Juana commanded. There was a fire in her eyes. Every woman in the room stopped talking and turned their attention to her.

"We cannot change the rules of men," she said. "We can, however, stand up and be strong." Juana paused for a moment, as if she were looking for some faraway thought to help us all understand her meaning. "Perhaps we can make peace with Titian's painting by considering Veronica Franco. Do you know her?"

No one said anything, so Juana told us her story.

"Veronica Franco is another Venetian, like Titian. She is a poet and courtesan and has challenged the notion that women can only be one of three things: married, widowed, or a prostitute. She belongs to the category of women known as the *cortigiana onesta*, the 'intellectual courtesan,' distinguished from the *cortigiana di lume*, the common harlot. Veronica and other women like her are well-educated and can lay claim to considerable literary and artistic accomplishments. But, they cannot claim to have the purity of virgins, a trait so prized by our culture."

"But what does this have to do with making an abduction seem to be a thing of beauty?" the queen asked.

"Another brave question," Juana said, "and perhaps the answer is nothing."

There was an undercurrent of whispering among the ladies.

Juana spoke again, loud and strong. "What I am saying is that we must not be afraid to speak. Veronica Franco saw the ways in which women and men are each powerful in their own way. We must find what power we do have and use it to help others."

Juana's words stuck with me. Sometime later, I discovered that

Veronica Franco had written on the topic of women's power. She published a broadside that made its way into intellectual circles throughout Italy and all the way to the Spanish court. When I found one of these broadsides being thrown away, I kept it. She posited that women need only realize their power in order to wield it. She set her intention to be an example for other women to follow. I read her words often and always treasured her strength of character.

I wished I could have invited Veronica Franco into the room that day to speak about Titian's painting with us. The way I saw it, she was a woman who had chosen her own destiny and was not hiding behind her father, her teachers, or the Church. No one in the world was protecting her but herself. She asked nothing from men but to be treated as their equal.

We live in a world in which a highly acclaimed artist like Titian is lauded for showing that the king of the gods can have any woman he wants in whatever way he wants. For women to suggest that we are equal to men has always been a lot to ask. Still, we must ask.

Sofi stopped her story and I stretched my writing hand.

"I have heard of *The Rape of Europa*, but I have never before heard of Veronica Franco. Is she still alive?"

"No," Sofi said. "She died in poverty in Venice in the early 1590s. But, I have heard that she wrote two books of poetry and started a home for abandoned women and their children."

"Another woman doing good work in the world. I wonder if I could find her poems."

"That would be most interesting, wouldn't it?" Sofi asked.

I nodded. It occurred to me that Veronica Franco was a woman of great courage, while I was frozen in fear to say what I needed to say. I took a deep breath. "Sofi, I am with child." As I expected, she looked at me with great surprise. "Are you ashamed of me, then?" I said.

"Dear Paola, no! How could I be ashamed of you? Myself having been in a similar position long ago, I know the anguish you feel. Have you told Francesco? Your father?"

"You are the first person I have told."

"How do you feel?" she asked.

"I wake up each morning feeling queasy and as though I hardly slept.

164

I'm worried."

"Oh, dear one, what are you most worried about?"

"Born outside of marriage, what stigma will this child carry? What scorn will I receive?"

Sofi wrapped me in her arms, and I rested my head on her shoulder.

"If I were you, I would not be so certain this child will be born outside of marriage. You must write to Francesco immediately. I am certain he will ask your father for your hand."

"That is my other worry. That he will not wish to marry me."

"Forgive me for contradicting you, my dear, but I think you are wrong about that. Francesco will want to marry you. We must celebrate this new life that is coming." She called Giulia to bring wine.

Feeling a bit queasy, I only took a small sip. Sofi and I sat together in the inner courtyard of her house with the afternoon sun warming us. We did not talk anymore. I thought about myself and the child that is coming. I realized I had not been abducted by anything other than my own desires. And as Veronica Franco suggested, I do have power. I must not be afraid of it.

II

I reconfigure every earthly wall,
lay flat the weathered rocks, a bridge to make.
And there upon new ground, I will awake
to carry in my heart the dream of all.
No stolen kiss, no rift, no harried fall
can throw me from this course. Make no mistake
into the fray I go, my life at stake
and if fate makes me bend, then I must crawl.
"Fear not," the angel said, and it is true.
The day will come when I, unbound, must leap
to cross a sea, or sky, or hallowed hall.
Never once forgetting that love accrues
and reflects how wide, how tall, how deep
life's treasured gifts, these riches large and small.

Sofonisba

While Paola has many worries, news of the child lifts my heart. I sent a messenger to her this morning telling her to please stay home for a few days. I want her to rest and take care of herself. She will need some time to compose a letter to Francesco and also speak to her father. Neither will be easy.

Today was the first day with my new sitter, Roberta Bruzzone. It was a pleasure to meet with her. She was a ray of sunshine and the exact opposite of my first impression of her husband. We sat in the courtyard and talked as I noted her oval face, high cheekbones, and long, thin nose. Her light brown hair was full of lovely curls pulled tight in a bun on top of her head, with a few that escaped to frame her face in the most pleasing manner.

"Forgive me if I repeat myself," she said. "But ever since you painted my husband's portrait, he is a changed man. It is as though seeing himself through your eyes, he sees himself in a new way."

"I am pleased to hear that, Signora Bruzzone. As for your portrait, do you have any requests about how you would like to be shown?"

"Honestly," she said, "I have not thought about it. What do you think?"

"Well, I thought to depict you here in the courtyard, if that is agreeable to you. Seeing that it is spring, and with so much new green out here, that will be a good background for your wonderful green eyes."

"Signora Anguissola, given your great success in painting a portrait of my husband, I trust you completely in these matters."

After she left, I felt so full of life that I spent some time with my story. A dark chapter, to be sure. But having had such a pleasant time with Signora Bruzzone, even this dark chapter could not pull me down.

During those first years at the court, I made a friend in the kitchen, one of the cooks who had come with Isabel from France. Her name was Marie. She would save treats for me and always had a kind word. She understood that I was feeling out of place and that I missed my family. I think perhaps she felt the same way. She invited me to come to the kitchen any time it pleased me. When the bustle of royal life excluded me, I often sought her out. And even if she was busy herself, she would make us both a cup of warm milk with honey.

Marie had developed a bond with a kind man she had met at court named Juan Pablo, who served the king in a variety of capacities—stable hand, sheep shearer, ironsmith, stonemason, and porter. It was also Juan Pablo's unfortunate task to build the pyres where heretics were burned at the stake.

One night, over warm milk and conversation, Juan Pablo joined us. He told us about an event that had taken place not too long before the marriage of Philip and Isabel, before Marie or I had arrived at court. Juan Pablo had accompanied the king and several other noblemen and their servants to Valladolid in the north. On the day the royal contingency arrived, there was a large crowd gathered outside the city walls at the burning place.

Juan Pablo described how he and the other servants built the pyres by stacking dry straw and wood to prepare for the mass burning. That day, there was a murmur in the crowd that this particular execution was going to include people whom Philip knew personally. They had done something unfavorable in the eyes of those leading the Spanish Inquisition and so were sentenced to death. The rumor was that the king was looking forward to this event.

"At the appointed time," Juan Pablo said, "I saw the condemned being led onto the public square. When an old friend of the king passed on his way to the pyre, he turned to Philip, saying, 'How can you look on and allow me to be burned?' The king replied without a shred of remorse, 'If it were my own son, I would fetch the wood to burn him, if he were as wicked as you.'"

It troubled me to know the man responsible for paying my wages could be so cold-hearted, and afterward, I began to distrust him. It was a feeling I could not share with anyone—no one, except God in my prayers at night. I worried about the queen, too, but I had no means to help her or even inquire as to whether his brutal nature ever emerged when they were alone together. It was not my business to pry.

———————————————

Paola

As Fabia and I walked to Sofi's place today, the morning sun warmed our faces and flitting birds serenaded us from tree branches, green with new buds.

"You see?" Fabia said. "New life is all around us. You must not fret."

I have confided my situation to her, and she knows how worried I am. She is right, though. Everywhere I look, I see new life coming forward as spring approaches, and I realize my place in that fecundity.

Sofi was waiting in the courtyard when we arrived.

"How are you, my dear?" she said.

I could feel her concern. "I've been in my room the last several days, trying to write poetry, but few words came."

"Anything else?"

"I wrote to Francesco."

Sofi's eyes fixed on me. "Good," she said. "And how did you put it to him?"

"I told him a child is coming. I suggested that we ought to marry sooner than he planned. It will take some time for my letter to reach him, and more time after that for him to write back. Between now and then, I will worry about what he will say."

"I think you can rest assured that he will want to marry you. Why wouldn't he?"

"I want to think you are right, but I have no way of knowing. Perhaps he is not ready, or perhaps he will not appreciate being forced into marriage. And then, there is my father. I am going to have to tell him soon because before too long, he will see with his own eyes that I am with child."

"It is a lot to contend with. I am here for you if you need my help."

"You do help me. The only way I can get through all this worry is to sit with you and write down your story. It helps me to ponder the trials of someone else's life, not my own."

"I have had plenty of trials in my life. If they help you, then recounting them will serve us both."

BELONGING

One of my biggest problems while I was living at the Spanish court was feeling as though I did not really belong anywhere. I tried to be a good friend to Isabel, and because I could speak to her in French, and also because we both admired beautiful fabric, she came to trust me in a way that she did not trust many others.

Isabel especially enjoyed having a dress and hat made for the portrait I painted of her in 1563. The dress was black velvet with pearl-embroidered red silk sleeves that peeked out from the slits in the arms of the over-jacket. This dress was made for her before she got pregnant. She was vibrant and in good health at that time, and I wanted to show off her great beauty and strength of character. I think I was able to capture both those attributes. Of course, as I always did with my sitters, I painted her face while she was in the room with me, but I spent many long hours working on the details of her jewel-studded jacket, her lace collar, and the beadwork of her hat when she was not there.

I loved dear Isabel from the beginning, from the very first time I laid eyes on her frightened and uncertain face. Fortunately, she was full of inner fortitude, and once she and I began her art lessons, much of her sadness fell away.

"You know," she once said to me. "When I put lines on a page, I feel like I am opening a door into a new place, a world that I can walk into any time I like."

Isabel understood how the blank page was hers alone, one that she could fill with whatever she wanted, things that no one could take away from her or claim as theirs. It was an honor for me to share drawing with her, to make creation possible, to bring her some relief. In a world where she had to appear perfect at all times, being able to relax in the garden with a piece of chalk and a drawing board was a great and mighty gift.

There was another person who I felt was in need of my help at the Spanish court. That was Don Carlos. Although I had seen him at the wedding, it took a while for us to meet face-to-face. I will never forget the day that his aunt, Juana, brought him to my chamber. I was tidying my workspace—cleaning paintbrushes and reorganizing my pigment jars—when there was a knock on my door. Before I could answer, the door swung open and Juana came in like a cold wave, pushing a pale boy on her tide. He appeared to be drowning.

Without so much as a greeting or an inquiry into my state of health, she said, "The king would like a portrait of this boy. You will begin now." The look on Don Carlos's face broke my heart in two. Everything about him was dark. He reminded me of an abandoned stone house crumbling in a fallow field. He stood a bit hunched over due to his crooked spine, the deformity he had been born with.

I reached out my hand to him. "Greetings, young prince," I said. "Won't you sit down?" He neither took my hand nor spoke. He did not look at me.

His aunt pushed him toward me. "Answer this lady, stupid boy!" she nearly shouted, then she spun around and was gone, leaving Don Carlos like a dead branch in her wake.

He would not raise his eyes to meet mine and instead cowered in the spot where he stood. It looked like he wanted to crumple down to the floor and vanish. I sat down in front of him and waited. As soon as I was seated, he joined me on the cold stone floor. He sat with his head lowered and his legs crossed. He was such a poor, neglected soul.

"Tell me about yourself," I said in the gentlest voice I could muster.

He was so pale and pinched. He looked like he had been kept in a dark room for far too long. He needed sunshine on the back of his neck and to be surrounded by green leaves and the fragrance of flowers. Even as far grown as he was, he needed to run outside and fall down in soft grass. He needed to study clouds.

I tapped him on the knee. "Will you come with me to the garden?"

He looked up, and although he did not actually smile, I could see a glimmer of interest in his eye. I stood up and reached out my hand, which he did not take. Instead, he walked to the door of my chamber and I followed. And that is how my friendship with the son of the King of Spain began.

Our first real conversation began with birds. We were out on maybe our third or fourth walk together, just silently moving through the flowers and herbs, when a flock of swifts swooped over us.

"I wish I could fly," he said.

I was about to ask "Why is that?" However, I decided it would be better to simply agree than to question him on his dreams. So I said, "That would be nice, wouldn't it?"

His eyes widened and he looked right at me with disbelief.

"Where would you go if you could fly?" I asked.

He looked down at the grass and remained silent.

"Is there some special place you would like to see from the sky?"

He looked at me as if to make sure that I really was expecting an answer to my question. My steady gaze must have calmed him.

"I would like to go to the New World," he said. "I would like to see what everyone is talking about, the Aztec temples. The parrots and jaguars. And all the gold! I would like to see where all the gold comes from."

"That is a long way to go," I said. "Are you sure you could fly that far?"

"If I had wings, I would fly as far away from here as I possibly could."

When he said that, I held out my hand to him, and for the first time, he took it. For the rest of that walk, we held each other's hand. "Will you let me paint you?" I asked. "You know, your father wants a portrait of you."

"My father? My father doesn't want to have anything to do with me. But I like being with you, Sofonisba. You are bright like Queen Isabel is bright. Did you know that I was supposed to marry her?"

I had heard this gossip whispered among the ladies-in-waiting. The story was that because Don Carlos and Isabel were the same age—born just a few months apart in 1545—their marriage would one day bring Spain and France together.

"What happened?"

172

"I don't know. That was the thought when we were young. But then something changed. Father decided he should marry her himself and make an heir to the Spanish throne. He wanted a better boy than the one he already had."

I did not know what to say to this, so I just kept listening.

"I like Isabel so much. She is like you. She is kind and does not treat me like there is something wrong with me. She talks to me and makes me laugh. We are good friends."

I felt like he was trying to tell me that despite the shroud under which he lived, he did have the ability to engage in common friendship. I was glad to know that he and Isabel had formed a bond.

Not long after that conversation, Don Carlos agreed to let me paint his portrait. He was a challenging but compelling subject. I showed him in a three-quarter view in a richly embroidered orange doublet and ermine-trimmed cape. I tried to give some hint of warmth to his face, as there was not much there. I hope that when people look at this portrait, they see not just a stony, cold-hearted young man but someone who was—more than anything—aching for love.

I did not want to upset Sofi, but her words about Don Carlos frightened me. A child unwanted by its father has not much chance of having a good life in this world. What if Francesco does not want to be a father? I hate to imagine that I might be raising this child on my own, but I must be prepared for the worst. I must get through this either with Francesco or without him. I have no choice but to carry on.

III

Life's treasured gifts, these riches large and small,
are not measured by merely what is seen.
Words alone cannot conjure what I mean.
The Spirit, I confess, reveals all.
We come from Heaven to heed the call
as sleeping winter trees in spring come green
and golden crowns make visible their sheen
until the end when every king must fall.
I'll find delight in the smallest of things,
gather flowers, feathers, grasses, and stones
for building sheltered nests both near and far.
I'll hear birdsong in what my own heart sings,
and life will grow within me and be known,
as joy springs forth and shines, a blazing star.

Francesco

My father's new vineyard is located in a place both desolate and beautiful. On the north side of our land the verdant hillsides of Alcamo roll gently to the Mediterranean Sea at the Port of Castellammare. The southern edge is dominated by Mount Bonifato, which looms up out of the earth like a sentinel that sleeps with one eye open, watching over me. There is a deserted castle up there, the Ventimiglia family castle, and an old water reserve called the Funtanazza. The road leading up to the castle is marked near the top of the mountain by a stone entryway that the locals call the Porta della Regina, the Queen's Door. I have gone up there on horseback a few times, and I've found that the mountain speaks of something from an earlier time. Next time I go there, I will take my sketchbook. If Sofi were here, she would pack a basket of food and another full of drawing supplies and say, "Let's make a day of it!"

Mount Bonifato is flanked by two river valleys. On the west is the Fiume Freddo and on the east, the Fiume Jato. Perhaps because so much water flows through this general area, the soil is rich and crumbly, a good blend of sand, silt, and clay. According to my father, who remains in Tuscany for now, this is exactly the type of soil grape vines find pleasing. I can understand why he felt it would be a worthwhile endeavor to cultivate a vineyard here, and I understand why he needs me to watch over it. My father's cousin has already done a good deal of the preparation. The trellises are built and the vines have been planted. My job is to tend to them and make sure they are happy as they make their way toward the sun.

My little house is just one main room with a large porch that offers a good view of the vineyard. I wake each morning just as the sun begins to light the world. In that still, quiet time I am affirmed in my decision to venture to this lonely, fertile place. And yet I left so much behind. At one time, I thought I was brave to leave the grape farmer's life to pursue studies in art. I was fortunate to find Signora Anguissola, who was willing to teach me. But soon, I could see that I would never be able to make a living as an artist. As satisfying as it was to pick up a piece of chalk and recreate the world before me on paper, art was never going to allow me to prosper, build a home, or provide for a family. I am grateful to Sofonisba for teaching me how to look at the world. But now, with my hands in the soil instead of holding chalk, I see the land itself as material of another kind.

As I journey through the rows of vines each day, my mind wanders. I catch myself staring at the clouds, missing Paola. I wonder if she misses me. I also wonder if she would like it here. She is accustomed to the activity of Genoa. I'm afraid Alcamo would feel isolated to her. Perhaps nearby Palermo would be more to her liking. When we marry, we could make our home in the city. It would not be that hard for me to come out here for several days each week to tend the vines. I've only been away from Paola for a short while, but already, it feels like an eternity. Despite all the uncertainties, I'm ready to ask Signor Vespucci for his daughter's hand in marriage. As I have been digging in the earth, I have been crafting a letter in my mind. I won't wait another day.

Paola

I have been thinking about something Francesco once told me about vineyards and how the earth waits quietly for the plants to come. I suppose I am something like the earth right now, waiting for new life. This thought was with me when I greeted Sofi today.

"Are you feeling well?" Sofi asked when I arrived. "You look tired."

I was embarrassed that she noticed. "I am well, but I must admit, growing a child is hard work."

"Never having experienced that myself, I can only imagine. Are you sure you feel up to working today?"

"Honestly, Sofi, I think most of my trouble comes from my insistent worry about how Francesco will respond to my letter. Transcribing takes my mind off my own concerns for a time and gives me something else to think about."

BIRTH

Four years into my time at court, news came in the spring of 1564 that Michelangelo had died in Rome. Even though I had only known him for a short time, his death brought me profound grief. While others around me were lamenting the passing of a great genius of our time, I was grieving the loss of a teacher and friend. He had taught me so much. As I lit a candle in his honor, I vowed to always "speak through the language of pigment on canvas that which is in my heart," as he had encouraged me to do.

I wanted to pass that same dedication on to my two sisters, Lucia and Minerva, both of whom continued to paint after I left Cremona. I had been corresponding with them regularly since arriving at court. Not only did we exchange letters, but each of them would send me drawings that I critiqued and sent back with my comments for ways to improve, similar to the way in which Michelangelo had first helped me.

Minerva especially seemed resolved to follow in my footsteps. Not having many models, she mostly drew her own face by looking in a mirror, much as I had done when I was young. I was happy to receive her self-portraits, and I used them to make a painting of her. I depicted her wearing a medallion with an image of the goddess Minerva on it. I was proud of that picture because I painted it without having her sit for me. Also, the portrait brought me comfort. When I looked at the painting, I felt as though Minerva was with me. I missed her, and all my sisters, a great deal.

Early in 1565, I received a letter from my father with the news that Lucia had died in childbirth. This was the dear sister who had accompanied me to Rome and been with me all through my time of learning with *Il Divino*. Not only was my teacher gone, but now, my dear companion, too. This was almost more than I could bear.

The queen was so kind in helping me manage all this grief, despite having just had a miscarriage of her own and losing twin girls.

"It is not so bad," she said as she recovered from her own trauma. "At least they were not boys. That would have angered the king."

Her view on having lost two babies who happened to be girls was disturbing to me, but I tried not to dwell on it. Who was I to say how she should view the loss of her own offspring? In my time of grieving, she consoled me the way any sister would. She released me from my teaching duties for a while, and I was grateful for her understanding as I took the time I needed to heal.

Gradually, I was able to make peace with the loss of Lucia. There was always something going on at court that could sweep me away from my troubles. In May of that same year, there was a trip planned to Bayonne, where Philip and Catherine de' Medici were supposed to meet and discuss the problems they—two Catholic leaders—faced from the rising tide of Protestantism. Philip did not wish to go, so he sent the Duke of Alba in his place. Isabel made the journey, of course, because it was a chance to see her mother and her fifteen-year-old brother, who had recently taken on the mantle as King Charles IX of France. Isabel asked me to accompany her. I was grateful to prepare for the trip as it provided a temporary distraction from my grief.

The overland journey to Bayonne was enjoyable, and once we arrived, there was a good deal of celebration that went on for several days. Of course, I was not privy to the negotiations, but I assume things went well because the general atmosphere at the French court was welcoming and pleasant. Every night, we were treated to some form of entertainment, music, dance, or theater.

On our last night, we were presented with a theatrical performance of Trissino's *Sophonisba*. The adaptation that was performed for us had some comedic overtones. I must admit it was hard for me to see the story of the woman who ended her own life as anything but tragic.

Still, the others seemed to find the play quite entertaining, and afterward, those who perceived the connection wanted to know how I came by my name. I felt honored by their attention and told them a little about my father's appreciation for Carthaginian history. I did not tell them, however, that Sophonisba's story had always been upsetting to me. I did not wish to ruin their enjoyment of the play.

The next morning, as I watched Isabel and her mother embrace, I had one of my premonitions. I sensed that this moment would be the last time they would see each other in this life. I cast out the thought, hoping I was wrong. But sad to say, my premonition did ultimately come true.

Soon after our visit to Bayonne, Isabel became pregnant again. This time the pregnancy went much better than her first one. But sadly, the birth was difficult. She developed a fever and, after the baby was delivered, the doctor bled Isabel—a barbaric practice, in my opinion, that nearly ended her life. Worse, though, was Isabel's feeling of utter despair. She had failed to give the king a son. For his part, the king did nothing to assuage her worry. Isabel gained strength in time, but it took much longer for her to look on her child's face with any semblance of love.

In contrast, the birth of Isabella Clara Eugenia in 1566 was like a burst of light in my life. She was a beautiful child and just looking into her sweet, innocent face brought solace to me as I continued to grapple with Lucia's death. I cannot be sure this is true, but perhaps my own adoration of the child was what enabled Isabel to finally realize her daughter deserved and needed her love. Once Isabel succumbed to the feelings she had tried to bury, the queen became a good and loving mother.

Little Isabella flourished with so much attention, and life in the queen's chambers was filled with joy. Isabel began to draw her daughter's face, her sleeping form, her tiny hands and fingers. The drawings were another way to keep the king's cold heart at bay.

Then, a year later, another letter from my father nearly sent me to the floor in my own despair. My sister Minerva had died in yet another struggle to give birth. To lose two sisters in such a short span of time was truly devastating. Thinking back on it now, I do understand how—with a certain convergence of circumstances—a person could be tempted to end their own life.

"Perhaps we'd best stop," Sofi said. "This tale might carry too much woe for either one of us to bear today."

"It is a bit frightening," I said, "to think childbirth can be such a deadly matter."

"It isn't always that way, of course," Sofi said. "My own mother bore seven children and was very much alive and well into old age but yes, it does happen, and I am sorry if I have upset you."

"I will be all right," I said, although I was not completely sure my words were true. On my walk home through the market and past San Siro church, I knew Sofi's story had sunk deep into me. The worries I had worked hard to conquer began swirling in my head anew.

Before today, my worst fear had been that Francesco would be too ashamed to marry me because I had become pregnant outside of marriage. But after hearing about Sofi's two sisters, and remembering my own mother's problems with keeping a pregnancy, I am afraid. My fear that either the child or I won't survive this birth has its cold grasp around my neck.

Whenever I feel agitated like this, I turn to poetry. The poem I wrote today for my heroic crown expresses a more hopeful view of life. In the days and weeks to come, I will strive to be more like the brave speaker of this poem.

IV

As joy springs forth and shines, a blazing star,
I anchor strong and safe beneath the lee.
I choose if I will go by land or sea
and seek a course that leads me on and far.
I'll unwrap blessings that already are,
despite the ones who say, *You are not free.*
To them I say, *Leave me still, let me be.*
I won't close tight the door once left ajar,
and look instead for those full on my side—
faithful friends in the vineyard of my heart—
who will stand straight beside me, always fair,
who gently flow like shells upon the tide,
sharing with me always the sacred part.
I disown shame, it drains and shows no care.

Sofonisba

This afternoon, I finished another productive sitting with Roberta Bruzzone. The ivy in the courtyard and the end-of-day light is a flattering backdrop for her skin tone and lovely green eyes.

"Am I easy or hard to capture?" she asked as she donned her gloves and prepared to leave.

No one has ever asked me this question, but I had no trouble answering. "You are a wonderful subject, Signora. Your attitude and demeanor make it a joy to paint your portrait."

"And what about my husband?"

I imagined she already knew the answer to this question so I told her the truth. "Your husband was distracted and unhappy. So no, he was not easy to capture in paint. Not at all."

"I'm sorry you had to contend with his dark moods."

"In the end, it all turned out well. That is what's important."

"That is true," she said, placing a lovely green velvet hat on her head. "I will see you next week, Signora."

"I look forward to it!"

Now that she has left, I want to spend the rest of the afternoon writing. These next few memories are ones I feel I need to write myself.

TROUBLES FAR AND NEAR

There were so many stories that came from my friend Marie. Being in charge of the kitchen and all the servants, she received information from many quarters. The things she told me during our late-night talks sat heavy on my heart and led me to harbor a creeping regret about being employed by the court, despite my love for dear Isabel. One night in the kitchen, Marie talked of the king's disdain for anyone who was not Catholic.

"King Philip is determined to preserve Spain as a country devoid of heresy," she said. "Protestants, Jews, Muslims, all should be destroyed in his view. He has forbidden Spanish students to study abroad because he does not want them to be exposed to different beliefs."

I remembered what Signor Barosi, the cheesemaker, had said to my father about Philip when he was just a prince and I was just a girl in Cremona. So while I was alarmed by these stories about Philip's efforts to suppress anyone who is not Catholic, they did not surprise me.

And it wasn't only in Marie's kitchen that I heard these things. There were similar conversations among the ladies-in-waiting, conversations often led by Juana. She made no attempt to hide the king's most drastic actions.

"My brother has followed in our father's footsteps with great determination to convert the Moors in southern Spain to Catholicism," she announced one day.

"Is it true," one of the ladies asked, "that the king is planning to make an edict that will order the Moriscos to abandon their customs, clothing, and language?"

"And if that should fail," another chimed in, "he plans to expel them to Tunis and Morocco?"

"From what I have heard my brother say behind closed doors, all that is true," Juana said. "And if he does what he says he will do, tens of thousands of people who have familial roots going back for centuries stand to be cast away. Furthermore, he has said that when he expels them, Spain will keep their children under the age of seven. In his mind, the children belong to the country, not the parents."

These revelations horrified me. How could I continue to work for someone who had so little compassion for others? But where would I go? What would I do? I could not simply leave my post at the Spanish court. More than that, I could not leave Isabel.

Meanwhile, Don Carlos was becoming increasingly volatile.

One day, he beat a servant for no apparent reason. Soon after that, he set fire to a house in the village because its owner had accidentally splashed the prince with water from a bucket. And yet it was something else entirely that finally drew the king's attention to his son. Philip had heard a rumor that Don Carlos was planning to go to the Netherlands to join forces with his father's Protestant enemies.

The king confronted his son on this matter and the two stormed through the halls of the palace, embroiled in a shouting match. They overturned chairs, broke dishes, and drove everyone—servants and nobles alike—into their rooms. In the course of this argument, Don Carlos tripped and fell down a flight of stairs, suffering a serious head injury. The king called a doctor who performed a trepanation on the prince's skull to release the pooling of blood. A long period of recuperation followed. And although the prince's health would have kept him from going anywhere, his father made sure Don Carlos's room was kept locked.

I asked permission to visit the prince, and the king allowed me to do so. Seeing Don Carlos—a prisoner in his own room—with his head bandaged was distressing enough, but even more disturbing was the way he went in and out of clarity of mind. One moment, he knew who I was, the next he did not recognize me. The lost boy whom I had befriended and who had come to trust me seemed no longer to exist.

DEATH

It took a while, but after several weeks, the veil that had covered Don Carlos's mind lifted. Not only did he recognize me when I visited him in his convalescence, but he was also appropriately concerned to hear that Isabel had endured another difficult and nearly fatal delivery in giving birth to a second daughter, Catalina Micaela.

"Can I meet this child?" he asked.

When Isabel felt well enough, we took the infant to visit Don Carlos. Some of the ladies-in-waiting tried to discourage us, saying that Don Carlos was a danger, but Isabel and I both knew differently. He was grateful for our visit and appreciated that Isabel trusted him to hold the new baby. After that first visit, we brought little Isabella, too, and the four of us sat together on the floor on many occasions, playing with a ball of yarn. We threw it, kicked it, and used the yarn to play string games. I think the visits were healing to Isabel and Don Carlos both.

These visits helped me too. Although I felt more and more like I wanted to detach myself from the king and his cruelty—not only toward non-Catholics but also toward his own son—I wanted to belong to a family. Isabel, Don Carlos, and the children gave me that gift.

As the two infantas grew, my service to the royal family changed. I was no longer only the queen's painting teacher. I gradually began to play a part in the upbringing of the queen's daughters. One day, I was taking care of the infantas and I brought them to Don Carlos's room for a game of yarn ball. I found Isabel already there. She and he were holding hands, looking out the window together. Not talking. Just sitting. As for Don Carlos, he had found in Isabel someone who cared about him. I know that meant a great deal to him. She could see right through his anger and violent, irrational outbursts. Isabel gave Don Carlos the gift of friendship and unconditional love, a rare thing among royalty, it seems.

One day, I asked Don Carlos if he had really planned to go to the Netherlands to thwart his father. He replied, "Since I have never been a son to him, what does it matter?"

The lucidity of his response led me to see that he was not as damaged by his fall as some had suggested.

One July day in 1568, nine months after little Catalina Micaela was born, news came to the queen's chambers that Don Carlos had died in his room. What was worse, as the day went on, we learned that there was no clear cause of death. Some suggested that the king himself had arranged to have Don Carlos poisoned. Such a damning idea was dismissed by many, but I knew how ruthless the king could be and I could not rule out the possibility.

The queen was crushed by the loss of Don Carlos and took to her bed. When I visited her, I found her room dark as a tomb. She had closed all the drapes, including her bed drapes. I approached her bedside and called her name.

"Let me be," she said in a voice so small, I could barely hear it.

I did not want to ignore her wish, but I also felt it was imperative to draw her out of the darkness.

"May I open the drape, dear one?"

She did not respond, so I pulled open the bed curtain and sat on the edge of her bed. At first she turned away from me, but I put my hand on her back and said nothing for a while. Then I started to talk. I told her about the first time that I had ever talked to Don Carlos, when he had expressed his wish that he could fly like a bird. I offered to her the idea that perhaps he was free now, his soul soaring. Perhaps he was able to find some peace.

The queen turned and looked at me with a face red from crying. "When I die, Sofi, please promise me that you will watch over the infantas. Please don't let any harm come to them. They will always love you like a mother, you know."

I saw then how heavily death weighed on her, so I promised her that *if* she were to die, I would watch over the princesses. Then, she asked me to open the *cassone* at the foot of her bed and take out the embroidered coverlet I would find there. The stitching was intricate and beautiful. It was a piece that would belong on a marriage bed. She said she wanted me to have it.

"Someday, Sofi," she said as she pulled herself up, "you will marry. You must."

"Highly unlikely," I said, adjusting the pillows under her head. Then, as if an idea had just sprung in her heart, she smiled broadly and took my hands in hers.

"I am going to tell the king that he needs to find you a husband," she said.

What a laughable idea, I thought. But I did not want to laugh at my friend. "You should spend no more time worrying about me, Your Majesty, and just take care of yourself."

Isabel smiled at me. While I was not convinced that her idea was a good one, at least it had given her a reason to smile.

Unfortunately, from that time on, Isabel's suffering only increased. She had migraines, fevers, and nephritis, which made even the briefest of walks painful. And unconscionably, she was pregnant again. It seemed the king would not let up until she gave him a son or died in the attempt.

On the third of October, the ladies-in-waiting learned that Isabel had been found in her bed early that morning in a pool of blood. I remembered my own pool of blood long ago, and I did not stop to ask anyone's permission to go to Isabel. When I entered the queen's bedchamber, the court doctor was there, as were several French ladies-in-waiting, and also the royal priest. The king knelt at her bedside, holding his wife's hand and sobbing. When he saw me, he motioned for me to come near. There was so much pain in his eyes. I could see that he truly did love her.

I put my hand on Isabel's forehead and felt her skin on fire. I said her name, and her eyes fluttered open. For the briefest of moments, she looked into my eyes and smiled. I wanted to pick her up and carry her away from death, but there was nothing I could do. I smoothed her damp hair and kissed the top of her head. Philip asked the priest to come forward. I stepped away from the bed, and the king nodded at me in gratitude. As the priest gave Isabel her last rites, I left them and went to my own room to cry.

By noon that day, Isabel of the Peace was dead. She was twenty-three. I was devastated, but I knew I needed to appear strong and comforting to little Isabella, who was just old enough to know what it meant that her mother was gone.

With Isabel's death, the whole court was thrown into disarray. The queen's household would be dispersed and all the French ladies-in-waiting sent home to Paris. My own situation was uncertain. No one had said anything to me about whether I would stay or go. Luckily, my friend Marie had by that time married Juan Pablo, so she was not required to leave. While I awaited news of my fate, Marie and I continued our late nights in the kitchen drinking warm milk with honey. I don't know what I would have done without her during that tumultuous time.

The most urgent task for the king was not to determine what to do with an inconsequential painter from Cremona, but rather to find a new queen. It was not so much about raising the two little girls because there were plenty of Spanish ladies-in-waiting, not to mention myself, who were there to ensure the well-being of the king's daughters. But the queen's role was a job of its own. There were protocols to follow and appearances to uphold. There were state functions to attend and dignitaries to welcome. And most importantly, male heirs were required. No royal subject wanted to think of a king without a queen, and especially without a male heir.

Philip had two young daughters. He had a son and three former wives—Maria of Portugal, Mary Tudor, and Isabel of the Peace—all dead. This did not bode well in the minds of people watching. Clearly, Philip needed to find a new queen, and he needed to find her quickly.

KEEPING A PROMISE

During this unsettling time, I wrote to my father and mother, informing them how bereft I felt in the aftermath of Isabel's death. I expressed the desire to come home. It took a while, but I did eventually hear from my father. Seeing his script on the page brought both my parents and all of Cremona immediately to me. If I could have somehow curled up inside his script to feel the warmth of my loving family, I would have done it.

Dearest Sofonisba,

You are welcome home any time. Your mother and I will receive you with open arms. I will turn your studio back over to you—I admit I have been using that room again—and I will send out queries to find you new portrait commissions. Never equate returning home to Cremona as a sign that you have failed. You have not failed!

With all the love in my heart,

Papa
29 May, 1569

As much as I wanted to go home, I was afraid returning would cause me to lose whatever momentum I had gained as a painter. If I went back to the terrace of my parents' home, I could paint portraits of my family and our servants, and Papa might find me an occasional commission, but I knew the move would mean the end of my life as a professional artist.

Despite my anguish over the harsh practices of the Inquisition, there was still much at court that was good. I valued the influx of visiting dignitaries and the companionship of friends like Marie. I thrived on hearing about things that were new and startling, like the story of Veronica Franco, the woman who taught me something about my own power. The court was a hub of knowledge, art, and diplomacy. I could still paint if I went home, but my work would take place in a much smaller arena. I selfishly did not want that for myself.

And I could not forget my promise to Isabel, to stay near the infantas and watch over them. I felt it was my destiny to show my dear friend's daughters that their lives need not be small. With the early foundation my father had set for me by giving me an education, I had opened a door to a world that very few women had passed through before me. I felt the weight of what this meant for Isabella and Catalina on my shoulders. I had vowed to Isabel I would stay, and I did not want to break my promise.

FIDELITY

I was astonished at how quickly Philip found a new wife. Anne of Austria was the daughter of Emperor Maximilian II, who was married to Philip's oldest sister, Maria. At the time of this new union, Philip was forty-two and Anne was twenty-one. She was a pleasant and kind young woman. She was not as concerned with fashion as Isabel had been, nor did she laugh as much. However, she gladly took on the role of mother to the two infantas, and for that, she deserved great credit. Furthermore, she eventually gave the king a son, Philip III. While Anne and I did not share the same deep connection that I had experienced with Isabel, we did share a love for the children, and so we became friends.

Of course, when Anne arrived at court, new portraits were needed. To expedite the process, Coello painted one of Philip and I painted one of Anne. I wanted to capture Anne's kindness and generosity of spirit. In the portrait, her gloved right hand rests on the back of a chair, holding her other brown leather glove. It is a similar pose to the one I had Isabel take in her portrait. It helped me to have a standard pose for my sitters because my familiarity with the structure of the image allowed me to focus on what I loved most:

the details. Anne wore a sumptuous black velvet gown decorated with silver and gold embroidery and pearl and gold buttons. The dress had bell sleeves that revealed more fitted sleeves underneath, accentuated by bands of gold and finished with delicate lace cuffs. Her ruffled lace collar showed off her pleasant face, crowned by blond hair and topped with a black velvet cap embellished with gold embroidery, pearl beads, and two fluffy ostrich feathers.

I sometimes worried that when future historians viewed all the artistic output from the Spanish court, they might mistakenly attribute my painting of Queen Anne to Coello. But when such anxiety arose, I would remind myself that anyone who knew anything about me and my work could see that I had painted her portrait. One of the hallmarks of my style is to create a warm and rosy look on my sitters' faces. In my paintings, you can imagine the individual is about to smile and speak to you. I captured this incipient liveliness in the portrait of Anne quite well.

Over time, I had developed a method for depicting my sitters' hands by showing the crux between the thumb and the first finger in a distinct curving V-shape. If you hold your hand out in front of you, as though you are about to take hold of a cup or a door handle, you will see the curving V that I am referring to. In the world of art, hands reveal a lot about an artist's fluency and style. In my portrait of Anne of Austria, you can see all the things I've described as recognizable characteristics of my work: the finery of her clothing, the warmth in her face, and the curved V-shape applied to the crux of her hand. No one could argue that this painting was by Coello.

Not long after Isabel died, the king asked me to paint a double portrait of his daughters. I wanted to capture their personalities, so sweet and warm and full of curiosity about the world. I thought it would put them at ease if I invited them to bring their pets to the sittings. Isabella had a parrot named Saint Sebastian that the king had given her and Catalina had adopted a spaniel that had been hanging around the kitchen. She named him Pepito. I was happy to include these friends in their portrait. Also, a dog in a painting symbolizes fidelity, and I wanted to indicate that the infantas, despite their young age, were faithful to the memory of their dear mother.

My practice of asking my sitters to stay still only while I worked on their faces was a very good strategy with the infantas. I was able to do some sketches to capture their expressions and then lay down color onto the canvas to get their skin tones set. I planned out the composition, their poses, and where and how to include Saint Sebastian and Pepito. Then, I let them change out of their gowns and the wooden hoops underneath and had one of the maids take them out to the garden so they could run and play.

I kept their dresses in my room and spent a much longer time working on the details of their matching brocade gowns with high lace collars. There was quite a lot of embroidery delineating the edges of the dresses and decorating the padded caps at the shoulders of their sleeves. Black velvet sashes embroidered with gold thread fell from the shoulders of each dress. I made sure to emphasize the gold fleur-de-lis decorations in the headpiece that Isabella wore in her hair, this being a French icon for the lily flower, and of course another detail to honor her mother. Everything about those little girls was a reflection of their mother. Their smiles, their laughter, the sparkle in their eyes.

Working on the infantas' portrait made me miss my friend so much, but it also made my heart feel light. I liked to think that wherever Isabel was, she knew her girls were loved.

Paola

I have been trying for so long to think of the right words to tell Father about my situation. I imagine two possible reactions. Either he will be joyful and suggest that we contact Francesco right away, or he will disown me.

I was about to leave with Fabia today to visit Sofi and do some transcribing for her, something I have not done for a while. As I opened the front door, I heard footsteps hitting fast on the stone floor and Fabia grabbed my arm to stop me. I turned and saw my father running toward us from his office.

"Paola!" he said, waving a paper. "I have news for you, for us. Don't leave yet!"

Almost breathless, he reached out and pulled me to the bench near the door. "Sit with me for just a moment," he said.

I could not imagine what his excitement was about, so I sat down with him. He handed me the paper. "Read this. And tell me what you think."

Dear Signor Vespucci,

I write this letter regarding a matter of the utmost importance to all concerned. I write to ask for your daughter's hand in marriage. I am in love with Paola, and I hope you will deem me a worthy son-in-law. I know she is your only daughter and that you rely on her in your business.

I have spoken to my father about this and we have a proposition to make. In lieu of the traditional dowry, we ask that you bring yourself to Palermo with Paola and join us by purchasing a share in the vineyard. We would like to see the winery be successful and feel that this will be best accomplished with you as a partner. I await your reply with hopefulness in my heart.

Most sincerely,

Francesco Rossi
26 March, 1606

I looked at my father and burst into tears.

"No, no tears!" he said. "Our answer is yes! Yes, you will marry. And yes! I will go."

"Father, I have something—"

"No, it's all right. I think I know."

"What do you mean, you think you know?"

My father cleared his throat and looked askance. "Well, I have noticed you are looking a little rounder, as your mother was with you. And how tired you are. Also, you have not been going so often to see Signora Anguissola."

"When were you going to say something?"

"I was waiting for you. I knew you would tell me when you were ready."

I grabbed his hand and made him stand with me, wrapping my arms around him. All the worry that had been tormenting me these past many weeks vanished in a breath.

I looked at the letter again. I recognized that the date on Francesco's letter is the very date I wrote to him. This means he had not yet received *my* letter when he wrote to my father—our letters crossed. I was overjoyed to realize that Francesco had proposed marriage without any provocation from me. And I never would have imagined my father being so willing to start fresh in a new place, in a new profession.

"Maybe you should pay a visit to Signora Anguissola today, like you intended," he said. "I think she should be told of these new developments."

At the mention of Sofi, my heart sank. A marriage proposal from Francesco is exactly what I have been hoping for. But when I go, who will help Sofi finish her story?

V

I disown shame, it drains and shows no care.
Naysayers will try to anticipate
and tell tales of me to humiliate
but I will rise above their unkind glare.
One thing is certain, I must always dare
to be my best self, thus never berate
the work that has been cut for me by fate—
the greater things that I have come to share.
God works with me in mysterious ways
shaping my faithful image, finely bred,
such radiance will one day be my all.
So rest assured in this, shame only pays
in sorrow. I look, therefore, high instead
for my heart and the songbird's gentle call.

Sofonisba

Early this morning, I put the last touches on the portrait of Roberta Bruzzone, finishing the rich, green texture of ivy in the background. When she comes to see it later today, it should be dry enough to safely transport. I hope she will be satisfied. I am excited to see her because she told me the last time we were together that today is her birthday. I am pleased that I was able to complete the painting in time for her special day. It always brings me joy to see opportunities for small kindnesses and to make sure I manifest them whenever it is in my power to do so.

After I finished with the portrait, I was cleaning my brushes when Paola arrived. She had good news to share. Francesco's proposal comes as no surprise to me. I knew he would ask. I did not foresee, however, the request to have her father join a new business venture. And yet, my former student was always one to see the importance of familial bonds. His idea to invite Signor Vespucci to come to Sicily was inspired, and I will tell him so the next time I see him.

Paola is distressed about leaving me with no one to help me finish my story. I told her that she must not give it a second thought. She insisted on transcribing for me today, and of course, I was happy to oblige. The story I wanted to share was a good counterpoint to her own pending adventure.

LEAVING

When the king married for the fourth time, he put forward a proposal for me. As a ward of the court, I was bound to no one other than him. Philip knew that I needed a way to move on with my life, away from the court, and so he presented the notion that I should be married. His pronouncement reminded me of the beautifully embroidered coverlet Isabel had given me when she was close to dying. It seemed likely that she had followed through on her intention to ask him to find me a husband. I never asked him to confirm that she had done this, but I doubt he would have thought of it on his own.

He offered to supply my dowry, which was very generous. I wasn't sure what to think. Getting married would mean new responsibility, and I wasn't sure how a husband—who might expect a doting wife—would react to me spending hours a day with my sitters. An artist's life isn't necessarily compatible with marriage. I was uncertain that any husband could be found who would understand that.

Still, I let the king know that if I were to marry someone, I would prefer to marry someone Italian. He told me he would keep that in mind. Soon after, he let me know he'd sent a message to a Sicilian nobleman named Don Fabrizio de Moncada, son of Francesco I, prince of Paternò and Viceroy of Sicily. He told me that Don Fabrizio was reported to be interested in art and poetry. He thought we would be a good match.

Don Fabrizio and I were introduced to each other one afternoon in spring, in a sun-filled sitting room where the king entertained visiting dignitaries. The king was there, of course, along with Juana, several ladies-in-waiting, and the infantas. It was important to me that the princesses be there, as their reaction to this prospective husband would be the truest measure of his character I could hope for.

I had a new brocade gown made for the occasion, and I must admit to being quite nervous about this meeting. I was seated when Don Fabrizio de Moncada was announced and entered the room. He presented himself well, with a look on his face that was both humble and self-assured. He was of medium height with broad shoulders and curly black hair cut close to his head. He had a pointy beard that brought to mind the memory of my beloved teacher from childhood, Signor Cavallaro—also Sicilian.

Don Fabrizio came straight to me and kneeled, placing a hand on his heart and bowing his head. To this day, I can see his hand on his chest, making a curved V-shape against his dark green doublet. I distinctly remember thinking that I must paint a portrait of this man.

"Greetings, Signorina," he said.

Although I was thirty-nine, I was still a signorina. "Greetings, Don Fabrizio," I said.

When he looked up, his smile was warm and friendly.

"Ah, Signorina. Please, you must call me only Fabrizio."

Somehow, I could tell by the look on his face that he was just as worried as I was that we might not find each other pleasing, which made me like him immediately.

Later, I asked the princesses what they thought of Don Fabrizio.

"He has a good smile," Isabella said.

"I like his beard," Catalina said. "He's nice."

Having their positive estimation of him, I knew that everything was going to be fine.

The plan was to marry at the Spanish court and then journey to see his family's properties in Sicily. Along the way, I would have the chance to stop in Cremona to visit my own family, whom I had not seen in twelve years.

It took an entire two weeks to pack a dozen years of possessions into just three *cassoni*. I had clothing, art supplies to sort through, fabric samples to take or leave, stacks of letters to organize, and other memorabilia from my time in Spain that I had to either keep or discard. I could not do this sorting with anyone else's help, although several of the maids—including dear Maria—offered to assist me. I kindly turned them all away because I wanted to go through my things myself and savor the memories that each item embodied. There were trinkets from Don Carlos and chalk drawings that Isabella and Catalina had made. I could not discard any of those items. They were all too precious to me.

During that time when I was preparing to leave, we had a new arrival at court—Princess Isabella's cousin, Prince Albert of Austria. He was eleven when he arrived and was a well-mannered, inquisitive boy. The Duke of Alba introduced him to me, and I liked the young prince immediately. He was bright and full of questions about painting, which I found endearing. He was quite attentive to his cousin Isabella, who was five at the time, opening the door for her or smoothing down a carpet so that she would not be in danger of losing her footing. My proclivity for premonition told me that perhaps Philip had brought the young prince to court with a purpose in mind—that is, to marry Isabella. It took some years for my premonition to be fulfilled, but they were eventually joined in holy matrimony.

Saying goodbye to people you know you will never see again is worse than death. Death is not a choice, but leaving is, and that is what makes it so hard. There were so many tears and hugs and the exchange of gifts. I gave Maria a small painting on copper of her and Juan Pablo. She cried at the sight of it. As for the infantas, I gave each girl a paintbrush. I had painted their names on the handles. Catalina gave me a drawing she had made showing the three of us together, myself in the middle with one of the girls on each side. Isabella gave me a bracelet of beads she said she had been collecting for quite some time.

"I found them on the ground, everywhere," she said. "And I saved them for you on this piece of thread." She tied the string of beads around my wrist. I wore it on my wedding day and for a long time afterward. The thread broke long ago, but I have kept the beads in a jar all these years. And Catalina's drawing is framed and hangs above my desk to this day.

Paola set down her quill and looked up from the manuscript with tears in her eyes. "How hard it must have been to leave those children," she said.

"It was terrible. I loved them as if they were my own daughters."

Paola was quiet, fiddling with the quill. At last she spoke. "I am going to miss you, Sofi."

"Oh, my dear, I will miss you too." I reached out my arms to her and we embraced. While I was holding her, I said, "I have been thinking. I have a favor to ask of you."

"Tell me," she said, standing back, still holding my hands. "I will do anything for you, my friend. You must know that."

"When you go to Sicily, I would like you to take the manuscript with you."

"But why, Sofi? How will it be finished?"

"Before you go, I will have you write down some important events in the second half of my life. I'm sure that with your poet's mind, you will find a way to finish the tale. And besides, one day you will have your printing press. I am sure of it. If anyone is going to publish my story, it will be you."

Francesco

Here in Alcamo, life is exceedingly quiet. My only companion is a local youth named Marco. I pay him to come from the village two afternoons a week to help me pull out weeds. Thank goodness I have someone to talk to now and then.

Coming to Sicily has been a true education. There is much about this place that is new and unusual, everything from the plants to the architecture, which shows Arabic influence. I had no idea what I was taking on when I agreed to come here and work for my father. I did not realize how lonely I would be. I have started to carry my sketchbook and chalk in my work bag, so I have them with me wherever I go. Sketching things makes me feel not so alone. I am especially intrigued by prickly pear cactus, brought to Sicily from the New World by Spanish conquistadors. I have drawn their strange green paddles bristling with dangerously sharp spikes many times. Beyond their beautiful spring flowers, the plant produces a red-orange fruit that is quite thirst quenching, once you learn how to peel away the needles.

Recently, I went on horseback to the top of Mount Bonifato and made some drawings of the gate known as Queen's Door as well as the old Ventimiglia castle. The place is in ruins and quite desolate. I long to show these places to Paola. I know she would write poems about them.

My sketchbook also contains all the drawings that I made during my time in Genoa. It wasn't quite a year, but I saw and learned a great deal while I was there. Each drawing brings back a memory. There are those first sketches I made of the old olive trees when Sofi took me up to the hills above the city. That was the day that our friendship began. There are sketches of my own hands and feet, drawings Sofi encouraged me to make in order to practice every day.

And then there are my sketches of Paola. When I look at those, my heart aches. I suppose that means I did a good job of capturing her beauty. Maybe I am not such a hopeless artist after all. I read the poem she gave me every night before I go to sleep, just like she asked me to do. I read it every morning, too, because it gives me strength to face the day. I have memorized the poem, and sometimes, I recite it out loud as I tend the vines.

> As seasons come and go without end
> and birds, the spirits of the air, fly free,
> I hope one day we'll meet again.

This morning, like every other morning, I was up early. I like to take advantage of the daylight before the sun gets too high and the heat too oppressive. My main task, to go along the trellises and make sure each vine is firmly anchored, is slow, careful work. It is important that it be done right, for if not, a stronger than usual wind off the coast could damage the vines.

"Signor!" Marco called. He ran down the hill from the house, excitement on his face.

He stopped before me, catching his breath. "A man on horseback brought this for you," he said, handing me a scroll with a "V" on the seal. It was far too soon for Signor Vespucci to have received my letter and sent one in return. As I broke the seal, I was hoping that Paola might have sent me a new poem.

Dear Francesco,

I hope this letter finds you well and that the vineyard is thriving. There is no easy way to tell you this, so I will just write the words. I am going to have a child. Our child! At the writing of this letter, I have missed my monthly flow twice. Only Fabia and Sofi know this news right now, but by the time this letter reaches you, I will have no doubt told my father, because my condition will soon be impossible to hide. I hope you find this news joyful and will make our union official by asking my father for my hand in marriage. I would be happy to be your wife and give you many more children in the years to come.

Please write to me and let me know your intentions. I remain ever faithfully yours,

Paola
26 March, 1606

I sat down and looked up toward Mount Bonifato to steady myself.

"Is anything wrong, Signor?" Marco asked.

"No, no. In fact, everything is right."

"What is the news?"

"I am going to be a father!"

"Congratulations, Signor," said Marco, sitting down in the grass with me. He took my hand in his and shook it. "That is happy news, indeed."

Me, a father. I inhaled deeply and took in the splendor of the world all around me, rows of grapevines, sparkling sea, clear sky, majestic mountain. My mind leapt ahead of me, imagining how wonderful it would be to hold Paola's hand in this place and marry her in God's sight. I looked at the letter again. If my memory serves me correctly, I think we wrote to each other on the exact same day, 26 March. Clearly, we are of one mind on the matter of marriage. I imagine that just now, Signor Vespucci might also be reading the letter that I wrote to him. Perhaps Paola is reading it, too, and now she knows that I have already done exactly what she asked me to do.

PART FOUR

Paola

Fourteen years ago, in the summer of 1606, I came to Sicily and began a new life with Francesco. Our wedding took place at the edge of the vineyard in Alcamo, with Mount Bonifato presiding over us. I will never forget the elation I felt knowing that our two lives would be entwined as one and that together we would make a family. We settled into a fine house in Palermo, which is about two hours from the vineyard by horse, an easy distance for Francesco to travel once or twice each week as necessary.

When our first child was born, we named him Lorenzo in honor of my father. Now we have a small army of our own with another child on the way. Some days, I look around me and see my sons—six fine lads, all as fine-looking as their dear father—and I cannot fathom how it is possible that fourteen years have gone by since I left Genoa. As for my father, his presence here has been a blessing. He has not once regretted his transformation from cloth merchant to vintner. Like the vines, all of us are thriving.

The only difficulty I faced when Father and I left Genoa, of course, was knowing that I was leaving my dear Sofi. Before I left, she and I sat together several times, and at her request, I made careful notes about aspects of her life that we had not yet touched on. She provided dates and a summary of events after her marriage to Don Fabrizio. I have read the manuscript many times over the years and I know her story—as far as we were able to go together—by heart. I don't know how, but someday, I will do what she asked me to do and write a good ending.

When I first arrived in Palermo, Sofi and I exchanged letters regularly.

But over the years, she found it increasingly difficult to write. At some point, Orazio acquired for her a pair of magnifying glasses that she could wear on her nose, but even that ingenious new invention did not help her as much as he hoped it would. In the winter of 1618, she wrote that her hands could not always be trusted to do what her mind wanted them to do. Her letters stopped coming.

So today, when a letter arrived marked with "OL" stamped on the wax, I was full of dread. When Fabia first brought it to me, I didn't have the courage to break the seal. I turned it over and over in my hands, assuming that it would contain the terrible news of my dear friend's passing.

Francesco knew I worried Sofi would not live much longer. "Would you like some help opening the letter, my darling?" Francesco asked, breaking my trance.

"Yes, please," I said, handing him the letter. "You read it."

I watched as his eyes took in the words, awaiting his confirmation of the thing I feared the most. But then, I saw a smile break on his face.

"How wonderful!" he said.

"What? Wonderful?" I grabbed the letter to read it for myself.

Dearest Paola and Francesco,

I hope this letter finds you well. Life in Genoa is the same as ever. The sea remains a steadfast source of income for me as I continue to deliver goods and passengers wherever they need to go. As for Sofi, she recently finished a self-portrait and declared it her last. She says she has no more strength to paint. As she approaches her 88th birthday, she wishes to come to Palermo. She dreams of Sicilian warmth and of being near the two of you and all the children. Through one of my contacts in Palermo, I have secured us a small house near the sea. We will keep the house in Genoa since it belongs to my family and will be a good place to store her paintings. We expect to land upon your shore in early September. We look ahead to seeing you and to whatever God has in store for us.

Yours truly,

Orazio
22 June, 1620

"I've always thought I would never see Sofi ever again," I said. "What should we do to prepare for their arrival?"

My husband put his hands on my shoulders and looked into my eyes. "Please don't worry about making everything perfect right away," he said. "There will be plenty of time." Then, he kissed my forehead.

"You are right. I am just so happy to know that soon, I will see Sofi again. Do you think she will want to continue with her stories?" I asked.

"I imagine," Francesco said, "that her artist's eye has kept her memory razor sharp. I am sure she still has many stories left to tell."

Since those first days in Palermo, the chores of life and being a mother have taken me away from poetry. But I've felt the need to return to my desk more than once since hearing from Orazio. Anticipating a continuation of Sofi's stories, I am compelled to return to my heroic crown of sonnets. It feels good to return to something I left behind so long ago. We all have a story to tell, and it won't be told if we don't take the time to write it. If there is anything I have learned in this life, it is that you never can be completely sure how stories will end until they do. Or maybe it would be more accurate to say that no story ever completely ends—rather, it transforms.

VI

For my heart and the songbird's gentle call,
I find the quiet music of the spheres,
these sounds that tremble lightly on my ears.
First light and last, their harmonies enthrall,
and ask no certain favors, big or small.
The mourning dove will woo me fast to tears
and swallows bring their trills so sweet and clear,
reminding me of why the trees stand tall.
I am the one who keeps my own fair words
and brings them forth as waves upon the sea.
I wrap myself in rhyme—a silken shawl—
that floats behind me as the wings of birds
and finds my gift unfold in poetry.
I won't be done until my words tell all.

When September arrived, I began coming down to the docks every afternoon, hoping to greet the *Sant'Agata* when it arrives. Today, Francesco and Fabia came with me, and we brought all the boys along as well. They ran like a band of marauding pirates along the pier, darting in and out among the fishing nets.

"Do you see that brown dot on the horizon?" Francesco asked. "I do believe this is going to be her."

I eventually discerned the distinct carving of Saint Agata on the prow of the ship.

"There is Sofi!" I said, to no one in particular. While still at a distance, I saw her standing near the prow, looking toward the shore. "Sofi!" I called out, waving my arms. I knew she couldn't hear me, but I had to do something because I could not contain my excitement. I was reminded of the story she told of waking her sister Elena in the mornings and saying, "Get up, sister! The day is here!"

With a calm sea, a light breeze, and only a few clouds dotting the brilliant blue sky, God had made September 5, 1620, a perfect day. It was a day of celebration, a glorious day to reunite old friends. I felt as though the whole world was exclaiming the message. *Get up, sister! The day is here!*

Once the ship docked and the plank was lowered, I could see that Orazio had caught sight of us amidst the crowd on the pier. He waved. I saw him saying something in Sofi's ear and she smiled.

Orazio assisted his wife down the plank. She held onto him on one side with Giulia, dear Giulia, on the other. Orazio has aged too, but not like Sofi. She wobbled on her feet and her upper back was hunched forward. She had the frail look of a seed pod split open, its contents dried by the beating sun. And yet, as she made her way toward me, I sensed the same warmth emanating from her that I had experienced the first time I met her in Genoa so long ago.

"Paola! Francesco!" Orazio called out. I rushed forward to greet them, and once we were finally a short distance apart, Sofi could at last see me.

"Paola! Is it really you?"

I grabbed her in my arms, "Oh, it is, it is! I am so happy to see you!"

"Welcome home to Palermo!" Francesco said, patting Orazio on the back. Then he turned toward Sofi. "Maestra, what a delight it is to see you again."

She cupped his face in her hands. "The delight is mine," she said. "I never thought I would see such a day as this!"

The boys were still running up and down the wharf and Francesco called them to us. They arrived in a tangle of arms and legs. "Boys, say your names and ages, please."

"Lorenzo, almost fourteen."

"Angelo, twelve."

"Tomasino, ten."

"Amilcare, eight."

"Orazio, six!"

"I'm Asdrubale," the youngest said.

Hearing this name, Sofi placed her hand on her heart.

"I am four," he said.

"So lovely to hear these names," she said. "Each one, a blessing."

"I am honored to meet my namesake," Orazio said, putting his hand on my son's head.

Little Orazio puffed up his chest and saluted the ship's captain.

"Let's get your things loaded onto the carts," Francesco said. "We brought two—one for people, one for things. Lorenzo can drive the cart with your things. Boys, lend a hand. We need to get these weary travelers home to rest."

As the men dealt with the cargo, Sofi turned to me. "When will this child come?" she asked.

It seemed her eyes were not so useless after all. "Two months, I think."

"Then we have come at the perfect time," Sofi said.

"Yes, you have," I said. "Perfect."

We delivered Orazio and Sofi to their new home and looked about with them to ensure all was well. There was some basic furniture already in the house, a table, some chairs, a bed.

"There are many things we did not bring," Orazio said. "We thought it would be best to purchase new things here."

"It's a lovely house, Sofi," I said. "I know you will be happy here."

"And, do you see?" she said, pointing to the golden light from the large window facing north. "The sea. I told Orazio I needed to be near water and the sound of seagulls."

We stayed to share a meal of bread, cheese, smoked sardines, and wine that Fabia had packed. We promised to return the next day to help Sofi and Orazio get other things they needed for their new home.

On the ride home, I felt full of joy and excitement. Once I sat down at my desk, my hand on the quill, the next sonnet in the crown almost wrote itself.

VII

I won't be done until my words tell all.
Finding new ways to gently push the veil,
and so reveal the mystery of this tale
that was sung to me when I was but small.
A snake who whispered at the garden wall
invited Eve to follow on its trail
to gain the knowledge of Good and Evil,
sacrificing Paradise with this call.
Like her, I know too well that choices made
sometimes bring joy and sometimes bring sorrow.
I go forth in awe, accepting the dare
and stake my claim on that which God forbade.
And so, I go to meet my tomorrow,
and print my verses high upon the air.

Francesco

When I first started my lessons with Sofi back in 1605, we sat in the grove of old olive trees high above Genoa and I told her that someday I hoped she would meet my father. And now, all these years later, here we are. Today I had the great pleasure of introducing my former teacher to my father, who only recently left the vineyard in Tuscany in the care of my younger brothers so he could join us in Palermo. Together on the terrace—Sofi, Orazio, myself, Paola, and our two fathers—we sat and enjoyed a bottle of our own wine in the late afternoon sun.

"It is wonderful to meet you, Signor Rossi," Sofi said. "I must thank you for allowing Francesco to leave the vineyard long ago so he could make his way to Genoa to find me."

"Ah, well. It is you who must be thanked, Signora, for giving him the opportunity to explore his dream and still find his way back to the vines. To art," said my father, raising his glass. "And to the education of the artist in each of us, no matter what age."

Sofi laughed, and together we all raised our glasses. "To art!"

"To that," said Paola's father, "I would like to add my thanks to Angelo and Francesco for inviting me to become part of this family enterprise. I have learned so much in this second profession. May we never be afraid to change our lives, even if it seems to go against everything the world expects of us."

"Lorenzo," Sofi said, "how was it for you when you left Genoa?"

My father-in-law took a sip of wine and leaned back in his chair. "Thinking back on it now, it was quite easy for me to sell my cloth business and move to Sicily. I would never have expected that to be the case."

"What did other cloth sellers think about your move?" Orazio asked.

"All my friends in Genoa tried to persuade me otherwise. Federico Barbieri, my friendly competitor, was especially disheartened. He thought I was abandoning him."

"I would say you did him a favor, Father," Paola said.

"Exactly," Lorenzo said, raising his glass to his daughter. "Over endless glasses of port one afternoon, I told him the change I was about to embark on would save him and his business because it made more room for him. At last, he understood and thanked me. We parted on good terms."

"To change!" I said, raising my glass.

"To change!"

"Speaking of change, how is your new home, Signora?" my father asked.

"It is perfect," said Sofi. "We are right near the water, not too far from here. It is bright and airy. And, we are just around the corner from San Giorgio dei Genovesi."

"That is a lovely church," my father said.

"It is," Sofi said, nodding. "We are glad to be near it because Orazio's extended family had a hand in helping to fund its construction."

"What a gift," Father said. "I understand that everyone laid to rest there has some connection to Genoa."

"Yes, that is true," Orazio replied. "It feels like a little piece of Genoa is here with us."

"I am just happy that we are near the water," Sofi added. "Any time I can feel the sea breeze on my face and hear seagulls, I know I am home!"

"To home," said my father, and we all raised our glasses.

"To home!"

"I think it is worth noting," Sofi said, taking hold of Paola's hand as she spoke, "that we are all home now. We are all blessed to be together again."

Sofi's words touched my heart. I sat back and observed how much she had aged since I last saw her. How lucky we are that she is still alive. It seems like it was only yesterday that I threw myself into the unknown and came here to Sicily to tend the vineyard for my father. When I think back to those first uncertain days, and then how everything changed when Paola and her father arrived, I realize how blessed I am.

When I welcomed our first son into the world, I wanted him to know three things: always be kind, carefully tend the vines, and learn how to draw. Of these, being kind is most important, with learning to draw a very close second. And yes, tending the vines cannot be ignored.

Paola

Today Sofi and I sat on the terrace of her new home. The house is up high on a bluff and I marveled at the pink, orange, and yellow cactus flowers that dotted the rocky terrain leading down to the shore. The sky was an azure dome above us, and the sea a sparkling ultramarine cloth that stretched out below us as far as I could see.

"It is beautiful here, isn't it?" I said.

"In my memory, yes. I wish I could see it now as you see it."

"I'm sorry, Sofi."

"I feel lost," she said. "With my sight so diminished, I feel that my oldest and dearest friend has left me."

"It must be a terrible thing."

"Some days, I feel so much pain behind my eyes that I wish I could just be gone from this world. But then I have an idea for a painting I would make if I still could. That makes me feel a little better. For a while." She smiled.

"What about the magnifying glasses that Orazio brought you? Did those help at all?"

"A little, but not enough. I can no longer distinguish one color from another. They all appear as shades of brown. And besides, it is not just my eyes that no longer function properly. My hands have grown unreliable. They have become so unsteady—painting is impossible."

"I am prepared to write for you again, if you wish," I said.

"I would like that," she said. "Very much."

213

I can't believe I am here again, on the island of Sicily. While my eyes may not see, my nose can tell that this is the place I came to nearly fifty years ago as Fabrizio's new bride. There is something in the air, dry and spicy, that brings memories flooding back.

My marriage to Fabrizio took place in 1571 on a spring day at the Escorial in Madrid with King Philip and Queen Anne in attendance. Fabrizio's parents made the long journey from Paternò. Our quiet ceremony was held in the king's chapel, and afterward, we feasted.

In the weeks leading up to the ceremony, I enjoyed many afternoon picnics conversing with my husband-to-be, learning about his family and what life was like in Sicily. We sat on a blanket in the shade and he told me about their house, situated on the opposite side of the island from where we live now, at the foot of Mount Etna. He told me about the rocky landscape of his home, the plants, and the Arab influence on the architecture. He told me it was at the Sicilian court of Frederick II that the thirteenth-century poet Giacomo da Lentini invented the form of the sonnet. I appreciated that he seemed to know what I would find interesting.

On one of our picnics, in the shade of an olive tree, Fabrizio asked me what it was like to meet Michelangelo. I told him how nervous I had been at first and how *Il Divino* had put me at ease with his gentle questions, how he revealed himself to be a person, just like the rest of us. I told Fabrizio the story of looking up to see the cherubs painted on the ceiling of Michelangelo's study and how that image had stuck with me throughout my life as a moment of joyful surprise.

Raising his glass, he said, "To more moments of joyful surprise!"

I touched my glass to his. "To joyful surprise!"

Those weeks we spent getting to know each other remain in my memory like a dream. Each thing Fabrizio did—each question asked, each gesture offered—was guided by his caring heart. He had a warm, amiable demeanor and a propensity to break into laughter at the slightest incitement. I was amazed that the king had found someone for me that I would have chosen myself, given the opportunity.

Throughout our wedding day, Fabrizio was deferential to me as we made our way through the official proceedings and into the evening festivities. As for our marriage bed, I will say that it easily fell into the category of joyful surprise. Other than my youthful transgression with Rinaldo, I did not know of such things. With Fabrizio, we discovered we were two pieces of an old puzzle, and I could not have asked for a better match.

As I listened to Sofi, I could understand that feeling of joyful surprise that comes with true love. It is the way I felt in Genoa when I first met Francesco. Every step I took was a step toward him. Then, he left for Palermo and I worried I would lose him, though looking back I see it did not take us long to find each other again. And now, despite how busy we are with life's chores and our brood of boys, we have not lost joy. He still brings me feathers when he finds them.

"I am writing again after a long lapse," I told Sofi.

"A creative soul cannot stay silent indefinitely," she said.

I know she is right, and I know I still have much to learn. I have lived in Sicily for fourteen years but have never before heard of the poet she mentioned, Giacomo da Lentini, the inventor of the sonnet form. What else is there in this world that I do not yet know?

VIII

I print my verses high upon the air
and cannot say that I have never sinned.
I find messages floating on the wind
and look for any door that stands ajar.
One foot on the other side, I'll go far.
My promise to you I will not rescind
despite how this story must one day end.
Upon this world, I leave no stain, no mar.
As joy will come to take me by surprise
and songs of angels lend their harmony,
in their glad verses I will find my worth.
They pull me upwards to unbounded skies.
I will be always new, forever free,
the grateful vessel of this bless'd rebirth.

215

Sofonisba

REUNION

The day after the wedding, Fabrizio and I left Madrid for the Moncada property in Sicily, where we would begin a new life together. We set our course through Cremona in order to visit my family. It had been twelve years since I had seen them. As our carriage approached the house that day in spring, my parents stood on the terrace, waving. Asdrubale, whom I had not seen since he was a lad of eight, had become a young man of twenty. At first view, I did not recognize my brother. What a reunion it was!

Papa was his usual self, full of energy. In some ways, it seemed like he hadn't aged a bit. He wanted me to talk, talk, talk and tell him about all the intrigue of the Spanish court. He wanted to know if I had a plan to continue painting in Sicily.

"Thanks to you, Papa, I will never stop painting," I said. "No matter where I live." My words made him smile.

Mama was her usual quiet self, still singing as she moved through the house, always making sure everyone was comfortable and had exactly what they needed to feel at peace. She asked me to name all the foods Fabrizio liked to eat and was pleased to hear that he had a fondness for artichokes because she did as well. She made sure we had them prepared in a different way at nearly every meal. Fabrizio and I were in Cremona for just two weeks, but in that short time, my mother made him feel he was welcomed into our family.

My sister Europa had grown into a beautiful woman and was

married to a Cremonese nobleman, Carlo Schinchinelli. They had a three-year-old son, Antonio. On our first afternoon home, Mama laid out a feast for us on the terrace. Afterward, when everyone was relaxing in the sun, my nephew kept pulling on Fabrizio's pant leg. Fabrizio eventually picked up the giggling boy, placed him on his shoulders, turned to my sister, and said, "Is this all right, Mama?" Europa nodded and smiled. Off they went through the garden, my new husband prancing and spinning with my new nephew laughing uncontrollably on his shoulders.

As for my youngest sister, Anna Maria, she was betrothed to another nobleman, Jacopo Sommi. In fact, due to my father's astute planning, her wedding was scheduled to coincide with my visit home. I have never forgotten that gift from Papa, who made sure I was there for my sister's special day. I took great delight in helping her fix her hair and don her dress for the wedding.

My ability to be present to see at least one of my sisters get married was good for all our hearts. I laughed with Papa about those naysayers from long ago who had said he was only educating his daughters to avoid the financial strain of dowries, the thought being that educated ladies would not make desirable wives. Papa educated us and paid the necessary dowries. His generosity in regard to his daughters clearly proved those cynics wrong.

Both Europa and Anna Maria had been very young when I first departed, but they had benefited from the artistic training I had given to Lucia and Minerva before I left for Spain. My two youngest sisters had continued to paint, and both of them were eager to show me their work. What a pleasure it was to see Europa's self-portraits and Anna Maria's two images of the Holy Family, one with St. John and one with St. Francis.

The time in Cremona also made clear how much I was still mourning the loss of Lucia and Minerva. Coming home to the place where they had once been so alive, I felt their deaths sting my heart. Papa had a painting in the house that Lucia had made, showing the young Jesus and John the Baptist greeting each other at Mary's feet. The scene took place inside a home. There was an unmade bed to the right of the main figural group and, in the background, Joseph read from a book while Saint Elizabeth looked on from the shadows. My sister had included a lamb at Mary's feet, symbolizing the sacrifice that was coming. All in all, it was a well-composed and beautifully executed painting. Seeing it brought tears to my eyes. Father said he was making arrangements to have the painting hung at the Church of Sant'Agata. It thrilled me to know that a religious painting by a woman, one with the name Anguissola on it, would grace the walls of the church. I felt hope grow in me for women painters everywhere.

Before Minerva died, she veered away from painting and became a writer and Latin scholar. She left a stack of manuscript pages, and Father said he was looking into the possibility of having her work published. I don't know if he ever succeeded in that, and I wish I knew where that manuscript is now.

The one sister I still needed to see was Elena. I wanted to visit her in the convent before continuing on our journey to Sicily, but Mantua was a bit off our southward path. I worried that perhaps Fabrizio would be opposed to this idea. On the contrary, he encouraged me to go as he had some business he wanted to attend to nearby, in Milan. So, although we had just gotten married, we went our separate ways for a short time, each to do what we needed to do.

MYSTERY

When my carriage arrived at the Convent of the Holy Virgin at San Vincenzo, I saw once again the towering oaks and the delicate lilies of the valley that I had seen years ago when I went there the first time to paint Elena's portrait. This time, my sister waited at the gate for me. I jumped out of the carriage and ran into her arms. We hugged, we cried, we laughed. My dear Elena looked exactly as she had looked twenty years earlier.

I picked up my small travel bag and we went straight to the chapel to light candles and pray. Then Elena took me to the cloister's inner courtyard and we sat together on a stone bench, enjoying the aroma of flowers and fruit trees all around us. I felt as though I was in a dream.

"There is peace here," she said. "We are a community of sisters. We pray, we eat, we learn. And you would be proud of me, Sofi, because I still sketch things, just like you taught me to do. Remember

218

how I fought you on the idea of drawing from feeling? Well, in the years since I came here, I learned what you were trying to tell me—to draw with the eyes of my heart."

"Did I say that?"

"Maybe not those exact words, but that is what I learned from your example. If I am drawing a tree, I understand the tree so much better once I feel its lines. Then I do my best to recreate them on the page. I can see that the tree is strong and rooted in the earth. At the same time, it is stretching its branches up to the sky. The tree gives shade, fruit, and a haven to the birds. It is a prayer spoken by God."

My sister's words touched my heart. It seemed to me that she had learned much more than I had ever taught her. What might my sister teach *me*? I wondered.

Later on, after a simple meal of broth and bread, we retired to Elena's room to prepare for sleep. The Mother Superior made a special dispensation for me once again, but this time, I was allowed to stay overnight in the cloister. The sisters provided a straw pallet and blanket that we laid out on the floor.

"What about you?" my sister asked after we were snug in bed, not unlike those days in our triangle room at Signor Campi's house. "What have you learned all these years?"

I did not know what to say. I had seen the goodness of Isabel and the sweetness of her daughters. I had experienced the generosity of Marie, and I had been present for many lively discussions with the ladies-in-waiting, pondering love, war, art, or the words of a woman like Veronica Franco, whose ideas filled us all with fiery questions about the world.

I had also seen the animosity and jealousy in a man like Coello and the darkness that abides in the mind of a king. I had seen a woman's strength in Philip's sister Juana, but also weakness in her contempt for Don Carlos. I had seen how far a person will go to destroy others who hold differing beliefs. I had seen how a ruler rules with a hard heart, closing his mind to the way his decisions touch countless people's lives, but also how this very same ruler could act with consideration for someone he admired or be reduced to tears by the death of someone he loved.

At first, I did not know how to talk about these contradictions, but it occurred to me that if anyone would understand the complexity of people, it would be Elena, who lived every day of her life so close to God. So I poured out my thoughts to her.

"We humans have a great responsibility," she said. "It is up to each of us to acknowledge the presence of Evil, and always, in our words and deeds, seek the Good, or as God would say, seek God. We know Evil is among us. But we must make the choice to dwell or not to dwell in the suffering on which it thrives. It can take a long time, but Good always wins."

As I drifted off to sleep, I reminded myself that Elena also bore the family name, Anguissola. She, too, was a lone snake. Different from me in many ways, but exploring her own inner strength as earnestly as I explored mine. I fell asleep that night feeling both agitated and strangely calm. I was grateful to be with my sister again, surprised to be thirty-nine years old and finally married, anxious to be on my way to a new life and a new home on the island of Sicily. I was unaware of any premonitions that night. I could not even begin to imagine what the future had yet in store for me.

———————————

Paola

The mention Sofi made the other day of the poet Giacomo da Lentini has sparked my curiosity. I asked Francesco to inquire with Father Vitale at the little church in Alcamo, and he in turn provided the name of a man who works at the archive in Palermo, Signor Luigi Conigliaro. Today I took the afternoon off from household duties and ventured to the archive with my big belly and a letter of introduction written by the priest. Francesco released our oldest son, Lorenzo, from his chores to drive the carriage and serve as my chaperone. My son was glad to help his mother as it meant a break from weeding and watering the vines.

I was a little nervous about meeting Signor Conigliaro, but I reminded myself of Sofi going to meet Michelangelo when she was much younger than I am now. If I could give birth to six healthy children with a seventh on the way, I could certainly meet an archivist and ask him about poetry.

Lorenzo stopped the carriage at the address on the Via delle Pergole. I was surprised by how small the building was. For a place that held such riches, the archive had an unassuming presence on a side street off the bustling Via Maqueda.

"I think I should stay with the horse and carriage, Mama. Don't you?"

"I think you probably are looking forward to a nap," I said, tousling his brown curls.

He grinned and wriggled away from me. "Really? Will you be all right on your own?"

"I will be fine, my love. Do not worry about your mother."

I knocked on the front door and a thin man with bright blue eyes opened it. He had a shiny bald head, and perched on his nose were magnifying glasses like those that Sofi had described.

"Can I help you, Signora?"

"I am Paola Vespucci Rossi. I am looking for Signor Conigliaro."

"I am he, Signora," he said, holding out his hand to me.

I grasped it and handed him my letter of introduction. He glanced at it briefly.

"Come in, come in!" he said.

I stepped over the threshold and he handed the letter back to me.

"Welcome to the Archives of Palermo, Signora. How can I help you?"

"I am seeking information about the poets in the circle of Giacomo da Lentini."

"Wonderful! Follow me," he said, then led me down a hallway, through an elaborately-carved doorway, and into a long, high-ceilinged room lined with study tables. Light poured in through a row of windows that ran all the way around the room just under the ceiling. My eyes were drawn to a large stained-glass window on the far wall. In the late morning sun, it glowed with rich hues of red, blue, green, and yellow. If I had not known I was in an archive, I would have thought I was in a church.

"Please, Signora, sit and be comfortable. I will be right back with various materials related to Giacomo da Lentini for you to peruse."

Alone in the light-filled room, I felt at peace and grew curious about the imagery of the stained-glass window. The window was divided into three sections. As I moved closer to better study it, I saw that each section represented a different mode of art—painting, music, and literature. As I looked more carefully, I saw that in each section, women and men were shown working together in the activity of creation.

Signor Conigliaro returned with an armful of folios, and I asked, "Who is responsible for this stunning stained-glass window?"

"Ah, the window. Everyone who sees the window is intrigued by it." He set the stack of folios on the table in front of me.

"It was fashioned by a man named Pietro Romano in the fourteenth century," he said. "The story goes that he had a mistress who was also an artist, and that she played a significant role in the design of the window. Sad to say, we do not know her name."

"What a shame," I said.

"It is indeed a glaring omission in the historical record, Signora. But I hope these poems will cheer you," he said, gesturing to the folios. "May I ask, what is it that has inspired you to seek out the poets in the circle of

Lentini?"

"Well..." I hesitated for just a moment but decided there was no point in hiding who I am. "I am a poet myself, a writer of sonnets. I heard about Lentini recently and I wanted to learn more about him."

"How delightful!" he said. "You are the first poet to visit me in at least half a decade. What specifically would you like to know?"

"I would like to learn about the origin of the sonnet form and who the poets were in his circle. What did they write about? Also, were any of them women?"

"As far as we know, Signora, these poets were all men. But having a connection to Alcamo, as you do, you might be interested to know that one poet in Lentini's circle, Cielo d'Alcamo, came from that very place. He is best known for his long poem 'Rosa fresca aulentissima.' I have the manuscript right here."

"How interesting. Thank you."

"Before I let you read in peace, Signora, you might like knowing that the lyric poetry of the Sicilians drew its inspiration from the lineage of the troubadours going back to the eleventh century. In their view, man was the servant and woman the superior. Also, these poets enriched the expansion of language, moving away from Latin to the vernacular, creating a much broader literary standard."

"And this use of the vernacular was furthered by Dante, was it not?"

"Indeed, it was," he said. "And then by Petrarch and Boccaccio after him."

"Everything is connected, it seems."

"That is true, Signora."

The archivist reached into a cupboard near the work tables and pulled out a quill, ink, and paper. "In case you want to make notes," he said.

"Thank you."

"I will be in that little room next door if you need anything else."

I began by reading the poem by Cielo d'Alcamo. It was written as a dialogue between a man and the woman he is attempting to woo. I recognized a fair amount of sly humor in the poet's words, and I copied down many of the lines. I looked forward to telling Sofi about this—a poem about a fresh and exceedingly fragrant rose, a metaphor for the beautiful woman who is driving the man crazy with desire. I was sure she would find it most entertaining.

Two hours went by quickly and I was feeling some hunger pangs. I thought of poor Lorenzo sitting outside in the carriage. If he had taken a nap, he was probably awake and ready to go. I felt I had absorbed enough Sicilian poetry for one day.

"Signor Conigliaro?" I called out and he came right away.

"Did you find some interesting threads?" he asked.

"Yes, this was most illuminating. Thank you so much for your time and attention."

"You are welcome, Signora. Please come and visit the Archive of Palermo anytime."

"I will, thank you." I took one last look at the stained-glass window's iridescent, glowing colors. I thought about the unknown woman who had helped design it and wished I knew her name.

As I left the archive, I knew I would go home and make time to work on the next poem in the heroic crown. I am approaching the end of the cycle.

IX

The grateful vessel of this bless'd rebirth,
welcomes the day, for time is running out.
I stand tall on the mountain where I shout
kind words of love for all I know of Earth.
Brave action overflows whatever dearth
as I make my way toward the final bout
and trust that I will leap, no shred of doubt.
Compassion is the seed of friendship's worth.
Be clear! Never alone in what we do,
soul matched to soul, the lineage we seek.
Love will be the flag we raise, unfurled
and hate will be undone by what is true
bringing balm to others, the bold, the meek.
I yearn to sing, make peace in this world.

Sofonisba

CALLED BACK

In 1572, after only a year in Paternò, where Fabrizio and I had begun to build our life in a lovely house together, we returned to Madrid. The king wrote to call me back to the Spanish court, saying that his sister Juana—of all people—needed me. She wanted me, not Coello, to paint a portrait of her son, Don Sebastian. She said that only I was capable of capturing his warmth and humanity.

I must admit to feeling no small amount of satisfaction at her preference for me as a painter. I always had mixed feelings about Juana because of the uncaring way she had treated her nephew, Don Carlos. Still, I was honored that she would choose me over the official court painter to create a portrait of her beloved son. Also, the king mentioned in his letter that he was not in the best of health, and that at times, his pain was almost unbearable. I got the impression that he wanted to see me again, so I felt compelled to answer his call. These people were my second family, and I wanted to help them. My dear Fabrizio was an accommodating soul, always putting the needs of others first. He was more than happy to journey back to Madrid with me. And so, we did.

The return to Spain and to all my friends and loved ones there opened a joyous new chapter. It was such a blessing to be reunited with the two infantas and to sit with them again in the afternoons to draw, play yarn games, and braid their hair. I was amazed at how much they had grown in one short year. I still enjoyed the occasional late-night talk in the kitchen with Maria, and I was also grateful to have the chance to get to know Queen Anne more fully. In every way imaginable, I was glad to return to court and settle into my old chamber, but this time with a husband by my side.

I got to work right away on the portrait of Don Sebastian. I painted him in a three-quarter view wearing a royal blue doublet. His youth had been spent in Portugal, away from his mother. She had given birth to the boy there, but her young husband died while she was still pregnant.

When Philip called his sister home to serve as regent while he went off to England for his marriage to Queen Mary, Juana decided it was best to leave the baby with her late husband's family. Later on, she regretted that decision. She told me that much of her malice toward her nephew Don Carlos was born of the anger she felt at herself for leaving her own son behind. When he was a grown man, Don Sebastian came to Madrid to see his mother and forgive her. I think she forgave herself too.

As for the king, he was definitely not well. He could not walk at all due to the gout that inflamed his limbs, so he spent most of his time in his chambers or in his study. He was always in his movable chair and would even sleep in it at times. He had a special portal made so he could peer into the Escorial's interior church sanctuary without ever having to leave his room. He had begun to do a lot of praying.

The year 1573 was fraught with opposites. I was married to a kind man, I was back at the Spanish court with my dear princesses, and I had plenty of portraits to paint. But bad news came to me in September when I received a letter from my brother.

Dearest Sofi,

It is with a heavy heart that I must tell you of Father's passing. He died two weeks ago, peacefully in his sleep. I would have written sooner, but I have been preoccupied with the burial and putting his affairs in order. I woke up this morning and knew I could not wait a moment longer to inform you. Take heart in knowing that Papa's death was not painful. We said good night to him after an evening of singing madrigals by the composer that Mama loves

226

so much, Orlando di Lasso. You remember, "O Occhi Manza Mia." That was one of her favorites by him. Papa had the bass, I the tenor, and Mama the soprano. We all missed having you as the alto, and Papa was the one who said so. The next morning, he was gone. Please know that I am helping Mama through this time of grief and that you need not worry about making the long trek back to Cremona. Our father was a great man and he will be missed by many, not just his family, but by the entire city of Cremona. His good works will live on.

With much love,

Asdrubale
28 July, 1573

I was devastated by my father's passing. I tried to distract myself with painting, but my grief was so deep that I could not concentrate. Fabrizio worked hard to help me through that dark time. He brought me fresh-cut flowers every day. He sat with me, held my hand, and walked with me through the palace gardens. He held me in his arms when I cried. Fabrizio gave me strength to carry on with ordinary life even though I wanted at times to curl in a ball in the dark and sob.

My brother helped as well. The words that Asdrubale wrote about Papa in the letter also guided me. *His good works will live on.* I took that fact to heart, and eventually, it did comfort me. I began to see myself, and my whole life, really, as one of his good works.

Princess Isabella was about seven years old at that time. Although she was so young, she remembered how it felt to lose a beloved parent. She sat with me, much like her mother, the queen, had done years earlier when my sister Lucia died. Isabella asked me for stories about my father, so I told her my favorite one, about the time he brought paper and chalk to me and Elena when we were girls, just about her age. She listened to all this with empathy and understanding quite remarkable in someone so young. I wish she could have met my father. I think she would have loved him as a grandfather. I know he would have loved her.

As Isabella grew, I continued to share with her more stories about my father and the dreams he had, not just for me, but for all his daughters. In this way, I felt I was meeting two aims: first, to make sure my father's good works endured in the world, and second, to impress on her that her life should never be limited by others' notions of what was possible. I told her how Father had argued with his friends on many occasions about the worth of women, and how important he felt it was to educate us all. I told her how he always put me, the firstborn, first.

Isabella, wise for her years, understood. We had many such talks over the next few years and our bond—not unlike mother and daughter—deepened. When the day came that she began her first monthly cycle, she came to me in tears.

"Why do I have to bleed like this?" she asked me.

I'd had the same question my whole life, and all I knew was that it was simply part of being female. I told her it had to do with the female body's ability to bear children.

"Well, I don't like it," she said.

I remember smiling and thinking, *No one does. Absolutely no one.*

When Isabella was twelve, she asked me to paint her portrait. She was not much younger than her mother had been when she came across the Alps to marry the king. Of course, I agreed. We dressed her in a fine cream-colored silk gown with elaborate brocade sleeves and an intricately-crafted lace collar. She wore a velvet hat encrusted with pearls and gold braid.

I showed her in a pose similar to the one her mother took in the portrait of 1563. Isabella's right hand rested on the back of a chair. The face looking at me during our sessions was so much like her mother's that it took my breath away. On her finger, she wore the ruby ring that her mother had worn in her portrait. I could hardly believe this budding young woman was the daughter of my long-ago friend.

Around that time, Coello, the court painter, softened his attitude toward me. Perhaps in his mind, I was no longer a threat to him because I was married. He acted with much less contempt toward me, and I was grateful for that. I continued to assist him with the many portraits of nobles coming and going from court. While he never actually complimented my work, I think he valued my help, and I no longer tried to undermine his efforts by withholding information from him or hiding his tools. As my sister had said to me in her humble way at the convent in Mantua, "It can take a long time, but Good always wins." I came to understand that she was right.

In the spring of 1578, Queen Anne gave birth to a son, Philip III. This birth marked the beginning of a jubilant new era, and the king became noticeably happier, as if a great weight had been lifted from his shoulders. At last, the Spanish throne had an heir apparent. There was great happiness at court and a reason to celebrate.

But in our personal lives, the pendulum swung back to sadness when Fabrizio received news at the end of that same year that his father was gravely ill. He was called to return to Sicily. While Fabrizio was prepared to go home alone, he expressed the desire to have me with him. He had been my solace when I needed him. How could I not accompany my husband home?

I explained to the king that I needed to depart once again, and of course, since I did not really belong to him anymore, he agreed. While our first trip to Sicily had been jubilant, the second trip—just seven years later—had death on our heels, chasing us down.

DEATH CHASING

Just before Fabrizio and I left Madrid, I received a letter from Asdrubale telling me he was on his way to Genoa to collect some new batches of Latin manuscripts he planned to translate. So it happened that when we passed through Genoa, I was able to see my brother. When he learned that we were on our way to Sicily, he asked if he could join us. For a long time, he had been doing research on the circle of thirteenth-century poets that had gathered around Giacomo da Lentini. I was worried about him leaving my mother alone in Cremona for so long, but he assured me that she would be happy to know that he and I were together. He sent word home to her and the three of us left Genoa together.

When we arrived in Paternò, we quickly learned that my father-in-law was doing much better than he had been at the time the summons was sent. This was good news, and it did not take long for Fabrizio and me to agree that now that we had left Spain for a second time, we ought to stay in Sicily and resume our life there. We were able to secure a house not far from the one we had lived in for a year at the beginning of our marriage.

The new house was smaller, but quite cozy. Best of all, it had a spare room for Asdrubale, who chose to stay with us for a while. My plan was that one day, I would use that room as my studio. We reclaimed all the furnishings that had been stored after we left Paternò. Fabrizio's parents gave us some other items we needed, like bedding, dishes, and silverware. They even helped us locate a housemaid and a stableboy. We were settled in our new home in late December and were able to celebrate Christmas Eve Mass with Fabrizio's parents at the nearby church. It was a joyous time, and as 1579 began, I felt blessed.

By mid-January, however, Fabrizio began to complain that his arms and legs felt as though they were filled with lead.

"I am getting old, Sofi," he said.

I tried to convince him that this feeling was due not to his age, but was more likely due to the weariness that comes from travel, worry, and too much happening too fast. But soon, all Fabrizio wanted to do was lie in bed and sleep. The initial aches got much worse and my poor husband complained of terrible pain in his head and his extremities. He also developed a fever.

Whatever he had, it was not the plague. I had lived through two waves of that horrid sickness during my long life—the worst when I was in Milan in the late 1550s—and this was not that. This was something I had never seen before. When a violent cough set in, I called for a doctor, but he, too, was puzzled by the mix of symptoms. He advised me to do my best to keep my husband comfortable. Fabrizio lost his appetite, so I tried to give him a little broth each day. All I could do was keep a cool cloth on his forehead and hold his hand. A few more days went by and instead of improving, he got worse. One morning, he awoke from sleep having trouble breathing. He could not speak. I felt as though I was watching him slip into an abyss.

All I could think at the time was, *How could this be happening?* Within two weeks of the first signs that something was wrong, he fell into a deep sleep. And then, he simply did not wake up. I am not sure how much pain he suffered as his life drained out of him. I, on the other hand, suffered a great deal, as I had been powerless to save him.

Fabrizio and I had been together for seven good and peaceful years. I could not believe that I had become a widow in the blink of an eye. If not for Asdrubale's presence, I might have taken my own life, because truly, without Fabrizio, I did not know what I was going to do.

ENDING AND BEGINNING

The sun seemed to mock my grief by shining brightly in a crystalline blue sky on the day we buried my husband in the Moncada family cemetery. My mother-in-law gave me a black lace widow's veil, and we stood together hand-in-hand as Fabrizio's casket was lowered into the earth.

"It should have been me," Signor Moncada said, tears in his eyes.

Signora Moncada embraced me and said, "You made him a very happy man, Sofonisba. I am so sorry you must endure this loss."

"Signora, I lost a husband, but you lost a son," I said. "Grief does not pick a winner. We both lost someone important to us."

That very afternoon I sat down to write a letter to King Philip to tell him what had transpired. It took several weeks, but eventually I received a letter in the king's own hand, expressing his sympathy and inviting me to return to court.

With my father and now my husband both gone, I felt that perhaps I had no other choice. But my brother thought differently. One evening over dinner, Asdrubale explained.

"Settle things as quickly as you can," he said. "Then come home. It would make Mama so happy, Sofi. And me, too. You belong with us in Cremona."

Even though I would have been happy to see the princesses again, I knew they would soon be married and would no longer live in the palace. The more I thought about it, I was not sure that returning to the Spanish court was really in my best interest. It did not take much to convince me that Asdrubale's idea was truly the better choice.

My brother wanted to remain in Sicily for a while to continue his research on the Sicilian poets. He offered to close up the house for me, to take that responsibility off my hands.

"You can go home as soon as you like, or do you want to stay with me?" he asked.

"I think I need to leave behind all the sadness and go back to Cremona and Mama."

"And do you mind traveling alone?"

His question was important for me to consider. Women traveling alone are suspected of evil-doing. *Where is her husband, her father, her chaperone?* People whisper and are loath to imagine a woman might have a plan of her own. What's more, I had never traveled alone before.

"I think I can do it. I am ready to go."

The next day, I booked myself a ticket for a sea voyage from Palermo to Livorno. From there, I would hire a coach to take me to Cremona. It was time for me to go home.

DEPARTURE

On the morning that I was to set sail, Asdrubale took me and my three *cassoni* to the dock to board the *Sant'Agata*. The quay was bustling with travelers and porters loading a number of different ships that were heading to many different ports.

"I will make sure your things are put into the hold," he said.

"Thank you, my darling Asdrubale. Good luck with your research."

"Goodbye, dear sister. Travel safe."

After a quick embrace, I made my way up the plank and onto the ship. When I reached the deck, I looked back at the dock and waved at my brother. He put his hand to his lips and sent me a kiss. I sent one back to him.

When I turned, I was met by a dark-haired young man with deep blue eyes. He stood on the ship's deck and looked to be about my brother's age. He reached out his hand to me.

"Signora Anguissola?" he said.

I took his hand in mine. "I am she."

"Welcome aboard the *Sant'Agata*. I am Captain Orazio

Lomellino, at your service."

Orazio Lomellino looked awfully young to be a ship's captain, but his demeanor was strong and confident.

"Our journey to Livorno should be about five or six days at most. I hope you will be comfortable, and that you will let me know if you need anything. I will have my deckhand, Pietro, show you where your cabin is."

And so I went below deck with Pietro to find my cabin.

I was happy to see that I had a small window, which allowed me to peek out at the world, even if that world would soon be only the sea. My cabin was on the side of the ship that faced the dock, and I could see Asdrubale talking to two porters. He handed them coins to load my *cassoni* onto the ship. He could not see me, so I did not attempt to get his attention. I just took comfort in knowing that my brother was taking care of me and that I would eventually see him again in Cremona.

Before too long, I felt the ship begin to move. I closed my eyes and prayed for a safe sea journey on the *Sant'Agata* with Captain Orazio Lomellino at the helm.

NORTH STAR

My first two days at sea were strange and lonely. The sea was rough and it was all I could do to keep down a little bread and water. I spent all my time in my tiny cabin under a woolen blanket. During the second night of the trip, I awoke from a terrible dream.

I dreamed that I was with Asdrubale and we were playing on the banks of the River Po. In real life, I am eighteen years older than my brother, but in the dream, we were much closer in age, both about ten. It was at first a beautiful, sunny day and we were enjoying ourselves immensely, looking for pebbles along the river's edge and chasing frogs.

At some point, the weather changed and the sky grew dark. Heavy rain pelted us and the river quickly began to swell and churn. Asdrubale, just a few feet away from me, lost his footing and was pulled into the swiftly moving water. I tried to run to him, but my feet were held by mud and I could not move. Flailing, he called my name, but I could not help him. I could only watch, helpless as he drifted farther and farther away.

Then, some brambles in the water caught him and held him in place. I managed to extract myself from the sucking mud and drag my way to him as the rain continued to batter us. I came so close, but just as our fingers touched, the water surged and pulled my brother into the current. I could not grasp him and he was swept away.

I awoke with my heart pounding, remembering the look of terror on his face. In time, my breathing slowed and I knew my dear brother was safe, just as I had left him in Palermo. But the dream left me with a feeling of being utterly alone in the world. I missed Fabrizio. I missed my father. I missed my girls in Spain, and I missed my brother who had stayed in Sicily while I ventured on alone.

I needed air. I put on my cloak and felt my way in the dark through the cabin level of the ship and onto the deck. Standing there in the middle of the vast sea in the middle of the night, the sky bejeweled by stars took my breath away. It was the most beautiful tapestry I had ever seen. The firmament.

"Signora Anguissola!" Captain Lomellino's voice startled me. "Are you unwell?"

I pulled my cloak around me tightly. I did not want the captain to see me in my nightclothes. "I'm fine, thank you."

"You have been below deck since we left port, and I was starting to worry about you. It was my plan that if I did not see you tomorrow, I was going to knock on your door and make sure you would come up here for some sunshine and fresh air."

"As you can see, I came of my own accord," I said.

"Yes, you did. Are you sure you are all right?"

"I am truly fine. Thank you."

The captain looked up at the night sky. "I suppose now I can show you the starshine instead. That is a different kind of light for the soul."

"What kind of light would that be?" I asked.

"Ah, Signorina. The light of the stars is very ancient. And not only that, but taken together, the stars tell us stories about the gods and goddesses of long ago."

"Mythology," I said.

"Exactly, mythology. The belt of Orion, the chair of Cassiopeia, and Pegasus, the winged horse. The two bears, Ursa Major and Ursa

Minor. Without the star at the end of the tail of the Little Bear, I would not know how to get us home."

"The North Star?" I had heard of this and I suddenly had the urge to make sure this ship's captain knew I was learned.

"Exactly. The North Star. That is what all ship captains use to guide our ships home. See it?"

He pointed to a spot in the sky where there were so many stars that at first I did not know which one he was pointing to.

"I'm not sure. Where is it?"

"You see the body of Ursa Major? Those stars that make a kind of rectangle shape?"

I nodded.

"Imagine a line that connects the two stars on the edge of the rectangle, and follow the line straight up until you come to the pole star. You see?"

I did indeed see. I could not believe that I was nearly fifty years old and no one had ever shown me the North Star, or that I had never looked for it on my own.

"And if we follow that star, we get home?"

"Yes. Sailors use that star to get our bearings, to know if we are on course. It is a real gift from God, the North Star."

I pulled my cloak around me a bit tighter.

"Would you like to sit down, Signora?"

Captain Lomellino offered me a little stool, so I sat. He sat too.

"How many times have you sailed this sea?" I asked.

He looked at his feet and chuckled. "I have lost count. Do you think that is strange that I don't know?"

"No, I don't think it is strange at all. I understand very well. I can't tell you how many paintings I have painted."

He smiled and we were quiet then. I wanted to ask him many questions. *When did you become a sea captain? What do you love most about the sea?* Instead, I said nothing and just listened to the sound of the wind in the sails.

Being quiet with him under the sea of stars was not unpleasant at all. After a while, I started to feel very sleepy and a little chilled, too.

"I should go back to my cabin," I said.

The captain stood and helped me to my feet. "Good night, Signora. Tomorrow, if you wish, we can meet here again and you

235

can tell me all about painting."

"Painting. Yes. Tomorrow."

"Tonight, I hope you sleep well." he said.

"Good night, Captain Lomellino."

"Good night, Signora."

I returned to my cabin and thought about my dream of losing Asdrubale to the raging river. I realized the person I wish I could have saved was my dear Fabrizio. I had to accept that my husband was gone and that his death was not my fault.

Safe under my blanket and feeling the gentle rocking of the sea, I turned my mind to the North Star and drifted to sleep with thoughts of setting a new course.

FRESH GIFTS

The next morning, I felt better than I had the first two days, and I went up to the deck to feel the sun on my face. I found the two stools that Captain Lomellino had set out the night before still in the same spot. I took my seat and looked out over the railing of the ship at the expanse of water and the horizon in the distance, where the water met the sky.

The ship's crew members were mostly young lads. They moved swiftly about the deck, winding and rewinding rope, carrying bundles, mopping up water that had come over the side in the night. I saw the deckhand Pietro, the one who had helped me find my cabin the first day. He nodded to me and went on with his tasks. Captain Lomellino, who had come up behind him, patted the young deckhand on the shoulder before calling out to me.

"Signora Anguissola!" he said. "I am happy to see you up and about."

"Thank you, Captain," I said. "I feel much better."

"I'm glad. This is for you." He had a basket in his hands and removed the cloth to present me with bread, cheese, and figs. "Normally, Pietro would have brought this to you, but I wanted to deliver it myself and make sure you were all right."

"How kind of you. Thank you."

"Eat, and enjoy the view. I will see you later." Then Captain Lomellino returned to his duties.

I ate a fig with a bit of cheese. Then I went below deck to stow the remainder for later and gather my sketchbook and some chalk. I spent the afternoon drawing the details and activities of the ship—the rigging, the sails, the deckhands moving about their tasks. It was a fascinating world and I enjoyed making sense of it with lines on paper. I looked forward to my next conversation with Captain Lomellino.

REUNITED

Pietro brought an evening meal of dried sardines, bread, and a pear to my cabin. After I finished eating, I ventured up to the deck hoping to find the captain. The stars once again filled the sky with light. The moon was only a very thin sliver, low on the horizon.

You have returned, Signora," he said when he saw me. "Welcome to the rising of the new moon."

"Thank you. How lovely that such a small sliver still sends a path of light over the sea."

"I never tire of looking at the moon making its journey up and down the night sky. Whether waxing or waning, the moon is my faithful companion."

I had never heard a man speak of things so poetically, not even my dear father.

The captain cleared his throat. "Well, enough about the moon. Tonight, if I recall, our subject is painting."

"Yes," I said, thinking for a moment that he could tell me anything and I would want to hear more. "What would you like to know?"

"I have so many questions," he said. "I don't know where to start. First of all, how did you learn such a thing? It's not like rigging a sail to capture a person's likeness."

I told him the story of drawing Elena's face in the earth and how drawing with chalk came naturally after that. I told him how my father had sought training for me, and that my teachers taught me the recipes and techniques for painting.

"But my ability to create a person's likeness was somehow in me from the very beginning. Still, it took a great deal of practice to find my own style and to learn how to bring my sitters to life."

"How wonderful that your father arranged training for you so that you could develop the talents God gave you. Tell me more about your father and about your home."

I spoke of my father's work in helping other men start businesses and also how he used his knowledge of Roman history to teach me many things about the world. I shared my stories about climbing to the top of the clock tower and exploring with Elena along the River Po.

"What about you?" I said. "Tell me about your family."

"My memories of home are not so happy," he said. "My father was a ship's captain too, and he was often gone for months at a time. My mother cried often, raising four children by herself. I vowed I would never be like him. So, while I followed him in his profession, I have never married."

The sound of the waves lapping against the side of the ship took on a regular cadence, almost like a musical composition.

"Your family name, Anguissola," he said. "That is Latin for 'lone snake,' is it not?"

"Indeed it is."

"If I may share something very personal with you, I think it is a name that applies well to the way I have lived my life," he said. "For so long, I have been quite alone in the world. Do you feel that way about your name? Is it a reminder to you of who you are?"

"Very much so, yes," I said. "I have felt set apart from others my entire life."

The captain nodded and then turned to look out into the darkness.

"I should probably go to my cabin before the sea lulls me to sleep here on the deck," I said.

He held out his hand to me and said, "Thank you for sharing your stories of home, Signora. And thank you for listening to me."

I took his hand in mine and said, "You are welcome." Then we said good night.

As I lay in bed, I wondered if it was wrong of me to be attracted to the captain. The spark I felt when I was in his presence reminded me of the way I had felt when I was Signor Campi's student and held hands with Nico. Part of me felt ashamed to allow such a feeling for a man so soon after Fabrizio's death. Another part of me felt elated.

238

I fell asleep feeling not so much the lone snake, but rather—for lack of a better word—reunited.

On our last night at sea, I ventured up to the deck once again and found the captain standing at the railing, peering off toward the dark horizon. I approached the railing myself, and instead of taking my customary seat, I stood next to him.

"Signora Anguissola, we will arrive in Livorno soon," he said. "And I..." He cleared his throat. "What I mean to say is that I hope Livorno will not mark the end of our conversations. If it would suit you, Signora, I would like to see you again."

It was exactly what I had wished for but could not express. "Yes, I would like to see you again, too." My heart was pounding so hard in my chest that I was sure he must hear it. "But, please, would you call me Sofi?"

"Sofi," he said. "And you must call me Orazio." Then he took my hands in his and brought them to his lips.

I saw in his eyes that we shared more than being two people alone in the world. Once this bond blossomed between us, there was no turning away from the joy of being together.

YES

Within a month after my return to Cremona, Orazio came to visit me and meet my mother. He arrived at our house with a beautiful maiolica bowl filled with artichokes, and he looked every bit as handsome as I remembered him, maybe even more so.

"Sofi told me that you are fond of artichokes," he said to my mother.

"This sea captain of yours is quite wonderful," she said, taking the bowl.

"That he is," I said, taking his hand in mine.

On that first day in Cremona, I took Orazio on a walk through the town. I wanted him to see Sant'Agata church since it shared the name of his ship. It is one of the oldest churches in the city. He admired the sculptural decoration and the stately Ionic columns on the front portico. We strolled to the city center and spent some time wandering in the market. He bought pistachios, and we sat on a bench in the shade of the Torrazzo.

"Would you like to walk to the top of the clock tower with me?" I asked.

"If you think I am up to the challenge?"

He laughed so easily that any fear I had of our reunion faded away.

I hadn't made that walk in quite some time and the climb was not as easy for me as it had been when I was younger. We stopped many times in our ascent and looked through the tower windows, surveying the countryside around Cremona.

When we finally arrived at the top, I was quite out of breath.

"Let's rest for a moment," he said.

High above the world, Orazio took my hands in his and looked into my eyes.

"Sofi, I would like you to come to Genoa and marry me."

The statement—so direct, so full of urgency—made my legs falter. The year was 1580 and I was nearly forty-eight years old. Orazio was twenty years younger than I was. But he wanted to be with me. And I wanted to be with him. Because I no longer had a father, no one in my life needed to approve of this union. It was up to me to decide.

"Yes, I will marry you. Yes!"

A SECOND MARRIAGE

Orazio and I were wed in Genoa. We had a simple ceremony at San Siro on 22 May, 1580. Asdrubale was home from Sicily by then, and he and my mother made the journey from Cremona to be with us. I was pleased that my brother had made it possible for Mama to be present for this happy occasion. No one from my family had been in Madrid with me when I married Don Fabrizio. This new wedding, quiet as it was, brought true joy to my heart.

After the ceremony, we went to Orazio's house on the Carubeo Auri Genue, the place that would become my new home, and we celebrated in the courtyard with a meal that Orazio prepared for us himself. He grilled a sea bass he had caught early that morning, sprinkled it with roasted pine nuts, and served it with olives and artichoke hearts. We also had plenty of wine. I could tell that Mother was pleased by his caring and kindness, not to mention his cooking abilities.

"You know," she said. "Too often in this world, marriage is not about choice or true love. Your father and I did not marry because we loved each other. Our union was good for the businesses of our fathers."

I refrained from asking my mother to say more, but Orazio was not so hesitant. "What was that like?" he asked.

"Luckily, we learned to love one another. As Sofi will tell you, Amilcare Anguissola was an admirable and caring person. Easy to love."

Yes, that was true. My father had a big heart, and being near him made others want to respond accordingly. The fact that my mother and father learned to love one another over time is not surprising, nor is it a unique story. Many people manage to do this.

But sometimes, love really does come first.

Paola

It has been such a joy to hear the story of how Sofi and Orazio met. I am also delighted to learn that Sofi's brother had an interest in Lentini and the Sicilian poets. The other day, Sofi and I were sitting on her terrace in the morning sun, preparing to transcribe. I asked her if she knew what had happened to Asdrubale's research on this topic. She said she did not, but she suggested that we write to him to find out.

"What a wonderful idea!" I said. Just then, I felt the flow of water between my legs. I told Sofi what was happening.

"Giulia! Giulia, come quickly," Sofi called out. Giulia came right away and saw me bending forward.

"Signora Paola, are you all right?"

"The baby is on its way," I said. Feeling the first stab of pain, I grabbed my belly. "Giulia, run and ask Francesco to bring Fabia in the carriage."

"Wait," Sofi said. "Before you do that Giulia, please take Paola to my bed."

So with Giulia's help, I shuffled to Sofi's bed and waited for Fabia to come and serve as my midwife for the seventh time. Sofi sat with me and held my hand. I tried to keep myself distracted from the recurring pain by talking. "Do you remember the words of Signor Campi, Sofi?"

"Which words are those, my dear?"

"You remember. You told me that when he was teaching you how to grind lapis lazuli, he said, 'Take a deep breath and press down hard!'"

"Of course I remember."

"I have thought of his words every time I have given birth."

We laughed together at that thought, and before too long, Francesco and Fabia arrived. My husband stood back, but he did not leave the room. As with all my other deliveries, he sat nearby and bowed his head in prayer.

I had already survived six easy labors. Thankfully, this one was no different. Within just three hours, I pushed the child out into the world.

"It's a girl!" Fabia announced.

She cleaned the baby, wrapped her, and laid her in my arms. At first, all I could say was, "You are here, you are here."

Sofi and Francesco were smiling with tears in their eyes on either side of the bed.

"Oh, my little one, you are so beautiful," Francesco said to our daughter. "We already know what your name is."

"Sofonisba," I said.

"Welcome, tiny one," Sofi said, taking her namesake into her arms.

Sofonisba

Once Orazio and I married, we settled into the house on the Carubeo Auri Genue, and he let it be known throughout the city that I was available to paint portraits. The 1580s was the decade in which my early premonition about living and thriving in Genoa came true. In Genoa, I transformed from "the maiden painter from Cremona" to a well-known and sought-after artist. I set up my studio on the upper floor of our house, and soon commission requests began. My husband also secured a permit from the city administrators that allowed me to offer drawing lessons to the sons—and even daughters!—of Genoese minor nobles. I never had a lot of students, but over the years I had a few, and that was enough to confirm that I truly was a Maestra.

I suggested to Orazio that we occasionally open the house to guests for evenings of wine and conversation. It seemed to me that together, Orazio and I could build a strong and vibrant community of artists and thinkers. We hosted writers and weavers, silversmiths and shipbuilders, musicians and merchants who sold everything from bread to books. I made a special invitation to the women of Genoa so that men were not the only voices. Topics like the defeat of the Spanish Armada or the pillaging of gold from the Americas led to heated discussions, as did new developments in poetry, music, and art. Everyone had an opinion, so it seemed, and I wanted to hear them all.

"I have never before been so eager to entertain the company of others," my husband told me one evening after a particularly spirited gathering. "You have made me a new man, Sofi."

It pleased me to know I had brought joy to Orazio's life. I was reminded of the days long ago in Cremona when Papa held court with his friends on the terrace, and I was just a young girl listening to every word. Now, I was an old woman and an active participant in such gatherings. At last, I had a place at the table.

Even in the midst of all this lively activity with new friends and new ideas, death was quietly lurking. In 1584, I received a letter from the Mother Superior at the Convent of the Holy Virgin at San Vincenzo telling me that Elena had died. She was only fifty years old. My dear sister, who had once asked me to draw a likeness of her face in the earth, was gone. I sometimes wonder what I would have become if she had not made that request. Would Papa have ever seen that I had an artistic inclination? Would I have been given the opportunity to study with Signor Campi? Although Elena and I had our differences when we were growing up, her spirit was always a comfort to me.

Like Papa, my sister died in her sleep, and I hoped that meant she did not suffer. Her body was interred in the convent cemetery, and I knew that soon I would journey to Mantua to put flowers on her grave. I left for Mantua, and along the way, I stopped in Cremona to gather Mama and Asdrubale. The three of us went together to sit at Elena's graveside and let our grief flow. I'm sure I was not the only one who saw how small our family had become.

One of the many benefits of settling in Genoa was that I was close enough to Cremona to return home on quite a few occasions. Mama was getting older, and while she seemed to be in good health, I knew death could take her any time. I tried to visit as often as I could between my many painting commissions to let her know how much I loved her.

On one of my trips home, I brought some sheet music by her favorite composer, Orlando di Lasso. She had a special place in her heart for him—not only because of his music but because she also admired his life story. At the age of twelve, he had been kidnapped on three occasions by different choirmasters, all of whom were desperate to have him sing in their choirs. He grew to be a choirmaster himself, but more importantly a composer of extraordinary music for voice.

Mama's favorite work by di Lasso was called "O Occhi Manza Mia," O Eyes of My Beloved. One evening, we sang it over and over, enjoying each verse and the yearning chorus of the love-struck suitor.

"This song makes me think of your father," she said. "I miss him so."

That evening still shines bright in memory. Mama sang soprano, I sang alto, and Asdrubale, tenor. If Papa had been alive, he would have taken the bass, but missing Papa, we enlisted the gardener, Niccolo, to stay late and join us, enticing him with wine and olives. Together, the four of us sang madrigals far into the night. I will never forget how Mama's eyes shone in the candlelight as she sang.

As it happened, that visit was the last time I saw her alive. Before I left, she gave me a bundle of things she had embroidered—pillows, table runners, a man's doublet.

"For Orazio," she said. "Take good care of that fine man."

"I will, Mama. I promise," I said.

I was not in Cremona when she died. I learned about her passing in a letter from Asdrubale. He told me that on the night she died, they had said their usual "good night" to one another and that when morning came, she was gone. Just like with Papa and Elena, Mama's death was apparently peaceful. I am grateful that for a short while, I lived close enough to my mother to sing with her.

FIRST TEACHER

Returning to Cremona regularly in those years also gave me the chance to see my first teacher, Signor Campi. He had continued to paint in Milan for many years, but he eventually retired and returned to Cremona. On the day I visited him, he was grieving the loss of Signora Campi, who had died not long before. I was sorry that I did not have the opportunity to reunite with her before her passing.

I hope the time I spent with Signor Campi in conversation that day did a little something to lessen the pain of his loss. We sat together in the quiet of San Sigismondo church with his paintings all around us, and I mourned the loss of two mothers: my own and Signora Campi, who treated me like a daughter when I lived in her home. I was also reminded of the day when Elena and I had sat on the floor of the church arguing about my presumptions to be a creator.

"What is it about the creative life," I asked my old teacher, "that seems to take hold of a person? How does this happen to some people and not everyone?"

"I think the spark is there in all of us, but not everyone answers the call," he said.

"It is harder for women, though. We are not allowed to answer the call."

"Yes, you were lucky to have a father who recognized that you had talent. But don't lose sight of the fact that you put in a great deal of effort, Sofonisba. You worked hard."

"You know, I had the opportunity to pass much of what I learned from you to a young woman painter at the Spanish court, the daughter of Alonso Coello. Teaching her helped me to better understand my craft."

"Having a willing student is always a helpful enterprise. You helped me in that way. Did you know that?"

"I did not," I said. I had never realized that I might have been a help to Signor Campi, but as soon as he said it, I understood completely.

"I think there is a sense of responsibility that comes with the creative life," I said. "And that spark needs to be passed on."

"I think you are correct in that, dear Sofonisba."

In that instant, I realized that I had become the teacher. We were both artists, each walking our own distinct paths.

"Mark my words, Sofonisba Anguissola," he said. "One day, more people will know your name than know mine. You have lived up to your name, the Lone Snake! I have been a minor name in Cremona and Milan. You are making history. If people know my name, it will only be because I was, for a short time, your teacher."

In 1588 I received word that Alonso Sánchez Coello had died at court. I had hoped to hear that Coello's daughter, Isabel, would take her father's place as official court painter. She was a skilled and sensitive artist, and having worked side by side with her father for many years, she held a respected place at the court. But instead of passing the torch to the daughter, Coello's male assistant, Juan Pantoja de la Cruz—who came to help after I left—took over the role.

And although Coello was never a friend to me, his daughter most certainly was. I was well aware that a father's death is never an easy thing, so I made sure to send a letter of condolence to Isabel. I also wanted to thank her for having so often helped me with preparing canvases and grinding pigments. In return, she wrote:

Dear Sofi,

What a happy surprise to receive your recent letter. I am glad to know that the years are treating you well and that you continue to paint in Genoa. Thank you for your kind words about the passing of my father. I know he never paid you the respect that you deserved, nor did he ever acknowledge your remarkable abilities as a painter. But they were impossible to miss, your abilities, and I know he saw them. I am grateful that while you were here at the Spanish court, I was able to learn from your knowledge and your example.

Not being named the new court painter came as no surprise to me, although secretly I hoped I would be proven wrong in my expectation. I have not let my disappointment stop me from drawing every day, and I have been working on a series of sketches of birds. Perhaps the subject is a bit odd, but they are fascinating creatures, and so richly colored that I am eager to begin painting them. I imagine a whole flock of small canvases. So, wish me luck!

I will be forever grateful to you, Sofonisba, for the guidance you provided me over the years. Because of you, I know I can do the work that I desire to do, even if no one else sees any value in it. If my work gives me joy, then that is enough.

Best regards to you always,

Isabel Coello
27 April, 1588

I was deeply moved by Isabel's letter. There is nothing better in this world than to feel as though something I have done has inspired someone else—especially a woman—to do what is in her heart.

COPIES

One spring day in 1595, Orazio came home from a trip to the port of Naples with a big smile on his face.

"I have something to show you, my darling, that I think will make you very happy. First, come to the table and sit," he said.

I sat and he spread before me a stack of drawings. There were several versions of Asdrubale getting his hand bitten by the crab and some of my sisters as they appeared in *The Chess Game.* There were also quite a few versions of one of my self-portraits, the one in which I sit at the clavichord. And yet I had not drawn a single one.

"Copies?"

"Yes, copies. Of your work, my love."

I was glad my husband had suggested that I sit down. To know that one's work has been copied is one of the greatest compliments there is. Being copied means that someone wants to keep your work in mind, wants to learn from your example. As I looked more carefully, I could see the drawings were not all by the same hand. To think that many aspiring artists had seen my work—or seen drawings of my paintings—and then felt moved to make their own copy was truly a marvelous and unexpected revelation.

"Where did you find these?"

"There is a bookseller in Naples. Whenever time permits, I visit him when I pass through there, to see what new books he might have. And when I paid a visit to him this last trip, he said he had something special he wanted me to see."

"How did he come by these, I wonder?"

"I asked him that very question. He told me that copies of the work of famous artists come to him from various sellers quite frequently. Whenever he saw a drawing that referenced you, he purchased it, hoping that one day I would venture into the shop so he could offer them all to me. Of course, I bought the whole lot!"

I was speechless. On each drawing, somewhere on the page, the person who drew the image had written the words "after Anguissola." Seeing my own creations reflected back to me in lines drawn by many different hands, I felt as though I had arrived at some new pinnacle, a place even more elevated than the clock tower in Cremona.

"People know my name."

"Indeed they do, my love."

Except for that time long ago when Michelangelo had copied my drawing, I had no idea others had done the same. Orazio's gift showed me that I was important to other artists. For the first time, I felt as though I might actually be famous.

ISABELLA

In the autumn of 1598, word spread throughout the region that Philip II was dead. I was saddened to hear of his passing. I imagined that there would be a great deal of ceremony surrounding the king's death, with a large public memorial on the grounds of the Escorial. I wanted nothing more than to see Isabella and Catalina and make sure that in this time of grief and upheaval, my infantas were both comforted.

Isabella and I had done well over the years, staying connected through letters. Despite the great distance between us and the many years that had passed, our bond of affection for one another never faded. On the occasion of the king's death, I began drafting a letter to her, but before I could finish and give it to a courier, a letter arrived with her seal on it.

Dear Sofi,

I write today to tell you of two occurrences, one sad, one happy. It seems likely you have already heard that Father has died. Philip II is no more and I grieve. Philip III will take the throne. All the while my half brother was growing up, Father made sure that he received better attention and tutoring than Don Carlos ever received. Now, this better-educated, better-groomed boy is a man and he will be the new king. I'd say he has a good and gentle spirit, and while he is sometimes swayed by his advisers, my hope is that he will rule well.

Now, the happy news. I am to marry Prince Albert of Austria! As you know, he has been a friend to me since we were children, and now he will be my husband. Before Father died, he included in my dowry the Netherlands for Albert and me to rule together. We intend to do what we can to bring an end to the bloodshed in the region. Enough with religious and political upheaval. It is time for peace.

Dearest friend, I beg a favor of you. I will be passing through Genoa on my way north and I would like to stay with you and have you paint my betrothal portrait. Would you do this for me? You will paint something so much better than anything Pantoja de la Cruz could ever conjure. Albert is traveling separately from me, so you won't have to worry about keeping both of us! I begin the journey soon and there won't be time for you to write back. Knowing you, I am going to trust you will do this for me. I will see you in Genoa in about a month's time.

With love always,

Isabella
14 October, 1598

For Isabella's arrival in Genoa, the whole city took on a festive atmosphere. On the day that her retinue arrived, flags and flowers decorated the Via Garibaldi, and people lined the streets to wave as her carriage passed. Of the many invitations she received from noble families offering her a place to stay while in Genoa, she chose to stay with us. What an honor that was.

When she stepped out of her carriage at our home, Orazio and I were there to greet her.

"Welcome to Genoa, Princess Isabella," Orazio said, bowing deeply.

"Thank you, Signor Lomellino. You are gracious to receive me."

She turned to me. "Sofi! You haven't changed a bit."

"Well, you have!" She had grown so tall and she made a commanding presence.

"When do we begin?" she asked. "I am not going to be here as long as I would like, and I want you to have as much time as possible to make me look like a ruler."

"That won't be hard to do," I assured her. "Let's have you finish this day with some refreshment and rest. We'll start first thing tomorrow."

The next morning, we sat together in the studio. She wore a deep maroon velvet jacket decorated with a swirling pattern of seed pearls. The early light streaming in made her look all the more radiant.

"Since our time is short, I plan to keep this portrait somewhat small. I hope that is agreeable to you," I said.

"Whatever you think is right, Sofi, I will be happy. You know," she said, "when Mother died, you took her place. You raised me, and I am so proud to have an artist for a mother."

"Ah, no one could take her place." But I knew what she meant. I thought of Isabella as my daughter. I put down my paintbrush and embraced her.

Then we looked into each other's eyes for a long moment and a thought occurred to me. "Since this is most likely going to be our last goodbye, I have something for you." She gave me a quizzical look, a look I had seen on her face so many times when she was a child. "Wait here," I said.

I returned to the studio with a small box, the one Signora Campi had given me when she and Signor Campi left for Milan. In it was the heart-shaped gold locket that her mother had given her. Isabella opened the box and smiled.

"It is lovely, Sofi. Thank you."

I closed the clasp at the back of her neck and then explained the significance of the gift. "Just as I received this gold heart from someone whom I considered to be a second mother to me, so should you."

Isabella admired her new necklace in my studio mirror. "I will wear it always, and always, I will think of you."

I worked on the portrait every day. Some days I needed Isabella to sit with me, but many days, she was free to meet with various noble families, all eager to court her favor.

After two short weeks, it was time for Isabella to go. Her retinue was headed first for Milan, and then onward to the court at Brussels. When she climbed into her carriage, the streets were again full of flags, flowers, and well-wishers. And while the world beyond my door looked festive and bright, a well of sadness opened inside me. Because she was going so far away, I knew this was the last time I would see my infanta.

"Goodbye, dear Sofi," she said with tears in her eyes.

As the carriage pulled away, Orazio stood next to me and took hold of my hand. He knew how much it pained me to say goodbye. Before long, our street was silent. While I kept myself busy for the rest of the day, I found myself imagining what Isabella's life as a ruler would be like. Like her mother, Isabella was a bright light. I knew that peace would follow her wherever she went.

LAVINIA

As I had discovered when Orazio brought those copies of my work home from Naples, my art had been circulating far and wide for quite some time. It was humbling to know that my example had served to inspire other artists, some of whom, I discovered, were women. Because of my accomplishments, the few women who were making their way forward as artists occasionally wrote to me, asking for guidance or advice.

One whom I had the chance to meet was Lavinia Fontana. She learned her trade from her father, a painter in Bologna. At the end of the last century, Lavinia became known for painting portraits, religious pictures, mythological pictures, and even church altarpieces.

She wrote to me in the late 1580s requesting an introduction to King Philip, which I was happy to write. This introduction led him to commission her to paint an altarpiece showing *The Holy Family with the Sleeping Christ Child* for the Escorial.

Lavinia came to Genoa in the spring of 1604 to thank me. She was on her way to Rome from Bologna. She had been summoned by Pope Clement VIII to paint his portrait. On the day she visited me, new green buds were just coming out on the branches of the potted trees in the courtyard. We sat in the midday sun, two artists side by side, two women artists. I was so pleased to meet her.

She spoke of her upcoming commission for the pope but quickly moved to more personal topics, telling me about the new studio she planned to open in Rome and her eleven children.

"Eleven children! How do you manage all that?" I asked.

"I am lucky to have a husband who helps me," she said. "Not only does he care for our children, but he serves as my agent, making sure my commissions run smoothly and my work is well-placed."

"A helpful husband is a great blessing, indeed." I felt I could say this with firsthand knowledge, having been blessed with two supportive husbands. What I did not realize until we met is what an inspiration I had been to her.

"When I saw a sketch made from a self-portrait of you at the clavichord," she said, "it sparked me to do the same. I also had a clavichord, and playing it always calmed my mind."

"I harbored a wish that my paintings of women playing music would encourage fathers to give their daughters musical training," I said. "Little did I know my painting would inspire another woman to show herself actually playing a musical instrument!"

"When I set out to tackle this same theme for my own self-portrait, I especially appreciated your inclusion of a maid in the background."

"What was it about the maid that interested you?"

"With her presence in the composition, you opened up a window on a space," she said. Lavinia pulled out a drawing from her portfolio, a sketch made from the painting. "You see?"

Indeed, I could see how she had used the presence of the maid to create a deeper and more dynamic setting for the action. The maid approaches the artist from behind, holding open a book of sheet music. And beyond the maid is an alcove with a window through which daylight enters the room. The artist looks straight out with her hands on the keyboard. She looks as though she is ready to stand and welcome her guest, the viewer.

"I think you far surpassed me in creating a believable space," I said. I held up my glass of wine to her and she blushed.

Then she raised her glass and said, "To women who create space!"

"To women who create space!" I replied.

"Well, I will tell you this," she said, putting the sketch away. "That is the one painting I am most proud of, and I'm not sure I would have ever thought to do it if I had not seen a sketch of your painting."

"You honor me, Signora," I said, raising my glass again. "To women who inspire each other."

"To women who inspire."

We sat quietly then, and I pondered just how strange we were, and also how similar. I offered her the plate of figs.

"Tell me about the controversy over your paintings of female nudes. I think there is one of the goddess Minerva that has caused a great stir?"

She laughed. "So, you have heard about that."

"It has been a subject of many conversations, yes." Lavinia's inclusion of female nudes in her paintings had caused much uproar among some of the men at the gatherings that Orazio and I had been hosting. They thought it was scandalous for a woman artist to paint a nude woman.

"You know, I simply asked my sisters and cousins to model for me. It was something that I felt ought to be in the repertoire of a woman painter. And why not?" she said. "Clearly, male artists have painted the female nude more than once. Why shouldn't women painters do this as well?"

"Why shouldn't they, indeed?" We raised our glasses again.

I was sorry to say goodbye to Lavinia, but she was on her way to meet the pope, so it was not right to detain her any longer, though if I could have done so, I would have. She was the first woman I met whose life mirrored mine.

In 1614, I learned that Lavinia had died. She was the first woman artist to paint large scale religious paintings for churches, something

255

I had always dreamed of doing. Before her death, Lavinia was elected to the renowned Academy of San Luca in Rome, a rare honor for a woman. It was heartening to know that another woman artist was not only making her mark, but surpassing me in fame and fortune.

Paola

Sofi and Orazio have been our neighbors for several months now. It's a blessing that our houses are so close, but while I can easily walk the distance, Sofi cannot manage it. She's still lively in mind, but at eighty-eight, walking is not so easy for her anymore. On Sunday afternoons, Orazio brings her to our house in their new carriage so she can visit little Sofi and I can write more of her story.

Recently, we've gone deeper into how she views her place in the history of art. As Sofi speaks, I hear a litany of women singing to me through time—Vittoria, Veronica, Lavinia, and Sofi herself, each woman passing her song to the women who follow. All these women have gone outside the role that men would assign them. Such an endeavor is not easy and many men will stand in the way. But, some men—Amilcare Anguissola, Signor Campi, Orazio, my own Francesco—will find a way to help. I have learned much from Sofi's example. I hope that someday, I can share her stories with a wider world.

When she comes today, I will tell her my idea about this chorus of women, this lineage of brave mothers, daughters, and sisters who sing to us through time.

X

I yearn to sing, make peace in this world,
a fine and fearless dance my mother taught.
Because life's greatest gifts cannot be bought
and a heart wide open will rise and whirl.

The right steps arrive, as the dance unfurls,
to a stirring tune that defies all thought.
Only love makes light, makes the load less fraught,
as my mother shared her wisdom like pearls.
In my own aching soul, this truth I know,
sorrow will raze the mind so hard it burns
and love, once gone, creates a wound that stings.
I wish she could have stayed. She had to go.
But to a grieving heart, light will return,
and as with each new song, I rise on wings.

Sofi and I sat in the shade of the olive trees near the edge of the terrace, with little Sofi sound asleep in the cradle between us.

"I wonder if you see yourself as part of a lineage, Sofi," I said.

"A lineage," she repeated. "What do you mean?"

"Not a familial lineage, but a lineage of wisdom and strength passed from one woman to another over time."

A breeze rustled the leaves of the olive tree, and high in its branches, a sparrow sang. "I haven't ever considered that." She paused for a moment. "But I can say that all my life, I have seen women help women. Maria helped me. I helped Isabel. I remember when I first met you fifteen years ago, I saw a young woman who was determined to help me by carrying my words into the future."

"I am still determined. I hope that is what I will do, dear Sofi."

"I know, and I am grateful."

"Do you think men are standing in our way?" I asked. "There are so many things we cannot do of our own volition. We cannot own property, start a business, decide our own fate."

"Are men purposely standing in our way? Some men, perhaps. But not all men. Not my father, nor your father."

"My father? He still resists my wish to pursue the printing press. He says he has his reasons, but I don't understand his reluctance. I need his help and blessing in this matter, but he will not give it."

"I think one day, he will."

Sofi looked up into the branches of the tree and I waited patiently as she formulated her thoughts.

"Do you remember long ago the story I told you of the Bona Dea?"

"I do—the Good Goddess."

"Yes, the Good Goddess. It was Papa who told me about her and how—in ancient Rome—her sanctuary was open only to women. It was a place that men could not go."

"I remember you told me how much that surprised you when you were young."

"It did. I think it was Papa's way of telling me that women can join together their efforts and gradually regain some power in the story of the world. In order to do this, I think we must always look for the good in all things."

"That reminds me of the words that Elena once had for you. Do you remember? I have read it in your manuscript many times."

"I do," Sofi said, recalling her sister's words. "'We must always seek the good, or as God would say, seek God.' The older I become, the more I see that to be true."

Little Sofi made a cooing sound in her cradle.

"And you see? My namesake agrees!"

"Ah, she does. I think she is also probably hungry!" I picked up my daughter and loosened my blouse to feed her.

"I do believe," Sofi said, "that someday men will recognize women as equals. I think progress is already being made."

"I hope you are right, for little Sofi's sake."

"You know, Paola, sometimes I imagine Papa and I having a conversation in which we reminisce about the time when I was young in Cremona. It is as though he is standing right in front of me, telling me how happy he is to see me and how proud he is of all that I have accomplished."

"What a lovely thing to imagine."

"Yes, and then we muse together on how much fun it would be if he could only point to my example and say to Signor Barosi, the cheese maker—the one who had so vehemently challenged my father on the topic of women being educated—'See? I told you so!'"

Today, we had a visitor from Naples, a bookseller named Marcantonio Abruzino. He is the same bookseller who once sold Orazio a stash of copies drawn from Sofi's paintings. Signor Abruzino has become fond of Rossi-Vespucci wine, which our family has been exporting to the mainland for quite some time now. Signor Abruzino wanted to meet the people in

Alcamo responsible for his favorite drink.

Orazio brought the bookseller down from Naples on the *Sant'Agata* and introduced him to Francesco. The first thing the three men did when the ship arrived this morning was head out to Alcamo to visit the vineyard. Later in the day, everyone came to our house, including Sofi, my father, and Francesco's father. We sat out on the terrace, enjoyed a large platter of olives and cheese, drank wine, and talked about the conditions in Sicily that make it such a good place to grow grapes.

"It's all about the soil," my father-in-law said.

"Well, God bless the soil of Sicily," Signor Abruzino said. He raised his glass, closed his eyes, and took a blissful sip. "I'm so grateful that you have been sending your product to Naples. I wish I could get the printers in Venice to send me their books!"

"What do you mean, sir?" Francesco asked.

"I dream of a day when I won't have to go quite so far away to acquire my inventory," the bookseller said. "I look forward to a time when more presses are operating in the South."

"Really?" I said. "Are there no printing presses in this region?"

"None!"

"That is very interesting," I said.

"What is your interest in the woes of a poor bookseller, Signora?"

I looked at my father, who avoided my eyes, but I am certain he could read my mind. "In fact," I said, tentatively, knowing full well I would upset my father, "I hope one day to operate a printing press of my own."

"Is that so?" he said.

"Yes, that is my plan." I wanted to know more from him. "How many people are needed to run a successful printing press?"

Before he could answer, my father jumped into the conversation. "My daughter has big dreams," he said, as though to apologize for my query.

Thankfully, Signor Abruzino answered anyway. "Ideally, it is best to have several people, as there are many different tasks involved in printing, not to mention the need for someone to go out and find the business."

"Find the business?" Francesco asked.

"You know, someone to go around to apothecaries, shops, theaters, and the like to find what people need. To further one's profit. Alongside the publication of books, of course."

"So, it is not just books that are created by printing presses?" I said.

"Heavens, no." Signor Abruzino took another sip of his wine. "In fact, a press can profit best by creating a whole range of ephemera from theater playbills and broadsides to shop signs and musical scores."

Musical scores. I had never thought about printing musical scores. All these years, I have only been thinking about books because I love them so much and because of my desire to print Sofi's story. It never occurred to me that there were many other things in this world that need printing.

"I love to hear the conversation of men and women sitting around a table together," Sofi interjected. "So different from the world in which I grew up."

"What world is that, Signora?" asked Signor Abruzino.

"A world in which women never spoke at the same table as the men. I believe this is changing. We can see it happening right here, today," she said.

"An astute observation, Signora. Times are changing, aren't they? Have you thought of writing a book about your life?" the bookseller asked.

"Have I thought about writing a book?" Sofi laughed. "As it happens, Paola and I are already writing it. We have been for many years."

"Now, that is a book I would like to read someday," the bookseller said. "The life of a woman artist!"

Then he turned to me and said, "When you publish this book, Signora, please let me know. I will gladly find a place for it in my shop."

"I will do that," I said, glancing at Father, who avoided my eyes.

"My wife is herself a poet," said Francesco. I think he sensed my father's discomfort and was trying kindly and gently to change the subject.

"How wonderful that you have settled here in Sicily, then, in the birthplace of the sonnet. Are you familiar with the School of Lentini?" the bookseller asked.

"Indeed, I am. I have been looking at his poems and those of others in his circle."

"Well, that is even more wonderful. When Orazio takes me back to Naples, I will send him home with a book for you. It is a series of sonnets that Lentini wrote in correspondence with other poets. I think you will find it most intriguing."

"How kind of you, Signor Abruzino. I look forward to reading it."

Evening has come and everyone else in the house is sleeping. I could not sleep and have lit the candles on my desk so I can work on the next sonnet and think more clearly about all that I heard today. Little Sofi is snug in her cradle, and as I look at her sleeping so peacefully, I can only wonder what the world will be like when she is my age. It was interesting to hear Sofonisba and Signor Abruzino talk about how the world has changed since Sofi was a girl. I wonder what other changes will come and if I might be part of that progress. Perhaps someday soon, if my father will help me start, I will be the first woman to own her own print shop.

Signor Abruzino certainly opened my eyes to what a printing press will entail and the many opportunities that I had never considered. I suppose I can forgive Father for being cautious all these years in the matter of starting a new business. I just wish he would assure me that he sees value in my dream. Perhaps what he heard today from Signor Abruzino has also opened his eyes to some new thoughts. After all, he was once a cloth merchant and now he is a vintner. My father has proven himself to be good at changing.

XI

And as with each new song, I rise on wings,
I see from high that which the future sees,
never missing the forest for the trees.
For lack of knowledge waits to strip all things
of the great delight that creation brings.
Thus, I hold myself tall when caution flees
and put no stock in prayer on bended knees,
for I have learned there are no puppet strings.
Taking my steps within this life I live,
I walk a path beyond obscurity.
Forward I go, strong in my own heart's worth,
to find the joy that only art can give.
Then as I rise and aim with certainty,
my feet stay planted firmly on the earth.

A few days after Signor Abruzino's visit, I sat across from my father at his writing desk to once again present my case.

"So, what do you think?" I said. "You heard what our new friend from Naples had to say about the lack of printing presses in our region."

"Signor Abruzino did say that."

"And yet you remain resistant," I said, feeling the heat rise from my stomach to my head.

"Paola," he said, laying his hand upon mine. "Think about the baby, your duties to your family, to Sofi."

"I do hear what you are saying, Father, but if only—"

"I also heard him say," Father continued, "that a printing press needs several dedicated workers. I know this is your dream, my darling, but you have a household full of young children, and all the men in this family are busy growing grapes and making wine. Now is not the time to put out a large outlay of money for equipment that we will not be able to put to use."

"But, Father—"

"I think it is better to wait. Perhaps when the boys are grown, a couple of them can help you in this work. Now is not the time to start a printing press. Please put this out of your mind for now."

Out of my mind? The printing press is not only in my mind, it is in my body, my heart, and my soul. But he did say "for now." Those are two words that I will not soon forget.

Francesco

I am back in Alcamo this week tending to the vines and mulling over Signor Abruzino's recent visit. The azure sky has not a single cloud, and while the sun is hot, enough breeze comes down from the mountain to cool me as I work.

As I pruned the oldest vines today, I thought about how upset Paola is with her father's lack of interest in supporting the printing press. She tells me every night how disappointed she is in her father and his lack of trust in her. I try to calm her. I wish I had the money to do this for her on my own, but the grape harvest is never assured and I cannot predict from year to year what surplus funds we might have. Still, she has been waiting her whole life for this, and I want nothing more than to make my dear wife happy. For now, I do what I can.

I wiped the soil from my hands and gathered cut vines. They'll be stored in the old stone barn to dry for fuel. Nothing is wasted here.

"Francesco!"

I looked up to see my father-in-law coming down the hill from the house. He wore a wide-brimmed hat to protect himself from the sun. He stood at the end of the row I was pruning.

"Father," I said. "The last time I saw you look so worried was when you first arrived in Sicily so many years ago with a pregnant daughter. What is troubling you today?"

"I need your advice, my friend."

"How can I help?"

"I have been telling my daughter for so many years that I cannot support her idea for a printing press."

He stooped to gather the remainder of the old vines, and we walked together up the slope toward the barn.

"Well," he said, "I want you to know that with every passing year, I am putting away the money so that one day, when I die, I can leave her an inheritance that will make it all possible."

I felt a knot twist in my stomach to hear this plan of his, to hinge the gift of the money to his death. His passing could be years away.

"Why do you not tell her?"

"Telling her now seems cruel. Knowing my intention does not take away the fact that she must continue to wait. If the money comes to her after I am gone, the gift will be a happy surprise for her."

"But if you told her you are planning to leave her an inheritance, I think she would take heart, don't you?

"I'm not sure. She is a very impatient person, my daughter."

"Well, that is true," I said. In the barn, we laid our bundles at the edge of the heap already dry enough to burn. "How can I help?"

"Talk to her for me? Assure her that one day, she will have the funds she needs to realize her dream. Please tell her to trust me in this."

"I will tell her." I reached out my hand to him, and he took it in his. "I promise."

Sofonisba

THE FUTURE

When the illustrious Flemish painter Peter Paul Rubens came to visit me in Genoa in 1618, I was sure I must be dreaming. Of course, meeting me was not the only reason for his visit. He was primarily on a diplomatic mission for his patron, Archduchess Isabella—my Isabella—who had appointed Rubens to be her court painter in 1609.

As soon as he walked into our home, he reached out his hand to me and said, "Signora Anguissola, please call me Pietro-Paolo." I found it delightful that he used an Italianized version of his own name. Rubens was a tall, thin man with reddish-brown hair and beard, sparkling brown eyes, and a stylish turned-up mustache. Sitting with Orazio and me under the lemon tree in the courtyard of our house in Genoa, he told us about the activities at the northern court.

"You can be proud of Isabella," he began. "She and Albert are leading the dialogue between the factions that will bring much-needed peace to the region."

I never doubted Isabella's intentions for reconciliation, but it was good to hear this news. Then the artist opened a portfolio and pulled out some sketches, placing them on the table.

"When I get back, I will begin full portraits of the two of them to document their roles as benevolent leaders. Isabella asked me to bring these sketches to you so you can see what I am working on."

There she was, my little infanta, in her sovereign role. My heart nearly burst with pride for all she was achieving. "These are so lovely."

"You are welcome to keep them," he said. "I have many more in my studio at home!"

"Thank you so much," I said. "I will treasure them!"

Giulia came out to the courtyard with a tray of figs, hazelnuts, and sweet cakes and three glasses of wine.

"Please, Pietro-Paolo, sit down and enjoy some refreshment," I said.

Once we had filled our plates and began to eat and drink, he said, "I have heard a great deal about you, Signora, from Isabella."

"What did she tell you?"

"She told me that you spent almost two years in Rome and that you not only met the great Michelangelo but studied with him. Tell me, what was he like?"

"Michelangelo may have been known as *Il Divino,* but he was full of humility. He was a truly kind and generous mentor."

"You know, I was born thirteen years after Michelangelo died," Rubens said. "I wish I could have met him."

I shared many of my stories about my time with Michelangelo. Rubens seemed to be especially moved by the story of the artist going back to his *Pietà* to carve his initials into Mary's sash.

"We all want to be remembered for the work we have done, don't we Signora?"

"Yes," I said. "Yes, we do."

The afternoon progressed pleasantly in his company. While Rubens talked, he shared his excitement about the many new directions taking place in Northern painting, innovations that he was certainly leading, although he maintained a quiet humility regarding his place in the shift toward a new visual expression. He talked about movement, color, and sensuous application of paint— all things that were being heralded as part of a new style that was moving away from the solid, earthbound, sharply delineated art of the last century. On the one hand, this was very interesting to me. At the same time, I worried that I was part of an era in painting that was at its end.

Every day since the day I met Rubens, I have reminded myself that everything I do connects me to the future. It may be a future that I cannot see, but still, I feel it. I know the future is waiting for me.

———————————————

Orazio

I have become old. Not so old that I cannot work, but my body tires too easily these days. I marvel at how well Sofi, who has twenty years on me, has managed. Until quite recently, she maintained a great deal of stamina. But when she found she could no longer paint, she began to show signs of her age in other ways, too.

I see how healing it is for Sofi to be around the children. Angelo and Tomasino are especially enamored of her. They constantly watch out for her, asking if she needs anything. They are natural caregivers, and I wonder if they won't grow up to be doctors one day. Or taverna owners.

Today, as Sofi and I enjoyed the sunshine on our little balcony overlooking the sea, she took my hands in hers.

"I wish I had been younger when I met you so we could have had children," she said.

I squeezed her hand. "You would have been a wonderful mother," I said. "What's the matter, dear Sofi?"

She held back her tears. "I feel like I am leaving this life and there is nothing I can do about it. I can't paint anymore, I can't write. I can't go back the other way."

"No," I said, acknowledging her pain. "We cannot go back the way we came."

"Recently, I thought I was ready to go, but suddenly now, I am not so sure. I realize I am afraid to go forward alone. Over my long life, I have grown to take pride in my name, the Lone Snake, thinking that it reflected well on my strength and ability to endure, to be a good artist. But so much of what I have done was done with the support and kindness of others."

"My dear, you are not just a good artist, you are a great artist," I assured her. "And you most definitely did that on your own. Others may have helped you, but you were responsible for developing your talent, my love. You did the work. Remember that."

"I keep thinking of a passage from near the end of Dante's *Paradiso*," she said. "In it, he talks about how Heaven does not exist in any set place, except in the mind of God."

"It is comforting to think of Heaven in that way," I said. "Not one set place, but more a thought in God's mind, burning bright with the power of love."

She turned to me and looked deep into my eyes, as though looking for an answer. "I am afraid of being alone in death," she said. "For so long, I have imagined that when I die, I will see all my sisters again. My father and my mother. Don Fabrizio. But I am starting to have doubts. What if that is not what happens? Was I such a sinner that I will be stuck in Purgatory for eons, waiting to get to Paradise?"

"Oh, Sofi." I pulled her close to me and smoothed her silver hair. "I am no theologian, nor am I a poet. I do know that the physical body cannot contain us forever. At some point, we must go back to the sea and sky. We must connect again with Creation. Please don't be afraid. I do think Dante is right that Heaven is not a place. And while I cannot tell you what it will be like for you when you go, I do know that I will miss you with all my heart. If you are afraid that your life and your name will be lost, you need not worry. I will not let that happen. Paola will not let that happen." I gave her my kerchief to dry her tears.

"Orazio Lomellino," she said, smiling. "You are so dear to me."

Paola

I was at my desk this morning, working on the next sonnet in the crown. I began with the last line of Sonnet 11: "My feet stand firmly planted on the earth," which is a fair reflection of how I view my life at this time. I am planted, waiting to blossom. I need to stop thinking my father doesn't want to help me. I think he does, but the timing is not right. I am in the planting season. Fruition will come. Just as I wrote down that thought, my dear husband came up behind me and placed a bouquet of roses between me and my notebook, like a stage actor right on cue.

"What is the occasion for this?" I asked.

"I just want you to know that I love you." He kissed the top of my head.

"I have no doubt about that, my love. What do you really want me to know?"

"I want you to have faith that your father is going to help you start the printing press someday. Just not right now."

"And how do you know this?"

"He told me so."

I brought the roses to my face and inhaled deeply.

"I will be patient, my love. Thank you. Can I tell you something else?"

"Always."

"I have an idea," I said.

"Let's bring Sofi to live here with us when Orazio is away," Francesco said, finishing my thought.

"How did you know that was my idea?"

"I know you too well, my love," Francesco said. "I know you worry about her being alone when Orazio goes out to sea, even with Giulia there.

We have the spare room, and I imagine Sofi will greatly enjoy the small balcony facing north toward the sea."

"Yes, she will. And here with us, she and I can keep working on her story easily. She will always have the children nearby, which I know brings her great joy."

"Let's make it so, my love."

Francesco

It is hard to believe, but after all these years of growing grapes and making wine, I still have it in my heart to make images. The lessons I learned from Sofi in Genoa have not left me. I am constantly framing the things I see in my mind's eye, imagining what it would look like if I could put the pictures in my head down on canvas.

Mind you, I never graduated from sketching to painting. Sofi and I talked about the processes of grinding pigments and priming canvases, but I never had the opportunity to do any of that. I gave up on the idea of making art and left Genoa too soon to gain all that I could have gained had I been able to stay and work with my teacher. But that was not what my life was meant to be. My life was meant to be here, in Sicily, in the vineyard. I am father to six sons and one daughter, husband to my wife, and partner to my father and father-in-law. What else is there for me to be? I am content.

I often think about the many different paths my life could have taken. If my mother had gotten her way when I was a child, had she not died too early, I might have been apprenticed to an artist in Florence, and who knows, I could have become a great painter. But then, I never would have had a reason to go to Genoa to seek out a teacher. If I had not been shown Vasari's *The Lives of the Artists*, I might never have heard of Sofi. If Dario had not treated me with such contempt because I was studying with a woman, I might never have stepped foot in San Siro to clear my head of his taunts. And then I would never have been standing in just the right place at just the right moment with Father Valeriano, who, for some

273

reason, knew he should introduce me to Paola.

Paola changed my life, and how lucky we are that she and I both have fathers who understood that what is best for business might actually be to put love first and let business follow. That seems to me so much better than creating marriages based on putting business first and expecting love to grow. It does happen. But I aim to put love first, and I am determined to do that for my own sons and my one precious daughter when the time comes for them to marry. Unlike most fathers, I will not be an arranger of marriages. I will encourage my offspring to make their own choices in life.

When I first went off to Genoa to study art, I went because I had the idea that I wanted to create lasting things. Growing grapes for wine seemed so transitory to me, whereas art seemed like something that could last. And it is true, art does last. But so do people and families. I can see now that the enduring thing I have made is my family. I cannot know everything my children will accomplish, but one day, they will have children of their own. I hope my legacy will be passed on through the generations.

I have taken on the task of teaching the boys to sketch. I have given all six of them, even little Asdrubale, sketchbooks. I think back to Sofi's tale of "paper and chalk," and I think about how she taught me to look at the world. The boys do seem to enjoy the opportunity to look at things with fresh eyes. Recently, Lorenzo took his sketchbook with him up Mount Bonifato to have a view looking down over the vineyard. The sketches that he made of the landscape from the perspective of the birds are quite remarkable, and I told him so.

Having Sofi in my life again makes me realize how much I have to be grateful for. I will never forget that day we sat under the olive trees and I told her about my mother. I see now all these years later that Sofi has always been like a second mother to me. How grateful I am that my mother has at last come home.

Paola

Sofi has been living with us for almost a year now. Even when Orazio is not at sea, she stays here, because it is easier for her to stay in one place. Orazio visits every day. Sofi and I no longer do much writing. Her past has caught up to her present and it seems she has no stories left to tell. And yet, as her biographer, I find there are still things worth recording. Just the other day, she told me a story that is not from her past, but from her present—right now—so of course, I added it to the manuscript.

WORDS

Little Sofi and I were playing in the garden together earlier today. As always, I was sitting in my chair and she was running about, bringing me things. Pebbles, flowers, a feather. When she brought me a stick, that gave me an idea. I wanted to show her how to draw.

"Find me another stick, dear child—a long one, please," I said.

I bent forward in my chair, as far as I could, and with the long stick that little Sofi had found for me, I was able to draw circles, squares, and triangles in the dirt. My namesake obtained her own stick and followed my lead, giggling with delight as she made shapes and lines in the earth.

I am grateful that I have been able to spend these days with little Sofi. I hope that she will grow up knowing that her life is important and that she can do whatever she sets her mind to doing. The words of my long-ago teacher, Signor Cavallaro, come back to me now:

"Never forget that your life is important, Sofonisba."

No matter how old and wise I get, I cannot stop wondering what I am leaving behind. My paintings, yes. I hope they speak for themselves. But if they are lost, misattributed, or forgotten, I have this story written down in words that will shine light on these images far into the future.

Asdrubale once told me something that the Roman poet Horace wrote: *littera script manet,* which means "the written word remains." The paintings will be there, but without the words to tell the story, the origin and meaning of the images will remain a mystery. I thank God for the lasting nature of the written word. I count on my words to stand with my paintings far into the future, into a time when I can no longer speak for myself.

Sofi's words ring true for me, too. I find that as I get closer and closer to completing the heroic crown, I know that what I write matters.

XII

My feet stay planted firmly on the earth
as I reach my arms upward to the sky
like birds, those spirits of the air that fly
and feel my grateful heart arise in birth.
The nurture of these seeds I must ensure
to harvest the wealth that comes by and by,
vowing always to do and not just try,
for only in this does my life endure.
Here is my story and these are my gifts
given to me by teachers far and near,
kept safe as a rose poised to uncurl.
I stay at last, in this place my heart lifts,
where joyous songs of love ring true and clear,
as flowers find their bloom and clouds their swirl.

Orazio

My recent conversation with Sofi and her concerns regarding the afterlife prompted me to seek out one of the church fathers at San Giorgio dei Genovesi. My mission was to secure a contract for a tomb in the church, where my dear wife's body can be laid to rest after she dies. Father Giovanni agreed to meet with me.

When I entered the church, its soaring architecture made me feel small and insignificant. This is one reason I have not found it particularly comforting to visit churches. If I am going to feel humble somewhere, I would much rather experience that feeling in the immensity of nature, not in a structure built by man. I still feel my true home is on the open sea, under the dome of the sky. That is the place that always makes me feel grateful to be alive. That is the place where I met and fell in love with Sofi.

Nevertheless, it was impossible to deny the beauty of the church, with its elegant white marble columns gracing the sides of the nave. Father Giovanni came out from behind the altar and gestured to me to follow him. He led me to a little room that was filled with spare vestments, jeweled crosiers, and stacks of gilt plates and goblets for communion.

"Welcome, Signor Lomellino. Won't you sit down? How can I help you today?"

"Thank you, Father. I would like to inquire about a tomb for my wife, the painter Sofonisba Anguissola. She is still alive at this time, but I am looking to the future."

"Signor," he said, clearing his throat. "There is no precedent for the entombment of a woman in the church."

"But my wife is a renowned artist who spent forty years of her life among the notable people of Genoa whose families contributed to the building of this church. Mine included, I might add."

"While that is all true, the fact remains that we do not bury women in the tombs within the church."

"Where do you bury them?" I asked.

"There is a graveyard a little way up in the hills. That place is for the remains of women."

"But surely, the Church can make an exception for a woman of her stature. She is far more than an ordinary noblewoman. She studied with Michelangelo and served at the Spanish court."

"It is just not possible, Signor Lomellino. I am sorry. And now, if there is no more I can help you with, I have to prepare for Sunday's Mass."

Of course, I will not mention my conversation with Father Giovanni to Sofi. But I have not given up yet. I cannot accept his answer, and I will keep asking him or someone with more authority until I am successful in achieving my wish for her.

Paola

The year is 1623, and it has been two years since Sofi moved in with us. She is getting more and more feeble as time passes. Fewer and fewer are the days that she leaves her bed. Then two weeks ago, a letter arrived that brought us the sad news of Asdrubale's death. He was seventy-two. The last of Sofi's siblings is gone. Her sadness was deep, and I half-expected that this event would bring her own life to an end. Eventually, she seemed to get past the grief, finding comfort in Orazio, in me, in Francesco, and in all the children, especially little Sofi.

On days when she feels strong enough to sit, Orazio carries Sofi out to the garden wrapped in a cotton coverlet and sets her in her chair. We put out figs, wine, and cheese. She speaks very little and eats even less, but I believe she can feel how much we love her. Just the other day, we gathered like this and Francesco began to sing a Sicilian folk song. Soon all the boys joined in, and little Sofi and Asdrubale did a partner dance. It was clear from the smile on the elder Sofi's face that she knew we were celebrating her existence.

It is delightful to watch the two Sofis together. To see the ancient artist wrapped in cotton, sitting in the shade of the lemon tree while her namesake tells her stories and brings fresh gifts from the garden. Just this morning, Sofi crawled onto her Nonna's lap. I scolded her and told her to get down. But, the artist shook her head and held tight to her granddaughter.

I wish I knew how to paint because I would like to put that memory on canvas with lines and colors. Since I cannot do that, I will have to write a poem.

279

The Weary World

Come the day when the weary world shines new
the youngest one among us brings you flowers.
Fresh gifts—young to old and back again—hold true.

She finds her place in you as we count the hours
and my heart grows heavy as I face your end,
hoping death brings you shelter in God's bower.

My mind paints pictures, makes these colors blend
as I depict you in this perfect hue
and find the grace in art to which we bend.

It's been a year since Asdrubale's death, and each passing day I am grateful he did not take his dear sister with him. Some days are better than others for her. On her good days, she still finds the energy to laugh and enjoy life.

Last week we received word from a messenger that the Flemish painter Anthony van Dyck is in Palermo and would like to meet the great painter Sofonisba Anguissola. I am anxious to have a visitor since parts of the city are under siege by the plague.

"Perhaps it is not the best time to entertain a guest," I said.

"We must entertain him," Sofi said. "You must have heard of Anthony van Dyck, the child prodigy."

"I have."

"You know, then, that Van Dyck studied under Rubens and began gaining a reputation for being a genius with a paintbrush by the age of fifteen."

"Yes, he has been heralded as quite a prodigy."

"And, not only that," she said, "but Van Dyck renders fabric beautifully. His father was a silk merchant and his mother a master of embroidery. Now, that is a painter after my heart!"

Clearly, she is pleased that the young artist requested an audience with her. At least ten times since I agreed to the visit, she has told me she cannot wait to meet him. I admit I am feeling a certain amount of excitement myself just now because I have completed the thirteenth sonnet. There is one last poem to write and then the crown will be complete.

XIII

As flowers find their bloom and clouds their swirl
when eyes smolder dark and lips blossom red,
fair hues lead us on to what lies ahead
and nothing fades when the painter's brush whirls.
The creator makes fair smiles, gentle curls
smoothing the ground on which poor feet have tread.
Passing all logic to touch hearts instead,
the artist finds poetry in the world.
Go then, for these are the tasks we must do.
Build color on color, make bright the way
and remember that we can move the strings
by poetry and pictures, it is true.
Makers we are of all we do and say.
The proof of life is held in all these things.

Yesterday, Van Dyck arrived at our house. When Fabia brought him out to us on the terrace, he immediately went down on one knee. He took Sofi's hand in his.

"Good afternoon, Maestra," he said. "It is an honor to meet you."

"The honor is mine, Signor," she said. "Please, sit."

Van Dyck is a handsome man with reddish-brown hair and beard, of medium height and quite trim. He seated himself across from Sofi and pulled a sketchbook from his satchel.

"I have been recording everything I am seeing on my journey through Italy. Would you allow me to draw a portrait of you in my book, Signora?"

"I would be honored." Her smile confirmed her joy. "Be careful not to show me too close, or with too much contrast high or low that will accentuate the shadows of my wrinkles!"

"I will be careful, I assure you." As he began to sketch, he continued to converse. "Tell me about your teachers, Maestra. From whom did you learn the most?"

"I hesitate to say who taught me the most, as I learned something important from each one of them. But, I suppose it was Bernardino Campi who truly made me the artist that I am."

"And Michelangelo? What was he like?"

"He was incredibly kind and patient. Also quite generous. He was a busy man and much sought after, but he made time to help me. Thanks to his friendship, I gained a great deal of confidence in myself."

I had not seen Sofi so lively in quite some time, so engaged in conversation.

"You have recently been living in Genoa, sir," she said. "Tell me, what do you think of my former city?"

"Genoa is wonderful," he said.

Van Dyck opened his sketchbook to a watercolor painting showing a view of Genoa and handed it to her. She brought the book close to her face.

"I venture into the hills above the city often to relax my mind," he said.

"Oh, the hills!" she exclaimed with delight in her voice. "Do you know the olive groves there?"

"I do! I love those trees. And you know, Signora, the people of Genoa still speak of you. They greatly miss your presence."

"That is kind of you to say," Sofi said with a small catch in her throat.

Francesco joined us on the terrace and bowed to Van Dyck. "Greetings," he said. "Welcome to our home."

"It is a blessing to be here, thank you."

"I heard you just now speaking about Genoa," Francesco said. "May I ask, is there still a taverna by the sea called the Barbarossa?"

"There most certainly is. I go there often, in fact."

"Is Giuseppe still there?"

"That he is. You know him, I take it?"

"I knew him well. I lived above the Barbarossa for nearly a year when I went to Genoa to study with Sofonisba."

"Well, I will take him your greetings."

"I would be grateful. Also, would it be too much to ask for you to take him a case of our wine?"

"Not at all, but only if I may have a couple bottles for myself as well!"

"Of course!" Francesco said. "I will prepare a crate before you go."

Van Dyck possessed such a light spirit. His ease in our midst made him seem like family. Sofi listened with rapt attention, a look of peace and contentment on her face.

"You know," she said, after a lull in our banter. "I can no longer paint, so I am not a painter anymore."

"But you will always be a painter, Signora, because your paintings still exist. I have seen many portraits you painted in Genoa. The vibrancy of your sitters has made me want to meet you for a long time."

"That means a great deal to me. Thank you."

The two artists fell silent. To keep the conversation going, I brought up a new topic that I thought might please Sofi.

"Have you visited any lace shops in Genoa?" I asked Van Dyck.

"Yes, I have. I bought several exquisite pieces for my mother."

"I hear your mother is an expert at embroidery," Sofi said.

"She is indeed. She is highly sought out by many clients in Antwerp because of her ability to create such beautiful designs with thread."

"My mother was also adept at this art," Sofi said.

"Well, you see, Maestra. It is proof that we are cut from the same cloth."

"So we are, good sir. So we are."

Van Dyck left this morning with our good wishes and the wine Francesco had packed. Before he bid us farewell, the artist showed me the notes he had made from yesterday's meeting, along with his sketch of Sofi. I asked if I could copy his notes and told him about the book she and I have been working on. He told me it would be an honor to share his perceptions of the artist. In his sketchbook, he noted her failing eyesight, her good memory, her quick spirit, and her kindness. He also documented her request that he not highlight her wrinkles. As I copied his words, I saw he had incorrectly written that she was ninety-six. Actually, Sofi will turn ninety-two this autumn. I should have told him so, but it did not seem appropriate to correct someone as celebrated as he.

After he was gone, Sofi remained in the glow of his visit. "He was so kind and generous," she said. "He sounded like a man with chestnut brown hair. Was his hair brown?"

"Brown, with a reddish sheen," I said.

"And did he have a mustache?"

"Yes, he did have a mustache."

"And he said we were cut from the same cloth, didn't he?"

"Yes, he did say that. And it is true, you are."

Seeing how joyful Sofi was to meet Van Dyck, and how his words of praise affected her, I was inspired to sit down and write the fourteenth poem in the crown of sonnets this evening. By the light of my candle, the final poem seemed to flow out of me as naturally as water flows in a stream. If there is one thing I have learned from Sofi over the years, it is that the only way to get past adversity is by staying true to one's own heart. As her story has unfolded, I have witnessed the great heights she reached with her art—despite all obstacles—through her dedication to herself. I know I have that ability in me as well. I see her story as my story. At last, the circle is complete.

XIV

The proof of life is held in all these things.
Where am I going and why did I come,
what are the various parts of my sum
and what miracle does my own life bring?
My answers await for the bell to ring
or lightning to strike me fast, leave me dumb.
My questions have faded, so I must run,
seeking melodies no one else can sing.
I will go then, upon a sea so tossed
that safe repose may seem a thing unmet.
From wick to flame, I light an inner star.
With that, no road is wrong, I can't be lost.
Returning always to my heart to rest,
if ever from myself I wander far.

EPILOGUE
1642

Paola

In November 1625, Sofonisba clung to the tree of life by only the thinnest stem. For a week, she lay in bed and did not want to be moved out to the terrace for air and sunshine. She had no appetite, but she did enjoy having me place a cloth soaked with cool lavender water on her forehead.

Orazio, Francesco, and I sang to her. We held her hand and read her poetry. Then one dreary afternoon, she reached for me. "There is something—" she said. She took my hand and told me that she would see what she could do once she got to Paradise to make sure I would realize my dream of starting the printing press. We also talked about publishing her life's story. She said, "Please make it a good one." I promised her I would.

At the beginning of her final week, she was still taking tiny sips of broth from a spoon that Orazio offered her. By the end of the week, she did not have the strength to swallow. All we could do was keep her warm and comfortable.

On the morning Sofonisba died, the sun poured into her bedroom and sparrows sang. I put fresh roses in a vase at her bedside. It was the eleventh of November, my daughter's fifth birthday. All of us were by her side, including little Sofi, who held her Nonna's hand. I imagined the cherubs from the ceiling of Michelangelo's studio were in the room with us.

Sofi's breathing was shallow and weak. She moved her lips to say something, and I put my ear close to her mouth. She whispered the same words she used to say to Elena: "Get up, sister. The day is here!" Those words took every last bit of energy she had. With that call to her sister, my dear friend and mentor was gone.

We buried Sofonisba on 16 November, 1625, in the church of San Giorgio dei Genovesi. Thanks to Orazio's persistence—having started the request well before her death—Father Giovanni finally granted Sofi a final resting place within the church. Her tomb is near the front of the nave, to the right of the altar, very close to the side wall. She is the only woman entombed there.

While we mourned her passing, Orazio and I kept ourselves busy by talking about how we could best organize the inventory of drawings and paintings still in his possession. Much of her work remained in Spain, and we knew we would never get that back. There were some paintings in Cremona, we imagined, but we did not know what exactly had happened to them after Asdrubale's death. The only things we knew we had for certain were the few paintings that had come with Orazio and Sofi to Palermo and those still in storage in the house in Genoa.

With Sofi gone, Orazio returned full-time to his shipping business, so there were long stretches of time that he was away from Palermo. I continued to work on my poetry and raise the children with Francesco. He continued teaching the boys, and little Sofi too, about the many steps involved in tending the vineyard. My father was a big help to us all. His grandchildren adored him. As did I. Not a day went by that he did not thank me for encouraging him to change his life. Despite our early misunderstandings and his long-standing hesitancy to aid me in starting the printing press, I loved my father.

When he passed away in 1630, Father kept his promise and left me money that he had been secretly saving for many years. *For the printing press*, he wrote in a note to me. I framed that note and hung it over the desk in my study. When I look at it, I think back to when I was just a girl of eighteen and he told me a printing press was "far too revolutionary." It makes me smile, and I have a feeling that wherever he is, he's smiling too.

In 1632, with the help of Francesco, his father, and our sons, we opened Lone Snake Editions, the first printing press on the island of Sicily. Through my connection to Signor Conigliaro, my friend at the archive, we found a vacant shop right near the archive on the Via delle Pergole. For the grand opening, Signor Abruzino, the bookseller from Naples, came down and made a speech. He congratulated me on what he said was sure to be a successful publishing endeavor for a long time to come.

That same year, seven years after we buried Sofi, we celebrated the one-hundredth anniversary of her birth. Orazio was able to add an inscription to her tomb, honoring her artistic excellence and his great love for her. Once the inscription was made, her tomb became even more sacred to me. I visited often in the afternoons to sit surrounded by the cool marble of the sanctuary to think and pray, speculating on how Sofi was still so fully alive inside my heart. I would have conversations with her about my hopes and fears for the future, and I marveled at the feeling that somehow over the years, she and I had almost become one and the same person. So many times, I saw myself in her. I understood how she worried about what would become of her work, as I too have wondered what will become of my poetry.

But as Francesco once said to me, Sofi's art is in the world and the art will speak for itself. We cannot control it, but we can name it, and we can recognize all that it took for her to bring it forth. He was right. I am glad to play a part in keeping her name alive.

1632 was also the year my daughter turned twelve. Little Sofi—who was no longer so little—made a commitment to help me with the press.

"Leave the vineyard to my brothers!" she said. She vowed she would never marry but would instead devote her life to helping me with the business.

I told her I would never allow such a sacrifice from her.

"It is not your choice, though, is it, Mother?" she said. "Isn't this what you have taught me?"

Further, she said that she had learned from Nonna Sofi that it was more important to do good work in the world than to be married.

"Besides," she said, "I can get married like Nonna did, when I'm thirty-nine." I decided not to argue with her about this because I needed—and wanted—her help. I needn't have worried about what Francesco might think, for he said, "Love comes first, my darling, and if what Sofi loves most is the idea of helping you with this printing press, then I will not steer her otherwise."

Signor Conigliaro loaned us some manuals about setting type, inking the pages, and pulling the prints. We learned by doing and let ourselves make a lot of mistakes. As Signor Abruzino had once explained, there are many different jobs to do at a press. Francesco gave the boys an option. The two who put forth the clearest arguments regarding their desire to help their mother with the press were free to leave grape farming. Lorenzo and Asdrubale, the oldest and the youngest, said they would like to help.

For Francesco, that was argument enough. I was grateful to have their assistance with the physical labor involved in running the press. I took the lead role on keeping the account books, having been well-trained in such work during my younger days, thanks to my father. Sofi took the role of going out to find business. She was very good at that, and over the years, we've made a name for Lone Snake Editions by printing broadsides for an array of clients from poets to apothecaries. Now, after ten years, we are about to publish our first book, *The Lone Snake*.

When I look back on Sofonisba's life and art, I wish I could show her the new developments that have been taking place in art in the seventeenth century. Francesco's father has a merchant friend who comes down from Holland every few years. The last time he was here, about a year ago, he brought with him the most amazing images. These were delicate drawings by an artist named Rembrandt van Rijn. I remember one in particular of a child learning to walk. Sofi would have loved his work. There were small canvases, too, "genre scenes" he called them, by Gerard van Honthorst, an artist who had clearly learned something about light and shadow from the work of Caravaggio, the same artist who had once stormed into Sofi's birthday celebration. In each one there was a sense of place and interaction between the characters depicted. There was warmth, intimacy, smiles, and laughter—all the workings of life itself.

Long ago, when I first began to serve as her scribe, Sofi showed me *The Chess Game* and explained to me how it was that she came to create it. Having limited access to subject matter, she invented her own. It was such an engaging image. Her depiction of her sisters clustered around the game drew me into the scene, making me feel as though I was right there with them on that sunny afternoon on the terrace, battling over the chessboard. I realize now, that in *The Chess Game*, Sofi invented something completely new in 1555—a genre scene. Something that no one had ever done before. Seventy years later, other artists caught up with her.

She was deeply observant, my friend, and she was resourceful. She used the limitations placed upon her as a woman artist in a man's world to innovate, to use her stumbling blocks as her victories. She was ahead of her time in so many ways, and she made it her job to show people engaged with one another, sharing moments of joy and tenderness. That is who she was. That is how I will always remember her.

If you are sitting somewhere in the future holding in your hands a book with the title *The Lone Snake* on the cover, please know that it was made not by one person alone, but rather by a small band of people working together over time. I thank my mother for poetry, my father for his willingness to change, and my husband for his love. I thank my sons for their companionship, and I take a special bow with my daughter for her hard work and dedication. Then, I applaud the artist for whom she is named. For without Sofonisba, there would be no story to tell.

As we all discovered—including Sofonisba herself, I think it is safe to say—the Lone Snake was never truly alone, and only together with the help of loving companions did she achieve victory.

And now at long last, I will put down the fifteenth sonnet, made of the first line of each sonnet in the crown. I could have done it long ago, but I wanted to wait until the book was ready to go to press. I can feel Sofi smiling down on me at this very moment as I write, saying, "Get up sister, the day is here!"

XV

If ever from myself I wander far,
I reconfigure every earthly wall.
Life's treasured gifts, these riches large and small,
as joy springs forth and shines, a blazing star.
I disown shame, it drains and shows no care
for my heart and the songbird's gentle call.
I won't be done until my words tell all
and print my verses high upon the air.
The grateful vessel of this bless'd rebirth,
I yearn to sing, make peace in this world.
And as with each new song, I rise on wings,
my feet stay planted firmly on the earth.
As flowers find their bloom and clouds their swirl,
the proof of life is held in all these things.

Acknowledgments

I first want to thank Barbara Stretchberry, who in 1995 was associate managing editor at *New Moon: The Magazine for Girls and Their Dreams*. She asked me to write an article about Sofonisba Anguissola. I had not heard of this artist, so I went in search of information. Luckily, there was a biography by Ilya Sandra Perlingieri (Rizzoli, New York, 1992) filled with images of Anguissola's art and a wealth of primary research. After my piece appeared in the March/April 1996 issue of the magazine, I continued to think about the artist and all the questions I had about her remarkable life. I imagined a novel would be good place to find answers to those questions.

I began a journey to write a book that took more than two decades to complete. Early on, I tried to write a story for young readers, but I soon realized that was not a good fit for what I wanted to say about the artist. From 2007 onward, I was becoming a poet, and I did not have the capacity to tackle writing a novel. Still, Sofonisba never left my side. Every few years, I would return to her and try again. She told me her dreams and shared her thoughts and feelings about her life. She asked me to call her Sofi.

In January 2017, writer-colleague Jennifer Morales hosted JanNoWriMo (January Novel Writing Month), and I signed on. My first 50,000 words showed me I had a lot to learn. I wanted Sofi to write in her own voice, but I also wanted to present a perspective that offered a view of her after death. I tried having her speak from beyond the grave. That was a disaster.

My son, nineteen at that time, introduced me to the book *The Name of the Wind* by Patrick Rothfuss, an epic fantasy told to a scribe. At last, I had my solution. I needed someone younger than the artist to serve her in this capacity. And so, Paola was born. It is not surprising that this character presented herself to me as a poet. She brought Francesco with her to provide a romantic subplot to Sofi's story. It took nine more drafts to get to the book you are holding in your hands. As you might imagine, that process involved numerous people I must thank.

Thank you to Jennifer Morales for organizing the group that kickstarted my final push to write this story. Thank you to Barbara Alvarez, Karyn Glass, Carolyn Graham Tsuneta, Tom Jacobson, Maeve Quinn, Jarie Ruddy, Laura Shovan, Sofia Tanski, and Mitch Tuchman for help and encouragement along the way. Thank you to my creativity coach extraordinaire, Sarah Sadie, for helping me visualize the story and to believe in my ability to translate it into words on a page.

Thank you to Andrea Eis, Cory Gooch, James D. Graham, Susan Hering, Chris Keledjian, Heidi Morford, Galia Peled, and Barry Waguespack for reading various drafts of the manuscript and offering feedback. To Rebecca Albiani, thank you for your enthusiasm for this story and for helping me avoid historical misinformation. To Joel Isaacson, thank you for your insightful feedback and for bringing to my attention newer scholarship on Anguissola by Michael Cole in *Sofonisba's Lesson* (Princeton University Press, Princeton, N.J., 2019).

Thank you to Giulia, Antonella, and Fabia, kind women in Milan, Genoa, and Palermo who were not just my Airbnb hosts, but who provided me with maps, ideas, and encouragement. Thank you to Manuela in Cremona for driving me to the River Po at sunset. Thank you to Roberta and Alessandro in Rome for teaching me to make cavatelli from scratch. In Palermo, thank you to Rossella for teaching me to make involtini. Thank you to Emanuele and Malik for two completely different tours of the city and to Melania for her warm smile and the Molti Volti t-shirt.

Thank you to the staffs of the Weather Center Cafe and Paradigm Coffee and Music, two wonderful places in Sheboygan, Wisconsin, where I spent many mornings writing and drinking mochas.

A huge thank you goes to my patient and meticulous editor, Signe Jorgenson. Her insightful reading of the first "finished" version of the book helped me see what I was doing right and where I was falling short. Her work in the final stage of the editorial process has been invaluable.

I am especially grateful to Dawn Hogue, editor and publisher at Water's Edge Press, for believing in me and in this story. In 2019, she surprised me by putting a draft manuscript on my Kindle so I could take my novel with me to Italy. I read it while sitting in the piazza in Cremona, riding the train from Genoa to Rome, and visiting Sofi's tomb in the church of San Giorgio dei Genovesi in Palermo. Dawn logged many hours of reading and reviewing to suggest revisions to the final two drafts. I thank her for keeping my spirits up through the last stages of this process. I also thank her for her thoughtfulness in designing the cover and the interior layout of the book, and finally, for publishing it.

I thank my family: Georg, Rosanne, Illia, Michael, and Owen for their encouragement, questions, and support over the many years in which this story gestated. Then, as Paola herself said, "I applaud the artist.... For without Sofonisba, there would be no story to tell."

INDEX OF PAOLA'S POETRY

Lisa Vihos received her BA in Art History from Vassar College in 1981 and an MA in Art History from the University of Michigan in 1985. She worked as an art museum educator for twenty years in Los Angeles and then in Sheboygan, Wisconsin, where she currently resides. Since 2011, Vihos has published four chapbooks of her poetry and has received multiple awards from the Wisconsin Fellowship of Poets and the Wisconsin Academy of Sciences, Arts & Letters. She has served as an organizer for 100 Thousand Poets for Change and been a five-time guest blogger for the *Best American Poetry*. She has edited three poetry anthologies and was the founding poetry editor of *Stoneboat Literary Journal*, a post she held for ten years. In 2020, she was named the first poet laureate of Sheboygan where she hosts the podcast, *Poetry on Air*.

Visit her at lisavihos.com

Made in the USA
Columbia, SC
28 May 2022

61015057R00186